THE MANE EVENT

THE MANE EVENT

SHELLY
LAURENSTON

B
BRAVA

KENSINGTON PUBLISHING CORP.
http://www.kensingtonbooks.com

BRAVA BOOKS are published by

Kensington Publishing Corp.
850 Third Avenue
New York, NY 10022

All Kensington titles, imprints and distributed lines are available at special quantity discounts for bulk purchases for sales promotion, premiums, fund-raising, educational or institutional use.

Special book excerpts or customized printings can also be created to fit specific needs. For details, write or phone the office of the Kensington Special Sales Manager: Kensington Publishing Corp., 850 Third Avenue, New York, NY 10022. Attn. Special Sales Department. Phone: 1-800-221-2647.

Brava and the B logo Reg. U.S. Pat. & TM Off.

ISBN-13: 978-0-7582-2036-3
ISBN-10: 0-7582-2036-7

First Kensington Trade Paperback Printing: October 2007
10 9 8 7 6 5 4 3

Printed in the United States of America

To my mom who always had faith in me.
To Christina L. who has faith in me still.
And to Cypress B. who knew I could do
anything I wanted . . . as soon as
I stopped all the whining.
I love you all.

Contents

CHRISTMAS PRIDE

Chapter One

"They found the body last night."

Mace Llewellyn watched the police activity going on in front of his Pride's home. He knew when he saw one of the Pride males waiting for him at LaGuardia Airport something was wrong. Still, hearing that a Pride male had been found with the back of his head blown out did take him by surprise. But only for a moment. He shrugged his shoulders. "And?"

Shaw, one of the more recent additions to the Pride, smiled. "I'm just doing what she asked me to. She said to pick you up at the airport, and that's what I did."

Rubbing his hand over his head, Mace sighed. Damn Pride bullshit. He didn't have time for this. Or for *them*. His sisters and cousins. Waiting in that house like fucking queens of the Serengeti. They still hadn't figured it out. Mace no longer wanted this. The day he signed the papers making him the property of the United States Navy, he ceased to belong to the Pride. Fourteen years in service had made him a man with a purpose.

He had two goals in his life at the moment, both of which involved his future. The first would work itself out with few problems. He would finally start his own business. He already had the financial backers and a partner. The second would be more difficult. He needed to find a woman. Not any woman, but the woman who had haunted his dreams and fantasies for longer than he could remember. The woman who deserted him more than twenty years ago. True, they had only been fourteen at the time but, damn her, it was the principle of the thing. He would find her. He would find her and he'd claim her.

The potential reality that she may be married with six kids or living in Istanbul as a nun never crossed his feline mind. He knew what he wanted. So he would have her. But, as usual, his sisters were in his way.

"Not sure why I should care."

"Neither am I. Personally, I'm glad to see Petrov gone."

Mace gave the man a sidelong glance, unable to hide his smirk. "Did you kill him?"

"Oh please." Shaw studied his fingernails. Then he unleashed his claws and studied them as well. "Do you really see me bothering with killing him?" He looked at Mace. "I mean . . . really?"

The man had a point.

"Besides, he did know how to party. Petrov had . . . exotic tastes. So, anyone could have killed him." Shaw resheathed his claws. "And what did you do to your head?"

Mace rolled his eyes. "Couldn't exactly have a mane in the United States Navy, now could I?"

"I guess." Shaw cracked his big neck. "She probably just wants to see you. You are her only brother."

And the only Breeding Male of the Llewellyn line.

No. They would not have *that* conversation again. About his duty to the Pride and the Llewellyn name. He'd done his duty for his country. The Navy reluctantly cut him loose. He wasn't about to go back into another service that would last a lifetime.

And he sure as hell wasn't about to let them trade him out to another Pride like a New York Mets pitcher.

Shaw, however, clearly enjoyed his life. As the top Breeding Male of the Llewellyn Pride, he couldn't ask for better. For some, being a Pride male was a great existence. The females fed you, bore your cubs, and made sure you lived comfortably. In return, you simply needed to help them breed when they were ready and protect them and their cubs from other Pride males. On the surface, it seemed great. For some it was. But not for Mace. He wanted more. He wanted his own mate. In particular, the girl he'd lost so long ago. She would be his and his alone. He had absolutely no intention of being in service to the Pride females like some rutting bull.

"I'm not coming back."

"Don't care. I could care less what you do. Although I would like you to get out of my car now."

With another sigh, Mace grabbed his duffel bag and stepped out of the Mercedes that Shaw picked him up in. He didn't go through the front door with all the media activity, but went around to the side. Several uniformed cops and a Pride male stood by the side entrance. The Pride male glanced at him, scrutinized his shaved head, and then let him in with a laugh. Mace fought the desire to snap the man's neck. A fight he almost didn't win.

He slipped into the back of the house, through the kitchens. The staff glanced at him but kept working. The holidays were their busiest time because of all the balls and charity events. Although Mace didn't know a less-spirited group than his sisters when it came to the holidays. Mace reached the other end of the kitchen, pushing the swinging door open, when his phone rang. He dug into the front pocket of his jeans and pulled out the cell phone.

"Yeah?"

"Hey. It's me." Watts. An old friend who knew how to find information whenever and wherever he needed it.

"What did you find out?"

"She's still living in New York. Divorced." Mace closed his eyes and let out a silent breath. He'd hate to start killing people at this stage in the game. Especially some poor schmuck who happened to marry the wrong woman. "And you'll love this. She's a cop. NYPD."

"Really?" He knew that had always been her dream, but he always wanted to be a hockey player. That didn't mean he ever strapped on pads and joined the New York Islanders.

Mace glanced out one of the big windows looking over the garden. He saw them standing around. Uniformed cops drinking coffee and talking amongst themselves. Mace looked down the hall leading to his sister's office.

"Are you still there? I've got more."

"Tell me later. I gotta go." Mace closed his phone. He licked his lips and tried to slow his breathing. She couldn't really be here . . . could she? But hell, if she were then he'd always been right. A sign from the goddess Druantia, Queen of the Druids, herself—she belonged to him. She would always belong to him.

He made his way to his sister's private offices, hearing the arguing before he even reached the door. He could hear her getting good and frothy with someone, too. Not surprising. Last thing the Pride needed was a bunch of cops searching into their lives. But Petrov had not only been his sister's employee and one of the Breeding Males, he lived on the premises. Since a shot to the back of the head usually indicated murder, the cops had every right to check the house.

Of course, all that logic wouldn't mean a damn to Missy, leader of the Llewellyn Pride females, his oldest sister, and the official family pain in the ass.

Mace turned the corner, one more hallway away from his sister's office, when he smelled her.

He stopped. Cold. It took him less than a second to recognize it. He knew it better than he knew his own name. Implanted on his adolescent brain more than twenty years ago, his adult brain still remembered it. In fact, his adult brain acted like his adolescent brain used to. It stopped functioning. All it wanted to do was wrap itself around the owner of that scent and purr. The cat in him wanted to stretch out his body and rub his face into that scent.

He'd been right. She *was* here. That explained his sister's anger. She hated her. Hated her whole family. Missy would never let her anywhere near the Pride home . . . unless, of course, she had no choice.

He came around the corner, slowly moving into the secretary's office. One more door and he'd reach Missy's office or, as he liked to call it, "Destination: Hell." He could hear his sister dressing down someone behind the closed office door and he didn't envy the man, but he had something much more important right in front of him. He had her.

She stood in front of the window overlooking Columbus Circle with her back to him. She didn't seem moved at all by the yelling coming from Missy's office. She radiated calm. Her energy centered. Her arms folded in front of her chest. Not nearly as tall as the women in his family, she stood no more than five foot eight or so. But curvy. Ripe. A brick house. She'd filled out in all the right places. She'd cut her auburn hair so it brushed thick against the collar of her leather jacket. As he glanced down the length of her sumptuous body, he could see the woman armed herself better than most SEALs. A gun holster bulged large behind her leather jacket, and a smaller ankle holster on her right leg under her black slacks. It also looked like her left leg sported a holster with a small blade, which he seriously doubted any other cop in the state would consider legal.

Her phone vibrated against her hip. She easily slipped the small device out of its holster, glanced at the caller ID, and answered. At that point, he almost dropped to his knees and crawled to her. That voice. That goddamn, fucking voice. Like ten miles of bad road in the hot desert, but she'd somehow tamed that brutal Bronx accent. A bit of a disappointment, though. He loved that accent on her. She used to wear it like an old leather jacket. Now she kept it muted, controlled. Kind of like her. He smiled and wondered what it would take to get back that Bronx girl he knew and still loved. Thankfully, though, there was nothing she could do about that voice. He closed his eyes for a brief moment and let her voice roll over him like a rough wave.

"I thought you'd never call me back. You won't believe where I am." She laughed and his balls tightened. "Missy Llewellyn's house . . . no, I'm not lying. How could I make that up?"

She scratched her long neck. The desire to lick the same spot nearly strangling him. "Jesus Christ, don't you read the papers? One of her people was killed in Battery Park. A couple of joggers found him. What? Nah. So, any message you want me to give her?" Her body began to shake as she stifled a laugh. "Well, I don't think I'll give her *that* message. Geez. And you said I hold a grudge."

After a few more moments, her body stiffened. "No. I can't. I'm working, that's why. Yes. Even on Christmas day. Besides, I hate Christmas. I have moral issues with celebrating it." He frowned to keep from laughing. She had "moral issues with" celebrating Christmas? The crap she could come up with still amazed him.

"Look, I gotta go. No, I'm not arguing about this." She closed the phone and slipped it back into its holster.

Dear God, the woman was still beautiful. After all these years. All this time. And he bet he could have her pants off and be inside her in . . . he glanced at his watch. *Thirty seconds.* Yeah. That would work.

Desiree MacDermot stared out the windows of the secretary's office and waited. Well, waited and fumed. Leave it to her oldest sister to ruin her moment in the sun. Here she stood in their archenemy's house, moments away from throwing the rich heifer's ass in the back of a squad car, and what does her sister say? "Are you coming to Mom and Dad's for Christmas dinner?"

Why of course I am. I also plan to remove skin from the most sensitive parts of my body and rub salt into the open wounds.

Because isn't that what the holidays are all about—letting your family make you wish you were an orphan?

Dez shook off her sister's clear attempt to make her miserable. How could she be miserable when she had grand plans of making Missy Llewellyn cry? Missy, who seemed to love nothing more than to make the MacDermot sisters' lives hell. Apparently, it wasn't enough that all three of them had earned the right to be at the exclusive Cathedral School of Manhattan by earning top-level scholarships. Or that their parents worked damn hard to get their daughters the best they could afford. No, to Missy and the other Llewellyn sisters, none of that meant shit. They only cared about one thing—the fact the MacDermots were poor, Puerto Rican–Irish girls from the Bronx. And they wanted to make sure they never forgot it.

Maybe God would decide to smile down on her and she'd be

able to piss off Missy so much the woman would do something stupid. Oh, if Missy would only hit her. Then Dez could handcuff the bitch and dump her butt in a holding cell for a few hours. Maybe the hookers would make her cry. Like she made Dez cry all those years ago on that muggy late-August day.

"You'll never be good enough for him."

That's what they told her as all four sisters circled her like a pack of wolves. She never forgot those brutal words, but she never let them hold her back either. Far from it. She probably should thank Missy. Without her inherently evil nature, Dez may not have had the guts to become a cop. She decided then and there to prove Missy Llewellyn wrong, and as far as she could tell, she had. Dez realized now these people, with all their money and connections, weren't nearly good enough for *her*.

Desperately fighting the smile that threatened to spread across her entire face, she suddenly realized all her fantasies seem to be coming true at one time. The thought of putting Missy in a squad car actually made her nipples hard.

Nope. This was quietly turning into the best day *ever*. Like someone hit her in the head with her Christmas gift five days early. It almost brought a tear of happiness to her eye. Nothing would ever beat this. Absolutely nothing.

"So where the hell have you been?"

Dez shuddered. Man, that voice sounded familiar. She only knew of one person with a voice like that. A freaky little kid who had to be the smallest fourteen-year-old she'd ever remembered seeing with the lowest voice she'd ever heard. She spun on her heel . . . only to be faced with a god, if she did say so herself. Big. Like some kind of beautiful linebacker. A shaved head with a serious five o'clock shadow issue, and gold-colored eyes. Eyes that, at the moment, were staring at her like a slab of prime rib. No. This couldn't be Mace Llewellyn. Her heart dropped. True, this man was pretty, but she saw pretty every day. The Mace she remembered wasn't pretty, but he always knew how to make her smile. She learned over the years that was a hell of a lot more important than looks.

"Well . . . answer me."

Uh-oh. Nutcase alert. How come all the good-looking ones were insane? "I'm . . . uh . . . sorry. Do I know you?"

He crossed big arms over a big chest and smirked at her. "Take a minute. Let it come to you."

She blinked and tried to remember all the exits out of the room in case the gorgeous nutcase went postal.

"Still waiting."

It hit her. Like a slap to the forehead. But . . . no. It couldn't be. It wasn't humanly possible. But that superior tone. That haughty expression. That damn smirk. That killer voice that had deliciously matured with age. All together, they really could only belong to one person. The one person she'd been waiting more than twenty years to see again.

What happened to the boy she remembered? Apparently, this . . . this . . . *man* replaced him. Oh, and what a man!

But no matter how different he looked, she still knew. Maybe those freaky gold eyes gave him away. Or those gorgeous full lips that, even at fourteen, she hadn't been immune to.

Or maybe the way he stared at her. Like he spent every waking moment imagining her naked.

Only one person ever looked at her like that. Well, only one person ever looked at her like that where she didn't have the overwhelming desire to rip eyes from sockets.

"Oh my God—Mace?"

Time had done wonders for her. Some women never looked as good as they did in high school, especially at thirty-six. But she did. Better. She still had those killer eyes. Gray with flecks of green. He used to stare into those eyes during biology class as they faked their way through the experiments. Of course, that's when he wasn't staring at that beautiful face with that cute, little pug nose or that incredibly hot body. She'd been an early bloomer, wearing a healthy C cup while the other girls were just moving from training bras. All of that didn't matter, though. Not to Mace. That was just the cherry on top.

For him, it had been more than her big tits and luscious

mouth. Dez actually liked him back then. Just the way he was. Ninety pounds soaking wet, barely five foot three, a head of hair he couldn't control, and the attitude of a giant. Most people didn't like Mace. Dez, however, found him funny and smart. Even his sisters never saw him that way. To a fourteen-year-old, that meant everything to him.

Then she left him. Walked out of his life and never came back. At the moment, Mace was completely ready to push her up against the wall and demand she tell him how she could leave him like she did.

For years, a part of him kept expecting to see her again. Although he always wished he could forget about her. Lose himself in some of the other women he met since he last saw her saddle shoes walking down the school hall and out of his life. But he never could. No matter how hard he tried, he could never forget about her. Hell, he still dreamed about her. She was older in his dreams, thank God, but his dreams didn't do justice to the woman now standing in front of him, an NYPD badge hanging on a chain around her neck.

"Mace Llewellyn? Is that you?"

So, she did remember him. Good. Now he could tell her what a bitch she'd been for leaving him. For breaking his fourteen-year-old heart into a million pieces and stomping on it with her saddle shoes. He geared himself to do it, too—until she smiled at him. A smile that practically knocked him on his ass.

After all these years, the woman leaped beyond perfect. Especially when she literally threw herself at him, her arms looping around his neck.

"Jesus, Mace! I can't believe it!"

His eyes almost rolled to the back of his head when she pressed her curvaceous body against his. Without even thinking about it, he wrapped her in a bear hug and lifted her off her feet. She actually squealed, which sounded strange with that voice of hers.

"I don't believe it, Mace!" He didn't either. How did anyone smell this good? How was it humanly possible?

She laughed. "Stop sniffing my neck!" She pushed against his shoulders and leaned back, but he wouldn't let her go. "I can't believe you're still doing that."

"You smell good."

She rolled her eyes. "Whatever."

"So?"

"So, what?"

"Answer my question."

"Your question?"

"Where the hell have you been?"

"Aw, Mace. Gimme a break." She tried to pull out of his arms, but he held fast. "Are you going to let me go?"

"I'm comfortable. Answer my question."

"My family moved, Mace. To Queens. My sisters and I went to a different school. I assure you it was nothing personal." He stared at her. "It wasn't!"

"Did you write me?"

"No, Mace."

"Did you think about me?"

"Oh, come on!"

"What? It's a valid question."

"You know, you come from one of the wealthiest families in New York. You could have tracked me down if you really wanted to see me that badly."

"I was in military school."

Dez tried not to laugh, but it was a sad, weak attempt. "Sorry. I guess I just have a hard time imagining you taking orders from . . . you know . . . *anybody*."

"What's that supposed to mean?"

"Come on, Mace. It's me."

He gazed down into her face. "Yeah. It sure is you." Their eyes locked and, for several moments, they did nothing but stare at each other.

Dez shook her head. "Okay. Put me down."

"Why?"

"Mace!"

He dropped her, forcing Dez to rock back on her heels. This, of course, forced him to grab her ass to steady her before she fell back.

"Hands off, Llewellyn. Or I'm turning your nads into a necklace."

He smiled as he released her. "Well, you haven't changed."

"Neither have you. I see Captain Ego still lives."

No other woman existed who he let get away with calling him that. He glanced down at himself. "I haven't changed? Not even a little?"

"I don't mean physically, you idiot." She punched him lightly on the shoulder, blinked in surprise, and suddenly felt the bicep under his leather jacket. "I definitely don't mean physically."

He grinned at her, enjoying that his body seemed to have her so distracted. "You doing all right there, beautiful?"

"Oh, shut up."

"At least tell me you missed me."

She nodded as her voice softened. "Yeah, Mace. I missed you. You were my best friend."

Best friend? He never wanted to be her best friend. He wanted to be her boyfriend. He wanted her parents to catch them on their couch making out. He wanted to buy her one of those tacky ID bracelets with his name on it. He wanted to tattoo "Property of Mace Llewellyn" on her forehead.

"Stop frowning, Mace." She reached up and ran her hands over his brow. A move she used to do a lot in school. Often the only thing that kept him calm back then. The only thing that kept him from tearing idiot jocks and rich assholes apart with his newly sprouted fangs. "It's been over twenty years, Mace. Let it go, bonehead." She ran her thumb down his nose, spreading her hand out so her fingers cupped his cheek. He leaned into her hand and she smiled that smile.

Even after all these years, she knew just how to handle him. How to contain the beast within his heart without even trying. Oh yeah. This woman was destined to be his. And nothing would get in his way now.

"*What the hell do you think you are doing with my brother?*"

Mace growled and wondered how much prison time a man would do for tossing his sister into the East River.

Mace's body tensed against her hand. Then she heard that Mace growl. He only used that when something really pissed him off. Poor baby, seemed he still didn't get along any better with his sisters than she did with her own.

She looked over her shoulder at the beautiful Missy Llewellyn. Unlike Mace, Missy hadn't changed much. Still lean, gold, and beautiful. Pretty much the exact opposite of Dez whose least-favorite uncle still referred to her as "the pudgy one."

"Well? Answer me." And still mean as a snake.

Oooh. A pissed Missy. Dez loved this. She could have been good. She should have been nice. But come on. The entire homicide department didn't call her The Instigator for nothing.

Dez turned to face Missy and leaned back into Mace's chest. Then, for the hell of it, she grabbed his big arms and wrapped them around her waist. Initially, she surprised herself with her physical reaction to Mace. Throwing herself into the arms of a man she hadn't seen in twenty years really wasn't her style. But just the sight of him brought back that fourteen-year-old girl who could never get enough of Mace and his inherent weirdness. But now? Well, using Mace to torture his sister—just a Dez party.

She smiled at Missy. "Your brother asked me to come with him to a hotel for some wild, dirty animal sex . . . and I said lead the way."

Oh yeah. If looks could kill, she'd be nothing more than a greasy spot on the woman's carpet. Apparently, Missy still felt Dez didn't deserve her brother. Which only made the whole thing that much more fun. Of course, Mace tightening his grip on her body and nuzzling her neck—that didn't hurt either. She wasn't surprised, though, when Mace played along. The two of them together had always been trouble. The nuns always separating them in class, giving them detention, calling them evil incarnate and condemning them to the fiery pits of hell. Ya know . . . whatever.

Seemed some things never changed.

"So, Mace, I get off work in a couple more hours."

He shook his head. "Baby, I can't wait that long. Let's go bang this out in my sister's office. You know. To take the edge off." Dez wrestled the part of her that wanted to take Mace up on that particular offer and kept the game going instead.

"That is sooo romantic, Mace. I never knew you were so romantic."

"There's a lot about me you don't know yet. Besides, Missy's desk is a nice, sturdy mahogany. We could go at it like wolves on that thing, and it wouldn't budge."

Ah, the Mace she remembered. The smart-ass kid who tortured people on a daily basis for his own amusement, and his sister was no exception. Actually, Dez knew he went out of his way to torture his sister and that he enjoyed every minute of it.

Yup. Her day just kept getting better and better.

Could his day get any better? The woman of his dreams cuddled up in his arms and his sister in an almost violent rage. A few more minutes of this and he would start purring and not stop.

"Mason," his sister spit that out between clenched teeth. "I need to speak with you. In private."

Mace watched her. He wondered how long before she snapped.

"Now!"

Well that took all of ten seconds.

He watched her rigid back stalk into her office.

"Ooh, Mace. You're in tru-ble," Dez whispered in a singsong voice.

He pulled her closer to him. He couldn't help himself. Did she have any idea exactly how tasty she was?

Another cop came to stand beside them. He glared at Mace, but Mace ignored it. He wouldn't let anything distract him from the woman in his arms.

"We're out of here."

"What? Why?"

"Got a call from the lieutenant. They're pulling us. I've been informed we have enough information for this investigation and we are not to harass Ms. Llewellyn any longer. And would you two stop whatever you're doing?"

"Hey, B! You're harshin' my buzz."

With an annoyed groan, the man turned away from them. Dez looked at Mace over her shoulder. "Mr. Llewellyn, I do believe your sister made a call."

"I believe you're right, Detective." His sister had a lot of political connections and was not shy about using them whenever it served her.

"Too bad. I had such plans of torture for her. And they all involved her desk." Smiling, Dez turned, reached up, and kissed Mace on the cheek. He'd had many women do much more intense things to him over the years, but none of it felt as good as that simple kiss. "It was really good seeing you again, Mace."

She pulled away from him and he grudgingly let her go.

"And I'm glad you're doing okay. Although I never doubted you'd do any less." She motioned to her partner. "Let's get out of here, B."

The male left. Dez followed behind, but Mace stopped her with one word. "Wait."

Dez looked at him, curious why he wanted her to wait. Actually, she found herself curious about a lot of things when it came to Mace.

"Go out with me tonight. Dinner."

She laughed at what was clearly an order as opposed to a request. "No."

"Why not?"

"You don't even remember my name, Mason Llewellyn." He hadn't said her name even once in the last ten minutes. It hurt to think he'd so easily forgotten about her, but when you looked like Mace now did, how could you remember all the women? Especially one who you hadn't actually slept with.

Dez turned and headed down the hallway.

"Desiree." She froze as his low voice slid across her skin. "Patricia. Marie. MacDermot. Dez for short."

Dez spun around, her mouth open in awe. "How the hell did

you remember all that?" He even included her confirmation name. No one knew her confirmation name except the parish priest, and that's because he really didn't like her much.

"I remember everything about you, Dez. Absolutely everything."

Her breath caught on a sigh. Her heart began to beat faster. And she suddenly wondered if Mace could *feel* her blood racing through her veins.

After a few moments, she shook herself. "You're still doing it, Mace." *The bastard.*

"Doing what?"

She grinned and glared at him all at the same time. "Torturing me."

He leaned against the doorjamb, his arms crossing in front of him. He took all of her in. From those cute little feet, past those magnificent breasts, straight to those gray eyes and auburn hair. "Baby, I haven't even started."

She closed her eyes and took a deep breath. After another moment, "I'm outta here, Mace."

This was not how his fantasy went. She kept turning him down. Didn't she know? "Yes" to dinner today. "Yes" to marriage tomorrow. Dammit, he had a schedule to keep. A schedule that involved getting her sweet ass into bed as fast as humanly possible.

"When will I see you again?"

She walked off down the hall. "For your sister's sake, you better hope never."

Then she was gone. But this wasn't over.

Not by a long shot.

Dez got in the passenger side of the car, leaning her head back against the seat and staring up at the roof of the Chevrolet.

"Don't do it, Dez."

She glanced at her partner of four years. "Don't do what?"

"Get all bunged up over this guy. He's rich. He's a Llewellyn. And he can have any piece of ass he wants in this town."

"I'm a piece of ass." Dez grinned. "That guy from last week, who believes aliens were talking to him and that's why he tried to set his neighbor on fire, said I was fabulous."

Bukowski, chuckling, started the car. "And he was right, even though he wasn't the healthiest man we've ever arrested. But a guy like Llewellyn would never realize it. So don't waste your time."

"I know. I know. A girl can fantasize, though."

"Yeah. Sure."

He pulled out into traffic and headed back to the precinct.

Mace Llewellyn. Back in New York and looking tastier than anything she'd ever seen before. Who knew he'd turn out like that? She'd always thought of him as adorable back in the day. The cute boy who sat next to her in science class, making her laugh by mocking everyone around them while trying *not* to stare at her breasts. He'd been brutal, witty, and her biggest crush ever. Now, however, well . . . now the man was a god. He had to be at least six foot four and well over two hundred pounds, without a single ounce of fat on him.

Initially, she'd been unimpressed with the males she caught glimpses of while waiting around for Missy. Too pretty. Too glossy. Too . . . clean. They wore Armani suits and seven-hundred-dollar watches. They were all blond. No, not blond. Gold. Seriously gold. Their skin. Their eyes. Their hair. It was hard to believe these people lived in New York. *Her* New York. Where you found every shade, every hue, every color under the freakin' rainbow.

As far as Dez was concerned, her family represented true New York culture. Her father a good Irish boy from Hell's Kitchen. Her mother a sweet Puerto Rican from the Bronx. Together those two people created one brown-skinned daughter who looked like she just arrived off the boat from Cataño. Another redheaded daughter with pale skin who looked like she should be on Broadway in *Riverdance*.

Then they made Dez, who dangled between both worlds. Her straight brown hair had a reddish tinge. Her skin seemed to have spent too much time in the sun. Plus she had the same damn freaky-colored eyes as her dad.

Mason seemed to have the same problem. He belonged and he didn't.

He always had the golden hair. The golden eyes. Even that golden skin. But now he had something rough and ready about him. He had stubble on that strong, square jaw. He recently shaved off that golden hair, although it seemed to be fighting its way back. His pensive gold eyes showed he'd seen a lot of the world over the past twenty years. And based on the brutal scar that cut across his neck, the world had been pretty hard on him.

Yeah, but Bukowski probably hit it right on the head. A guy like Mace was way out of her league . . . if she had a league. It's not like she dated much once her marriage to "The Idiot" ended four years ago.

Still, the fourteen-year-old Mace used to give her this little tingle at the base of her spine when he would smile at her in biology lab. This adult Mace, though, made her entire body tingle—violently.

She didn't even think Mace noticed her back then. He always treated her like a sister he didn't actually hate. After seeing him now, though . . . well, she really hoped he didn't actually look at his own sisters like that.

Dez had changed. And all for the better. No longer the painfully shy girl trying to hide huge breasts behind a load of books so the jocks would stop trying to grab her, this Dez reeked of attitude and confidence. Almost cocky. Even the way she moved. She walked with her back straight, head held high, breasts straining beneath a burgundy turtleneck sweater, daring a guy to touch them. And seeing the way she moved, Mace had no doubt she would snap the neck of the first fucker who tried something.

Yup. He still wanted her. Had to have her. And, like a gazelle running past him on the African plains, he would do whatever necessary to get his paws on her.

Mace looked at the door that blocked him from his sister. With a heavy sigh, he walked toward it and prayed they got along better this time. He wasn't sure he could handle any more stitches on his throat.

Chapter Two

"What exactly were you doing with that . . . that . . . police person?"

Mace's feet sat comfortably atop his sister's desk, and his eyes stared up at the ceiling.

"Well, if you hadn't interrupted us, I probably would have laid her out on your desk and—"

"Mason Llewellyn! This is not funny. That idiot is a cop—believe it or not—and she's trying to prove that *I* had something to do with Alexander's death. She actually asked me if *I* killed him."

Mace watched his beautiful sister. She took after their mother. He took after his father. And they got along about as well as that pair did.

"Did you?"

Missy glared at him. "Of course I didn't!"

"Just checking. I know how cranky you can get."

"You're enjoying this, aren't you."

"As a matter of fact—"

"You have no idea what's going on."

Something in his sister's tone made him stop. Something tired . . . and scared.

"You're right. So why don't you explain it to me."

Missy began rubbing her temples. A sure sign her stress level just hit a new high. "I don't know. I think someone's trying to take over the Pride. Force the males out."

"You're telling me lions *shot* Petrov?"

"I said I don't know."

"Clearly."

An unspoken rule among shifters—never fight against another shifter with anything but your fangs, claws, and hunting skills. One of the reasons few lions shed a tear over the loss of the Withell Pride a few months back. Using poison on your claws? Tasteless.

"You sure it's not hyenas? I know I've been away for a while, but you can't tell me you're getting along with them."

Missy sniffed. "Hardly." No. He didn't think things had changed that much. Not when Missy still sported a scar on her back from a childhood fight with a hyena. They were the only shifters Mace knew of born with their fangs and the belief that everything around them existed simply to be their prey.

"Just be careful, Mason. If some other males are planning to take over, I'm not sure if they'll see you as a threat or not."

Males always left the Pride they were born to, but since the Llewellyns were one of the "civilized" Prides that traded their males out, his existence created a bit of a problem and a threat to outsiders trying to claim his sisters and cousins as their own. With his money and name, the Pride could get three higher-level males for him.

Of course, that particular thought made him want to retch.

Although, Mace really wasn't worried. He learned a long time ago how to survive without the Pride. He'd been the hunter and the hunted. Trapped in the middle of firefights with seemingly no way out. He'd killed. Humans. To protect his men and himself. His days of pampering had disappeared as soon as he went off to the Naval Academy.

But his sister's concern almost made him feel like he didn't hate her. Almost.

"So what do you want me to do?"

"Nothing at the moment. Just keep breathing."

"And then what?"

"I don't know yet. I don't want some renegade males trying to take over this Pride. Sherry had two cubs last month by

Petrov." Missy shuddered. "I'd hate to think what they'd do if they got in."

He didn't want to ask the next question, but his stupid sense of duty and loyalty wouldn't allow him to do any less. "Do you need me to stay here?"

"No. Shaw and Reynolds won't stand for it, and I don't need you three snarling at each other over breakfast. Besides, we have some important people coming over for a holiday banquet tomorrow. And since I know you won't clean yourself up for it—"

Mace held up his hand. "A simple 'no' really would have answered my question."

"Where will you stay? And don't say your apartment. It won't be safe."

He wanted to say "between Dez's thighs," but that would simply set his sister off again.

"Actually a buddy of mine from the Navy is coming to town. He and his Pack are staying here for the holidays. I can crash with them for a while." He looked up to find his sister staring at him in horror. "Is there a problem?"

"Did you say Pack?"

"Yes."

"You're friends with a . . . a . . . dog?"

"He prefers wolf, but yeah, I am." He actually considered Smitty his brother. They'd saved each other's life on more than one occasion.

"But . . . you can't be friends with him."

In theory, maybe. They were Pack and Pride, dog and cat; he and Smitty should be the worst of enemies. Especially with the Pack–Pride war that had been going on for decades. But the military created strange bedfellows. Guys who had to rely on each other for their survival. Smitty was and always would be one of his best buds. Even if Mace caught him on more than one occasion licking his own balls.

"You know the funny thing is, Missy, I'm really not asking your fucking permission."

"Don't you dare curse at me, Mason! I'm not one of your military cohorts or that slut from the Bronx." Mace looked back up at the ceiling. Five minutes with his sister and he felt twelve years old again.

"Now," she continued, "are you at least going to come over for Christmas? I have a gift for you."

Mace glanced around Missy's office. There wasn't one sign that in five days the world would be celebrating Christmas. It could easily be the middle of August for all the decoration that his sister had up.

"Are you even celebrating Christmas?"

"Don't be smart. The living room is quite decorated. I just don't like tinsel and things in my office."

He didn't even have to ask to know that his sisters hired someone to decorate their living room. No way would the Pride's females lower themselves to something as middle class as putting up a Christmas tree.

"We'll have to see. I may be busy."

His sister's gold eyes narrowed. "Not with that woman."

If he were lucky, Christmas day his cock would be so far inside Dez MacDermot, going anywhere would be a physical impossibility.

But to his sister, he shrugged. "You never know . . ."

Dez cringed as her boss slammed his door closed. But before she could walk away, he snatched it open again. "And I better not see your ass until after the New Year!" He slammed it again.

Dez glared at Bukowski as she headed back to her desk. "*I* didn't even do anything."

"You did ask her if she killed Petrov. I think your exact words were, 'You whacked him, didn't you? You sadistic bitch.'"

"Sadistic heifer. And it was just a question."

"Uh-huh. Well, your 'question' now has you on a lovely vacation until after the holidays."

"Still doesn't seem fair."

"Maybe not." Bukowski threw himself into his desk chair. "But your dad is the one who golfs with the lieutenant every couple of weeks. Whatcha wanna bet he went on and on about his poor baby working every holiday?"

Who knew bringing her dad to an NYPD function would cause all this trouble? She introduced him to her lieutenant, and once the men found out they were both former Marines, they got along like a house on fire. Then they started golfing several times a month with some other Marines. Dez knew it would only be a matter of time before her father found out that she really didn't have to work during the holidays. With her seniority and vacation time, she could take the entire month of December off.

But Dez worked the holidays for a reason. Because anything had to be better than another Christmas with her sisters. There were just so many times a woman could hear she was a failure with men and in her career before it really started to hurt.

Dez flopped herself into her chair and glowered at a wall. The current situation did not bring her happiness.

"So what are you going to do?"

She glanced at Bukowski, then back at the wall covered in "wanted" flyers. "Pretend it didn't happen."

Her partner chuckled. "Good luck with that."

Dez turned her chair around and glanced at the Petrov file sitting on her desk. She examined the picture attached to it. Petrov had been a handsome man, no doubt about that. But nowhere close to Mace.

Closing the file, Dez glanced up briefly when she heard someone settle into the chair on the other side of her desk. When big feet propped up on the vast amount of paperwork in front of her, she looked back up.

Yeah, that sure was Mace Llewellyn staring at her from the other side of her desk. Just staring. Like he used to. Like he knew where she'd buried the bodies of all her goldfish after their unfortunate "accidents" or what she did with her sisters' toothbrushes on more than one occasion. The all-knowing, all-seeing Mace stare, and it still made her crazy.

She raised an eyebrow. "Why are you here?"

He mockingly gave her the raised eyebrow back. "You never gave me an answer."

"Yeah. I did. In fact, my exact words were 'no'."

"Yes, but I've chosen to ignore that until I hear what I want."

Dez laughed. "Jesus, Mace. You really haven't changed all that much, have ya? You're still . . . you."

"Are you talking about my bountiful charisma and overwhelming charm?"

Okay. The hysterical girl-giggling had to stop. A mature woman of thirty-six, she had a divorce under her belt and a healthy mortgage. Acting like the football team captain asked her out to the prom was not, in any way, remotely mature.

"Mace—" Dez stopped and looked around the room. Yeah, she had every idiot's attention. "Don't you people have something to do?"

As one, "No."

She growled and looked back at Mace. She blamed him for what would certainly be hours, maybe even days, of precinct gossip. "Mace. I can't go out with you."

"If you're worried arresting my sister will come between us— really, that's not a problem. I'm pretty sure it will bind us tighter together. Besides, we made plans . . . involving Missy's desk."

"You know I was only torturing your sister."

"So you were just using me?" He actually sounded wounded. "Like a whore?"

"Mace . . ." She stopped and rubbed her eyes. Of all the places he could be doing this, her precinct should not be one of them.

"You're doing it again."

"Doing what?"

"Trying to make me crazy."

The look he gave her was pure predatory male. "I like you crazy."

Christ, did he just growl that?

After all these years, Mace still worked her in all the best parts. Making her feel uncomfortably warm . . . and seriously wet.

Flash-flood warning wet.

Her desk phone rang. She should have been grateful for the

distraction from Mace, but she grimaced instead. She did not look forward to this.

Apparently afraid she wouldn't get the phone herself, Bukowski reached around Mace and picked up the receiver.

"Detective MacDermot's desk. Well hi, Mrs. MacDermot, how are you?"

She held her hand out. "Gimme the phone, you—" She bit back the curse she had at the ready. It took her years to beat that Bronx girl out of her system. She wasn't about to let her loose again. Especially in front of the one person she still wanted to impress.

Bukowski tossed the receiver to her. She caught it and brought the phone to her ear. "Hello?"

"Hi, baby."

"Hiya, Ma."

"So, I hear you're available for dinner on Christmas."

Jesus Christ, did the lieutenant have her father on speed dial or something?

"Well—"

"Don't you dare lie to me, Desiree MacDermot!" The acid tone that still made her cringe zipped across the line. "Dinner will be at six. Bring pie. Love ya." Her mother hung up. As always, the woman was short and to the point.

Dez dropped the phone back in its cradle. This Christmas had gone to hell fast.

She looked up and saw gold eyes staring at her. Actually, they were devouring her.

Holy shit.

The woman was fucking gorgeous.

"Don't look at me like that, Mace."

He dropped his feet to the floor. "Like what?"

"You know like what."

He leaned on the desk, his chin resting in the palm of his hand, and he waited. Waited for her to realize they would be together.

"What, Mace? *What?*"

"I'm waiting on you."

"Don't bother." She casually waved him off. "Apparently I've gotta go buy pie."

She sounded so despondent, he couldn't help but smile. "Not a big fan of the holidays?" He'd have to work with her on that. He loved Christmas but had never been able to really celebrate it with his own family. He really wanted Dez to enjoy Christmas as much as he did. Right now, however, she looked like a puppy that got her tennis ball taken away.

"The whole season brings me out in a rash. I usually work during the holidays, but now, because of *your* sister, I've gotta deal with them."

"Them?"

"The family."

He understood her pain. Of course, his sisters weren't about to demand his presence to anything, especially if there might be a chance he'd end up embarrassing them. And since Mace went out of his way to embarrass them that would be a damn good worry.

"Oh God. I gotta go shopping now." She buried that beautiful face in her hands. "I hate holiday shopping."

"You know what? I gotta go shopping too. We should go together."

She started to drag her hand through her hair, then abruptly stopped. She shook her hand out and crossed her arms in front of her chest. "Have you always been this pushy?"

"I'll buy you a hot chocolate."

He watched her fight that amazing smile. "Go away, Mace."

"You're going to leave me to the tender mercies of these cruel New York streets? All alone? On Christmas? No family?" He sighed, giving her his best "sad look." He'd perfected it over the years with quite a few sympathetic barhooks. "Missy doesn't want me around for her big Christmas banquet tomorrow. She says I'll embarrass her in front of all her friends."

Dez damn near growled in anger. "You're her brother. How could she do that to you?" *Yes!* He had her. At least . . . well . . . he *did* have her.

"Hey, hoss." Bobby Ray Smith, also called Smitty by his closest friends and the entire United States Navy, grabbed a chair from one of the other desks, pulled it up next to his, and sat down. "They do have some beautiful women in this city." Why, oh why, did he meet with Smitty first before coming here? *Cause you're a dumb ass, Llewellyn.*

Smitty suddenly caught sight of Dez. And like the dog he, literally, was . . . "Well," he stated with that slow easy grin that got him more pussy than either of them would ever be able to count. "Hello, darlin'.."

The two shook hands, and Mace had the overwhelming desire to rip Smitty's arm from his socket.

Dez caught sight of the anchor tattoo on Smitty's forearm. "Navy?"

"Yup. Got out a few months ago." Smitty's slow drawl seemed more annoying than usual. "And Mace got out yesterday. Huh, hoss?"

Mace nodded.

"Navy, Mace?" She actually sounded disappointed.

"Now darlin', what's wrong with the Navy?" Smitty still hadn't let her hand go. Suddenly Mace hated his best friend.

"Nothing. Except it will never be the Marines."

Dez pulled her hand away as the men glanced at each other. "You were a Marine?"

Dez glared at him. "You don't have to sound so shocked, Mace. And I wasn't just a Marine. I was an MP, baby. Sergeant MacDermot when I discharged."

Smitty gave that damn charming smile. "He was commander. I made lieutenant. We were SEALs together." Normally, Mace would have no problem with Smitty dropping that bit of information. Amazing how much sex that little admission would get them. But he didn't want the flea-bitten bastard making his moves on Dez.

"Wow." Dez seemed less than interested. "That's really impressive. Bet that line got you a lot of oral sex too, huh?"

Smitty blinked. "You think I'm lyin'?"

"No. Not at all." Dez shrugged. "I just don't care, uh . . ."

"Bobby Ray Smith. But you can call me Smitty."

"Of course you're Smitty. Because everybody in the military has a friend named Smitty." The two smiled at each other. Nope, Mace didn't like this one goddamn bit.

"So . . ." Dez glanced at Mace with one raised eyebrow. "Smitty, are you enjoying our fair city?"

"Oh yeah. You know, Mace is taking good care of me and my kin."

"Kin?"

Uh-oh.

"Family."

"Oh?" Another glance at Mace. "Your *family* is here. And do they get along with Mace too?"

Mace had to look at Smitty for that himself. He always sensed that most of the Pack barely tolerated him.

He should have known, though. Being Southern, Smitty would never say anything anyone would consider cruel in front of strangers.

"Oh yeah! My momma says Mace is her sixth son."

"Really?"

"My sister's with me too, and she loves her some Mace."

"Does she now?" Dez turned to Mace. Boy, did she look annoyed. "You haven't changed one bit, Llewellyn."

He leaned back, crossing his arms in front of his chest. "I never said I had."

"But you did lie to me?"

"No. Missy really doesn't want me to come to her banquet. I simply don't give a shit."

"And if that happens to play on my sympathies, you conniving bastard?"

"I know what I want, Dez. You know how I am about that. Remember the Ring Dings?"

She pushed her hands through her hair. He kept frustrating her. *Good.* "We are *not* discussing the Ring Dings, Mace. Christ, we are too old for this. *I'm* too old for this."

"So, say you'll come out to dinner with me and then I'll stop."

"No."

"I refuse to hear that."

She turned to Smitty. "You tell him, Smitty. Tell him I said 'no'."

Smitty gazed at her. "You sure have some pretty eyes, darlin'."

Dez looked startled, then she beamed. "You are as bad as he is."

Mace realized in that second the two of them were having a "moment." *Well, that's not acceptable.*

"Jesus, Dez. What's that?"

Dez, following where Mace pointed, turned to look behind her. While he had her temporarily distracted, he took his other hand, wrapped it around the back of Smitty's neck, and slammed the man's head into Dez's desk.

When she snapped back around, Mace watched her innocently, Smitty gripped his forehead, and Dez's partner began to hysterically laugh.

"What did you do?"

Mace blinked. "Nothing."

Dez stretched her legs out on her couch and studied her painted toenails. That and waxing her brows were her only female indulgences. It was Christmastime, so her color of choice this week? A merry red. She smiled, wondering if Mace would like that color on her.

She shook her head. Mace Llewellyn. Back in her life after all these years. Persistent as ever too. Only now he was persistent about her as opposed to the Ring Dings. She wondered why. Why his sudden interest in her? They'd been friends throughout ninth grade. Very good friends. The move to Queens had been quite the ordeal, and when she'd finally gotten up the courage to see him . . . well, his sisters got to her first. They made it clear that with her Bronx accent and less-than-sparkling manners, she would never fit in with him or his family. In the end, she'd be nothing but an embarrassment for him.

Dez sighed and glanced at the television. Sirens from one of her favorite episode of *Cops* blared incessantly while a police dog took down a perp. The man kept moving, and the dog only bit down harder. If he stopped moving the dog would stop biting. Suddenly she knew how that perp felt. She kept moving and Mace kept biting down harder.

Damn. She kept doing that. Thinking about Mace Llewellyn. Why couldn't she get the man out of her mind?

Because he reminded you what that hole between your legs is really for.

She shook her head. She didn't have time for this or for him. Being a cop was her priority. Always had been. Always would be. Just ask her ex. And she wasn't about to go through *those* conversations again. So Mace would have to back the hell off.

Yeah. Good luck with that.

A big, wet tongue slathered across her ear, and she turned her head just enough to get another lick right across her face.

"Yuck!" She pushed her dog's giant paws off the couch, but for some reason that seemed to indicate he and his brother should join her on her large sectional. Suddenly she had a hundred-and-fifty-pound dog resting against her back, the other splayed across her lower legs.

"You two comfortable?" They both answered with a snort. When she'd gotten home, she'd put the two through their paces while she wore the bite sleeve. She loved working her dogs. It made a day of being a New York cop easier for some unknown reason. Maybe because she had an outlet for her stress and two amazingly well-trained and very protective dogs to show for it.

"So, what do you guys think? Mace Llewellyn—the man of my dreams? Or another schmuck looking for his chance at these beautifully painted toes?"

Her dogs whined. They'd barely tolerated her ex. They definitely wouldn't make room for some new guy Dez always sensed wasn't exactly a dog person.

"Don't worry, guys. I remember the rules. Love me. Love my dogs."

Dez leaned back against her furry Rottweiler-sized pillow and watched some stupid perp run from a man wearing a uniform holding a gun and yelling "Freeze." *Then they're shocked when they tazer their butts.*

Dez grabbed a bowl of chips. "Why do they always run?"

*   *   *

Mace should have known better. Drinking Uncle Willy's moonshine continued to be a bad idea. Especially when you were horny and desperately wondering whether the woman of your dreams moaned or growled during sex.

"You're thinking about her again, aren't ya."

Smitty sat down on the floor next to Mace. Poor drunk bastard. Of all the things Smitty could do, holding his liquor had never been one of them.

"I'm crazy about her."

"She's got big tits. What were those anyway? Triple Ds?"

"I'm sensing that knot on your forehead was not enough of a clue to keep your grubby dog paws off my woman." And they were *definitely* triple Ds.

"Don't get me wrong. She wears those big tits well. But they're big. *Huge!*"

Christ, drunk Smitty was annoying. Wolves simply couldn't hold their liquor.

Mace sighed. The evening started off nice enough. The two friends went to dinner. Discussed their new business plans. Flirted with the waitresses. Well, Smitty flirted. Mace watched and thought about Dez. Walked around Times Square. Started a fistfight. Ended a fistfight. Talked their way out of an arrest. Made their way down to Avenue A. Chatted with some very nice hookers. Talked their way out of an arrest by cops pretending to be nice hookers. Ate some pizza.

They could have kept going, but around two A.M., they found themselves back at Smitty's hotel room with two bottles of 'shine and a minibar chock full of junk food. Really, the two of them didn't need much else. An hour and a half later and Smitty was falling-down drunk while Mace found himself longing for a woman who kept staring at him like one of those nutcases she probably faced everyday on her job.

"Bobby Ray Smith, where are you?"

Mace nudged Smitty. "You are so busted."

The hotel room door flew open and Sissy Mae Smith stormed

into Mace's room. He didn't even know she had a key. "Dammit, Smitty!"

"What?"

Mace looked up at Sissy Mae, a very pretty girl version of Smitty. Mace learned to love the younger woman as his baby sister. He'd protect her exactly like Smitty would. There were very few people in his life he cared that much about. The fact that several of them were wolves still confused him to no end.

"You have got an entire city waitin' to be explored and what the hell do I find you doin'? Sittin' here drinkin' with Mace!" She smiled at Mace. "Hey, Mace darlin'. How ya doin'?"

"Fine, Sissy. Thanks for asking."

"How come you're nice to him?"

"Cause he's Mace and he already lives here. But you, you idiot . . ." Smitty drunkenly waved his baby sister away, and Sissy kicked a couch cushion at his head.

She glared at Mace. "Although I don't appreciate the great lion dragging my big brother down to the very pits of hell."

"Do you mean Long Island?"

"And what is going on with your hair?"

Mace ran his hand through the unruly locks on his head that had been sprouting all day. "Mane's growing back in."

"Weren't you damn near bald when we saw you this afternoon?"

"It grows fast." While on active duty, he had to shave his head every day to keep his C.O. off his back. But letting his mane grow back became his first step toward being a civilian again. Besides, he got the feeling Dez would like putting her hands in his hair. He knew he *wanted* her to put her hands in his hair. Preferably while he gently sucked her clit into his mouth.

Sissy Mae sniffed. "Lions are freaks."

Mace saluted Sissy with his Mason jar of 'shine. "Thank you kindly, Sissy Mae."

Smitty awkwardly pulled himself to his big wolf feet. "Would you like to live here, little sister?"

Sissy Mae turned her glare on her brother. "What are you

talkin' about now, you drunken idiot? And what in the hell happened to your forehead?"

Mace raised his hand. "That was my fault."

"I'm talkin' about movin' the Pack here. At least . . . part of it."

Sissy Mae scowled. "Why the hell would we . . ." Mace watched as she realized the implication of her brother's words. The Smith Pack of Tennessee had too many Alpha Males among Smitty's four brothers. One of the reasons he left the Pack and joined the Navy. Mace met Smitty when a high-ranking officer with jaguar blood decided to create a SEAL team made up of shifters only. It worked surprisingly well, and they did a lot of damage over eight years. When the team disbanded, Mace and Smitty decided they were ready to leave the military. Smitty got out six months before Mace, and the infighting between him and the other Smith brothers got pretty ugly.

Mace knew he'd never go back to the Pride, so he made Smitty an offer. It seemed logical the two friends should start a business together. Smitty agreed. Yet he didn't want to leave his baby sister. Although Mace didn't think she'd ever let him.

"Bobby Ray Smith, are you saying we should leave Tennessee and move to New York City?"

"Yup. That's what I'm sayin', Sissy Mae Smith."

Sissy threw herself into her brother's arms. "*Yes!* I was hoping that's what you were gonna say! I love this place! It's so exciting!" She looked at Mace. "Are we going to be working with you?"

"*You* are not going to be working with Mace. *I* am going to be working with Mace. You're going to find something nice and safe to do—like knittin'."

Sissy Mae laughed. "Yeah, right. So, Mace, are we going to be working with you?"

Smitty stumbled away from his sister.

"Now listen up, little sister—"

Sissy Mae slapped her hand over her brother's face and shoved him onto the couch. By the time he landed, he was snoring.

Mace watched two big feet stand in front of him. Wolf females always seemed to have the biggest freakin' feet. She crouched in front of him and smirked. "What's the matter, Mace?"

"What makes you think something's wrong?"

"You haven't been pompous or superior in the last ten minutes. So somethin' must be wrong."

Mace shrugged. "The woman of my dreams turned me down."

"For marriage?"

"Dinner."

Sissy Mae shook her head. "Is this the girl you've been talkin' about since I met you?"

"Desiree MacDermot. The woman I've been waiting for all my life."

"You know, my momma's right about you. You are a wolf in lion's clothin'. Get all bunged up over one woman. I can't even get Smitty to do that and he *is* wolf."

"That's not helpful."

"You want helpful, Mason?"

"Yes. I want helpful. Make yourself useful, woman."

"Fine. Call her as soon as you wake up."

"What?"

"Call her as soon as you wake up and ask her out."

"Why?"

"Trust me on this."

"I'm not a morning person."

"Mace . . ."

"Okay. Okay." He glanced over at Smitty, then back at the man's sister. "Let's write *Omega* on his forehead again. He hates that."

Chapter Three

Dez woke up cursing. The ring of her damn cell phone completely disrupted her lovely dream involving Mace, her, and her handcuffs.

She grabbed for the phone on her nightstand. Knocked it off. Reached down and grabbed for it. Fell out of bed. Hit one of the dogs in the process. Wrestled the phone from the dog's mouth. Then groggily crawled on all fours back into her warm and cozy bed.

"MacDermot," Dez mumbled into the phone, assuming it would be work.

"Hey."

Dez's arms went out from under her when that voice tore through her dazed, sleep-drowned mind, and she landed flat on her face. Mace and that voice of his slid all the way down to her clit and moved in.

Why the hell was he calling her? What the hell was his deal? And how the hell did he get her number anyway? All right. Forget that last stupid question. He probably had a full background check done on her by now. The man was a SEAL, after all.

Not knowing what else to say, Dez hit him with the first thing that came to mind. "Who is this?"

She crossed her eyes. Well those brilliant phrases kept rolling right from her mouth. *You're such an idiot, MacDermot.*

"It's Mace."

"Oh," she replied casually like she didn't almost come from

his "hey" alone. "Hiya, Mace." She used her shoulder to cover the mouthpiece on her phone, shoved a pillow over her face, and yelled into it. After a moment, she calmly went back to the conversation. "What's up?"

She heard him stretch. "Nothing. Just checking on you."

She closed her eyes and her legs. Took a calming breath. "Oh. That's sweet."

"I'm known for being sweet."

"No, you're not."

He laughed softly and she bit her lip to keep from moaning. Really . . . is there anything better than the gravelly six A.M. voice on a man? Dez didn't think so. And Mace had one of those in spades. She may have to dig out her vibrator. *It has to be around here somewhere.*

"You're right. I'm not." A moment of silence descended, and Dez wondered if they already ran out of things to say. She should have known better. "You just getting up?"

"Not really. It's only six A.M. and I don't have to go to work. So, I'm just lying here."

"Really?" She heard his body move, the sheets rustle. She imagined him naked and in bed. She closed her eyes. Okay. She needed to stop doing that right now. "What are you wearing?"

Oh no! They were *not* going to have this conversation. She couldn't handle it. Hell, she couldn't handle *him*. "Christ, Mace, we haven't had one of these conversations in a long time."

"Yeah, but at fourteen they were relatively tame. We're much older now."

"Don't remind me."

"So?"

"So what?"

"What are you wearing?"

"I'm not discussing that with—"

"Are you naked?"

"No!" Dez rolled her eyes. Good God, the man could be persistent. "A tank top and baggy shorts."

"Panties?"

With a throat clear, "No."

He purred. At least that's exactly what it sounded like. Purring. She didn't remember him purring before.

"Did you . . . did you just purr?"

"Yup. I'm thinking about you with no underwear."

"Jesus, Mace. You're killing me."

"Is it making you wet?"

"Mason Llewellyn! We are *not* having this conversation."

"Why?"

"Well, I am hoping to eventually arrest your sister for murder."

"I'm hoping you arrest my sister for murder."

"Oh."

"You're running out of excuses."

"I am not."

"Your nipples hard?"

"Mace!"

"Give me something. I'm dyin' here." Every once in a while, Mace suddenly reminded her he was born and raised in New York when a little bit of an accent reared its ugly head. It usually only happened when he got emotional or, if she remembered her school days correctly, horny . . .

She ground her teeth together. She would *not* have phone sex with a guy she hadn't seen in more than twenty years. Even she wasn't that desperate. "What do you want from me, Mace?"

There went that damn purr again. Deep. Low from his gut. Primal. "Everything."

Dez closed her eyes. *Good answer.* But also the wrong one. She didn't have everything to give. She was a cop. Born a cop if you happened to ask her dad. The one thing in her life that made her truly happy. The one thing she did really well. She couldn't give that up for Mace. She couldn't give that up for anybody.

"You got quiet all of a sudden. What's wrong?"

Dez sighed. "I'm thinking about the price I pay to be me."

Mace chuckled. "What's so funny, Llewellyn?"

"You. You haven't changed one damn bit."

"Are you kidding? I am not the person you used to know."

"No. You're the person I always knew you were."

Dez pulled herself up to a sitting position. "Is that right? And what deep insight do you have about me right now?"

"That's easy. You're thinking you're not about to give up being a cop for me or any man. Aren't you?"

Dez placed the phone on the comforter and scowled at it. She had the almost overwhelming desire to run from the room screaming. She forgot Mace used to do this to her all the time. That he saw what no one else saw. What no one else wanted to see. Sometimes her own family included.

"Pick up the phone, Dez."

She shook her head. *It's not a picture phone, you idiot!*

"I can hear you breathing. So pick up the phone—*now*."

Dez grabbed the phone and put it to her ear. "How did you . . . when did you . . . ?"

"Come out to dinner with me, Dez."

"No way!" She would not be dating Rasputin anytime soon.

"You either come out here for a nice, normal dinner or I come there . . . and who knows what I'll tell you about yourself."

Would that be before or after her dogs rip his arms off? Or she fucks him on the porch. You know . . . whatever.

"This is—"

"Blackmail. Yes. I know. I'm a rich, white male not afraid to use the power of his position." She rolled her eyes, imagining Mace's smile as he spouted that load of crap. "So come out with me anyway. Just dinner. I promise."

"Mace—"

"Come out with me, Dez." His voice actually got lower. How? "Come out with me tonight. Please?"

The "please" caught her off guard. She didn't remember Mace ever asking for anything except the salt or ketchup. And then only out of politeness. Now he wasn't being polite. The man practically begged. She thought about that for a moment. She had someone like Mace Llewellyn *begging* her to go out with him? Had hell frozen over? Were pigs flying?

She let out a shaky breath and she knew he heard it. Closing her eyes, she wondered how huge this mistake would turn out to be.

"Okay. I'll go out with you."

"Good."

"But just dinner. Don't go gettin' any wacky, adolescent ideas."

"Who? Me?"

"When and where?"

"Eight o'clock. You pick the place. Any place you want."

"Any place? You know, I have very expensive taste when other people are buying."

"*Any* place."

"Okay. Well, I heard there's a Van Holtz steakhouse that opened up in the Village." Another long, rather deafening pause. "Is there a problem there, Mace? A little out of your price range, perhaps?"

"Smart-ass, and no. That's not an issue."

"You're not a vegetarian or something, are you?"

Mace's almost-hysterical laughter at her offhanded remark seemed a little excessive, but she chose to ignore it. "Well then?"

He cleared his throat. "Okay. Fine. You want Van Holtz? We'll go to Van Holtz."

"Jesus, Mace. I'm not asking you to choose a political party here."

"Might as well be."

"What?"

"Nothing. So eight, in the Village, front of Van Holtz restaurant. That work for you?"

"Perfect. I've gotta do some shopping anyway. So, I'll see you then. 'Kay?"

"Yeah . . . so . . . are your nipples hard or not?"

"Bye, Mace."

She closed the phone. *This is such a mistake.*

Dez flinched when her phone rang again. She flipped it open. "I'm not telling you if my nipples are hard."

"That's good. Cause I really don't wanna know," stated a female voice Dez didn't recognize.

"Who the hell is this?"

"Is this Detective MacDermot?"

"Who's askin'?" She shook her head. The reappearance of Bronx-Dez. She thought she'd buried her . . .

"Look, I got some information. On Alexander Petrov." Dez sat up a little straighter. True, her removal from this case made this a slightly inappropriate conversation, but why scare off a potential lead with that unnecessary bit of information?

"Okay."

"Can you meet me?"

"Where?"

"The Chapel. At eleven-thirty."

The Chapel. A hot Village club she could never hope of getting into without her badge. "Isn't there another place we can—"

The woman cut her off. "I'll be there. You won't have a problem getting in."

"You work there?"

Dez received a long pause. For a moment, she thought the woman hung up. "My family owns it."

Dez bit the inside of her mouth to prevent herself from saying something stupid. An effective technique she learned years ago. "So, you're a Brutale?"

"Yeah. Gina. Gina Brutale. Meet me there at eleven-thirty. Tell the guy at the door you're there to see me. Give him your name but don't say detective . . . and try not to look like a cop." Brutale hung up.

Dez closed her phone and glanced at the clock on her nightstand by her .45. This would work nicely. Dinner with Mace at eight o'clock. Having to handle work at eleven-thirty kept her from doing something monumentally stupid. Like going back to Mace's hotel room or giving him a blow job in the restaurant bathroom. You know, whatever . . .

Mace turned over in the king-size bed and buried his face into the pillow. That woman's voice would be the death of him. Knowing she sounded like that when she woke up turned his cock into a lead pipe. He couldn't wait to experience that for himself. Waking up with Dez growling next to him. He would experience it, too. He'd waited too long for this. For her. She simply had no idea what she did to him. She never did.

Mace went back to sleep and dreamed about him and Dez. And Dez's handcuffs . . .

Dez stood next to her partner as they waited for the M.E.

"Don't forget, MacDermot. You're not here."

"Nope. Right now I'm out singing carols."

"Let's not push it."

John Michaels, one of the city's best M.E.s, pushed open the double doors. "Good. You're both here." He motioned to them, and they followed him inside. Alexander Petrov's naked body lay out on a metal table.

"I want to show you two something. Here." He pointed to the man's throat, and both Dez and Bukowski leaned over and examined the area.

"What is that?"

"Claw marks."

Dez frowned. "From a dog?"

"Awfully big claws for a dog, in my opinion. Plus something's not quite right."

"What do you mean?"

He motioned to her, and Dez went and stood in front of him.

"If an animal clawed his throat, we would have found three to four swipe marks here." He tapped one side of Dez's neck. "Or here." He tapped the other. "Or both."

"Okay."

"But what I found on this vic is very different."

"Like what?"

"There's a bruise across his throat. Four claw marks on the left side of his neck and one on the right. Which would imply this . . ." He wrapped long fingers around her throat. Four on one side. His thumb on the other. "Now pull away from me, Detective." Dez did, and Michaels's gloved fingers painlessly slashed across her flesh.

The two stared at each other. "Holy shit."

Bukowski stood next to them. "I don't get it. What am I missing?"

Dez looked at her partner. "How many animals you know got thumbs?"

Dez and Bukowski stood on the street corner while she pulled gloves onto her hands. As soon as Bukowski pulled out one of his rare cigarettes, she knew he was freaking out. "What's with you?"

"Doesn't this whole thing freak you out in the least?"

"Nah." Dez shook her head. "A real puzzle to solve. I live for this stuff. Besides, it's probably some wacko wearing a clawed glove or something."

Bukowski smiled. "You're a weird one, MacDermot."

"So my sisters keep reminding me."

"Where you going now?"

Dez pulled her notepad out from her back pocket and checked her list. "Shopping for the family . . . that'll be fun. Gotta order those goddamn pies too. Dinner with Mace. And meeting with Gina Brutale."

"Gina Brutale? Why are you meeting with her?"

"She says she has information on Petrov."

"Dez, you're not supposed to be meeting with informants. You weren't supposed to be here."

"She called me directly. If you show up instead, we won't find out a goddamn thing. Don't worry, if I get anything really juicy, I'll make sure to let you know. Okay?"

"Be careful. Those Brutales are not a nice bunch of people."

"I know. I know. You don't have to tell me twice."

"And don't think for a second you slipped that bullshit about Llewellyn past me. What do you mean you're having dinner with him?"

Damn. She really thought she'd gotten away with that.

"He called me this morning and asked me out. Again."

"And you said yes? Are you high?"

"Not in years. And I don't see the problem. Mace Llewellyn is an old friend of mine. We're just having dinner. Nothing else."

"I saw the way he looked at you yesterday, Dez. That man has more on his mind than just dinner."

"I'm not discussing this anymore. I gotta meet the guys for coffee."

"Ask them, then. They'll tell you. Llewellyn wants one thing from you."

"Bye." She walked off, but she could still hear Bukowski yelling at her.

"I'm calling you tomorrow. And you better answer the fuckin' phone or I'm coming over!"

Why did every man insist on becoming her big brother? She had two sisters. More than enough siblings. So she didn't want a brother.

Funny, she had the distinct feeling no matter what Mace felt for her, it definitely wasn't brotherly.

Mace leaned back on his hotel room couch, his arms over his head, his legs stretched out in front of him. His T-shirt and long shorts stuck to his sweat-drenched body. He thought he'd be able to run Dez from his system, at least for a few hours, in the hotel's gym. But every second that passed brought him closer to seeing her again. The thought made his mouth water.

He thought his obsession for her rocked off the charts before. He'd been wrong. That had simply been the idea of her, without any knowledge of how she actually turned out. He could fantasize all he wanted to, but his subconscious knew she could be a far different person. Lazy. Mean. Nasty. She could be anything. Instead, she blossomed. Who knew being a cop would actually make someone *happy*?

That scared little girl who used to hide behind her books? Well, the strong, confident woman of Mace's dreams had replaced her. He hadn't been lying to her earlier. He always knew that woman quietly lived inside Dez. He always hoped he'd be the man to bring it out in her. But based on what he found out about her from Watts, she found confidence under the relentless tutelage of a Marine Corp drill sergeant.

Dez still seemed wary of him, though. Not surprising really.

According to Watts, her divorce turned kind of bloody. Her ex was a prosecutor who eventually became a defense attorney. The marriage lasted as long as her stint in the Marines but apparently wasn't nearly as satisfying for either of them. Since then she hadn't dated much, and nothing serious had come along.

Until now.

Mace flew beyond being serious about this woman. His feelings for her lived in another universe altogether.

The woman's very soul called out to him. He kept imagining what that body would feel like under him. What that voice would sound like in his ear when she was coming. Would she rip the skin off his back or just leave bruises? Did she bite? Or maybe she liked to be bit. Did her pussy taste sweet? Or a little salty? And did she mind being worn as a hat?

Mace groaned and glanced over at the hotel clock on the nearby end table. He still had hours before he'd see her again.

Smitty took his Pack out for a long lunch in Midtown. Mace glanced over at the bathroom. Nope. His cock was too hard to even think he could make it to the shower.

He reached into his sweatpants, pulling his cock free. He ran his hand along its hard length, immediately imagining Dez. Now she wasn't some hazy fantasy that he concocted. He knew exactly what adult Dez looked like, which only made him harder. Mace accessed one of his standard Dez fantasies, the one where he kissed her for hours. Not exactly *Penthouse* worthy, but it still ruled as one of his favorites. She had such gorgeous lips, he could spend his life kissing that mouth. In fact, he had every intention of doing exactly that.

Mace closed his eyes and let his head fall back against the couch. He started off slowly, stroking himself. Enjoying the feeling of his own hand. And he could almost feel her. *Dez's lips on his throat, his jaw, his mouth.* His grip tightened and he couldn't stifle a groan. *His tongue inside her mouth, her hands sliding across his chest.* His breath sped up as his strokes became stronger, faster.

One meeting with her and Dez had become a part of him. She

infected his blood. He could smell her scent. Almost feel her skin. That voice, though. That goddamn voice pushed him over the edge. It always had. His orgasm slammed into him and he growled Dez's name as his come spurted all over his hand.

Mace relaxed back on the cushions. *That woman is going to be the death of me.*

Dez walked up to the table outside the café. Not surprisingly, they weren't alone. Four gorgeous women surrounded them. Vinny caught her eye. The spark of desperation in those pretty blue peeps sent her a clear message. "Help me. These women are boring me to death."

Well, she couldn't leave her buddies hanging. Besides, it would be fun.

She walked up to the group, flashed her badge. "I'm sorry, ladies. But I'm here to arrest these men for their homosexual prostitution ring."

The group stared at her. She crossed her arms, which caused her jacket to move back, revealing the gun holstered at her side. "Start moving those asses, ladies. Or I start shooting."

It took them less than a minute to evacuate their seats. Dez threw herself into the one next to Jimmy Cavanaugh and put her feet on Vinny's lap. "Well, that was fun."

Vinny slapped Dez's boot-covered feet. "Why are we always gay in these scenarios you create?"

She grinned. "Because it makes you idiots uncomfortable. I live for that."

Dez ordered herself a large black coffee and an éclair from the waiter. Once he walked away, she glanced at the three men sitting with her. Three of her closest friends since her tour in Japan. They became friends because they were all products of the "Burroughs." Vinny Pentolli represented Queens, Jimmy Cavanaugh Brooklyn, and Salvatore Ping-Wei stood in for Manhattan. She represented the Bronx.

They were the toughest MPs she'd ever known. They took no crap but were fair. And she had become one of the most feared dog handlers because she had "Baby." No one messed with

Baby. No one came near Baby. No one looked Baby in the eye. No one but her. Dez had earned their respect by expertly taking care of four drunken sailors her third night on duty. Not hard when Baby had one of their throats in her maw.

The four of them served together for over a year until reassignment to different bases. Dez stayed in the Marines for only another two years after that. Then she came back to the city of her birth and became what she always wanted to be. A New York City cop. Five years ago, she walked into one of her favorite Irish bars and right into the middle of a bar fight. She and her partner at the time broke up the fight even though they were both off duty. When the proverbial smoke cleared she came face to face with her past.

Kind of like the day before when she saw Mace again. Only she just wanted to have a beer with the guys and catch up with old times. With Mace, she didn't want to do anything but sit on his face.

"You look awfully nice today."

Of all the people she would expect to notice the cleavage she decided to show in anticipation of her dinner later that night with Mace, Sal was the last of them. It always seemed like he didn't pay attention to much, like he existed in his own world. Yet, every few months or so, he surprised her by revealing that nothing really got past him.

"You're right," Vinny agreed. "She has on her *good* black jeans and her low-cut slut top." She glared at Vinny and took her feet off his lap.

"Showing some healthy tit action," Jimmy unnecessarily added.

"*I am not!*"

The three men laughed while Dez's face turned red.

"So what's the deal, MacDermot? I know you didn't dress up like this for us. You hate this season, so you're not feeling merry. And you're off duty since your unfortunate run-in with the rich and the powerful."

Dez waited until the waiter left her coffee and pastry and walked away. "Well . . . I have a date tonight."

The way they gaped at her was what she found so insulting. "I'm not lying."

"No. But are you delusional?"

"Blow me!"

"*Whoa!*" All three men reared back, and she inwardly groaned at the return of the foul-mouthed Bronx girl she had been. *Damn Mace!*

Vinny held his hands up, palms out. "Calm down, woman. You know we're kidding."

"No, you're not. And you're paying for my éclair."

Jimmy stared at her and Dez knew why he didn't spend a lot of time alone. She did really have the most gorgeous male friends. Although they were a little . . . different. Sal lived in his own world. Vinny brought being an egotistical prick to a brand-new high or low depending on your perspective. And Jimmy always seemed angry. She never saw him smile with anyone but the three of them. He probably came out of his mother's womb with that scowl permanently plastered to his gorgeous face. Sometimes she wondered if smiling might actually be painful for him.

"So who is he?"

"He's actually an old friend of mine. Just got back into town." She sipped her coffee, then said while staring into the coffee mug, "He's Navy."

Dez ducked the balled-up napkins thrown at her.

"Have you no shame?" Jimmy sighed.

"Oh, shut up."

The men took chunks of her éclair. "So who is this Navy guy?"

Dez swallowed at Jimmy's question. "Uh . . . Mason Llewellyn."

The silence that followed . . . kind of painful. Finally, Dez couldn't take it anymore. "*What?*"

Vinny barely smothered a laugh. "You expect us to believe you're dating a Llewellyn?"

"I'm not *dating* a Llewellyn. We went to school together. I told you about him."

"You went to school with a Llewellyn?"

"Well," Jimmy cut in, "I went to school with a Rockefeller. Of the Brooklyn Rockefellers."

Dez gazed down at her empty plate. They'd completely demolished her éclair. She inwardly sighed. Of course they didn't believe her. Why would anyone think Dez MacDermot would know, much less date, a Llewellyn? Especially one as tasty as Mace?

"She did tell us about him. They went to the Cathedral School together. He was her first big crush. A cute little guy who couldn't control his hair." The three of them gaped at Sal. "What?"

Dez pushed the empty plate away. "I'm always surprised when I realize you were actually listening to me."

"I listen. I just don't say anything unless necessary." He shrugged. "It felt necessary."

Jimmy leaned back, and Dez winced as the chair creaked loudly. All that muscle on one man often seemed kind of inhuman. Not a lot of chairs held him easily. "I'm not sure I'm comfortable with you going out with a Llewellyn."

Startled, Dez looked at her friend. *He's not comfortable?*

"I agree with you, Jim. I'm not sure you should go through with this." Now Dez turned her eyes on Vinny.

"Have you both lost your minds?"

"I mean, who is this guy?"

"And when exactly was the last time you saw him?"

"You know, I'd expect this crap from Bukowski, but not from you guys."

"Bukowski's uncomfortable with this too, huh?"

"This conversation"—Dez rapped her knuckles against the Formica table—"is over."

"Be careful, Dez," Jimmy stated earnestly.

"And don't sleep with him the first night," Vinny warned. "We know what a slut you can be."

Dez turned to Sal. "Do you have anything to add to this bullshit?"

"Yeah." Sal looked down from the ceiling he'd been staring

at. "Based on the structure of this building, if we removed that pillar back there, we could take out this whole block."

Dez sighed.

Mace sat down next to Smitty and glared at the man. "Could you explain to me again why we're here?"

"Because my sister wanted to come to Macy's. See all the pretty Christmas displays. Some people actually like this holiday, Mace."

"I understand why we're at Macy's. I don't understand why we're in the lingerie department of Macy's." It sure as hell wasn't helping his present situation. He kept imagining Dez in all the different panties and bras on the sales floor. It simply wouldn't make dinner an easy event if he walked in sporting a hard-on.

"You think I'm comfortable?" Smitty shook his head. "I'd rather be driving bamboo shoots through my fingernails than thinkin' about my sister in any of this . . . stuff," he growled. "And she better be gettin' somethin' flannel."

"Yeah, right." Smitty always wanted to believe his baby sister remained some kind of untouched virgin. At twenty-nine and seriously cute, Mace doubted that.

"I'll have you know wolf women are very into flannel."

"Not the wolf women I've known."

Surprised, Smitty turned to Mace, who smiled and shrugged. Smitty really thought he knew everything about him, didn't he? Foolish puppy.

"What can I say? I'm a male. They were three healthy females. It was the Philippines. Do the math."

"And after all that you think you can settle down with one woman? A human, no less?"

"Of course I can." Mace grinned. "Cause she's Dez."

"I met her, Mace. She's a nice girl and all, but I don't get it."

"Good. Keep it that way."

Smitty chuckled. "Man, hoss, you got it bad."

"I know." He stood up. "You better tell your sister to get a move on. I've got to head downtown soon. I am not going to be late for this."

Mace wandered away to check out all the lingerie. He wondered how long before he and Dez would be at the "It's okay to buy me lingerie" stage of their relationship. He hoped it would be tomorrow. Although even he had to admit that might be pushing it a little.

Or maybe dinner would prove she had changed after all. So much he'd rather stick his hand in an open flame instead of spending one more second with her. It would definitely make things easier since she insisted on being damn difficult about all this. Yet he wasn't holding out hope for that scenario either.

Mace had just passed a line of demi-cup bras that actually made his mouth water when he saw her. Looking beautiful and sexy—and desperate. She was talking to some short guy with no neck. Actually, no-neck was doing all the talking. Dez seemed trapped. She nodded as if she were really listening, but her eyes seemed to search for anyone who could rescue her. Eventually their eyes locked, and Mace could practically hear her screaming for help. He realized how much of their time together she did remember, when she made a move he hadn't seen in twenty years.

Dez ran her hands through her beautiful auburn hair, brought her fingertips over her ears, lingering on the right one as she gave it a gentle and subtle tug.

It had been their sign. The move they made when Amber Kollerici backed you into a corner to discuss the fun world of knitting or when Dominic Bannon had you backed into a corner threatening to pound your face in. Their secret sign for "Get me the fuck outta here!"

With a smile he didn't try to hide, he held up the bra and panty set he'd been eyeing and pointed at it. He raised an eyebrow. Immediately she caught on. *If I help you, you wear this . . .*

She scratched her forehead with one finger. The middle one. He laughed and went off to save his damsel in distress.

Wasn't holiday shopping for your family bad enough without having to add running into the ex-husband? Especially when he stopped to buy lingerie for his fiancée. Then she did that thing again. That thing her post-breakup therapist told her never to do when she met up with her ex to go over property splits or paperwork.

Ask him how he was doing.

Because Matt would tell her. He'd tell her in detail. And it was always bad. The man made über-money, lived in the poshest part of Manhattan with his hot, slut fiancée. Yet he always found a reason to complain about something—if not everything.

Already he'd been talking for a good twenty minutes about how everyone at his firm hated him. Of course they hated him. Matt made being an asshole into an art form. But, of course, that couldn't possibly be the reason. They didn't understand him. His brilliance had them all jealous, or they envied the fact he could buy a new car every other year. It definitely wasn't because he was an asshole.

For the billionth time since she realized her marriage had been a huge mistake, Dez kicked herself. What the hell had she been thinking anyway? That he might actually like her? That he wanted to be with her to raise a family? That he'd be okay with her being on The Job? She shuddered, thinking about those many arguments over her late nights and overtime schedule.

Well, that's what she got for trying to prove her sisters wrong. She wanted to show them she could get a man. That she could be happy.

Idiot.

Well, she had no one to blame but herself. All that aside, she still needed to get away. She just never knew how to politely get herself out of these conversations. At her very core, she still felt a little guilty over their breakup. So telling him to fuck off and storming away never seemed like an option.

Dez glanced around. She'd been shopping for her sisters and their brats when she found herself wandering around the lingerie department and thinking about Mace. She never worried about underwear too much, but she did have on her special, dark red lace panties with matching bra. Although she had no intention of letting Mace see her in them, she still couldn't bring herself to whip out the Hanes Her Way for this particular occasion.

Now, pricing all the great stuff they had available, she found herself thinking all sorts of dirty and morally appalling things she could do to Mace and that he could do to her. The nuns had been right. She was no better than Mary Magdalene.

"And you know the only reason he's trying to prove I'm using the firm's money for inappropriate purchases is because he's jealous of me."

Dez barely stifled a yawn when she suddenly felt someone's eyes on her. The intensity of it almost overwhelmed her. It licked across her spine, the back of her neck. It wasn't an unpleasant feeling. Far from it. She looked around, finally catching sight of Mace. One look into those gold eyes and her entire body clenched. She almost squirmed.

Why he was in the lingerie section she had no idea, but she would always be eternally grateful.

She screamed at him in her head. "Get that fine ass over here and save me!" Although that seemed kind of useless. She remembered the hand signals they came up with should they find themselves in such a situation. They went from, "Hey, when you got a minute, could you stop by" to *Get me the fuck outta here!*"

Dez really hoped she was using the correct one now. She'd lose her mind if she instead utilized the never-before accessed "We're going to the closet to make out. Come get me in twenty minutes."

Instead of rushing to her side, Mace held up a panty and lingerie set she would never try to pour her body into. Had the man lost his mind? Why the hell would he show her that? Then he wiggled his eyebrows at her.

Christ! Men truly were disgusting. She rubbed her forehead with her middle finger, which made him laugh.

He came toward her, but Mace never simply walked. No. He stalked. Like she were prey. This time was no different. As he moved toward her, she noticed he stared at her face. Then, as he got closer, his eyes moved onto her mouth.

Holy shit, he wanted to kiss her and seemed hell-bent on doing just that.

She swallowed. Hard. She didn't know what to do. Clearly the man was taking advantage of her current dire situation. And, clearly, she wanted him to.

God, did she want him to.

The whole time, her ex kept talking. But she'd stopped listening. She couldn't hear anything over her poor heart trying to burst out of her body.

Suddenly Mace was there. In front of her. Her ex's voice droned on for another thirty seconds or so, then stopped, since he was no longer the center of her attention. He'd always hated that. Hence the divorce.

Mace's arm slipped around her waist and he pulled her flush against his body. His head lowered toward hers, and for the first time she noticed Mace had a healthy head of hair. She frowned. She could have sworn only yesterday the man had been nearly bald.

His lips were inches away from hers.

"Don't you dare, Mace Llewellyn," she whispered in desperation. When did her life start spiraling out of control? She always had control. Or, at the very least, the illusion of it. But Mace, he wouldn't let her have even that. Not if he could help it.

"I'm just helpin' out, baby," he whispered back. Then his lips were on hers, and suddenly Macy's giant department store, three days before Christmas, completely cleared out and she and Mace were the only people left in the entire building.

That's how it felt anyway. She couldn't think beyond his lips taking hers. His tongue licked across her bottom lip and, like the weak-willed female she was, her mouth opened just enough for him to stake a claim. His tongue slid in and instinctually her tongue met his. She tasted spicy cinnamon and Mace. Both tasted wonderful. No one had ever kissed her like this before. Like they were taking ownership.

Her arms slid around his neck, his free hand finding its way into her hair. He gripped the back of her head and held her steady for his onslaught. Not letting her back away—like she even considered it an option. She wasn't going anywhere. Not at the moment anyway. It had been a long time since she'd been this close to a man. Any man. But to have a physical god like

Mace Llewellyn kissing her like he'd been waiting years to do this . . . well, a girl should never rush through that. And she didn't. She took her time exploring Mace's mouth and tongue.

Tonight would be brutal. Thank God she had something to do after their dinner or she'd be getting herself into all sorts of trouble. With just a kiss, Mace practically made her forget . . . well, everything. Everything but him.

Throat clearing. He kept hearing someone clearing their throat. Who the fuck would dare try to get his attention when he had the most divine tongue in his mouth?

He gripped Dez tighter, and she tangled her fingers in his hair. Damn, but the woman could kiss. She tasted so good, too. When he'd walked over to rescue her from the no-neck guy, he had no intention of kissing her. But the closer he got the more he found himself staring at those lips. Those perfectly shaped, full lips. Suddenly he forgot all about no-neck and could think only about Dez. Sweet, adorable, damn confusing Dez.

That throat clearing again. Well, that would start getting on his damn nerves. Regretfully, he pulled away from her, looking down into her beautiful face. He could smell her lust for him. He would bet Dez was as wet as he was hard. Maybe they could just go to the Ritz and have dinner after some serious fucking? Nah. Dez was too nice a girl for that.

Dammit.

"Excuse me?"

Mace glowered at the strange voice speaking to him. Without looking away from Dez, "Who is that?"

"That's my ex . . . Matt . . . uh . . . somebody . . ."

Mace beamed in absolute delight. She'd forgotten the man's name. The name that once belonged to her. *Good job, Llewellyn.*

Growling low, Mace turned just his head to glare at Dez's ex. The man physically blanched and probably didn't even realize he backed up several steps. Mace really wanted to shift right then and there. Rip the man's throat out and bring his lifeless corpse back to Dez as a kind of pre-wedding gift. Although right in the middle of Macy's . . . that might be a bit tacky. Even for him.

"Go. Away."

Whatever expression Mace had on his face, he didn't have to repeat himself. No-neck stumbled back a couple more steps, turned, and quickly walked away with a "See ya, Dez" tossed over his shoulder. Mace watched until he couldn't see him anymore, then he turned back to Dez. He still had her undivided attention. Good.

His hand slid around to cup her cheek, using his thumb to trace the line of her mouth. "That was better than I'd ever imagined. Like ten thousand times better."

Dez swallowed. "Good to know."

They gazed at each other, and Mace wondered if she'd be amenable to a quickie in one of the changing rooms. Just to take the edge off. Nah. She was too nice for that. *Dammit.*

"Mace Llewellyn! What the hell are you doin'? Let that little girl go."

Mace ignored Sissy Mae, but Dez apparently remembered they weren't alone. That they were actually in the middle of a major department store, making out in the lingerie section. Her hands suddenly released the grip she had on his hair and began to push on his chest as she pulled away from him.

He growled. Really, how attached could Smitty be to his sister? Would he really notice if Mace killed her?

She lost her fucking mind! What the hell was she doing? Why hadn't she decked him? Kicked him in the nuts? Set his hair on fire? Something! Other than kissing the presumptuous bastard back.

Her sisters were right. She had no friggin' sense.

"Are you okay, darlin'?" Dez looked into the face of a woman who had to be Smitty's sister. She looked exactly like him, only a smaller, girl version.

Dez took a deep breath as she took another step away from Mace. "Yeah. Yeah. Sure, I'm fine."

The woman took hold of her wrist with a vicelike grip. "Well, why don't you and I stop by the little girl's room. Give you a little time to compose yourself."

Mace suddenly tore his eyes away from Dez's face to glare at her rescuer. "She looks fine to me."

"That's cause you're a boy and you wouldn't know any better." She walked off, yanking Dez behind her.

Christ! What a strong female. Strong as an ox.

The two women wandered around until they discovered a bathroom, while the woman introduced herself in one long rush as "Sissy Mae Smith. Smitty's baby sister. Everybody just calls me Sissy. Or Sissy Mae. Some call me Mae. But I really don't like that. So you can call me Sissy. Or Sissy Mae," while dragging Dez into the bathroom with her.

Thankfully empty, Dez gripped a corner of one of the bathroom sinks and took in a couple of deep, calming breaths.

"That Mace sure does have a way, don't he?"

"You could say that." Dez splashed some cold water on her face. As she dried off with a paper towel, "You know, I've been up against guys covered in the blood of their coworkers. I've faced off against stone-cold contract killers who thought they had nothin' to lose. I've even gone toe to toe with a sixteen-foot python that had recently finished digesting its owner and I could tell he wanted me as the tasty dessert. And yet, none of that freaked me out as much as Mace Llewellyn does."

Sissy chuckled as she put on a dab of lip gloss. "Yeah, I know. That's our Mace."

Dez turned and leaned her butt against the sink, her arms crossed in front of her. She opened her mouth to speak but realized she had nothing to say. Or maybe she had way too much to say.

Sissy continued to touch up her makeup, but Dez could feel the woman watching her. She hated that. If there was something to say, then freakin' say it.

"What?" The woman caught her making out in the lingerie department; normal pleasantries one has with a stranger didn't seem to apply anymore. "Why do you keep staring at me?"

"Can I ask you a question?" Sissy's accent flowed as thick as molasses. And she spoke as fast as Smitty talked slow. If the two didn't look so similar, Dez would have never guessed they grew up in the same house.

"Why not?"

Sissy put her makeup away in her small leather purse and turned to face Dez. "You and Mace—"

"Whoa, Gidget. There is no me and Mace."

"My name's Sissy Mae. Or Sissy. Or—"

"What I'm trying to say is that there is Mace period. And Dez period. There is no combining of the two. We are two separate sentences."

"Not to be rude, but you may be screaming 'no way' now, but out there you were screaming 'dear God, yes!' So I wanna make sure you ain't about to hurt my boy."

Dez turned to face her. "Me? Hurt Mace? What are you, high?"

"I beg your pardon?"

"Look, Sally Mae—"

"It's Sissy Mae."

"Whatever. All I'm saying is, I couldn't hurt Mace. I don't think there's anybody who can."

"That's where you're wrong. You are his one weakness. Maybe his only one."

Dez stared at Sissy Mae. Her mouth open. The woman must be sniffing glue. She didn't think Mace had any weaknesses, but if he did, she couldn't be one of them.

"Honey, I don't know what load of crap he's told you, but I'm guessing Mace's only interest in me right now is that he didn't fuck me before."

"Well excuse me, darlin', for being a bit direct and crass here—but that's a huge load of bullshit."

Dez blinked in surprise. Like that, Sissy Mae went from charming, soft-spoken Southerner to a bitch on tractor wheels. "Look, Sissy—"

Sissy cut her off. "That boy has been drivin' me crazy with stories about your ass since I've known him. And I've known him for more than ten years now. Let me just say that, no offense, but I am tired of hearing about you. Trust me, if Mace only wanted to fuck ya, you'd have had your ankles around your ears by now. He's looking for more than that. So get ready for the ride, darlin'."

With that, Sissy stomped out of the bathroom, only to glide back in ten seconds later, her demeanor completely back to old Southern charm. "Well, come on, darlin'. The boys are waitin'."

Sissy Mae gave a charming smile, and Dez felt that need again. The need to find out where all the exits were.

"What exactly is your sister doing in there?"

"Telling Dez she should run for her life?"

Mace was in no mood. He checked his watch. If they left now they would end up at the restaurant a little early, but he had to get Dez away from these two. He admitted to himself the Smiths had truly become family. Because only family could embarrass and worry him this much.

Sissy Mae dragged Dez back toward them. "Mace Llewellyn. You be sweet to this darlin' little gal. I just love her!" Dez pulled away from Sissy and attached herself to Mace's side.

He leaned down and asked against her ear, "You okay?"

"Just keep me away from your hillbilly friends," she murmured back.

Mace kissed the top of her head and focused back on the siblings.

"The ballet? What the hell am I going to do at the ballet," Smitty barked.

"I didn't invite you, Bobby Ray Smith. It's only for me and the girls. So piss off." With that, Sissy Mae Smith walked off, or sauntered depending on your perspective, tossing over her shoulder, "Bye, Dez. It was nice meetin' ya."

"Uh . . . you too, Sissy Mae."

Smitty's big shoulders slumped in defeat. "Now I have nothin' to do."

With a wild look of relief, Dez clutched Smitty's arm. "You could come with us. To dinner."

Oh no, she didn't. "No, he can't."

Dez glared at him. "Yes. He can."

Mace glared back. "No. He can't."

"I don't see what the big deal is. I've got my SUV, I can drive us all down there."

"Smitty's got a date."

"No, I don't."

Mace took a menacing step toward Smitty, but Dez stepped between them. "You've got two choices, Llewellyn. Either Smitty comes with us or you go alone."

Smitty shrugged and in that slow drawl Mace suddenly detested, "Now, y'all. I don't wanna be puttin' anybody out."

Mace pinned Smitty with a look. "I hate you."

"Back off, Mace." Dez turned and rubbed Smitty's arm. "You're coming with us, Smitty."

"Well, if you insist." He smiled at Mace, and Mace's entire body tightened with the need to beat Smitty within an inch of his life. "Where y'all plannin' to go, anyway?"

"Van Holtz Steakhouse."

Smitty started laughing and couldn't seem to stop. Yeah. He'd never hear the end of this one. Mace Llewellyn willingly heading into Pack territory for one reason and one reason only.

Dez stepped away from the two men. "Is there a problem with this place I don't know about? I mean, do they piss in the food or something?"

"No. No." Smitty cleared his throat. "They are a fine, *fine* establishment. And if you like your steak bloody, you'll love it there. It's almost like they hunted it up that very mornin'."

"Okay." Although Dez appeared seriously wary. "Um . . . let me buy a couple more gift certificates and then we can go."

Mace watched her move off toward a cash register. Once out of his line of sight, he grabbed Smitty by the neck, lifted the man's entire body up off the ground with a roar, and then went down on one knee, slamming Smitty against the floor. The crowd of people milling around dashed away from the two men like they were on fire. No one was brave enough to step between them.

Mace released Smitty's throat and stood. "Just so we're clear," Mace sneered, barely able to control himself.

Smitty gave him a thumbs-up while trying to get his breath back. "We're clear," he wheezed out. Then Mace followed after Dez.

Chapter Four

She found it interesting how she kept having to remind herself to keep breathing. But Dez had to. She kept forgetting. Every time she looked up from her food and found Mace staring at her, she'd simply forget to breathe. She kept trying to find some flaw on him. Something wrong with his features or his hair or his teeth. Anything to make him less godlike and more human.

Yet she found everything about him perfect. From that voice that kept dropping impossibly lower every time they touched on the topic of sex to the way his gold eyes glinted in the dimly lit restaurant to the way his muscles bunched under his seen-better-days, black, long-sleeve T-shirt.

If she really intended to keep her Puerto Rican ass out of his bed, she should have never gone to dinner with the man. Because he still knew how to get to her. Still knew how to make her smile and pant. Still knew how to make her hot.

And she wanted his dick in her mouth so bad she thought she might start crying.

Is it actually wrong to toss a woman onto a restaurant table and fuck her senseless? Probably.

Mace sighed and continued to stare at the lovely Detective First Grade Desiree MacDermot. Dez who always made him smile. Always made him hard. Always made him crazy.

Still made him crazy. With those gray eyes, those amazing

breasts, . . . and that voice. That fucking voice still made him sweat.

He found her so distracting he completely overlooked the fact he'd spent the last three hours in the company of wolves. Owned and operated by the Van Holtz Pack, the Van Holtz restaurant chain had the best prime rib Mace had ever tasted. In retrospect, he was glad Smitty joined them. Smitty had actually been able to keep the wolves at bay and away from him. They clearly didn't like having Mace in their space, although all the Van Holtz restaurants were supposed to be neutral territory. Mace guessed that only applied to other Packs and not Pride.

It amazed him what he would willingly put up with for this frustrating and beautiful woman.

"What I'm not quite clear on, Dez, is how you didn't actually notice your husband moved out."

"*Ex*-husband. And I had a lot going on at the time. It was my first big case. A lot was riding on it. It just took me a while to realize he'd left."

"What's a while?"

She held the coffee cup between her hands and stared at it. "Three weeks."

Mace leaned forward and waited until she looked him in the eye. "You noticed after three weeks or he *told* you after three weeks?"

When she didn't answer but went back to staring at her coffee cup, he couldn't help himself. He laughed. Loud.

She glanced around as the entire attention of the restaurant turned toward them.

"Christ, would you keep it down? I'm not exactly proud of this."

"Sounds to me like he was boring and selfish and you should be glad the asshole is gone. I know I am."

She smirked and a blush spread across her cheeks. He liked that he could make a tough city cop blush.

She glanced up, clearly ready to change the subject. "Where did the redneck go?"

"I don't know. He does keep disappearing, doesn't he?" *And that's why he's family.*

"We should probably check the ladies' room."

Mace grinned. "Probably. Smitty's always had an easy time with women."

"Oh, and I'm sure you have a real struggle with women, Mace. I bet they ignore you and treat you like you don't even exist."

He smirked at her. "Only one does that."

She put down her coffee and ran her hands through her hair. She'd been doing that more and more as the night wore on. "I know you exist, Mace. Trust me. I *know*. But you forget, I was in the military. I know exactly what you scumbags get up to. Sorry if I'm not blindly diving into the deep end of *that* pool."

"So, you think I just want—"

"To screw the one girl you didn't? Yeah. That's what I think."

"Then you don't think much of me."

"I didn't say that. But you are a guy, Mace. A Llewellyn, true. But still a guy."

"Which means what?"

"Well, I did read that testosterone causes brain damage."

Mace snorted out a laugh as Smitty, reeking of some wolf female, sat back down at the table.

"What did I miss?"

"Dez was telling me how all men are mentally handicapped."

"I didn't say that," she corrected with a condescending smile. "I merely said that you all have"—she made air quotes with her hands—" 'special needs.' The reality is you guys really can't think past that thing between your legs."

"Damn, girl." Smitty wasn't used to women not immediately bowled over by his charm. "That is mighty harsh, darlin'. Lumping us in with any-ol'-body."

"Really?" Dez picked her coffee back up.

"Yes. Really. Mace is a good guy. One of the best. And I am a caring, sensitive male that has many, many layers. Don't let this tough, manly exterior fool you. There's so much about me you'll never understand."

Dez swallowed a mouthful of coffee. "You have a hickey on your neck."

Dez grinned at the two men as a waiter placed a piece of cake between them. He laid out forks for each. Smiled at Smitty. Leered at Dez. And practically spit at Mace. Man, the staff at this restaurant really didn't like him.

Smitty winked at her. "You're right, ya know. We're all scum."

Mace shook his head. "Thanks for the help there, bud."

"What can I say? She caught me in my lie."

"You admit nothing. Deny everything. Demand proof. Did you learn nothing in Boot Camp?"

Dez did like Smitty. She liked him a lot. But the man sure wasn't Mace. Darker in appearance. An inch or two shorter. Not as wide. She found herself surprisingly comfortable around him. Mace, however . . . well, she didn't actually feel comfortable around him. Not with her body tingling at the mere thought of him. She kept noticing things about him. Little things. Like the way he unconsciously scratched the scar on his neck or the way he kept pushing his blond-brown hair out of his eyes. Her eyes narrowed. *Wasn't he bald just yesterday?* No. That wasn't possible.

"Don't blame me, hoss, because she knows we're all brain damaged."

Dez looked down at the chocolate cake garnished with dark chocolate and wondered how she kept getting involved with such idiots.

Mace watched as Dez took her forefinger and swiped up some of the drizzle of dark chocolate sauce that decorated the plate as garnish.

She slipped her chocolate-covered finger into her mouth and sucked it clean.

Mace growled. He couldn't help it. If it were a practiced

move, meant to tantalize, he wouldn't have even noticed. But Dez did it because she clearly liked dark chocolate and was slightly tacky.

She frowned and smiled at the same time. "Did you . . . growl at me?"

"Sorry. Couldn't be helped."

"No reason to apologize. I've just never had a man growl at me before."

"You just weren't listening," both Mace and Smitty said at the same time.

Dez shook her head as she and Mace picked up their forks. "You two are such boneheads."

Smitty watched Dez for a second, then leaned forward. "Do you mind if I ask you a question, darlin'?"

"Only if you stop calling me *darlin'*."

"Now where I come from that's a term of endearment."

"Really? Well, where I come from *motherfucker* is a term of endearment. Want me to start calling you that?"

Mace almost spit his cake out, but now he knew Smitty was pissed.

"All right then, Dez. Mind if I ask you a question?"

"Ask away," she happily offered as she ate a bite of cake.

"You've never had great sex, have you?"

Swallowing her cake and damn near choking on it, "That ain't no question, Smith."

Well, hello Bronx accent. Welcome back!

"Oh, I'm sorry." Uh-oh. Smitty being sarcastic—not good. "I can phrase that in the form of a question if ya like. Have you ever had great sex?"

Dez leaned back in her chair, her arms crossing in front of her. She leveled that gray-green gaze in Mace's direction. "You're not going to help me out here, are you?"

"I could help you out, but I don't think that's what you mean."

"I'm still waitin'," Smitty pushed. Mace didn't know what his friend was up to, but he couldn't wait to find out, and to see if Dez punched him. The girl he used to know had a mean right hook; he could only imagine what this woman had in her arsenal.

"Well . . . I . . . uh . . ."

"Well-I-uh what?"

"Hey! I'm thinkin'!"

"If you have to think about it, darlin', you haven't had great sex."

"What exactly is the point of this conversation?"

"Simply pointing out a fact." With that, Smitty got up and disappeared again.

Now it seemed to be Dez's turn to growl. "Okay, now I'm starting to hate him."

Mace grinned. He was so okay with that.

Dez's face burned. She could probably fry an egg on it. How had this evening gone so terribly wrong so goddamn quickly? She'd lost control. *Again!* She never lost control. Whether during an interrogation or a perp walk or a tactical maneuver, Dez MacDermot never lost control. But with Mace staring at her and his country bumpkin friend twisting her words around, she felt like she dangled off a building without a bungee cord.

She'd already regressed to her old nervous habit of running her damn hands through her hair, saying the word *ain't* in a sentence where she wasn't mocking someone, and getting that damn accent back. Maybe Missy Llewellyn was right. She would always be that Bronx girl, no matter what she did.

"Dez. Look at me."

"No." Absolutely, unequivocally, kill-herself-first no.

"Desiree. *Look* at me."

Clenching her hands into tight fists, Dez raised her head and froze, trapped in that gold gaze. Trapped there as if the man had put shackles on her wrists and sat on her. Dez had no idea how long they were staring at each other. She felt Mace sliding through her body. Touching everywhere. Making himself quite at home. She couldn't look away and she didn't want to.

He didn't say anything to her. He really didn't have to. He said it all in those beautiful eyes of his. He wanted her. Would do anything necessary to get her. And, if she let him, he'd give her more than great sex. He'd give her never-able-to-walk-straight-again sex. The kind where she'd lose her soul.

Finally, Mace motioned for the check, but his eyes never left her face. "Come home with me, Dez."

On a sigh, "Okay." Dez blinked. *Helllloooo! Idiot alert! Have you lost your mind?* "Uh . . . I mean . . ." Dez pinched her leg to snap herself out of it. "I can't."

"Why?"

"Because I don't do one-night stands."

"I don't want a one-night stand. I want us to—"

"I don't do relationships either," she burst out suddenly, completely cutting the man off.

Calmly. "Why?"

"Because I'm a cop. Always was. Always will be."

"Not quite sure why that affects us."

"It does." She'd already been through this. Learned the hard way. Never again. "I've actually got somewhere to be." *Thank God.*

"At eleven-fifteen at night?"

"It is the city that never sleeps."

The check came, and she figured she needed to grab this chance to bail.

"I'd like to help with the tip." She tossed two twenties on the table. "Thanks so much for dinner, Mace." She stood up and walked around to his side of the table. She leaned over and kissed the top of his shaggy head. "I had a really nice time."

"You could continue to have a nice time."

Relentless bastard. She ruffled his hair like she used to when they were fourteen. "I'm outta here." She hadn't taken a step when Mace grabbed her hand. His fingers, warm and dry, interlaced with hers. In that one move the man went through her entire body. And that's when she realized they were no longer fourteen. They were no longer just pals. Dez suddenly saw them naked, sweaty, and fucking like there was no tomorrow. She knew Mace saw it too. Those gold eyes screamed at her, and she knew hers were screaming right back.

Nope. She needed to go. *Now.*

She took in a shaky breath. "Mace, I have to go." Oh hell. She needed to stop whispering.

"Don't. Stay, Dez. Stay with me." And she knew he didn't mean at the restaurant having more coffee and another piece of cake. He meant in his bed. With him inside her. And he'd make her scream. Again and again.

"I can't." She pulled her hand away. He let it go but not before dragging his big fingers across her palm. Who knew a simple move like that could rock her right down to her toes? And rock her it did.

Jesus Christ. What a man that boy had grown into.

Dez looked into those gold eyes. She knew a few more moments of him and she'd end up doing something really tacky. Like crawling under the table and giving Mace Llewellyn a blow job. She shook her head and backed away from him. This kept spiraling out of control. "I have to go, Mace."

He smiled. "Okay." She raised an eyebrow at that calm response but decided to let it go. Especially when she so clearly saw him slamming her facedown on the restaurant table and fucking her into oblivion. Yeah. In that moment she realized she'd overstayed her welcome.

"Have a great Christmas, Mace."

Then she practically ran out the door, heading to the club a few blocks away.

Mace had to wait a good five minutes before he could hope to comfortably stand and not embarrass himself.

That woman . . . that woman was *everything* he'd ever wanted. He'd known it all those years ago. Tonight only confirmed it for him. The kiss and that simple touch practically blew his boots off. And she felt it too. He could see it on her face. He could smell it. Her desire rolled off her in waves and practically knocked him from the room.

No, he wasn't letting Dez MacDermot get away. He'd take her down like his ancestors took down full-grown zebra.

Smitty finally returned to the table as Mace signed the credit card receipt. He smiled at his friend. "Well? Where did you go?"

"Well, nothin'. That girl's got a temper. I wasn't about to stay around for that."

"You were pushing her."

"Well, if I waited on you two to quit pussyfootin' around and get down to it, my grandchildren would be runnin' the Pack."

"I don't need your help, Smitty. I've got this under control."

"Really? Then why are you here alone?"

Mace stood up. "It's all about timing, Smitty."

"Yeah. Sure. Hopefully timing will keep you warm tonight, hoss."

The two men walked out of the restaurant. "You don't understand Dez. You can't push her. She needs subtle, refined encouragement."

"You forget. I watched that woman put away a steak. She ain't subtle."

"This is true. Excuse me." Mace moved past three men. "But then again, I'm not really that subtle either."

"Mason Llewellyn?"

Mace stopped and turned. He knew before he even turned around what he would find. If he hadn't already smelled them, Smitty's growling would have been a dead giveaway. He tolerated Mace well enough, but that was about it.

There were three of them. Large. A good ten years younger. Raw. Hoods. One didn't meet a lot of lion hoodlums these days.

"Yeah?"

"Wow. It really is you. I told these guys it was."

Mace watched the man closely as Smitty paced behind him. His wolf buddy did not like this one bit. Of course, he didn't like it much himself.

"You know, you and your Pride are real well known around this city. It's a real honor to meet you." He held his hand out. "Patrick Doogan. These are my brothers." Mace grasped the man's hand with his own. Cold, gold eyes sized Mace up. Debating his strength. His power.

"So, Doogan. What can I do for you?"

He glanced at his brothers. "Smart, ain't he? I told you he'd be smart. He knows we aren't stopping him in the street to just say hi."

"I know you didn't simply find me in the street by accident either. So can we cut the bullshit?"

Doogan grinned. A true predator this one. Not a soft bone in his mammoth body. "I wanna tawk to youse sometime 'bout ya sistas." The man's New York street accent painfully assaulted Mace's ears. Dez's made him laugh and turned him on, especially when she struggled to hide it. Not Doogan's. Mace wanted to slash the man's vocal cords with his paw. "See if we can discuss some ... uh ... possible business arrangements regardin' the Llewellyn Pride."

Mace shrugged. "Sure. That would be great. And you have sisters that I can have ... and fuck. Right?"

Doogan's eyes narrowed, while Smitty softly chuckled next to him.

"Since that is what you want my sisters for, right? To mate with you? To breed with you? To rub your fuckin' feet?"

"I don't like to be fucked with, Llewellyn."

"Then you shouldn't bend over and hand me the lube."

Mace couldn't believe how angry he felt, but discussing his sisters like high-priced collateral galled him to no end. True, on any given day he detested them severely, but still ... they were his sisters. *His sisters.* You don't talk about a man's sisters like you're buying hookers for a bachelor party.

He watched, fascinated, when the façade of one cat chatting with another turned to outright hatred. Doogan hated what Mace represented. What Doogan and his equally large brothers would never be.

"I'll have your sisters, Llewellyn, and I'll fuck 'em all."

"You're underestimating the women of my family. They don't play nice with others. They'll rip your cock off and show it to ya. And when they do, I'm going to laugh my ass off."

Mace turned to walk away, but Doogan's voice stopped him cold.

"Tell me, Mason. How's Petrov doing these days?"

Mace sighed. "You know why you'll never have the Llewellyn Pride?" He looked back at Doogan. "Cause you have no class."

In less than a second, Doogan was on him.

Dez pushed past the fifty or more people standing in line, waiting to get into the hottest club in the Village. She told the bouncer her name and watched him stare at her breasts for a good ninety seconds before letting her into the club.

Immediately Dez knew she didn't belong. This was not her kind of place. An Irish cop bar. A biker bar. The local bowling alley. Those were her kinds of places. Here she felt . . . old. Her gun pressed into her back under her leather jacket. She was glad that the bouncer hadn't checked her. She wouldn't like to be here without her weapon.

Packed to capacity, the club had the rich and the connected mixing with the famous and the drug dealers. Vice would have a field day in this place.

She walked to the bar. "I'm looking for Gina Brutale."

"Yup. In the back bar."

She headed toward the back part of the club, pushing her way through a throng of barely dressed, overperfumed people. She'd almost made it to her destination when she caught sight of him. All gold and beautiful. Talking to a lean, dark-haired woman. Dez moved over to him and tapped him on the shoulder.

"Mr. Shaw?"

He turned to her, and he was as beautiful as the picture of him in the Petrov file. Only now he seemed really annoyed. And not nearly as beautiful as Mace. She laughed to herself. Hopeless. Absolutely hopeless.

"Do I know you?" It would be real nice if he directed that question to her and not her breasts.

She leaned into him. She couldn't announce to the bar she was NYPD, but the man clearly had idiotic tendencies if he insisted on being out in the middle of the night after one of his business partners had so recently been blown away.

"Mr. Shaw, I think you'd be safer back at home, don't you? At least until we get a handle on this Petrov situation."

"Ah, you must be one of the detectives. Must be the one Missy threw out of the house." Shaw leaned into her and sniffed her neck. He grinned. "How is Mace tonight, anyway?"

Dez pulled away from him. What? Did the entire Llewellyn family know she had gone out with Mace? And did they all go around sniffing each other? *Oh whatever.*

"Mr. Shaw, I really think you should go home. Now."

Shaw leered at her and she raised her eyebrow, daring him to give her real attitude.

"I was leaving anyway, Detective."

"Good. Thank you. Cause I'd really hate to have to watch Forensics catalog pieces of your brain—like we did with Petrov."

Dez headed off to the back bar. As she came around the corner she caught sight of five women. At least, she was pretty sure they were women—they were a tad butch—sitting at the bar. They looked very similar, and Dez guessed a blood connection between all of them. It was the one nursing a straight scotch and staring sadly at the floor that had her complete interest, though.

The fourth kick to his ribs sent him flipping up and over. He landed on his hands and knees. Ready to shift, but holding back until he had absolutely no choice.

He saw one of Doogan's brothers going for the weapon he had hidden under his silk jacket and long cashmere coat. Mace didn't wait for him to get a good grip on it. He moved, catching the man's arm and twisting it back until it snapped. The roar of pain he let out shook the block and made people run. Doogan moved toward him because Smitty had the other brother and was definitely seconds away from snapping his neck.

"Ah, ah, ah." Mace pulled the man in his arms back so that his body practically resembled a U.

"Don't make me break him in half—cause I can."

Doogan stopped. He could see both of his siblings were seconds away from meeting a rather ugly death. Who would the cops believe? Three criminal hoods from the projects or Mace Llewellyn and his out-of-town Southern friend? Two decorated officers from the Navy.

No. Doogan wasn't stupid. Mean and evil, but not stupid. He held his hands up and backed away from Mace. Once far enough away, Mace pushed the man in his arms toward Doogan, and Smitty did the same.

Doogan took them both and backed away down the street.

"Stay away from my sisters, Doogan. Or next time I'll make sure this ends differently."

Doogan didn't answer, he just left.

Smitty resheathed his claws and wiped blood off his hands. "Well that was almost as much fun as the cops pretending to be hookers."

Mace smiled and grimaced all at the same time. His face and chest hurt.

"Shouldn't the cops be here by now?"

Smitty's innocent statement made Mace laugh outright.

His friend grabbed his arm and pulled him under a street lamp. "Let's see your face, hoss." He winced. "Yup. They did some damage."

"Thanks." Mace went to touch his face, but Smitty held his hand back. "I wouldn't have known if you hadn't pointed it out to me, Smitty."

"Don't get sassy with me, hoss."

"Sorry. I can't stop thinking about what would have happened if Dez had still been with us."

"That's easy. There would have been a lot of people dead. Between the two of ya. She got that look in her eye. She's a predator, son. And don't think for a second she ain't."

"Dez would be the least of their worries."

"My, my. We are awfully protective of a woman we haven't seen in years."

"Don't start, Smitty."

He chuckled. "You know, you look real shitty, hoss."

"Thank you very much." Mace moved his jaw around. At least it wasn't broken.

"So shitty you look like you need someone to take care of you."

Mace blinked in confusion. "Why? I'll be fine by tomorrow."

"Someone to take care of you, Mace. Tend your wounds. Comfort you in her very large, sweet bosom."

Mace shook his head. "No. No way, Smitty."

"Would you trust me?"

"That's a shitty thing to do. It's almost catlike in its evilness."

"See, your problem is you underestimate dogs. There's a reason many of us are let up on the couch, while they keep y'all in a zoo."

"This is a stupid conversation."

"We're stupid men. Stupid men who like their women big chested and loud."

"You think Dez is loud?"

"Nah. Sissy's loud. Your woman does have quite the voice, though. Like someone took a sandblaster to her vocal cords."

"I like her voice."

"I know dirt roads in the poorest part of Tennessee that are smoother than that girl's voice. Although, I have to admit, I did enjoy watching her suck that finger clean."

"It's almost like you want me to hurt you."

"Gina?"

Dark brown eyes that were almost black focused on her. Filled with such intense sadness, Dez hated that the woman freaked her out so much. But something about Gina Brutale set her nerves on edge.

"Yeah." She slid off her stool. "Come on." Gina sucked back the rest of her scotch and dropped the glass on the bar.

She glanced at the women with her. "I'll be back in a bit."

The women didn't respond. Instead, they stared at Dez. Perhaps the most uncomfortable experience she'd had in a long time, and Dez's job consisted of uncomfortable experiences. But the way they stared at her—that's what freaked her out. Like they were silently plotting which parts of her body would sauté well in olive oil.

Gina walked away from the bar and Dez followed her, glancing back once at the women. They were still staring at her. She fought the urge to shudder.

Gina walked to an office in a deserted part of the club and went to open the door, but someone pulled it open from the other side. A woman who resembled Gina stepped out. The two women stared at each other. Actually, they really glared. Almost vicious in its intensity.

Eventually the woman's brown eyes turned to Dez. "Who the fuck is that?"

"None of ya fuckin' business."

Dez rolled her eyes. This sounded like one of those typical arguments between girls in her old neighborhood. They usually degenerated into hair pulling until knives were eventually drawn.

She didn't have time for that.

"Can this wait? I gotta life."

Gina proceeded into the office. The other woman made to move around her but stopped and suddenly sniffed Dez instead.

Dez reared back. "Can I help you?"

She grunted. "Another one."

Dez had no idea what that meant, but she didn't have a chance to ask as the woman walked off.

Shaking her head, she entered the office, closing the door behind her.

"Interesting girl."

"She's a bitch." Gina slid on top of a highly polished mahogany desk. "And my sister. Anne Marie."

"My sympathies."

She snorted. "We all have our own personal hell. She's mine."

Dez took in the office. Fancy, but it didn't look very used. Lots of mahogany and glass. It didn't look like the office of a woman.

"Whose office is this?"

"My father's. But he doesn't come here very often."

Dez almost gave in to her desire to find out more about the well-known but rarely seen Gino Brutale. Instead, she forced herself to remember she was in this club for a reason. Not to see if she could find out more about Brutale's mob ties.

"So . . . you wanted to talk to me about Alexander Petrov's death?"

"Yeah. Ya see, he was . . ."

The woman struggled with her admission, but Dez didn't know why. "He was . . ." she coaxed.

Brutale stood tall, suddenly proud. "He was with me. He was my lover."

Dez didn't understand why Gina needed to fear admitting that information. Brutale was no youngster. She appeared to be in her early to midthirties. And it wasn't like Petrov ran some rival mob family, unless Missy was up to more than she realized. Which Dez seriously doubted.

Dez waited for Gina to continue.

"I saw him the night he died. When he left me that night, he was very much alive. I don't know if anyone followed him. I do know Missy Llewellyn would lose her friggin' mind if she knew about us."

Dez stepped forward. "And did she know?"

"I don't know. But he was going to leave her and stay with me. I don't know if he ever got around to telling her that, though."

"Petrov and Missy Llewellyn were . . . together? A couple?" Maybe, but who would put up with that heartless bitch?

"It's too complicated to explain. But, basically, she owned him."

What the hell does that mean?

"What do you mean she owned him? She had something on him?"

"No. But he belonged to her. She wouldn't take him leaving well. Especially if he were leaving her for me."

"Why you? What connection do you have with the Llewellyns?" A Jersey girl like Brutale wouldn't exactly be welcome at a Llewellyn banquet, and they both knew it.

"Our families have . . . a history, you might say. We've hated each other for a long time."

"Do you think Missy killed him?"

"I don't know. I really don't. Shootin' him in the back of the head, though, doesn't really seem Missy's style, ya know?"

Dez shrugged. "I couldn't tell ya."

"All I'm sayin' is, you need to look at Missy Llewellyn for this. Look at her close. She shouldn't be able to get away with this. Just cause he loved me and not her."

"Yeah. But are you sure he loved you?"

Brutale locked her beady dark eyes on Dez's face. "What?"

"Maybe you want me to focus on Missy because you want her to suffer more. Maybe Petrov wouldn't leave her. Maybe he didn't love you at all. So you got rid of him yourself." Dez didn't really believe that, but she wanted to see Brutale's reaction.

She wasn't disappointed. She blinked and suddenly Gina Brutale stood right in front of her. Their bodies almost touching. Rage and sorrow came off Brutale in waves, practically knocking Dez out of the room.

"I loved him. He loved me. Anybody tell you different, they're lyin'. We had plans, him and me. Plans to run this family together."

"Maybe your father wasn't okay with that."

"My father will do what I tell him to do. The women run this family. Not the men."

Well, that was new. "Okay."

Brutale glared at her for a long minute. Then she took one step back. Then another. Eventually a good five feet separated the women. But Dez still didn't feel safe. She wouldn't feel that way until she got the hell out of the building.

"But I will say this, Detective—whoever killed him better pray to the Mother Mary you get to them first. They better pray I never fuckin' find out. Cause I'll kill 'em myself. And I'll make sure they suffer for what they done."

Dez didn't doubt Gina's words for even a second. She wanted out of this building. She wasn't even supposed to be on this case. Suddenly, nailing Missy took a backseat to her basic survival.

"I'll keep that in mind."

"You do that."

Dez backed up from Brutale. She didn't feel comfortable turning her back on the woman. She grabbed hold of the door-knob, opened the door, and eased out into the club.

She cut through the enormous place, including the back bar where she found Brutale. She had to pass the same pack of women, only this time Brutale's sister was with them. As she moved past them, the lightest touch nipped her neck.

Reaching back, Dez grabbed the hand touching her and twisted until Anne Marie Brutale lay on the floor at her feet, howling in pain. Dez planted her foot in the woman's side and twisted her arm again. This time even farther away from her body. A few more inches and she'd break the bone at the shoulder.

"Don't you ever fuckin' touch me again." The grip she had on the woman she learned from the Marine Corps. The state-ment—that was all Bronx.

Gina Brutale walked in. She stared dispassionately at her sis-ter. It had to be the coldest look Dez had ever seen. As much as she detested her own sisters sometimes, Dez would never let anyone else hurt them. Not ever.

"I really hope I made myself clear." She twisted Anne Marie's arm a bit more for emphasis, pulling another brutal howl from her throat. The sound sent a nasty shiver up her spine. These people just weren't right.

Yeah. Dez wanted out of here.

She glanced around at the women watching her. None of them seemed very interested. She glanced down at Anne Marie. She had big, long nails. The kind her sisters never let her get be-cause they said they were "beyond tacky." She glared at those nails, suddenly very concerned with them, but she didn't know what the woman's tacky fashion sense had to with anything.

Dez finally released Anne Marie and backed away from the women. When far enough away, she spun on her heel and headed toward the front exit and home.

Mace crouched on the hard ground, his back against the pas-senger side of Dez's SUV, and impatiently waited. He didn't like to wait.

Of course, the knowledge that he would be going to hell for this, misleading a beautiful woman he was crazy about, didn't make the waiting any easier. At least, however, he would go to hell with a smile.

Mace wiped the last bit of blood dripping from his nose. Even with the blood in his nose, he could still smell Christmas in the air. He didn't know how all the scents he could detect reminded him of this particular holiday, but they did. He loved those smells. Actually, he loved the holiday, he'd just never been able to truly enjoy it. Even the times he'd gone with Smitty to his mother's in Tennessee. True enough, she always went out of her way to make Mace feel like part of the Smith family, even part of their Pack, but Mace never forgot he didn't belong. Of course, he didn't belong with his own Pride either. Instead, he'd have to make his own family. His and his alone. And every fiber of his being told him Dez was the one. She would be the one to make every Christmas special for him. Of course, she did seem to detest the holiday, but no one ever said Dez wasn't difficult.

He spotted her immediately as she came around the corner. When she caught sight of him, she slowed down. She probably couldn't make him out at first. Mace put on his most wounded expression and continued to wait. He didn't make any sudden moves. He had no doubt Dez would shoot him on sight if she deemed it necessary.

Dez slowly moved closer until she could see him clearly. Then she rushed to his side.

"Jesus, Mace." She knelt down next to him. "Oh honey." Her soft hands slid across his face. "Who did this to you?"

He shook his head. "It doesn't matter." He looked up at her and blinked, startled by what he saw. Sweat drenched her face and neck, which wouldn't seem odd—if this were the middle of summer. But it was December twenty-second, and definitely nippy out.

"Dez?"

"What, baby?"

"Are you okay?"

"Sure." Dez swallowed, closed her eyes, and fell face-first

into his lap. He stared down at her. *Dammit.* How many dreams and fantasies had filled his head over the years with Dez Mac-Dermot in this very position? Only then, he expected her fully conscious.

Mace carefully cradled Dez in his arms. "Dez, baby. Can you hear me?"

She didn't answer him. He wondered if someone had slipped a drug in her drink. He sniffed her. She smelled of hyena.

"What the hell have you been up to, beautiful?"

Why would Dez be hanging out with hyenas? He examined her body and after several long minutes found the tiniest scratch on the back of her neck. He sniffed the area and smelled the poison.

Tricky, fucking hyenas. They hadn't given her enough to kill her. That would have been too obvious, and she would have never made it out of the club on her own steam. No, they gave her enough so she would make it outside, maybe even to a cab, and then she'd pass out. Leaving her to the tender mercies of the New York streets. Or perhaps she'd pass out at the wheel of her car.

Mace wanted to roar his displeasure and start tearing some hyenas apart, but Dez was his main concern right now. He turned her head and brushed her beautiful hair away from the scratch. He licked the wound and spit. He did it six times until he removed all the poison.

"Okay, baby. Let's get you home." She didn't carry a purse; instead she had a slim leather wallet shoved into the front of her black jeans. He pulled it out and quickly glanced at her driver's license. He grimaced. Brooklyn. Christ, the woman lived in Brooklyn.

"Sure, you couldn't live uptown, could ya?" Mace stood up, Dez in his arms. Without much effort, he got her keys and got the woman safely bundled into her SUV. He sat on the driver's side and started the vehicle up. He glanced at her, a rumbling sigh coming from his chest. His beautiful Dez. He rubbed her cheek with the back of his hand.

"Let's get you home, gorgeous."

Chapter Five

Mace walked up Dez's porch with her in his arms. Without putting her down, he unlocked the door and walked into the dark house. His cat eyes could see her furniture clearly, but he went ahead and flipped on the light switch. He froze in shock.

How could he not? The woman's living room was a fucking winter wonderland. She had a fully decked-out Christmas tree with tinsel. Lights strung everywhere that were connected to the main outlet, so when he turned on the overhead lights all the Christmas lights came on too. She had stockings attached to her mantel. Three. One for her and two for . . . ? Sig and Sauer? He didn't want to know and he wasn't going to ask.

He smiled. As much as Dez bitched about the holidays, she clearly loved it as well. No one put in this much effort for something they hated when they lived alone.

Mace took Dez to her sectional couch. He liked this couch. Big and roomy. He wanted to fuck her on it.

He laid her down and checked her wound again. He'd cleaned out the poison, but he didn't want the area to get infected. He took off his jacket, tossing it across the floor. Then slipped Dez's jacket off her body. He had to pull her shirt away from her wound and realized that would eventually get in his way. With a shrug, he pulled her shirt off completely. Once again, he froze.

A lacey red bra covered those beautiful breasts. The red color contrasted beautifully with her brown skin. He could nuzzle between those breasts until the end of time, if she'd let him. Mace took a deep breath. This wasn't helping anything. He shook off his lust and went back to work.

Dez opened her eyes and glanced around the room. Home. Somehow, she managed to get home. The problem? She couldn't remember anything past stumbling out of the club. She looked down and realized her father's old New York Jets blanket covered her body. She still had on clothes, except for her shoes and her shirt.

And someone had turned on Nat King Cole.

She lay there and glared up at the ceiling. *What the fuck is going on?*

Mace had his cell phone next to his ear, his shoulder the only thing holding it up while he went through Dez's kitchen.

"The woman has nothing. I mean, I've eaten all her chips and her crackers and she seems to have an unhealthy love of beef jerky. But other than that—the woman has nothing."

"Now see. That's why you should get yourself a nice Southern gal. They always make sure everybody's fed and comfortable."

"Really? So . . . what's your sister doin' tonight?"

Smitty growled. "That ain't funny, cat."

Mace chuckled. "Actually, yes it is." Mace opened the refrigerator. "Well, she likes beer." He grabbed a pizza box, opened it, shut it in disgust, and put it back into her refrigerator. "Clearly food purchasing will be my responsibility."

"Uh . . . tell me, Mace. Have you actually let her in on the fact she's yours now?"

"No. But I will. She'll simply have to deal with it."

Smitty sighed. "So says the King of the Jungle."

"By these fangs I rule." Mace glanced around her kitchen again. His eyes caught sight of a bag and he frowned. "Smitty?"

"Yeah?"

"She has dog food."

A long pause followed his statement. "How much?"

Mace walked over to it and examined it closely. "It's a twenty-five-pound bag."

Another long pause. "Is there only one?"

Mace opened up a door leading to a pantry. There were a few things on the shelves. A few human things. But on the floor . . .

"Um . . . she has ten bags of twenty-five pounds of high-priced dog food. You know, the special kind you get from a vet."

Another long pause, then Smitty began to laugh hysterically. "Hey, ya'll. Hey!" he barked to his Pack. "Mace is in love with a *dog* person!"

Mace gritted his teeth as howls of laughter assaulted him. A truly humiliating moment.

"Are you done?"

"Sorry. Sorry. It's just fun to see how the mighty cats have fallen."

Mace rolled his eyes. "Well, I've been here two hours and I haven't seen hide nor hair of any dog."

"Didn't you smell 'em when you got there?"

"I'm wearing your jacket. So I thought that was you. You guys all smell alike."

Smitty growled again. "I do not smell like a dog."

Mace smiled. Nothing pissed off a wolf more than comparing him to a dog. Smitty didn't speak to him for three months when he found Mace drunkenly talking to a German Shepherd about Mother Smith's Tennessee mud pie.

"They're probably hidin'," Smitty offered.

"Hiding from what?"

"You, dumb ass. And what you wanna bet wherever they are, they've pissed themselves. Your little girlfriend won't be happy when she has to clean up the stains tomorrow."

"You really are enjoying this, aren't you?"

"Oh yeah."

Mace hung up the phone and went in search of Dez's stupid dogs.

*   *   *

Mace crouched down and looked under the couch. "Here, stupid, stupid dogs," he whispered softly in a singsong voice. "Come here, you little fuckers."

He wasn't sure when he knew Dez watched him, but he knew. He raised his head and found her staring at him over the arm of her couch.

"What are you doing?"

"Nothing."

"Where's my shirt?"

He glanced at a large leather chair across the room. "Over there."

"And why am I not wearing it?" When a woman spits that sentence out at you between her teeth, you can feel pretty assured she's good and pissed.

"I can explain everything."

"You better."

Mace stood up and walked around the couch to sit beside her. She pulled herself into a sitting position, her hand holding the green and white Jets blanket up to her chin. He did notice she had securely fastened back on her jeans the holstered .9mm he placed on the coffee table. She couldn't find her shirt, but she sure as hell found her gun.

"How do you feel?"

"Okay, I guess. A little shaky maybe. What happened?"

"You were drugged." Saying the word *poison* would freak her out. And he had no desire to explain the lifelong battle between lions and hyenas at this moment. "But you should be okay now."

She looked at him as if seeing his bruises for the first time. Her hand reached up and touched his cheek. "Oh honey. What happened to your face?"

Mace gazed at her lips and moved in slowly. Not wanting to startle her, but determined to taste those lush lips. But before he could reach heaven, her head snapped around. "Where are my dogs?"

"What?"

"My dogs." Her soft hand on his cheek suddenly grabbed a hunk of his hair and pulled.

"Ow!"

"They should have ripped you apart and left you for dead on my porch by now. Where are they?"

With a dramatic sigh, "I don't know."

Dez got to her feet, a Packlike growl rolling from her lips. "If anything happened to my boys—"

"What exactly are you accusing me of? Harming two smelly beasts that would happily run out in the middle of moving traffic?"

Dez threw down the blanket and began to search the room. Mace had to focus hard on her face so he didn't focus on the rest of that luscious body. Her body did things to him. Strong, almost painful things.

He shook his head. *Stop it, Llewellyn. You're wasting your time.* The woman didn't even notice him in the room.

Who was she kidding? Her dogs were somewhere. But waking up and finding one gorgeous hunk of man-meat crawling on her floor had stirred things in her she never thought existed. Things she wasn't sure she could actually admit to. It didn't help that seeing his face all bruised up almost shoved her right over the edge of "Stupid Things People Do," like letting him kiss her—again.

So finding her dogs seemed the quickest and simplest thing to do, given the circumstances.

Although she *was* starting to worry a bit. Her dogs should have greeted them at the door. They should have definitely gone for Mace's throat by now. He didn't seem like much of a dog person, but she couldn't see Mace doing anything to her "boys." So where the hell where they?

"You check under the bed?"

Dez practically snarled at the man who had quickly become the star of any and every fantasy she would ever have. He leaned back into her couch, his arms out over the back of the sofa. His incredibly long and muscular legs stretched out in front of him and crossed at the ankles. *My, he certainly has made himself at home.*

"My dogs don't hide under beds, Llewellyn."

"But did you check?"

"Did you see me go upstairs?" At his raised eyebrow, she snapped, "Fine. I'll check." She headed up the stairs to her bedroom. Her house wasn't big by any stretch of the imagination, but it had a backyard for her dogs, a second floor, and a huge dining room and gourmet kitchen she rarely used. Most important, though, it was *her* mortgage. Her place. So it didn't matter how big or small it was.

"Sig! Sauer! Where are you guys?"

"You named your dogs after a gun?" Dez jumped and spun around. Mace had moved up behind her and she hadn't even heard him. "Holy shit! The Christmas stockings were for them?"

She would not be having *that* conversation. "What the hell are you doing?"

"Besides being freaked out by your Christmas decorations—helping you find your dogs. The dogs you named after a weapon."

"They're cop-owned dogs. What did you expect me to name them? Fluffy and Poopsie-head?"

Dez walked into her bedroom. She could feel Mace behind her. Feel the warmth of his body. She could smell the man. And he smelled really good.

She mentally shook herself. *Snap out of it, MacDermot.* She crouched down by her bed and looked under it. And, to her utter disbelief, she found her two dogs. Cowering.

She reached for Sig. "Come here, baby."

Mace crouched down next to her and that's when Sig gingerly gripped her wrist in his maw and dragged her under the bed. He didn't hurt her. If she didn't know better, she'd swear the dog simply wanted to protect her.

"What in the hell?"

"You okay?" Mace held on to her ankle and she suddenly felt like a wishbone.

She pulled her arm away from Sig and slid back out from

under the bed. Mace grabbed her hand and helped her to her feet. She snatched her hand away. She had to. His touch made her uncomfortably warm.

"What did you do to my dogs?" She had no idea where that came from, but she couldn't shake the feeling they were hiding from Mace.

"Me? What makes you think I did anything?"

"Sig once took down a two-hundred-and-fifty-pound professional football player because he got a little too close to me in the park. And Sauer took on three, out-of-control pit bulls to protect me. These are not dogs that hide under the bed. And then you come to my house . . ."

Mace didn't say anything, he simply watched her.

Dez sat down at the foot of the bed. She ran her hands through her hair. *Someone obviously drugged me.* Why else would she sit on her bed, hardly worried about the unsightly rolls it would cause in her less-than-taut stomach, wearing her favorite lace Christmas bra and jeans, in front of the one man she'd happily wrap herself around like a boa constrictor? Meanwhile, her vicious, well-trained dogs cowered under her bed. Something was going on and she wanted to know what. And she wanted to know what right-goddamn-now.

"My dogs are hiding from you, Llewellyn. And I wanna know why. Or you can get the fuck outta my house." Christ, less than twenty-four hours around Mace and Bronx Dez came roaring back. But her intense anger kept her from feeling ashamed.

Mace watched her from under a mass of hair practically covering his eyes. Hair that had not been there the day before.

What in the hell is going on?

Damn dogs ruin everything. Typical. If he told her anything but the absolute truth, Dez and her detective mind would see through it in two seconds. That would be it for him too. For them. Dez needed to trust her partners, Mace knew that just from the few precious hours he'd spent in the woman's company. He couldn't lie to her. Not if he ever wanted her screaming his name while she came.

So, throwing centuries of Druid tradition and secrecy out the window, he faced Detective Desiree MacDermot head-on and told her the truth.

"I'm a shapeshifter. Specifically lion. My Pride is descended from Welsh Druids. Your dogs sense that and that's why they're hiding under the bed. That and they're big pussies."

She stared at him. He could almost read her thoughts. She was thinking, I have a nut in my house. How do I get the nut out of my house? He was expecting her to start inching toward the door any second. Or pull her gun and shoot him between the eyes.

But she didn't. Instead, Dez crossed her arms in front of those beautiful red lace–covered tits. "Prove it."

Mace gaped at her. "What?"

"Is this a full moon kind of thing?"

He stifled his roar. *Insulting little bitch.* "I'm *not* a were-wolf."

"Then prove it. Right here. Right now."

"You want me to prove it?"

"Right here. Right now."

Mace smiled. "If that's what you want . . ."

Yup. Leave it to Dez to find the one rich nut in New York City who wasn't afraid to drive out to Brooklyn. The one rich nut who thought he was a—what was it?—shapeshifter? *Oiy.*

Of course, Dez didn't grab the phone, lock herself in the bathroom, and call 911. No, she challenged the nut to "prove it."

Sure. Why not? Besides, she was wearing her gun and she had a lovely shotgun in her closet. Plus, it wasn't like she hadn't dealt with nuts before.

Still her dogs' whimpering, heard clearly even though they were still under her bed, gave her the first clue something really wasn't right. Mace's eyes started to look different too. Becoming glassy and reflective. And his scent became stronger. Filling the room, swirling around her.

Dez uncrossed her arms and let them hang loose by her side as she watched Mace carefully. She blinked several times, her brain unwilling or unable to process what she thought she was seeing. *Jesus Christ, were those fangs!?*

She stopped breathing when the hair on his head spread across his entire body. The gold locks burst into a full-on mane while spreading across his back. The brown hair that tumbled from under the gold covered his chest like a thick winter sweater. Then his limbs altered so he went on all fours.

The whole process took all of forty-five seconds, but it seemed like years. And with a shake of his body, Mace's unnecessary clothes flew across the room.

With those gold eyes she'd recognize anywhere staring straight at her, he shook out his mane and roared.

Her dogs bolted from under the bed and out the bedroom door. Dez wasn't sure she'd ever see them again.

She analyzed the situation quickly. Her .9mm probably wouldn't do any good. Nope. Not with this one. She needed the shotgun.

Dez shot off the bed and made it to the closet in record time, but before she even had her hand on the doorknob he slammed her up against the hard wood. The body against her, though, wasn't lion, but human. And all male if the erection pushing into her back was any indication.

"Breathe, Dez. Just breathe."

Breathe? How was she supposed to breathe? She leaned her head against the door and wondered why she couldn't pass out like any other normal woman. She shouldn't be strong. She should be weak and frail. By the time she woke up, he'd have eaten her legs off and she could die from loss of blood. Anything had to be better than dealing with the reality of *this* situation.

"I don't think you're breathing."

"Get off me, Mace. Now." Amazing. She sounded completely calm and rational. She tried to push away from the door, but that big, hard body refused to budge one inch. His hands held her hands flat against the wood so she couldn't go for her weapon. His naked flesh practically seared her exposed skin with its heat.

"You said you wanted me to prove it," that low voice purred in her ear. "And that's what I did, Dez."

He was right, of course. *The fuck*. Although he didn't have to sound so haughty about it. But who knew the world actually had people who could shift into something other than human? She happily went through life thinking people who believed in vampires, werewolves, and witches were nutcases. As a cop, she believed what she could see and it always had a plausible explanation.

Of course, a lot more things made sense now. All those weird "quirky" things that Mace always used to do so clearly spoke of . . . well . . . an animal. Smelling the back of her neck. The growling. The purring. That time he actually bared his fangs at a sophomore who tried to take his grilled cheese sandwich in the cafeteria.

Yet none of that made any of this easier. Especially not with her body being pinned by a guy who three minutes ago had shifted himself into the king of the jungle. A guy who scared her one-hundred-and-fifty pound Rottweiler dogs to death.

A guy kissing her neck.

"What are you doing?"

"What do you think I'm doing?" He asked just before his tongue swirled around that spot where her neck and her spine met. Her knees almost buckled, but she stopped by reminding herself that the guy *wasn't human*.

Her fingers dug into the wood. "Is this really the time for you to get horny?"

"Sorry, shifting does that to me. Shifting and you."

No, no, *no*! He wasn't going to get away with being charming now. "Mace—"

He cut her off. "I've wanted you since Mr. Shotsky's biology class."

Unbelievable. A naked freak has her slammed up against her own closet door so she can't get to her gun, but some trite bullshit about ninth grade had her creaming like a porn star. Exactly what was wrong with her? And could she pass it on to any children she may have?

Mace's hips pushed up against her, and she had to bite her lip to keep from moaning. "Christ, Dez. I wanna fuck you so bad, my whole body hurts."

Okay. She had two choices here. She could tell Mace what he wanted to hear. Get free and splatter pieces of him all over her nice wood bedroom furniture. As human she could probably use her .9mm on him.

Or . . . she could be honest with the big idiot.

"Mace . . ." She took a deep breath. "If you let me go now, I'm going to blow your brains out."

Mace didn't move. He barely breathed. This was the moment. This. Right now. If Dez really wanted him dead, she would have lied her ass off to get away from him and . . . well . . . blown his brains out. Instead, she warned him. Warned him that if he let her go, she'd kill him.

Okay. The woman had completely confused him. And how he handled it from here would decide everything for them.

"That's kind of a problem, baby. Me being partial to breathing and all." He nuzzled her neck and her heart started beating faster, but he didn't smell fear. He took that as a good sign and decided to barrel forward—slowly.

"Why don't we do this . . ." He slid one arm down her body, feeling the soft skin under his fingers. "Let's get rid of all this unnecessary paraphernalia. Make it easier for us to have a civilized discussion." He grasped Dez's holster with her .9mm in it, pulling it off her jeans and with practiced aim tossed it to her dresser across the room. It landed with a rather loud thunk, and Dez's body jumped next to his. But he still didn't smell fear. He smelled something else altogether.

Lust.

He lightly kissed the tip of her ear. "Any other weapons, Dez?"

Her forehead resting on the door, she muttered, "You don't expect me to answer that honestly, do you?"

He leered. "I guess I'll have to check then."

"Guess so."

Mace slowly dragged his hands down Dez's arms. He used every ounce of his self-control to not rip her jeans off and start fucking her from behind. A sudden move like that could blow it all. Dez trusted him. Trusting him even though she knew he wasn't human. Not completely. That meant more than he could ever say, and he wasn't about to ruin it by being . . . ya know . . . a guy.

Dez closed her eyes as his hands slid down her body, across her breasts, lingering for a moment at her nipples, which caused her entire body to convulse. *Damn sensitive nipples.* Every time her ex had touched them, she practically ripped his throat out. That wasn't the response she had with Mace, though. She wanted him more than she ever had before. And she'd wanted him a lot before. Yet knowing he was only partially human had changed everything for her. She dealt with humans every day. Every day she found herself disgusted and appalled by their bullshit. Trusting human-Mace seemed like a stupid idea to her. She didn't trust, understand, or really even like humans. She knew what they could do. The damage they could cause.

Animals, though, were all about survival. Mating, hunting, feeding—simply keeping their species alive. They didn't hurt each other out of spite. They didn't humiliate others to make themselves feel better. When they hunt and kill it is only for food, and they never do anything morally reprehensible to the corpse afterward. Dez understood animals. She always had. Now she understood Mace, and that made all the difference in the world for her. He was the first man she could ever truly trust.

Although that particular thought made her want to pass out.

"You stopped breathing again, Dez." She let out the breath she had been holding. "Good, baby. Keep doing that and you'll be fine."

His hands slid around her waist and he crouched low, bringing them down the outside of her legs. He found her secondary weapon in an ankle holster and a small blade strapped to the other ankle. He took those and tossed them on the dresser.

He returned to his crouch behind her. "Spread your legs," he ordered. She caught that moan before it could pour out of her mouth along with the potential begging that might follow. Silently, she complied.

Mace slowly dragged his hands up between her legs, his right hand sliding between her thighs and pushing against her crotch. Her whole body jerked like someone attached a live wire to her. She knew she was wet. Now he knew it, too, if that very primal grunt of satisfaction rumbling up from his chest proved anything.

He rubbed his hand against her crotch, and Dez dug her short nails into the closet door. "Anything else I need to be on the lookout for, Dez?"

She didn't answer him. Instead, she shook her head.

"What's the matter?" And she could hear the smile in his voice. "Cat got your crotch?"

By far, one of the stupidest things anyone had ever said to her, and in response, she burst out laughing.

He turned her to face him, and she looked down into that gorgeous face.

"It's going to be okay, ya know. I promise."

His body, still crouched in front of her, seemed more naked than most. Not that she'd never seen a naked man before. Hell, she arrested a lot of naked males over the years. But none of them, even the best-built Marines, had ever been like this. Something so raw and male exuded from Mace, the thought of *not* fucking him was becoming an impossibility.

"Now, if you're not going to tell me if there are other weapons, I guess we'll have to get the rest of these clothes off you." He grinned. A wicked, evil grin that almost dropped her to the floor. "Just so we can get a closer inspection, of course."

He unzipped her jeans, pulling them down her hips and legs until they puddled onto the floor. He tossed the jeans aside while he pulled his body out of its crouch and kneeled in front of her. He slid his hands back up her legs as he kissed the exposed flesh above her red lace panties. His hands slid under the lace to grip her ass, his tongue swirling right under her belly button.

Dez bit her lip. "At this point, Mace, I'm not exactly sure what you're searching for."

Gold eyes, so dark with lust they seemed black, focused on her face. "Do you really care?"

She blinked. "Care about what?"

"You're not paying attention, Desiree." He nipped the sensitive flesh of her lower abdomen. "I guess I'll have to work a little harder to make sure you don't lose interest."

Mace slid her panties off, and Dez wondered what the hell was going on. What the hell was she doing? And what exactly was Mace doing with his finger?

"Mace!"

He stopped, clearly annoyed. Although his forefinger seemed damn happy to have slid past her clit and buried itself deep inside her pussy. "What now?"

"Maybe we should—" before the word *wait* could come out, Mace started slowly finger-fucking her. Dez's back arched off the closet door. *Tricky fuckin' cat!*

Dez dug deep lines in the wood of her poor door. It had been so long since she'd been with anyone. So long since she had a man touch her in any way but friendship or while trying to outrun her after doing something illegal. She didn't want to blow this, but to be honest she had no freakin' idea what the hell she'd gotten herself into. Add in the fact Mace's cock was freakin' huge and you have a recipe for a Dez disaster.

Mace's free hand slid around her waist, pulling her close to him. He kissed and nipped her stomach and hips. "Touch me, Dez. I need to feel your hands on me."

Why did that surprise her? Maybe because Mace never seemed like he ever needed anything or anyone. "I thought cats didn't like to be touched, Llewellyn."

He licked her belly button. "Damn dog people. That's propaganda." He rubbed his face across her belly and thighs, his unshaven cheeks and jaw feeling rough against her skin. "We need affection, Dez. We just don't beg for it."

Dez grinned as she slid her hands into his hair. She now understood why Mace's hair was always out of control in high school. Because it had been growing into a mane. A real, honest-to-God lion's mane.

She closed her eyes and plunged forward. "I need you to kiss me, Mace."

Mace stopped moving. Even his fingers paused in their slow, steady movements.

"I loved the way you kissed me today." She looked down at him, brushing his hair out of his eyes. He watched her silently, and Dez realized how much she wanted all this. How much she wanted him. "Do you know I would have given anything for you to kiss me like that in high school? I would have given anything for you to even try."

Mace's gold eyes locked with hers. He slid his finger out of her and, as he slowly stood, he slipped it in his mouth, sucking it clean. Dez groaned as his exquisite body towered over her. He took her hands, their fingers interlacing. Palms against palms. Then he slammed them against the door, his body once again pinning her to the hard wood.

"I wish I'd known you'd felt that way, Dez." His mouth barely touched hers, and Dez briefly wondered if her lungs stopped working. "Because I've felt like that since the second I saw you. And I've never stopped." Then his mouth was on hers, and this time she couldn't stop the moan or the shudder that went through her entire body. Nothing had ever felt so good. Or tasted so good. Damn, but the man tasted so goddamn good.

He released her lips, burning a delicious line down her neck with his tongue and back up again. Eventually he stopped by her ear. "So, baby, anything else I need to get out of the way before I get down to the business of making you come so hard you'll think you're dying?"

Dez scowled. "Exactly how the hell am I supposed to even answer that, Mace?"

"That's easy. Just say, 'Please fuck me, master.'"

Dez laughed again. *Good.* When she laughed, she wasn't freaking out. He found that humor was the best way to deal with Dez. If he got too intense she would make a run for the door.

"What, exactly, is wrong with 'Fuck me, master'?" He slid his hands behind her back and unhooked her bra. When he slipped it off her body, he made sure that his hands touched her skin the entire time. Not only did he love the feel of her, but the more he touched her, the more aroused she became.

"You want a list, Llewellyn?"

He became thoughtful, truly wondering what the answer to his next question would be. "Do you trust me, Dez?"

He dropped her bra to the floor as Dez closed her eyes and, for a moment, Mace thought she might be in pain or trying to remember all the exits out of the room. Then he heard it. A soft whisper. Almost a sigh.

"Yeah, Mace. I trust you."

That was definitely the answer he had been hoping for, he just never expected to get it.

"Of course," she continued, "I've been told on occasion that I'm an idiot."

Mace slid his hand behind the back of her neck, pulling her toward him. "Since that still works in my favor, I'm okay with that."

He kissed her again, allowing himself the chance to explore her mouth. Enjoy her taste.

She trusted him. He wanted to roar it from the roof. Because to Mace that meant Dez MacDermot was all his.

Why did she suddenly feel like the weakest gazelle of the herd? With Mace kissing her, claiming her again. And she had a feeling this would only be the beginning. Whether she meant to or not, she'd given him what he wanted. Not sex because, let's face it, he could have had that anytime in the last eight hours. No, she'd given him what she hadn't given any other man besides her father. She'd given him her trust. The fact that this revelation seemed to move him to a new level of passion warmed her. Made her feel like the most important person in the universe.

But Mace always made her feel that way. That too-smart-for-his-own-good, scrawny kid acted like she was the queen of his universe then. She didn't realize until she'd gone to a new school, she used that feeling as her life raft. When things got too harsh at the Cathedral School, she knew she only had to go to two o'clock biology class. One look at Mace's funny, but so cute, little face would lift her day and make her feel like she could handle the hell until she escaped for good.

Of course, that little kid no longer existed. In his place was this man making her tremble simply by kissing her. His kisses, like his smiles, held such promise.

He stepped away from her and walked to the bed, gently pulling her along with him. He positioned her beside it, then kneeled down. He tugged her hand until she followed, kneeling in front of him. She had no idea where this was going, but he had her intrigued.

Mace kissed her neck, licking that sensitive spot right under her ear. Her breathing grew labored as he took both her arms and gently pinned them behind her back with his own. With that one move, her back arched and he lowered his head to capture a nipple between his lips. She jumped. Practically out of her skin.

"Hold it." He paused, his gold eyes watching her closely. She cleared her throat. "My nipples are really sensitive."

"Am I hurting you?" he asked around her nipple.

"No. No. Not at all. It's just—" She stopped. She saw the wicked intent in his eyes. The lust that said he wanted her screaming and coming until *he* was satisfied she'd had enough. "Jesus Christ, that's what you want."

He grinned.

She tried to pull her arms away. "Mace Llewellyn, you let me go!"

"Really, baby? You sure that's what you want?" He sucked on her nipple and her back arched again, practically throwing him off. She gasped, her head resting on the bed behind her. He put her in a position where she wouldn't be uncomfortable but where he had complete control.

Tricky son of a bitch cat!

"Mace . . ." She growled it. Her warning growl. But he only laughed.

"When you're ready to beg for my cock, baby, you let me know."

"Beg? I don't beg."

"Good." He released her breast long enough to grin at her. "Then when you do, you'll really mean it."

His mouth returned to her breast and she couldn't speak. It felt too wonderful. Too extraordinary. Too everything.

He only focused on her breasts. He teased. He licked. He sucked. He did practically everything but marry one. It didn't take long before her climax started sneaking up on her. That never happened before. She usually always needed to have a finger, tongue, or dick involved with her clit to even have the hope of getting off.

But as she sped within seconds of climaxing the bastard stopped. He pulled away and blew on her nipple or nuzzled her breasts. He did it over and over again. Constantly bringing her to the brink of an orgasm guaranteed to permanently blind her and then backing off. He kept it up for so long she was close to crying. Her entire body hummed like a tuning fork. Her hips wouldn't stop rubbing against him. Eventually, she told her ego to fuck off.

"God, Mace. Please."

"Please what, baby?"

"You know what, you asshole."

"Is that your idea of begging? Because it's sorely lacking." She glared at him as she tried to get her arms loose so she could strangle the fucker.

He licked both her nipples again, and she thought she might really start crying.

"Any condoms?" he finally asked.

Oh thank God! "Top drawer of my nightstand. By the Luger."

"My, you're awfully prepared. Expecting someone else, were we?"

"Mace Llewellyn." She really hoped he could hear the warning in her voice, because she was very close to losing it.

"You know, I can wait all day. So if you want to be bitchy . . ."

He lowered his mouth to her nipple and she bucked under him. "Okay. Okay," she sputtered desperately. "I got it as a gag gift from some of the other female detectives. For my birthday."

"Aw, baby. Did I miss your birthday?"

"*Mace!*"

"Okay. Okay." He laughed as he kept her arms locked behind her with one of his big hands while he reached over and dug into her nightstand drawer. "Christ, you have more guns," he muttered. He pulled out the box. "Whew. That's good. They're extra large."

"Mason."

He grinned like the evil cat he was, ripped open the box, and took out a condom. With amazing skill, he rolled it on his dick with one hand.

He grabbed Dez around the waist and tossed her up on the bed. By the time she landed Mace had already crawled up her body. He rubbed and licked his way along her legs, stopping to nuzzle her crotch and give a quick lick to her clit, which almost sent her over the edge—but not quite. He dragged his big body over her until they were face to face. He stared down at her and, for a minute, she thought he wanted more begging. But his hand reached up and cupped one side of her face. "You are so beautiful, Dez."

Dez looped her arms around his neck and opened her legs wider so Mace could fit comfortably between them. "That's really sweet and all but can that fuckin' wait 'til later?"

Mace chuckled. "Damn, Dez."

Growling low she rubbed her head against his chin. He'd done it to her a few times—she wondered if it would work on him as well. When she heard him purring, she knew it had.

With one quick, hard thrust, he slammed into her and she had never been so happy to have a dick inside of her before. She worried about his size, but she was already so wet, so fucking worked up, that she was thankful. His big cock filled her up and took her right to the edge. But Mace left her hanging there because he wouldn't fuckin' move.

She peeked up at him. His eyes closed, his face frowning in deep concentration, his sweat dripping onto her skin. She briefly wondered if she did something wrong. If she screwed something up. The one thing she really didn't want to screw up.

"Jesus Christ, Dez. You are so fuckin' tight."

She smiled. She couldn't help herself. She hadn't screwed anything up. She was actually doing damn well for herself. "So hot and tight. I'm going to lose my mind being inside you."

Dez leaned up, her mouth beside his ear. "Mace Llewellyn, you make me wait one more goddamn second and I really will start shooting." She brushed his cheek with her forehead and he brushed her back. "Fuck me, Mace. Please. Just fuck me—"

She didn't get a chance to say another word as his mouth slammed down on hers and he began fucking her in earnest.

By the third stroke, she climaxed around him. Her entire body clenching and pulling him in deeper. She screamed out, "Fuck!" Most likely waking up the lovely old couple next door.

She'd never come so hard before in her life. But Mace didn't stop, he kept going, shoving her right into a second climax and a third. Each one she prefaced with a "Fuck! Fuck!"

Suddenly Mace buried his face against her neck and announced his orgasm with an actual roar.

Dez smiled at that, leaning back against the warm sheets. Her eyes closing in exhaustion. Mace pulled out of her and, she assumed, disposed of the condom.

Sleep just started to take her when Mace poked her in the forehead with his index finger. "Hey, MacDermot. What are you doing?"

Dez opened her eyes to find Mace over her again. "Trying to sleep."

He raised an eyebrow. "We're not done."

"What do you mean, we're not—" But he cut her off by pushing his already-hard dick inside of her again. He stopped to put on a fresh condom, but other than that, he was as hard, if not harder, than before.

"You can't be—"

"That just took the edge off." He kissed her cheek, then leaned in next to her ear. "So, if I were you, baby. I'd get comfortable."

Holy fuck.

Mace woke up out of habit. He glanced at the clock next to the bed. It wasn't even six yet. He started to stretch and quickly realized he was alone. He growled. He'd waited a long time to wake up in Dez's bed. He always planned for her to actually be in it when he did.

He closed his eyes and listened. She had to be around somewhere. The television played in the living room. Naked, he went downstairs, stopping at the last step.

Dez, also naked, sat on her big couch. Her knees pulled up so her chin rested on them. He smiled. She was actually watching old episodes of *Cops*. He chuckled to himself. Such a cop . . .

She didn't even know he stood right behind the couch until he reached out and touched her shoulder. She actually screamed, jumped up, and stumbled back away from him, tripping against her coffee table and landing on it.

He didn't move, afraid he'd scare her more. It must have hit her. The truth about what he was. And like most humans. She wasn't ready to handle it.

"Jesus, Mace! Don't sneak up on me!"

Mace took a deep breath. He understood. It took a lot for humans to understand about shifters. About their lives and how their bodies worked and how they weren't evil, blah, blah, blah.

"It's okay, ya know."

"What's okay?"

"To be scared."

Scowling, "Scared about what?"

"About me. Being what I am."

"Oh, get over yourself, Captain Ego. You and your big but silent lion feet startled me. That's all."

Torn between being annoyed and wanting to fuck her on that coffee table, Mace decided to sit down on the couch instead. He stepped over the back and planted himself on the burgundy cushions.

"What's going on, Dez? Talk to me."

"Nothing's going on."

"Don't lie to me, Desiree."

She leaned over, her elbows on her knees, and ran her hands through her hair. After a few moments of silence, she took in a deep breath. "Petrov's body had marks on his throat. Claw marks. Except that the grip implied . . ." She looked at him with those beautiful gray eyes. "Thumbs."

Mace observed her closely. She must have the smoothest skin known to man. Except for the frown lines in her forehead, which she always had, her skin was flawless. Clearly, Dez lived a relatively clean life. No drugs. Very little drinking. And, until recently, very little sex and the difficulties that sometimes come with it.

"Are you going to answer me?"

"You didn't ask me a question, so I was staring at you instead."

She rubbed her eyes with the knuckles of her hands. "Mace, what am I going to do with you?"

"Well, we've got that big bed right upstairs—"

"Mace."

"Or I've been thinking about fucking you on this couch too."

"Mace!" She took another deep breath. "Mace. This clearly involves—you know—your people, and I'm not exactly sure how to handle this. It's not like I can go to my lieutenant and tell him there seems to be a rash of 'shifter killers' around."

"You don't have to. This stuff works out on its own. I just need you to stay out of the way, Dez. I can't have anything happen to you."

She leaned forward and ran her finger along the wound she recently unbandaged. "You mean like this? We both know this wasn't an accident."

Debating what to say, he glanced down at her feet. The nails painted a bright red, she wore a small silver ring on the second toe of her right foot. Damn, even her feet were cute. "It wasn't an accident, I just don't know why they targeted you. Unless they had something to do with it."

"They?"

He sighed. Things kept getting difficult. Well, more difficult. No point in lying now, though. "Hyenas." When she simply raised an eyebrow at him, he continued. "You know. Hyenas. Natural enemies of lions?"

"Yes, Mace. I know hyenas. I watch the Discovery Channel."

"They did this to you. I'm assuming whatever club you were in, whoever you met with, were hyenas."

Dez nodded slowly. He didn't think she understood, but apparently her NYPD attitude wouldn't allow her to show that weakness.

"There's one thing that confuses me."

"Just one thing," he teased. He knew this had to be freaking her out. It still amazed him she hadn't tried to go for her shotgun again.

"Yeah. The club I was at last night . . . Shaw was there. I mean, he's like you, right? He's attached to your sister?"

Mace nodded, surprised at how quickly she caught on. "Who did you meet exactly?"

"Gina Brutale."

"Yeah, they're hyenas all right." Mace realized exactly how lucky he was. "The Brutales are not to be messed with, Dez."

"I wasn't. She called me. Said she had information on Petrov. She said he was in love with her. Is that even possible?"

"Sure. You can fall in love with anybody. And I've heard hyenas are a wild ride in bed."

Dez glared at him. "Thanks for the info, Mace."

"Just trying to be helpful, Detective."

Dez ran her hand through her gorgeous mane of hair. "Brutale owned the club. The Chapel on Sixteenth."

Mace shook his head. "If they owned the club then that was hyena territory. I'm sure the club is considered neutral but, still, Shaw must be playing Russian roulette if he's hanging out there."

Mace watched Dez as her mind turned around all he told her.

She seemed to be less than interested in the fact of what he was. Not while she still had a case to solve.

"Brutale thinks your sister killed Petrov."

"Do you?"

She sighed. "No. Although I really wanted her to. I'm still not sure why me, though. What did I do?"

"You probably still had my scent on you when you went to the club." *When you were running from me.*

She held her hand up. "Okay. Please stop."

"What's wrong?"

"It's getting a little weird for me."

"What's weird, Dez? The hyenas? The lions?" He leaned down, his elbows resting on his knees, his hands clasped in front of him. "Or you smelling like me?"

Her eyes narrowed at the same time her nipples hardened. He almost smiled. He loved making her crazy.

"Well, your sister didn't kill Petrov. I don't think Brutale killed him. Shaw, however, could have or . . . you know . . ." She shrugged and watched him with those gray eyes.

"You know what?" She raised one eyebrow, and he exploded. "*Are you suggesting I may have killed the man?*"

"Now, calm down. It's only a suggestion."

"A very fucking insulting suggestion!"

"There's no reason to yell at me."

"You accuse me of murder and there's no reason to yell at you?"

"Is it still considered murder amongst your people?"

"Amongst my people? Are you fucking kidding me with this shit?"

"I'm simply asking the question."

"No, you're not. You're trying to find something wrong with me."

"I am not!"

"You are too! You know as well as I do that I got off the fucking transport yesterday. Petrov was killed . . . what? Two days ago? You know it wasn't me. And I would hope you thought more highly of me than that. Especially since you just fucked me."

"All I know is that you're not exactly human. And I only recently found that out."

"Bullshit. You know me better than anybody else, Dez. You've always known I wasn't exactly human. Didn't you?"

"What I do know is that it all makes sense to me now. You. Your sisters."

"We're naked. We are never to discuss my sisters when we're naked."

She stood up. "You know, they actually said I wasn't good enough for you. For you!" Dez pointed at him. "You're a freak."

"And you reek of normal. You surrounded yourself with a shitload of guns and the world's largest dogs so no one will get near you, and the first male that does, you accuse him of being a murderer."

"I didn't accuse you. *I made a suggestion!*"

The two glared at each other. Mace could feel and smell Dez's rage. He also sensed her fear. Yet he now knew it wasn't because of what he was, but her own fear of being hurt again. Of having anyone get close enough to touch the woman she had buried underneath her Kevlar vest. But he didn't have time for her bullshit. He was crazy about the woman. Madly in love with her. Probably from the first time he saw her all those years ago. So she would simply have to get over whatever little "issues" she had.

"Come here, Dez." He didn't mean to spit that out through clenched teeth.

"No."

"Come. Here." Well, that sounded like an order. Probably not good either.

"Fuck. You."

Well, this wasn't working. He watched her glare at him from no more than five feet away, but it felt like a two-hundred-mile chasm. His need to touch her became almost overwhelming. The desire to stroke her flesh. To lick that little pulse point on her neck. To kiss her. God, did he want to kiss her.

Mace leaned forward and gently grabbed hold of her hand. He gave a tug. "Come here, Dez."

Her anger receded as quickly as it came. She rewarded him with a shy smile. "Why?"

He tugged again. "Please."

Dez slowly moved toward him. He pulled her until she sat on his lap, facing him. Her strong legs straddled his thighs.

"The condoms are upstairs," she reminded him softly.

He pushed her thick silky hair off her face. Ran his hands across the soft flesh of her cheeks. "We don't need 'em for this."

Dez let Mace pull her toward him, his eyes on her mouth.

Could she be more of a bitch? No, she couldn't. Why else would she accuse the man of being a murderer? She knew he wasn't. A predator . . . definitely. A well-trained military killer . . . absolutely. But to gun someone down in cold blood? Nah. If for no other reason, Mace simply wouldn't bother. He simply didn't like or dislike most people enough to get up the emotion necessary to blow their brains out. He was a cat, after all.

"I'm sorry, Mace." The words were out of her mouth before she could hope to stop them. "I should have never said that to you."

He smiled and she almost came from the sight of it. "You're right." He ran his big hands through her hair and she moaned at the contact. She never believed hair could be an erogenous zone. Man, she'd been wrong about that. "You should have never said that to me."

"Can I make it up to you?"

"We'll have to see, now won't we."

As soon as his lips touched hers, a jolt went right to her pussy, causing her clit to actually spasm. From just a kiss. She never thought that possible. At least not for her. But with Mace, anything seemed possible.

He pulled her closer, his tongue sliding across hers, his strong hands moving across her back. She kept waiting for more, but he kept kissing her. Only kissing her. That's all he wanted. She sighed and melted against him.

Nope. She couldn't deny it. This man rocked her world. Her universe.

She squirmed against him. That flash-flood warning problem happening again. Her nipples were so hard they hurt. And Mace kept on kissing her, his hands never leaving her back or going below her waist.

Man, she was in over her head.

"You keep squirming, baby. You okay?" He licked her collarbone, but she could feel his smile against her hot flesh.

"Mace?"

"Yes?"

"Stop messing with my head."

"I didn't know I was. I've just always wanted to make out with you. It's a fantasy of mine. I figured this was as good a time as any."

She wanted him so bad she wasn't sure how much more she could take. "Well, it's not. So get on with it." Mace pulled back from her, and Dez groaned in disappointment. "What, Mace? What?"

"I'm enjoying the fact you think you can order me around."

She really did not like the sound of that. "Uh—"

"Put your hands on my shoulders and lean back a bit." Dez placed a hand on each shoulder and leaned her upper body back. Mace's right hand slid down between her breasts, across her stomach, pausing at her crotch. His thumb right above her clit. Without thinking, her grip tightened a bit on his shoulder.

"Look at me, Dez." She did. "Don't close your eyes. Don't look away. You understand?"

She opened her mouth to reply.

"And I don't need a thesis on this. Yes or no will do just fine."

She glared at him. "Yes. I understand."

"Good." Mace twisted his hand, pushing two fingers inside her and brushing his thumb over her clit. Immediately Dez's head fell back on a moan. Mace stopped. "See," he pointed out softly. "Clearly you don't understand."

Dez took a deep breath and looked back at Mace. *Christ, he's serious.*

She wanted to call him every name in the book—and she had

a big book—but she wanted him to make her come in the worst way. So, for once, she bit her tongue. Besides, there was something about not having to worry about . . . well, about everything that really turned her on. She'd never given up control to anyone before. Mace would be her first. She had the feeling she wouldn't be disappointed.

Mace stared at her for a moment. "Are we clear, Marine?"

Dez fought the urge to roll her eyes. "Yes. We're clear."

"Yes, we're clear . . . what?"

"Mace Llewellyn—" He swirled his fingers inside her, causing Dez to gasp.

"I'm waiting."

"Yes. We're clear . . ." Dez gritted her teeth. "Commander."

His grin almost blinded her. "I like hearing you say that. I wish I'd seen you when you were still active. Me being an officer and you . . . not . . . I could have had some real fun."

He would so be paying for this.

Slowly, he began pumping his fingers in and out of her. Taking his time. Dez promised herself again she'd make him pay for this . . . later.

Her eyes locked with his and she clenched her muscles around his fingers. He grunted in satisfaction as the pad of his thumb massaged her clit. Dez forced herself to look Mace in the eyes. It wasn't easy. All she wanted was to close her eyes and ride the sensations he inundated her with. Plus, those gold eyes burned into her, stripped away all her defenses. He took control, but in the process he made her feel strong, female, and sexy. No one had ever done that for her before. No one had ever bothered to try.

"Stay with me, Dez." Good God, that voice of his would be the death of her. His voice stroked her like his fingers. Only it touched her in places his fingers couldn't quite reach.

Dez's muscles tensed and her orgasm rolled up on her in one crashing wave. Mace, though, still wouldn't let her look away. She had a feeling his pleasure relied on her pleasure. His hard dick rubbed against her butt as his breath came in short, hard pants.

She dug her short nails deep into Mace's shoulders. Her entire body unraveled. Falling apart under his skillful hands. "Fuck, Mace. Fuck!"

His fingers picked up the pace, pumping in and out of her with one intent. "I wanna see you come, Dez. *Now.*"

She did. She broke into a million pieces all over the man's hand. And not once did she look away from those beautiful gold eyes.

She is so beautiful. Sitting around watching *Cops* or coming all over him, the woman was freakin' beautiful. He always loved getting a woman off, but something about Dez's pleasure, her joy at simply having an orgasm, absolutely set his hair on fire.

The woman held complete control of his heart and didn't even know it. He wasn't sure she even cared. Dez collapsed against him, her lips against his collarbone. Her fingers still digging into his shoulders. She belonged here. On his lap, right on top of his cock. Skin against skin. Heart against heart.

He could do it. He could make her love him. Even if he had to put up with those goddamn dogs, he'd get her to love him.

Mace rubbed his chin against the top of her head. "So . . . did that take the edge off?"

She chuckled against his neck and goose bumps broke out across his skin. "You could say that."

"Then can I get back to business?"

Dez sat up as he slowly removed his hand from what he now considered the most amazing hot spot on earth.

"Back to what business?"

He ran his still-wet hand over her bottom lip, leaned in, and licked it away.

Dez shuddered. "Oh. That."

"Yeah. That. You're not going to work today, right?"

Dez gazed at his mouth and shook her head.

"Good." He pulled her toward him. "Then kiss me, Dez."

Chapter Six

Dez woke up when her dogs licked her face. She pushed the two Rotties away and glanced around. Half on and half off the end of the bed, her body completely tangled up in the sheets.

"*Sitz.*" Her dogs sat. "*Plotz.*" Her dogs lay down. She trained them in German since they were German dogs. She glared at them. "Thanks for deserting me last night." They at least had the decency to look ashamed.

Dez sat up. The room was a wreck and she guessed she was too. She listened but didn't hear Mace anywhere. Maybe he left. Didn't want to be around for the morning-after awkwardness. Not that she blamed him. She hadn't been looking forward to that either.

Dez slowly stood up. She took a couple of steps to see if she could still walk. Surprisingly, she could. She thought for sure the man made her a cripple, her entire body sore as hell. Not that she actually minded.

She glanced at her nightstand clock. Already one o'clock. Well, if she were going over her parents' house on Christmas she needed to get the rest of the gifts. And order that goddamn pie.

The thought of facing last-minute shoppers didn't sound very tantalizing, but she didn't have much choice. Besides, her alternative? Sitting around waiting for Mace to call. She shuddered thinking she even would do that for one second of the day. Hell, there was no shame in the one-night stand. It had been a one-night stand, right?

Of course, nothing about this *felt* like a one-night stand. Far from it.

Dez stumbled to the bathroom, her two dogs trailing quietly behind, and took a shower. As she towel-dried her hair, she examined herself in the mirror. She did look well fucked, now didn't she?

Well fucked by a cat.

She waited for it. The freak-out over the cat thing. But it never came. Christ, either she'd become really jaded or she really didn't care. She thought about it for a moment.

Nope. She really didn't care.

Dez headed back to her bedroom but stopped when she heard noises from the kitchen. When her boys dived back under the bed, she knew what it was. *Who* it was.

Holy shit. He's back. She wasn't sure how to react to that. Although her body began to cream at the mere thought of him. Well, she would have to do something about that.

Still wearing her towel, she walked down the stairs and headed to the kitchen. She heard female voices chattering and assumed Mace turned on some female talk show. But when she opened the swinging door, she stopped and almost choked in horror.

"Well, well. Look who's up."

"And all dressed for the day, I see."

Dez glared at her two sisters as her mother placed a sandwich large enough to choke a rhino on a plate and sat it in front of Mace. He sat there showered, dressed, and, surprisingly, shaved. He even had on what appeared to be new clothes. Black jeans, black turtleneck sweater, black boots. On anybody else they'd look like dockworkers. On Mace . . . well, he didn't look like any dockworker she'd ever known.

Dez glanced around the kitchen and realized there were department store and grocery bags all over the counters. *He really has made himself at home, now hasn't he?* He grinned at her and shrugged.

"You had no food. A man could starve."

"But her dogs never will."

Dez glared at Lonnie while Rachel choked around the bottle of soda she swigged from.

"Why are you all here?"

"We came to see if you wanted to go Christmas shopping. We know how bad you are at that," Rachel offered.

"But we found Mace here all by himself bringing in groceries," Lonnie added. "And you nowhere to be found."

Mace bit into the sandwich, and when his eyes practically rolled to the back of his head, her mother beamed. "Eat. Eat, dear boy. A man your size needs food."

"You know when you called me about Missy, I had no idea you'd seen good ol' Mace from high school."

Dez couldn't believe the two bitches. Sitting in her kitchen like butter wouldn't melt in their mouths. As Missy and Mace's other sisters told her in no uncertain terms she wasn't good enough for their brother, her own sisters actively put down Mace. He's funny looking. He's short. He's strange.

Now they were acting like their long-lost brother turned up at their door.

Absolute bitches.

Before Dez could start getting good and frothy, her mother came around and hugged her hello. "How's my little girl?"

"Hiya, Ma."

"You look so pretty this morning." Then, in a tight whisper against her ear, "If you don't feed them, they leave."

Dez ignored her mother, instead mouthing "Fuck you" over and over to both her sisters. Who returned the loving sentiment with the finger and the word *whore* mouthed at her. This went on for a good fifteen seconds before her mother stiffened in her arms.

"You three stop that right now!"

The three women froze. Hard to believe that Lonnie was one of the most feared federal prosecutors in the country and Rachel had probably removed the top of someone's skull yesterday to get to their brain. And, of course, Dez was a well-armed cop and former Marine with a shapeshifter in her house. Hell, just a few hours ago, she had him between her legs too.

But a word from their mother still had them quaking.

"Sorry, Ma," all three mumbled as the tiny woman pulled away from her much-taller daughter. Dez almost exclusively took after her father. Unlike her sisters, there was nothing petite or delicate about her. Of course, that didn't seem to bother Mace too much.

"Well, we're going to leave you two . . . alone." Her mother raised an eyebrow, and Dez wanted to crawl into a hole. "And we'll see you on Christmas, Mace."

"Yes, ma'am."

Dez's head snapped up and she locked eyes with Mace. "I thought you had other plans." No way. *No way* could she let Mace spend that much time around her sisters. When it came to the worst lowlifes on the planet, Dez always kept total and utter control. But her family remained a whole different matter. Five minutes with them and they'd completely turn him against her.

"Nope."

"What about your sisters? Shouldn't you go to their house for the holidays?" She knew the whole family thing would get to her mother. Sure enough, her mother didn't disappoint.

"Oh, Mace. We can't take you away from your family."

"You're not, Mrs. MacDermot. My sisters aren't expecting me. Besides . . ." Those gold eyes turned to Dez. "Dez and I already had plans to spend the day together. Didn't we, baby?"

She wanted to say "No, we did not" but her sisters were waiting for that. Waiting to see something they could feed on. Mace knew it too. He had sisters—he knew exactly what he was doing. Fine, then. He wanted to spend time with her family, more power to him.

"How could I forget?" She rubbed her mom's back. "We'll be there, Ma."

"Good. Good. Don't forget pie."

The women headed toward the door, leaving Mace downing that sandwich like it was his first meal in six months.

Once at the front door, her mother leaned in conspiratorially. "I still like him. He's grown into a very nice young man."

"Ma, you don't even know him."

"Yes, but I'm never wrong about these things."

"Of course, it doesn't hurt he's a Llewellyn."

Dez glared at Lonnie, "Fuck you" on her lips. One look at her mother told her that would be a bad idea. The woman believed in the holiday spirit, even if she had to kick the shit out of you to make sure you were feeling it too.

Her mother hugged her. "See you soon, honey."

"Bye, Ma."

She walked out the door, but her sisters remained.

"The Llewellyns are powerful, little sister. Hope you know what you're doing."

"Why don't you let me do what I gotta do and you two do what you gotta do."

"Fine."

Then Lonnie snatched the towel off Dez and charged out the door, Rachel slamming it before Dez could get to them. Instead, she collided with the hard wood.

They were too old for this bullshit.

Dez kept her head against the door, unable to turn around. Not when she knew Mace stood right behind her.

"Here, baby. Here's a towel."

She reached back, unable to face the man, and grasped the towel he handed her. Of course, it was a dish towel and not much good.

"I hate you."

"You so wish you did. But tragically, you're crazy about me."

She wanted to argue with him, prove to him she hated him. That she still had control. But when his hands slid across her ass, she completely forgot what she'd been mad about.

So that was what a nice normal family was like. Yeah. He could get used to that. As much animosity that passed between the three sisters, fangs and claws never made an entrance. And before Dez arrived, the two women grilled him like he'd applied to the CIA. They didn't want anyone hurting their baby sister. He bet Dez had no clue.

No. He'd make sure they went to see her parents on Christmas. Besides, it would be nice to have a real Christmas dinner that didn't involve senators or a live wild boar they hunted and devoured raw.

He would worry about that later, though. Right this second, he had the most delectable ass staring at him.

He ran his hands over the curves and planes of her body, pulling her back against his chest.

Man, he had some great sex over the years, but nothing like that. Nothing like her.

He trapped her against his body, wrapping his arms around her, and leaned down close to her ear. "We didn't wake you up, did we?"

"No. I didn't hear you guys until I was out of the shower."

"Good. I wanted you to get all the sleep you needed."

She leaned back into him. "Why?"

In answer, he slipped his hand between her legs and gently stroked her. "You sore?"

She wiggled against him. "I'll live."

Then her stomach growled. Her head dropped forward in defeat. "That was more embarrassing than the towel."

Mace took pity on her. He dragged her to the kitchen, pausing long enough so she could grab the Jets blanket from off the couch.

"You need to feed. It's normal after all that sex." He sat her down at the counter in the large kitchen. A cook or chef must have once owned the house. The kitchen easily outstripped the rest of her place. The island in the middle of the room was made of stainless steel and marble. Shame Dez never used it. Still, he found himself liking her house more and more. It smelled like her. Well, her and those stupid dogs, but he could learn to live with that. He could learn to live with a lot to be with this woman.

"Your mother made you a sandwich." He pulled it out of the fridge and put it in front of her, along with a cold can of soda. He leaned against the counter next to her.

She stared down at the sandwich as she finished wrapping the blanket around her like a towel, covering everything from her chest down. "What's the meat on this? Antelope?"

He smiled. What a smart-ass. "Actually they were out. It's zebra."

She picked up the sandwich, brought it to her mouth, but stopped when she realized he was staring at her. "What?"

"I'm waiting for you to finish eating."

"Why?" He grinned and she turned completely red. "Oh."

"So hurry up."

"I can't eat with you staring at me. Talk or something."

"Well, when I started in the Navy I knew this guy—"

She cut him off by raising one finger. "No, and I mean *no* Navy stories. *Ever.*"

"What's wrong with the Navy?"

"Nothing. It's military stories in general. Nothing makes me crazier than listening to a bunch of males sitting around talking about their goddamn military glory that always ends with something about a barhook giving them a happy ending."

"Okay then. Of course that doesn't leave much. I was in for fourteen years."

She finally took a bite of the sandwich and now spoke around a mouth full of food. "Come up with something. You're smart . . ." She looked him up and down. "Basically."

"Okay." He waited until she took another bite of food. "My sister tried to rip my throat out once."

He pounded on her back to prevent her from choking. Eventually she swallowed and glared at him. "Don't do that!"

"Sorry."

She took a gulp of soda and leveled those gray eyes at him. "You know, your sisters are real bitches."

"Yeah. I know."

She went back to eating and talking simultaneously. "The worst thing my sisters did was hold me down and spit on me."

Mace grimaced. "I think I'd rather have her rip my throat out."

"There's an upside to both."

Mace watched Dez eat. He examined her long neck and strong body. Her arms well defined, probably from handling those two stupid but huge dogs. He noticed faded, jagged scars on her shoulder. Without thinking, he ran his forefinger across the indented flesh. "Where did you get these?"

Dez shrugged. "Baby."

"A baby or your baby?"

Dez grinned around her sandwich. "Neither. *The* Baby. My first working dog. I was a dog handler in the Marines. Her name was misleading." Mace guessed so when he made out at least a dozen puncture wounds on and around her shoulder.

"A dog handler, huh? Were you any good?"

"Nope. I was one of the best."

"Yet who knew you were really a cat person at heart?"

"I'm not. I just tolerate you because you have exceptional thighs."

Mace laughed. "So what happened with Baby?"

Dez swallowed a mouthful of food. "I'd only been working her about two weeks or so. I was pretty terrified of her, but I didn't want to tell my sergeant because I didn't want him to think I was weak or something." She shrugged again. "One night I was putting Baby up in her run, I took this chewed up old ball from her . . . and she didn't seem to appreciate that much. Next thing I know, she had me by the arm and had dragged my ass into the run with her. Then I woke up in the hospital, covered in bandages."

"Jesus, Dez."

"It's the risk you take being a dog handler. You're gonna get bit."

"You were mauled."

"Samey-same, G.I."

"Did they put her down?"

"Nope. They blamed me. They were going to give her to another handler, but I wouldn't let 'em. I was determined to train her ass myself. The other handlers suggested I take her on a Nature Walk. I thought about it, but I just couldn't."

"A Nature Walk?"

"Don't ask." She took another bite and spoke around the food. "Anyway, when I was done, we were the tightest team out there. I could control her off-leash with hand signals alone. Of course, no one could get near me. She protected me like you wouldn't believe."

Mace touched the faded scars again and goose bumps broke out over her flesh. "What happened to her?"

"Typical military bullshit. They gave her to another handler. New C.O. hated me. Bad move, though."

"Why?"

"The next handler . . . she took his hand. Literally."

"Charming."

"Baby was all about the charm."

He stared at the one-third left to her sandwich. "You done yet?"

"God, you're pushy. I forgot how pushy you are."

"No. That's not pushy. But I can be pushy." He took the rest of her sandwich and shoved it in his mouth. He chewed. Swallowed. "Now are you done?"

Dez bit back a smile. Mace Llewellyn. Always a royal pain in the ass. Now *her* royal pain. So she might as well enjoy it—and him—while it lasted.

Dez slid off the stool and stood in front of him. Gold and beautiful, the man could completely change his molecular structure with a thought. *How cool is that?*

"I'm still hungry, Mace."

He sighed dramatically. "Fine. There's a bag of chips on the counter."

Dez shook her head while she undid his belt buckle. "Not good enough. I need a little more protein than that."

Mace took a deep breath, watching her closely. "Oh."

"That the best you can do, Llewellyn?"

"At the moment—yeah."

"I see." Dez unzipped his pants. As she dropped to her knees, she dragged his black jeans with her, unleashing that enormous dick. With the tip of her tongue, she licked off the small bit of pre-come already glistening on the head.

She glanced up. Mace had his arms stretched out across the counter, as if nailed to a cross. His eyes closed, his head leaning back. She smiled. *Cocky bastard.*

"These jeans new?"

His head snapped forward. "What?"

Such urgency flooded his voice, it took all her strength not to bust out laughing. "I said are these jeans new? They look new."

He swallowed. "Um . . . yeah . . . got them this morning."

"Locally?"

His fingers dug into the metal of her island countertop. Even his claws came out. "Yes."

"The sweater too?" She tugged on it. "It's nice. I like it."

He glared down at her. "You're killing me, Desiree."

"I know, baby."

"What do you want?"

"I want you to ask me—nicely."

"I don't ask."

"Cause you're a Llewellyn?"

"No. Cause I'm a cat."

"But I'm a—what was it? A *dog* person. And dogs beg for my attention. I want you to beg."

"I definitely don't beg."

"You will if you want my mouth around your dick anytime this millennium."

Dez leaned forward and let her tongue swirl around the head. Once. She pulled away, her eyes locking with his, and licked her lips.

With a deep and painful groan, Mace's head fell back again. Dez stifled a laugh.

"Ask me, Mace. Ask me nice."

There was a long pause, then she heard Mace's gruff voice talking to the ceiling. "Please, Dez, for the love of all that's holy—put my cock in your mouth and suck me as if your very life depended on it."

"See? That wasn't so hard, now was it, baby?"

Without waiting for him to answer, Dez opened her mouth and eased Mace's huge dick in until the tip hit the very back of her throat. She closed her lips around the engorged flesh and sucked. Hard.

Mace gave a catlike hiss, and Dez had the feeling her countertop was suffering some serious damage. *Oh well.* It came with the house.

She pulled back until only the head rested in her mouth. She laved it with her tongue, then sucked on it. With a sigh of pure enjoyment, she deep throated him again. She didn't know blow jobs could be so enjoyable. Her ex always made her feel like they were obligatory. The job requirement for being his wife.

It didn't feel that way with Mace, though. All she wanted from him at the moment was his pleasure. She stroked his dick with her mouth, sucking hard when she pulled back, licking when she went back down. She brought her hands up between his thighs and gently took hold of his balls. They were tight, and she knew he'd come soon. Normally, she'd pull away and finish him with her hand. But there was no way she was doing that. She wanted him to come in her mouth. She wanted to taste him in the back of her throat and know she brought him there.

His hands tunneled through her hair. He tugged, forcing her to look up into his face. Without releasing her grip on his dick, she did. He stared at her as if seeing her for the first time. Then his eyes closed, his body tightened, and with a kind of scary, kind of sexy roar, he came. She sucked and swallowed until she drained him dry.

Dez finally released her grip on his dick and that's when he yanked her to her feet by her hair. Startled, she barked out a curse, but it got lost in his mouth as he crushed her in a brutal kiss that made her entire body ache. She knew he tasted himself in her mouth, but that seemed to only fuel his lust.

Mace yanked the blanket off her body and pushed her toward the wall.

"I swear, Dez. The things you do to me."

* * *

Even in the wildest, dirtiest dreams he used to have while trapped in his bathroom, he never imagined that Dez would be this hot, this willing, this wild. She was much more than he ever hoped for. And she belonged to him.

Her hands moved along his shoulders and down his chest. Now that she knew he craved her affection, she never stopped touching him. Which is what he wanted. She pulled his sweater over his head and tossed it across the room while he toed off his boots and kicked his jeans after them.

Once naked, he forced her against the pantry door with his body. She gasped, and it rippled against his skin.

"Wait. Wait."

"What?" He didn't mean to growl that at her, but his need for her nearly overwhelmed him. And her naked body against his . . . *damn.*

"We used up the condoms last night."

"I'm a SEAL."

"And?"

He reached over to the counter, digging into one of the bags. He pulled out the box of condoms. "We are always prepared for every contingency."

She took the box. "I didn't even know they had boxes of fifty."

"That should last us a day or two."

Dez squeaked and tried to bolt past him. He caught her around the waist, pushing her back. "What are you doing?"

"Running for my life. Much more of this and I'll be walking like I've been in the rodeo."

"You complaining?"

Dez frowned, deep in thought.

"Fine." He started to walk away, but Dez's hand on his rapidly growing cock stopped him in his tracks. "I didn't say leave."

"You didn't say stay either."

She pulled him toward her, using his cock as a handle. She kissed his chest, nipped the flesh.

"Stay, Mace. Stay with me."

*   *   *

Wow. This certainly couldn't be Dez MacDermot. The bitter ex-wife of a lawyer who told everyone in his office she was a cold fish with a dry pussy. Dez now realized the man was an asshole, because she was anything but cold.

She looked up and was startled by Mace's expression. Intense and desperate were the words that came to mind. Funny, Mace never seemed like that before.

He stared down at her without saying anything. Simply stared. Then his hand came up and cupped her cheek.

She cleared her throat. "You're making me nervous."

"Why?"

"I've never had anyone look at me like that before. I can't tell if you're falling for me or if you're going to kill me using my own kitchen knife."

He laughed, which eased the moment for her. "I have claws. Don't need the kitchen knife."

"Well, that's good to know. Now I can sleep peacefully."

He pulled her naked body flush against his. Just her skin against his had his cock rearing right back to life. "Exactly which one is scarier?"

"You falling for me."

Mace shook his head. "I'm not falling for you, Dez."

"Oh." *Damn.* "Good."

"I've already fallen. Head first."

Oh shit. "Um . . ."

He smiled. "Um?"

His hand lazily traced patterns across her chest, around her nipples, and under her breasts. She started to squirm from the pleasure of it.

"Mace, maybe we're movin' a little too—"

He cut her off. "Actually, I fell for you a long time ago, Dez. The day you dropped your books at my lab station and sweetly asked 'Youse mind if I sit here?'" Dez smirked at Mace's accurate portrayal of the Bronx accent she'd so desperately tried to curb. "And it's not my problem if that freaks you out."

"Do you even care if it freaks me out?"

CHRISTMAS PRIDE 123

"No."

Christ, could the man be more like a cat?

Mace pushed her hair off her neck and licked her wound. "That still hurt?"

"Mmmhm . . . what?"

"You're not paying attention, Dez."

"Mmmhm . . . what?"

He grabbed her ass, pulling a squeak out of her. "Pay attention, baby."

"What is it with you and ordering me around anyway?"

Mace leaned in, his nose right against her neck. He breathed in deep and sighed. "I love how it makes you smell."

Oh, that's a damn good answer. She could get used to these shifters. She understood their logic better than she understood any human's she'd ever met.

Dez pushed at Mace's shoulders. "I don't think that's good enough, cat." He watched her, concern on his handsome face. He didn't want to hurt her. Man, was she falling for this guy or what? That couldn't be a good thing.

She stood up on her toes to get closer to his face. "I don't take orders from any man." She looked him up and down. "*Especially* you." She quirked an eyebrow, and Mace's concern turned to amusement. Well, amusement and lust.

He pushed her back against the wall. "You'll do what I tell you to." He grabbed her arms and pinned them above her head. "And you'll enjoy it."

Could a woman spontaneously come? Dez felt perilously close.

So that banging at her front door, not a welcome intrusion. Especially when it set her dogs off to full-on warning barks, and some rather scary fangs burst from Mace's gums along with a growl that quickly became a roar erupting from his throat.

She heard Bukowski's voice as Mace released her and protectively wrapped his arms around her body. "Dez, if you can hear me, open this fuckin' door!"

"Who the hell is that?" Mace snapped. He really needed to find a way to control those fangs of his.

"My partner." She pushed past Mace, grabbing the green and white blanket off the floor. "Stay here. I'll get rid of him." She glanced at him over her shoulder as she wrapped the blanket around her body. "And feel free to stay hard."

She moved toward the door, eager to get back to Mace with his enormous dick and killer voice. Dez had no idea what Bukowski wanted, but it better be good.

As she neared the door, she heard Bukowski again. "Answer me or I'm breaking it down!"

Dez's body froze, but not her mouth. "*Don't you dare!*"

Her dogs stopped barking, running to stand protectively on either side of her. Fighting to control her anger, Dez snatched her front door open and came face to face with Bukowski.

Mace pulled his jeans over his painfully hard cock and thought about all the ways he could eviscerate Dez's "partner." He had no idea he could detest a man he barely knew, but the loud-mouthed bastard had interrupted their "playtime." Unacceptable.

When he heard Dez's "Don't you dare," he was all ready to go out there and kick some NYPD ass. But the smell of Irish Spring soap stopped him. He scented the air. They were moving through the backyard. Actually, they were right at the back door. He scented two . . . no. Three. Although only one of them used that particular soap.

Dez had guns hidden all over her house. He could smell the gun oil. The one in the cabinet under her sink was the easiest to get to. He crouched, his hands wrapped around the grip, when they came through the back door. Almost silently. If he'd been human, he wouldn't know they were there until they were on top of him.

Still crouched, Mace released the safety, spun, and landed flat on his belly. The barrel of his weapon pressed against a throat.

Hard to enjoy the moment, though, with a .45 slammed against his head.

* * *

"What the hell are you doing?"

"I kept trying to call you and never got an answer. I finally called your neighbors about an hour ago. The old couple next door. They said they thought they heard screaming last night."

Maybe Sister Mary Joseph had been right. *Dirty little girls like you, Desiree, get caught and dragged out in front of the town and stoned.*

"Get in here." She grabbed her partner by his arm and dragged him into her house, slamming the door behind her.

"Did that scumbag do this to you?" He motioned to the wound on her throat. It probably looked much worse than it felt.

"No. Of course not."

"Don't bullshit me, MacDermot."

Exasperated, she snapped without thinking, "Do you think I'd let some guy do this to me and then fuck him?"

"Oh my God! *You fucked Llewellyn?*"

"*I am not having this conversation with you!*"

Dez, busy wondering how much time she'd actually do for killing her partner, barely noticed when her dogs suddenly spun around and charged back into the kitchen. She doubted they suddenly regenerated the balls she removed years ago and charge Mace. Someone else was in that kitchen. And one look at her partner's face confirmed it.

Bukowski tried to grab her arm, but Dez yanked herself away from him, taking his sidearm with her. She headed to the kitchen but stopped dead in the doorway.

She lowered the gun to her side and took a deep breath to calm her exploding nerves. One false move here and she could destroy everything she held dear.

First, she ordered her dogs out with a barked "*schnell.*" Then Dez laid Bukowski's gun on the side table and calmly walked into the room. She walked up to the four men in her kitchen.

Mace had her gun, a sweet little .38, shoved up against Vinny's neck. Vinny had his Glock .45 against Mace's temple. Jimmy and Sal had their semiautomatics—no way legal in this state—trained on Mace's back. A Mexican standoff, and she could only hope to keep these four idiots from killing each other.

First, she focused on Jimmy and Sal. "I need you two to stand down." When they ignored her, "I need you two to stand down . . . *now.*"

Their eyes shifted to her and, so slowly she thought they were completely ignoring her, lowered their weapons. She wasn't out of it yet. Vinny was one of the best Marines she knew. Mace a government-trained killer.

She moved until she stood right next to them, her feet nearly touching both men. Slowly she crouched beside them and carefully placed her hands over each man's, pulling their weapons away and up. Mace and Vinny never looked away from each other. They finally released their hold on their weapons, and Dez quickly stepped away. After one glare, both Sal and Jimmy handed over their guns as well. They knew better than to fight her when she got like this.

They also knew she had no qualms about putting all their asses in prison for illegal weapons possession and forced entry.

She walked back toward the table where she placed Bukowski's gun and dropped the weapons there. She fought to control the shaking of her body. The thought of anything happening to her best friends or to Mace almost too much to bear.

She faced the man she held responsible for this bullshit. "Get in the living room," she spit out between gritting teeth as she handed him back his gun. "*Now!*"

Mace slowly stood, the dark-haired man following. They heard Dez leave the room with her partner, but they still hadn't looked away from each other.

Mace glanced over the men. The blond one sported a tattoo on his inside wrist. The Eagle, Globe, and Anchor. Marines.

"So . . . you guys interested in a job?"

Dez dragged Bukowski into the living room. "*Have you lost your ever-loving mind?*"

"You're sleeping with some scumbag whose sister you're in-vestigating for murder and you have the nerve to ask *me* that?"

"I'm not investigating her anymore. I'm off the case. As of now." Why should she pursue the case? She already knew the answers. "And I can't believe you dragged the guys into this ei-ther."

"They were as worried as I was."

"You could have gotten them killed. *In my house!* The man's a goddamn SEAL. He eats entire tactical units for fuckin' break-fast!"

Bukowski shook his big, shaggy head. He often reminded her of one of her dogs. "I thought you were smarter than this, Dez."

"Smarter than what? What is your problem with him?"

"I don't want you to get hurt." She sighed. Here came the big brother syndrome right on schedule. "No. Really. A guy like Llewellyn, all he's going to do is use you."

"You don't even know him."

"And you haven't seen him in twenty fuckin' years, but you went ahead and hopped right into bed with him."

"I don't hop."

"Dez, I don't wanna be cruel. But come on. A guy like that with somebody like *you?*"

She wasn't as hurt as she probably should have been. She knew exactly where she stood with Bukowski and, in his own brutish way, he wanted to protect her. Still, that seemed a little harsher than necessary. And she was about to tell him where he could stick that particular comment when the swinging door to her kitchen exploded open, the wood banging off the wall and coming off its hinges.

Mace stormed into the living room, amazingly pissed off in just his jeans. It didn't help his fly was only halfway zipped up, reminding her of what Bukowski forced her to miss out on. She could still taste Mace in her mouth.

Dez stepped aside as Mace strode angrily across the room. Usually the man didn't let anything get to him. Not with that military-trained feline personality. Yet here he was, protectively pushing Dez behind him as he faced off against Bukowski.

Great. Another male protecting her. How did she keep getting into these situations?

"If you've got something to say, why don't you say it to me?"

Dez glanced behind her. No sign of the other three. They must have left once they realized she was fine. They knew better than to stick around for her wrath. They'd seen the damage she could do when that MacDermot temper made its rare entrance.

"I wasn't talking to you," Bukowski barked angrily.

"Well, ya are now!"

Mace towered a good six inches over Bukowski, but both men refused to back off. *Idiots.* God save her from protective men.

She sighed. "Would you two just—"

"*Shut up, Dez!*" They both said it at the same time, never once taking their eyes off each other. It took all her strength not to grab the gun she kept hidden under her couch cushions and shoot both of them in the head.

Instead, Dez turned on her heel and headed back upstairs, her two dogs trailing faithfully behind. At least there were some males in her life that obeyed her. "When you two are done pissin' around me, feel free to let yourselves the fuck outta my house!"

Mace watched that cute ass walk away from him and he didn't like it one bit. Well, he liked the view. A lot. But he didn't mean to push her away. Not when all his future plans involved her.

"I swear to God, you hurt her—"

"Shut up. And get the fuck out."

"She told both of us to leave."

Mace ignored him, heading for the stairs. Bukowski stopped him with a hand on his arm. Mace looked at it, then at the man it belonged to. At least, the man it belonged to for the moment.

"Get your hand off me or lose that arm."

He didn't know what the little man saw, but his startled expression would be funnier if Mace wasn't already so pissed.

"Jesus Christ." *What is this idiot's name again? Bukowski?*
"You do care about her. I can see it on your face."

Sometimes full-humans are as dumb as dogs.

"That's brilliant deductive reasoning there, Sherlock. I'm surprised you don't run the whole fuckin' precinct. Now leave."
With that, Mace followed Dez up the stairs.

Chapter Seven

Dez snuggled under the covers, her face buried in her pillow. She should have remembered her Grandmother Fiona's words to her when she turned ten. "Honey, all men are idiots." As always, the older generation called it.

She didn't know Mace was in the room until he laid his long body out on top of hers. A heavy, muscle-laden man, his weight still felt good against her.

"Are you and Bukowski meeting at dawn for a duel with pistols? Or you going the Brooklyn way and using a couple of two-by-fours?"

He nuzzled the back of her head, licked her neck. His tongue dry and rough. *Well that's damn distracting.*

"Are you even listening to me?" she demanded as she turned over, pushing his big body off her. With a sigh, he rolled to his side and watched her. She ignored his obvious annoyance, wanting to get a few things straight before he started distracting her with that big dick of his.

"I can handle Bukowski. He's my partner. We've been in some ugly shit together, and I don't need you or anybody else stepping in and saving the day for me."

"But isn't that what Bukowski and those three guys did? Come in to save you from the big, bad lion."

"That's besides the point."

"Why?"

"I'm not fucking them! I don't care what they do. I care what you do."

"I'm unclear about your logic."

Dez grabbed a pillow, covered her face, and yelled into it. When she pulled it away, Mace still watched her impassively. Just staring and blinking.

"And you're fixing my kitchen door!"

Mace rolled those gold eyes and sighed. "Whatever." With a good yank, he snatched the comforter completely off her.

He couldn't believe she was giving him shit about that door. She let that asshole Bukowski walk out without putting a bullet in his tiny pea brain with that gun she had hidden in her couch. But she orders him to fix the door. Did she believe for even a second he would ever let that idiot talk to her like that?

He gazed down at her ripe body. The woman was absolutely perfect. She tried to shimmy away from him, but he trapped her with his leg. Didn't she know he was busy? He didn't need her distracting him with her nonsense.

"What do you want me to do to you?" he asked.

"Excuse me?"

"You heard me. What do you want me to do to you?" She didn't answer, and he finally looked up to find her glaring at him. "What?"

"You don't trust me."

Where the fuck did that come from? "What the hell are you talking about?"

She knocked his hand off her chest and pulled herself away from him. "You don't trust me to take care of myself. I can see it on your face. That's why you're so busy trying to distract me with those big lion hands of yours."

"That's a load of shit, Desiree, and you know it."

"Fine. Prove it."

He really didn't like the sound of that. "How?"

She slid off the bed and walked over to her dresser. He really hoped she didn't turn around with her gun in her hand. Although he wouldn't put anything past her.

He heard metal clink and she turned around, her handcuffs dangling from her index finger.

"Not on your life, MacDermot!"

"See? You don't trust me."

Tricky, manipulative, little dog lover! Mace closed his eyes and took in a deep breath. Look what she'd reduced him to. These shenanigans. Suddenly Pride life began looking better and better.

She pouted. "You don't have to trust me, Mace. It's okay. It's okay I trust you but you don't trust me. That's fine."

With a short roar, he stretched out on the bed, his arms over his head. "Let's just get this over with, shall we?"

He ground his teeth together to keep from coming in his jeans. He'd been thinking about something like this as soon as he realized she'd become a cop. Of course, she'd been the handcuffed, not the handcuffer.

Still naked, Dez stepped up on the bed and settled her curvaceous body over his chest, straddling him with her long legs.

She held the cuffs up in front of his face. "You sure, Mace?"

"Don't bullshit around with me, woman. Just do it."

"Okay." She leaned over him, her breasts in his face as she worked to secure his wrists to the bed frame. Being a cop, she hooked him up in about ten seconds. Even before he could get his mouth around her nipple.

She pulled away and smiled at her handiwork. "You've got huge wrists."

He smirked. "Thanks."

"It wasn't a compliment or anything. Merely a statement of fact."

He closed his eyes. The woman wanted to make him insane.

"Wanna see what I can do?"

Part of him wanted to say "No" and pout like a ten-year-old. But he was trying to be cooperative. It went against his very nature but, clearly, he would walk through fire for this woman.

Mace opened his eyes. On an annoyed sigh, "Yeah. Okay."

Dez lifted her right breast in her hand, leaned forward, and wrapped her tongue around her own nipple. Her breasts were large enough so it wasn't a challenge for her at all. Yet it was knowing she somehow discovered that little trick on her own— Mace swallowed. *Dear God in heaven.*

She licked her nipple, swirling the tip of her tongue around it. Mace could almost feel it on his own tongue. His cock strained against the hard material of his new jeans and in a few more seconds he'd end up destroying the bed frame to get to her.

Dez pulled back. "Cool, huh?"

All Mace could manage was a nod.

"Wanna see me do the other one?"

He nodded again. She held the other breast and repeated her actions, turning herself on in the process. He could smell it. And her squirming on his chest—so not helping.

She entertained him and her breasts for a little longer. When she finally pulled away, she'd begun panting. They stared at each other.

"Come here, Dez."

She shook her head. "No."

"Why?"

"I don't want to." Funny, she *smelled* like she wanted to.

"What do you want?"

Dez bit her lip. Then, taking a deep breath, she ran her hand down between her breasts, past her abs, and between her legs.

"Dez . . . what are you doing to me?"

"At the moment? Absolutely nothing."

Mace watched Dez's hand as she slid her middle finger inside her pussy, slowly drag it out, and across her clit. Why did she insist on torturing him? Okay. So he had tortured her *a little* the night before. And this morning. And in the kitchen. But nothing like this. This was killing him.

Her finger circled her clit as her hips slowly thrust against him. He watched her, completely entranced. How could he not be? She looked so gorgeous, riding him while she sought her own pleasure. One of the most beautiful things he'd ever seen and all he wanted to do at the moment was bury himself so far inside Dez he knocked her tonsils out.

It didn't take her long. Her head thrown back, moaning, saying his name. God, she moaned his name. With that voice. Before he knew it, she was coming. Her legs gripping his hips, her body shaking. When the spasms passed, she slowly looked down at him.

"Fuck me, Dez," he growled. "Or I'm buying you a new bed frame after Christmas."

"We left the condoms downstairs."

"Then get 'em. *Now.*"

Dez slipped off his body and walked out of the room. Great. Now *he* was panting. Mace closed his eyes and concentrated on the sound of Dez walking around the house. Anything to keep him from coming as soon as she touched his cock.

He heard her go down the stairs and into the kitchen. Heard her pick the box of condoms up off the counter. Heard her feet walking back the way she came. His cell phone rang and she stopped. He heard the swipe of metal against the counter as she scooped it up and headed back to the bedroom. He blinked in surprise, though, when he heard her answer his phone. Dez didn't seem like the type to cross those kind of boundaries, until he remembered he had caller ID on the front of it. Which meant only one thing . . .

"Well hi, Missy. How you doin'?"

By the time she walked into the bedroom, Mace was laughing so hard he could barely see straight.

"Yeah, it's me. Desiree. Although you can call me Detective."

She dropped the box of condoms on the nightstand, grabbing one before returning to Mace on the bed. She crawled back on top of him.

"Oh yeah. He's here, hon, but he's handcuffed to my bed right now and kind of sticky, which is my fault." She sighed. "Well, I can ask him to see if he wants to talk to you. But I was about to make him see God . . . oh. Well, you don't have to get nasty. Hold on."

She leaned over him, holding the phone to his ear until he could pin it against his shoulder.

He cleared his throat to stop from laughing. "Hello?"

"You stupid son of a bitch! Tell me that woman doesn't have you handcuffed to her bed!"

Mace should have been mad his sister yelled at him like a child, but with Dez kissing his neck and rubbing his nipples, he found it really hard to care.

"Is there a reason you called, because she's getting awfully insistent. And I must obey all her commands." Dez snorted as she moved down his chest. His sister became deathly quiet.

"What the hell does that mean, Mason?"

"That I'm the bottom to her top. The sub to her dom. The slave to her master." Dez began laughing so hard she rolled off Mace and right out of bed.

"Please tell me you're kidding?"

"I can't. I can't tell you anything. Not unless she tells me I can."

He stifled his own laughter as Dez's became more intense.

He could hear Missy's attempts to calm herself down. "Mason Rothschild Llewellyn . . . I will talk to you another time."

"Well, only if she'll let me talk to you another time—" He heard the click from the other end.

Okay. Even he had to admit that was one of the best moments ever. He released the phone, grabbed it with his teeth, and tossed it across the room.

"Get your ass up here, Desiree. *Now.*"

She crawled back up onto the bed, but she laughed so hard she'd begun to cry. She barely managed to get back on his chest. Then she buried her head in his neck, her entire body shaking with laughter. Christ, he could be like this until next Tuesday. He wasn't even sure she'd be able to find the key to let him loose. He shrugged. Looked like he'd be bed shopping come December twenty-sixth.

Chapter Eight

Mace woke up to a cold, wet snout in his ear. He growled and snapped. Dez's two dogs charged out of the room, leaving a lovely trail of piss in their wake. Great. Something else he had to clean up himself. Mace sat up and glanced at the dresser. Her badge and gun were gone.

Dammit, where was that woman? She kept disappearing on him. He knew she wasn't in the house. He always knew when she was around. He could sense her, feel her. So the question became where the hell did she go this time?

Sliding out of the battered bed—the bed frame another replacement he had to make—he quickly found something to clean the floor and then jumped in the shower. He just finished washing his hair, which now reached to his shoulders, when it suddenly occurred to him where Dez may have gone.

The one place where she could get herself killed.

Dez watched as Mace stormed out of her house, down the front steps, and headed . . . somewhere. Maybe he decided to bail. Thinking he could finally make a run for it. *Ah, who the hell am I kidding?* She knew Mace wasn't going anywhere anytime soon. If she wanted him gone, she'd have to do it herself. Part of her wanted to make that happen too. Before she got in too deep. Another part—the one attached to her heart—kept telling her to back the hell off. Her heart wanted Mace to hang around for as long as she could keep him. But how long could she keep him once she started working again? When she got late-night calls about a murder they wanted her on? Or when she had to leave in the middle of dinner? Or she missed his birth-day? How long would he put up with that?

She remembered her ex-husband's words as clearly as if he were saying them right in her ear at that very moment. "You just aren't pretty enough to put up with this kind of shit, De-siree."

Mace spotted her SUV. He stopped and stared at it. She found it fascinating to watch him move. He'd been right, of course. She always knew he was a predator. That he wasn't quite human. She'd known it deep in her bones.

He sniffed the air, then spun around, his eyes locking on her. With a growl, he stormed over to her as she calmly sipped her coffee.

"You're making me crazy!"

"I didn't do anything."

"Don't ya think I know that?" Mace sat down on the stoop beside her, his thigh barely touching hers. She suddenly wanted to crawl into his lap and let him hold her, but she had never been good with public displays of affection. Mostly because she didn't know how to do it.

"I thought you'd gone back."

"Gone back where?"

"To that club from last night."

"The one with the hyenas?" Had the man lost his mind? "Wow, I didn't know I had 'stupid idiot' tattooed on my fore-head."

He smiled and she immediately became wet at the sight of it. "Not stupid idiot. Big, bad cop."

"No way, cat. They tried to kill me once. Why would I push my luck? Besides, vice squad's raiding them as we speak."

Mace closed his eyes and gave a deep sigh. "You didn't."

"Oh, I fuckin' did." She took another sip of her coffee. "They can probably only close it for a night or two, but it will still give me such joy."

"You're crazy."

"There's no hard evidence of that."

Mace suddenly lifted her arm up and stretched out, his head in her lap. He placed her hand on his head. "Stroke away, baby."

She put down her coffee and started laughing. It seemed she didn't have to know how to show affection. Mace would command her. Actually, that kind of worked for her. If she wasn't in the mood, she could always roll his ass down the stairs.

Dez dug her hands into his wet hair and slowly pulled her fingers through the silky mass. After the third stroke, Mace began purring. Considering his head lay in her lap, damn near her clit . . . she shook her head. She really needed to get some kind of control around this guy or she'd end up embarrassing herself.

Mace rolled onto his back, his big feet planted firmly against the porch handrails. He smiled up at her with those beautiful eyes. His wounds from the previous night were already faded, but she'd probably have that scratch on her neck for the next couple of weeks.

Dez kept running one hand through his hair, marveling at how fast it had grown in, while she laid the other on his chest.

He took her free hand and held it between his. He slid his finger across her flesh, and Dez bit the inside of her mouth to keep from moaning.

"What do you want to do today," he muttered softly.

Fuck you senseless? "Whatever."

"We could go into the city."

"Yeah." Not a bad idea, really. "I still have some shopping to do."

"You know, Dez. For someone with 'moral issues' against this holiday, you sure do have a festive apartment."

She kind of hoped he wouldn't notice that. She should have known better. "I don't have a problem with the holiday. I have a problem with . . . with my . . ." Exactly how did he expect her to make a cohesive thought when he insisted on putting her finger in his mouth and sucking on it?

"Go on," he pushed, her finger still in his mouth.

She tried again. "I have a problem with my family." She

closed her eyes and shuddered as his tongue slid around her index finger. "They make me crazy."

"Like I do?"

"No, Mace. Not like you." *No one like you.*

"Good."

Cocky prick. She shook her head again. The man would never change.

"You know, we could stay here and fuck all day."

"Very subtle, cat."

His expression thoughtful, he said, "You seem real comfortable with what I am, Dez. Why is that?"

"Last night you said I was scared of you."

"I was wrong. You're not scared of the cat. You're scared of the man."

"Bullshit, Llewellyn."

"You're scared of where this is going."

"It's not going anywhere, Mace."

"The hell it isn't. You know I'm in—"

Her cell phone rang. "*Phone!*"

Mace jumped, his words cut short, as she scrambled to answer her cell. She didn't want to have this conversation. She wasn't ready for this conversation. And she damn sure never would be.

"MacDermot."

"Hey, darlin'."

Dez blinked. "Sissy Mae?"

She heard Mace growl and wondered how the hell the woman had gotten her number. "Sure is. What'cha up to today?"

Looking down at Mace, she saw the intent in his eyes. If she stayed here with him, he'd fuck her until she promised him anything and everything. Until she admitted how she truly felt. She wasn't even ready to admit it to herself.

She needed time. She needed to think. She needed for him to stop sucking on her fingers.

"What do you have in mind?"

"Why don't you meet me in the city for coffee or somethin'?"

"Well, there's just one thing—"

"Of course Mace can come." Apparently, everyone knew about her relationship with Mace Llewellyn. "He can keep Smitty company."

She glanced down at Mace. He'd taken her hand and slid it across his rapidly growing hard-on. With a healthy shove, Dez pushed him down the stairs of her porch.

"Ow!"

Funny. I always thought cats landed on all fours.

She smiled. "Yeah, Sissy Mae. I'd love to."

Mace turned to Smitty and held up two watches. "Which do you like better?" He motioned to one. "The Breitling?" He held up the other. "Or the Breitling?"

Smitty stared. "Is that for one of those breedin' males?"

"No. It's for me."

Smitty laughed and rubbed his eyes at the same time. "I think you're missing the point of this particular holiday. It's the season of *giving*."

"Yeah. And I'm *giving* to myself." Besides, he didn't do last-minute holiday shopping. He took care of that months in advance. That way he could enjoy the holidays buying for himself. He motioned to the jeweler. "I'll take this one. And that Tag Heuer I saw earlier, for a woman though."

The jeweler scurried off while Smitty shook his head.

"Pathetic, hoss."

"What? You want a watch too?"

"No. I don't wanna watch. I just can't believe you're buying her one."

"I don't understand why you sound so pissed."

"Cause my sister's driving me crazy. The Pack is asking all sorts of questions I ain't got answers for yet. And I'm freakin' horny as a dog."

"Well that's fitting."

Mace took the ladies' watch handed to him. He examined it closely.

"I'll take it. Wrap it up. I'll wear the other one now." He

turned back to Smitty. "So what exactly was going on with you and those wolf bitches at the restaurant?"

"Aw, hoss. That was me playin' around. That's not good enough. I need a woman."

"Then get one. Just stay away from mine."

"New watch. Dire warnings. She must be quite the party in bed."

Mace snarled and Smitty held his hands up. "Kidding. Calm yourself."

Taking the watch handed to him, Mace placed it on his arm. "Let's get this straight, Smitty. So there are no misunderstandings down the road. I love that woman. You even look at her wrong, I'm snapping your neck like a twig. Is that clear enough for you, hillbilly?"

Smitty sniffed in disgust, sounding more like a cat than a dog. "Crystal."

"So." Sissy Mae sipped her hot chocolate. "Is Mace good in bed?"

Dez choked on her black coffee. They sat at a small table in front of a quiet café. A chilly December day, but Dez wasn't in the mood to sit inside. She felt restless. She needed the fresh air, the energy of the people-filled streets. She loved the Village. Always had. And if she had a large fortune, she'd live here.

"Oh, I'm sorry, darlin'. Didn't mean to startle you."

"Yes, you did." Dez wiped her chin. She couldn't believe she liked Sissy Mae Smith. But she did. Sissy reeked of warmth, honesty, and a slight insanity that made Dez completely comfortable.

"Yeah. All right. I did." Sissy smiled. "I'm sorry, Dez. My brother's driving me crazy. It makes me mean-spirited."

"Why?"

"He's worried about this new business he's startin' with Mace. He's worried about me and our kin. And he needs to get laid."

"You know"—Dez leaned back in her chair—"that's a little too much information for me."

"That's too much information for anybody."

"And yet you felt the need to share."

"I worry about him, ya know? I mean, Mace got himself a nice little girl. I want the same for my brother."

Dez slammed her coffee down, startling her new friend. She should have known Mace had another woman. Some poor Navy wife waiting for him to come home for the holidays. "What's her name?"

"Who?"

"Mace's 'nice little girl.'"

Sissy raised an eyebrow. "I'm talking about you, darlin'."

"Me?" Now it was Dez's turn to be startled. "I'm not nice, Sissy Mae. I ain't little. And Mace *does not* have me."

She waited for Sissy to say something, but to her growing annoyance, the woman only folded her arms in front of her chest and stared at her.

Bitch.

Smitty bit into his hot pastrami on rye with spicy mustard. Mace almost laughed at the absolute rapture on the man's face.

"Like it?"

He received the thumbs-up, since Smitty was enjoying his food way too much to answer. For the next ten minutes, the men ate without once speaking. Although they did occasionally grunt at one another.

When their plates were clean, they leaned back with their sodas and sighed in satisfaction.

"So, hoss. Have you actually told her you're in love with her?"

"She won't let me. When I tried, she threw me down a flight of stairs."

"And you're not concerned about that?"

"There weren't that many steps."

"Mace . . ." Smitty rubbed his eyes with his thumb and forefinger. "She ain't a village of well-armed rebels, ya know. You can't just invade under the cover of night."

"But I have. And I will. Again. As many times as I have to. Until she admits she's crazy about me."

"And if she ain't?"

"If she *ain't* what?"

"Crazy about ya? Then what?"

He didn't want to think about it. He couldn't. He loved her too much to think about it. To worry she didn't love him. True, he could always find another woman, but he'd still always be alone. He'd be alone because he wouldn't have Dez.

Mace looked at Smitty and shrugged.

Dez answered her cell. "MacDermot?"

"It's Vinny."

Dez slammed her phone shut and took another bite of chocolate cake.

"Problem?" Sissy asked as she studied all the activity on the busy Village street.

"Nope."

The phone rang again. Dez answered it. "MacDermot."

"Don't hang up."

Dez hung up and took a sip of her coffee.

"How long are you going to torture them?" Dez had filled Sissy in on her friends bursting into her house and putting a gun on Mace. Although she left out the astounding blow job she gave him beforehand.

"Until they learn better."

"Sounds like they were trying to protect you. Friends like that are hard to find, darlin'. You should be grateful."

"I am."

"But you're going to make them sweat anyway?"

"Yup."

Dez's phone rang again. She glanced at caller ID. The number looked familiar to her but it wasn't one of the guys unless they grabbed someone else's phone.

"MacDermot."

"You fuckin' bitch!"

Dez grinned. "Ms. Brutale. Is there a problem?"

"Why are the cops here? Why are they tearing my fuckin' club apart?"

"Gee. I don't know." Dez licked her chocolate-covered fork.

"Bullshit, you bitch! You did this. And if you think for a second I'm going to let you get away with this . . ."

She wasn't surprised Brutale was pissed. Dez heard back from the officer in charge of the investigation. A big, biker-looking, old-school cop called Crushek, or Crush if you liked playing with fire. Several of Brutale's bartenders and waitresses pulled in for possession with the intent to distribute. They closed the club for at least the night, if not longer, depending on the Brutale political clout.

"Don't threaten me."

"I don't get it."

"Maybe you should ask your sister. She seemed to have a real problem with my presence at your club last night."

The silence Dez got back from the other end of that phone sent a chill up her spine. Not for her, but for Anne Marie Brutale. She didn't envy the girl. She got the feeling Gina didn't like her sister involving herself with her life.

"I understand," Brutale said, and hung up.

Dez shuddered. No, she didn't envy Anne Marie one bit. Of course, she didn't really feel bad for her either. The woman *had* tried to kill her, after all. The bitch had made her bed. Now she could freakin' lie in it.

"Everything okay, darlin'?"

"For me. Yeah."

Sissy's phone rang. She answered it, and when Dez realized it was a rather tense call from one of Sissy's other siblings, she decided to give her a little privacy. With her cup in hand, Dez strolled slowly past her coffeehouse. A cute place that had great hours, not closing until three or four A.M. She came so often many of the staff knew her by name. She continued to walk until she found herself in front of the alley beside the coffeehouse. A fairly large place with one entrance in front and another side entrance leading to the alley. A large brick wall spanned between the coffeehouse and the building beside it. A metal door oddly placed dead in the middle.

Dez stopped and openly stared. How could she not? She knew the woman. Anne Marie Brutale. And she recognized the man. How could she forget a guy she'd once arrested? Especially a guy who broke one of her ribs during the takedown? She wasn't sure about his name. Something Irish.

He had Anne Marie backed against the wall, one arm braced over her head. He leaned into her and she gave a freaky sadistic grin and shook her head. His free hand ran up her arm, across her collarbone, to savagely grip her throat.

"Do what I tell ya."

Anne Marie hissed, and Dez knew she saw fangs, even from here.

"Dez, let's go."

Dez turned her head to glance at Sissy Mae, who had already started off down the street. When she turned back in the alley, both Anne Marie and her pet criminal were gone. Dez looked around. She didn't understand. They couldn't have passed her.

Her eyes locked onto two doorways. One led back into the coffeehouse. The other led into the brick wall. Part of her itched to see what was in there. Itched to find out why a Jersey princess like Brutale would hang around with such a lowlife. Something deep inside told her it wasn't fucking, but something scary and dangerous. And she'd be an idiot to go follow them.

"Dez, come on, darlin'."

Dez stared into the alley a few more seconds, then followed Sissy.

From the bench, Dez watched Sissy Mae glide by on the ice. Impressed, Dez sighed. She had no idea Sissy could be so . . . graceful.

Funny, after thirty-six years this was the first time Dez had ever come to Rockefeller Center during the Christmas holiday. She hated the crowds, the tourists, and, God knew, she didn't skate. But Sissy Mae and Smitty wanted to come so badly, she didn't have the heart to tell them to go by their damn selves.

Sissy Mae glided by again. She moved with such confidence and skill. She could see the younger skaters watching Sissy with admiration. Until her brother slammed into her from behind. Dez covered her mouth and tried not to laugh. Although seeing Sissy sprawled out, facedown on the cold ice, made it kind of difficult.

Dez watched the younger woman snarl, drag herself to her feet, and take off after her brother. She'd never seen two siblings play so rough. Sissy Mae threw herself at Smitty, landing on his back. Using her body, she spun him up and around, knocking him to the ground while still attached to him.

"Holy shit."

She started to stand up, worried she would have to prevent the two from going to jail, when Mace's hand on her shoulder pulled her back onto his lap.

"Leave 'em alone, baby. They get like this."

Dez closed her eyes at the feel of Mace's chest against her back.

"You know, Dez, you never answered my question. Did ya miss me today?"

"No."

"Liar." Yeah. She was a liar. She'd missed him all afternoon. She had a great time with Sissy Mae, but she kept thinking about seeing Mace later. Seeing him naked.

He kissed the back of her neck, and Dez fought the urge to drag Mace into the nearest bathroom.

"Did you miss *me*, Captain Ego?"

"Oh yeah." He tightened his grip around her waist as he leaned in closer to her. "I missed that little sound you make when I graze my teeth across your clit. And the way you taste on my fingers and tongue. The way you dig your nails into my back when you're coming and that little thing you do with your hips when I'm going down on you."

"Stop."

"Stop? You sure?"

"Yes. I'm sure." If he didn't stop, she'd come while sitting on his lap without the man doing a damn thing to her.

Mace closed his eyes. Thank God she told him to stop. Much more and he'd have her jeans down and his cock jammed into her right in front of all of New York. He needed to get her back to her house. Or a hotel. Or an alley. He needed to fuck this woman and he needed it soon. Hell, he'd even brought a condom along . . . ya know . . . just in case.

He heard gasps around him. Mace looked up in time to watch Sissy Mae put her brother in a headlock and slam him face-first into a gate.

"How much longer can they keep that up?"

"Hours."

"That can't be good. Oh shit. Security." Dez started to stand up again but he pulled her back down.

"I'd really wish you wouldn't move right now."

"But I—" She stopped when he pulled her closer to his bursting erection. "Oh."

"Yeah. Oh."

"Well, what about Sissy and Smitty?"

"They can take care of themselves."

"Honestly, Mace, can't you control that thing?"

"Not around you apparently." He rubbed the back of her neck with his hand. "Let's get out of here, Dez."

She looked at him over her shoulder. He saw the lust in her eyes. A lust as strong as his. She opened her mouth to answer but stopped when her cell phone went off.

"Goddamnit," she angrily snapped as she answered her phone. "MacDermot." She nodded. "Yeah. Okay. Okay." She glanced at her watch. "Yeah. Okay. Yeah." She closed the phone.

"I've gotta meet Bukowski at a bar."

"You're kidding, right?"

"Nope. He wants to talk to me about the Petrov case."

"He can't do that over the phone?" He really had to stop growling things at her when annoyed and jealous. It did nothing but piss her off.

"Yeah. He can. But he probably wants to apologize too and he won't do *that* over the phone." She didn't seem pissed at Mace's tone, though. Instead, she acted like she expected the other shoe to drop—or for it to be thrown at her head. There was something going on and he had no idea what.

Dez rubbed the back of her neck. "You know, I'll understand if you want to—"

"Want to what?"

"Well, if you got stuff to do or somethin'. I don't expect you to wait for me while I take care of this." Why the hell wouldn't he wait for her? She wasn't running off to one of those bullshit charities his sister chaired or going off to Milan to watch polo like his mother used to—although she really only scared those poor horses. No. Dez had a murder case with her name attached to it. He still marveled at the fact she hadn't run screaming from him once she knew the truth. She hadn't gone straight to her C.O., given him the whole story, and had Mace thrown into the local zoo. Instead, she'd let him fuck her until they both could barely stand and then she fucked him back.

"Dez, the only thing I want to do at the moment is you."

She turned away from him. "Oh."

"Do you want to meet me back at . . . at your house?" He winced. He almost said "our house."

"No. You'll scare my poor dogs to death. I'm not sure they can handle much more."

Smitty and his sister stood in front of them. "Can you believe they asked us to leave?" Sissy demanded.

"All right you two. Get those skates off." Dez stood up, her hand digging into Mace's hair. An unconscious act, and that made Mace love her even more. "We're going to a real cop bar now."

"Like in *NYPD Blue*?" Sissy actually clapped her hands together.

Dez rolled her eyes at Mace as her hand stroked through his hair. "If that brings you joy, Sissy."

They both cringed when Sissy actually squealed.

Dez grabbed the door of McCormick's Bar; stopped; and looked at Sissy, Smitty, and Mace. "All right, you three. I have to work with these people. No fistfights. No growling. No purring. No threatening of body parts." She looked directly at Mace. "No grabbing of body parts. No embarrassing me. No pissing me off. Are we clear?"

The trio stared at her. With a sigh, she pulled the door open and walked in. Packed with cops from two local precincts, all trying to get in some downtime before going home to their families.

"I'll be back." She tugged the sleeve of Mace's jacket. "And you be nice."

"I'm not sure I like what you're implying."

Dez wound her way through the crowd, greeting friends and acquaintances. She loved this bar. Loved being around other cops.

She spotted Bukowski with Crush and headed straight toward them.

"I'm taking the Pack out clubbin' tomorrow night. Y'all should come. You know, if you can pry Dez's thighs off your face long enough, that is."

Remembering Dez's order of no fistfights, Mace instead pointed to Sissy Mae. "What exactly is your sister up to?"

Smitty turned to see his baby sister happily surrounded by four SWAT team members.

"Sissy Mae Smith!"

Mace watched Smitty storm off to rescue the four men.

"Didn't we almost arrest you a couple of nights ago?" Mace turned to find two women staring at him.

"No." He motioned to Smitty. "You almost arrested him."

* * *

"That's who I saw. Patrick Doogan. I busted him about seven years ago. My last year in uniform."

Crush threw back a shot of tequila, his big muscles rippling with the effort. The man resembled a small mountain. He wiped his mouth with the back of his hand. "I had a conversation today with one of my informants. A hooker. She said he bragged to her he took out Petrov."

"Why?" Bukowski asked the question, but Dez knew why. She now understood that Doogan and Mace were the same. At least breed-wise.

"Apparently he wants Missy Llewellyn."

"So he kills her accountant? Why not try online dating instead?"

A man of few words, Crush said nothing.

"What confuses me," Bukowski admitted, staring at his beer, "is how the thumb claw thing works."

Dez planned to make sure Bukowski went to his grave fifty years from now never understanding how the "thumb claw thing" worked. She knew he'd never be able to handle it.

"All this is really interesting, guys, but I'm off the case."

Bukowski and Crush looked at each other. Then Crush stood up and lumbered to the bar.

"Come on, Dez," Bukowski said. "This is me. I thought you were shittin' me earlier. I mean, when have you ever backed off a case? You're like a rabid pit bull."

"Not this time."

"Is this about Llewellyn?"

For once, he didn't sound pissy when he mentioned Mace's name. "Well, it does make things a little awkward. I don't want anyone to say I'm doing anything even remotely sniffing of impropriety. So, I'm off the case."

"Why didn't you tell me that over the phone?"

"Because I thought you might have something else to say to me."

He shrugged. "About today . . ." He looked back at his beer. "I'm sorry."

Dez kicked him under the table. "I know."

"So we're cool?"

"Yeah. Just stay out of my love life."

"Well, you've never really had one before, so I was a little confused."

Dez smirked. "Schmuck." She stood and said, "You stopping by my house on Christmas?" A standard tradition for the partners. Bukowski's kids loved getting their gifts and playing with her dogs, and it gave Dez a chance to catch up with Bukowski's wife, Mary.

"Yeah. It gives me an excuse to get us away from the in-laws. Besides, Mary has a gift for you."

"That's cool. I have something for the kids."

"You have actual gifts this year?"

"I always have gifts for your kids. It's my sisters' kids I always forget about."

The partners smiled at each other.

"I'm outta here, B."

"All right. I'll let you know if it gets interesting."

"Good. And I'll tell Mace you said happy holiday."

"Yeah. You do that."

She winced at Bukowski's sneer. No love loss between those two.

Dez pushed her way back through the crowd. She found Smitty about to start a fistfight with half the SWAT team, Sissy flirting with a couple of guys from the vice squad, and Mace chatting with two of her fellow female officers, which she didn't like one goddamn bit.

She shook her head. No wonder she loved her dogs. Because people never listened.

Dez grabbed Sissy with one hand, took Smitty by the collar of his jacket with the other, and yanked both of them toward the exit. As she passed, she kicked Mace in the ankle.

"Move."

By the time she got the siblings out the door, Mace stood next to her.

"Were my rules not clear?"

Smitty and Sissy pointed at each other.

"She started it."

"He started it."

With a sigh, she turned to Mace. "And what the hell were you doing?"

Mace smiled. "Being nice."

Dez growled as Smitty grabbed his sister's arm.

"We're leavin'. Talk to y'all tomorrow." He dragged her off to a taxi and literally threw the woman in.

Dez crossed her arms in front of her chest. "Patrick Doogan."

"What about him?"

"Is he after your sister?"

"You could say that."

"Mace, he's a problem. The man has a sheet longer than your dick."

"Wow, that's huge."

Dez sighed. "Would you focus."

"What did I say to you? This stuff works itself out."

"I don't know about that. When I was with Sissy, I saw him. He was talking to Anne Marie Brutale. I don't know how all the politics work with you people, but that don't seem too good to me."

Mace shook his head, "Yeah. That's not good."

"So what do we do?"

"*We* don't do anything. *I* will call my sister." He pulled out his cell phone. "Now, just stand there and, ya know, look cute."

She growled in exasperation as Crush walked out of the bar. He nodded toward Mace, raising an eyebrow at Dez. "You and a lion? All right, MacDermot." Then he walked off.

She turned to Mace. "Crush?"

Mace nodded. "Bear."

She watched Mace walk toward her SUV, telling his sister to shut up and listen.

"*There are bears?*"

Chapter Nine

Dez walked into her house, Mace behind her. He hadn't said much of anything on the ride back to Brooklyn. She asked questions about a bunch of different things, including the Doogans, but she got no more than one- or two-word answers back.

Once inside, Dez heard her front door close. She turned to ask Mace if he wanted a drink or something when Mace's big hands grabbed her leather jacket and yanked her to him. His mouth on hers, her jacket pulled off her shoulders and snatched from her back.

"I thought we'd never get here," he growled against her neck.

"City traffic. Blows, doesn't it?"

He walked her back until her ankles hit the stairs, then he pushed her down. Dez watched as he pulled off her sneakers, her jeans. No smooth or controlled moves from Mace this time. She could actually feel his desperation and she loved it. He wanted her and he wasn't going to be happy until he had her.

Her panties were the last to go, then Mace dropped to his knees, burying his head between her legs. His dry, rough tongue gliding along the wet folds of her pussy. Dez's eyes crossed as her entire body arched. She didn't know anything could feel so good.

His big hands slid under her ass, lifting her up so he had better access to her. He continued to lick, until he sucked her clit into his mouth.

Dez reached up and grabbed the staircase handrails, pulling her body off the floor. "*Fuck! Fuck!*" She really couldn't think of anything more eloquent to say. She was lost. Deserted in this place that Mace took her. The place where he *kept* taking her. Again. And again. And again.

Mace never meant to be so rough with her. He never meant to grab her and fuck her on her own damn staircase. But dammit, he couldn't help himself. The whole trip in from the city had been absolute hell. He kept smelling her, kept hearing that damn voice as she asked him questions. He couldn't even remember what she asked him. Not with that voice of hers rasping over every word. The way her left hand sat on the steering wheel and her right kept brushing her hair off her face.

Eventually all he could manage was monosyllabic answers to all her questions, and he had no idea if what he told her was even remotely true. He'd never wanted anything or anyone as badly as he wanted her. He had no idea finally fucking Dez would make him want her more. He thought it would be the exact opposite. He'd been so damn wrong.

"Fuck! Fuck!" He really did love hearing her come. She became that tough Bronx girl he knew so well. Not that well-educated detective who knew how to hide herself behind her badge. When she came, her whole body and soul became his. Add in that voice and he was in absolute heaven.

She grabbed the shoulders of his sweater and yanked him up her body. She still had on her Marines sweatshirt. He wanted to pull it off her so he could get a mouth full of tit, but she seemed equally as anxious. Her body writhing under him as she reached up and kissed him hard. She unbuttoned his jeans, pushing the denim past his hips. He lifted himself up and pushed his jeans down as far as necessary while taking the condom out of his back pocket. He whipped it on his painfully hard cock and buried himself inside her.

"God, Mace!"

He gripped her hips hard, pulling himself out, then slamming back in. She wrapped her arms around his neck, her teeth on his throat. There were no more words between them, just the sounds of their fucking. The sounds of him taking her body over and over. She let him, holding him tight and urging him on with her growls.

His orgasm began to come on fast, but he wouldn't let it explode. Not until he got Dez there too. Luckily, she left herself completely open to him. So damn ready for his cock she started coming so suddenly they both seemed surprised. One second she merely hung on for dear life, the next she screamed and sobbed into his neck. He let go then. Let his body come hard, knowing he'd be back inside her tonight as many times as he could manage.

It took him a second to realize he roared. Like a lion that had nailed the lead female of the Pride. He roared and she gripped him tighter. When he crashed on top of her, she wrapped her arms and legs tight around his body and sighed.

After a few minutes, he lifted himself up on his elbow. He looked down at her face. Her eyes closed, a faint smile on her lips. She looked absolutely stunning.

"Should I apologize?"

Her eyes opened and those gray beauties focused on him. "What the hell for?"

"For not trying to get you into an actual bed."

"Don't you dare."

She ran her hands through his hair. Before he knew it, she had him purring. No woman had ever made him purr before simply by stroking his hair.

Dez kissed his cheek. Nipped his ear. "Besides," she whispered, "beds are overrated."

Dez listened to her cell phone messages while Mace scooped out into two bowls the gourmet dark chocolate ice cream he'd bought that morning. After a few minutes, she closed her phone and grabbed a bowl and spoon.

"Everything okay?"

To enjoy a more leisurely fuck on the couch, they'd finally gotten their clothes off. Her jeans, sweater, sneakers were scattered around her house. But Dez's gun, cuffs, and badge were safely on the metal island she now leaned against. Her position allowing her the absolute joy of watching Mace walk around her house naked.

"Yeah. Three messages from Vinny and the guys. They feel guilty."

"You have protective friends."

"We used to watch out for each other when we were in Japan."

"Did you date one of them?"

Dez almost choked on her ice cream she started laughing so hard. "Are you kidding?"

The look he gave her over his spoon told her no, he wasn't kidding. She cleared her throat. "Not sure why it should matter to you, Mace."

"Because I made them a job offer today and I'd hate to rescind it because one of them fucked you."

"A job offer for what?"

"Smitty and I are starting a business."

"Something in high-level personal and business security or are you two just going to be bounty hunters?"

Mace straightened up in surprise. "How did you know?"

"Come on, Mace. You've wanted to save the world since I've known you. I mean, it makes sense. You milk the rich and famous, which will let you help those who normally couldn't afford you. People cops can't help. Unless you really are planning on becoming a bounty hunter."

"I don't see me being a bounty hunter. Having criminals tied up in my trunk would bother me. Cause really I'd rather shoot them in the head."

"It certainly will be fun watching you transition back into normal society." Dez thought about that for a minute. "You know, this could really work for you two. With your family's connections and Smitty's charm—you two could make a lot of money."

"His charm? What about mine?"

She knew he wouldn't appreciate her burst of hysterical laughter, but who the hell was he kidding? The man's charm was in his *lack* of charm.

She cleared her throat again. "Sorry."

"You never answered my question."

"About the guys? No, Mace. I never dated them." She didn't date at all while in the military. She had too many male friends. She knew what all of them were up to with women, and she made it her mission never to end up on the bad side of that situation. So she worked hard and kept her legs closed for four years. A lonely life, but she got used to it.

"Good."

"I'm glad I brought you such joy."

Dez glanced around. She'd put her dogs' food out and they still hadn't shown up to eat. "Where the hell are Sig and Sauer?"

"Under the table," Mace muttered, focusing on his ice cream.

With a frown, she crouched down and looked under her kitchen table. And there they were—cowering.

Poor things.

"At this rate they're going to starve to death."

"They'll get used to me." Dez chose to ignore that statement and what it implied. Instead, she stood up and finally asked him the question she'd wanted to ask him for a few hours now.

She took another spoonful of ice cream. "Smitty's like you, too, isn't he?"

Mace glanced at her. "Why would you say that?"

"Lots of reasons. But mostly because he has a happy spot."

"Every man has a happy spot. Some of us have several."

"Not that happy spot." She glanced down at the rest of her ice cream. Already full, she handed it to Mace. The man had a killer appetite. "He has one on the back of his neck. If you scratch it, his leg shakes."

Mace slammed the bowl down on the countertop. For some unknown reason, she didn't jump. She did, however, look at him like he'd lost his mind. "Is there something going on between you and Smitty?"

Ah. He *had* lost his mind. "Of course not. It just feels very comfortable with him. Kind of like with my dogs." She grabbed Mace's arm. "Oh my God. Is he a dog?"

"Wolf. And if you want to go out with him, you can, you know."

"Wha—"

"You know what? I'm lying. No, you can't."

Dez stared at Mace. *Holy shit, the man is jealous.* "First off, I don't wanna go out with Smitty. He talks too slow. I'd have to kill him. And second, what do you mean I *can't* go out with him? I can go out with anybody I want to."

This had to be the stupidest argument two grown people could have but, clearly, Mace didn't care. And apparently neither did she.

Mace stepped in front of her. He placed both of his arms on either side of her, the island at her back.

"Let's get this straight now, woman. You and me—we're a couple."

"I didn't agree to that."

"Don't care."

Dez let out an exasperated sigh and went to run her hands through her hair, but Mace grabbed her wrists.

She tried to pull her arms out of his grasp, but he held tight. "Mace, it doesn't work that way. We're not together because you say we are."

"Yeah, but if we fall in—"

With strength she had no idea she possessed, Dez snatched one arm away and slapped her hand over Mace's mouth. Hard.

"Don't. You. Dare."

Gold eyes stared at her. Few people knew how to read Mace's eyes. Mostly they simply freaked everybody out. But she always knew Mace's feelings from what she saw in his eyes. Like right now, she knew she'd hurt him.

"Aw, Mace, don't be hurt. Please. We're just not . . . we just can't . . . no."

Heaving a heavy sigh, Mace took her hand off his mouth and

kissed her fingers. He took both her arms and dropped them down by her side as he pulled her close. He lowered his forehead until it touched hers.

"I understand."

"You do? Really?"

"Yeah. Really."

Then she heard metal click as Mace stepped away from her. She tugged her arms and realized the son of a bitch had locked her to one of the thick metal supports attached to the kitchen island.

"I understand I need to convince you we're meant to be together."

"Mace Llewellyn. You let me go! *Now!*" Her dogs bolted from under the table and ran up the stairs.

"*Cowards!*" she bellowed after them.

Mace watched Dez try to figure out how to get herself out of her handcuffs. The woman simply continued to confuse him. One second it seemed like she couldn't live without his touch, the next he expected her to toss his ass out of the front door as soon as she came.

Full-humans were so freakin' difficult to read.

"When I get loose I'm gonna kick your *gringo* ass all *ova* this fuckin' kitchen!" Well that Bronx girl sure had come back with a vengeance.

Mace reached out and lightly brushed her breast with his fingertips. The woman's knees buckled. He caught her around the waist, worried she might hit the floor.

She growled at him. "Get off me, Mace. And stop starin' at me!"

"So confusing," he muttered more to himself than to her.

He reached down and slipped two fingers inside her tight pussy. Her head dropped against his chest.

"Dammit, Mace!"

He ignored her and instead said, "Christ, Dez. You're so wet."

"I am not." Except she moaned that statement. He pulled out

of her and this time she moaned in disappointment. He slid his two fingers across one of her nipples.

"You tasted so good earlier." He lowered his head to her breast and, before he even touched her, heard Dez's sharp intake of breath.

"Don't," she whispered. "Don't, Mace."

"Come on, Dez. Just a little taste." He sucked her nipple into his mouth. Her whole body jerked and he had to wrap one arm under her ass to keep her from dropping to the floor.

Immediately Dez's body responded. Her breath coming out in short, hard pants. Her chest rising to give him better access to her nipples while her juices flowed down her thighs and across the free hand he had between her legs.

"Tricky damn cat."

Smiling around the hard flesh sitting comfortably in his mouth, he brought his free hand up and squeezed the other nipple. He didn't have to get it hard, it already was.

"Shit, Mace!" that brutal voice cried out, and he realized he needed to be inside her again. He might as well have himself surgically implanted, because he couldn't think of anywhere else he'd ever want to be again. Not if Dez wasn't there with him.

"Still want me to stop, Dez?"

"God, don't stop, Mace. Don't—" He sucked harder and she began to break around him. "Don't ever stop," she begged. Then her whole body convulsed and she came hard, almost knocking him across the room. He held on to her, though. Kept sucking and tugging her nipples until she came again.

He released her and she sagged against him. He grabbed the handcuff keys lying with her badge. He unlocked her and held her sagging body against his. Dez's arms looped around his neck and he easily lifted her up, urging her legs to wrap around his waist.

With that, he turned and headed up the stairs.

"Don't you dare fall asleep on me, Dez," he whispered against her ear. "We're not even close to done."

Dez shivered in anticipation of the promises that statement

held as Mace carried her up the stairs to her bedroom. And if she wasn't so sexually overwhelmed at the moment, she'd kick herself in the ass. He was making her fall for him. She was, too. She was falling hard and fast. *And when you fall that hard and fast*, she thought desperately to herself, *you usually break something.*

Chapter Ten

It couldn't have been past eleven o'clock in the morning when he heard it. The most horrible sound. The kind of sound that drove men to kill, to destroy all they love, to destroy everything.

With a growl he stood up, went to the window, and threw it open. The carolers at the front of the house glanced up at him. They looked quite festive in their Santa hats and green and red sweaters, singing happily about Rudolph and his goddamn red nose.

Mace glared at the group and roared. A full-on, lion-protecting-his-Pride roar. The kind of roar that would travel up to five miles and let any other shifters know this territory belonged to him now.

The carolers stopped, screamed, and ran. He slammed the window down and turned back around. Dez kneeled naked on the bed, watching him with beautiful wide-awake eyes.

"What is wrong with you?"

"They woke me up. I hate that."

"Mace, I gotta live here. And weren't they from the church?"

"I thought I saw a priest."

Dez buried her head in her hands. She wondered if it were really hot in hell or just a little humid.

"Don't worry, Dez. They'll convince themselves it didn't happen."

Her head snapped up. "Look, Mace. I know you're a freak, but do you think you could be a little less freaky?"

Mace calmly walked toward her. All naked and glorious. Dez's body responded immediately at the sight of him—her breath leaving her in a soft whoosh, her nipples tightening, and the evidence of her lust pouring from between her thighs.

"You like me freaky."

She watched as he moved toward her with the grace of the animal he truly was, and Dez felt awe. Not only for what he could do, but for what he did to her. How he made her feel.

He stood at the foot of the bed. "Come here, Dez."

She shook her head. "No."

"You scared of me?"

She shook her head again. "No." Her eyes traveled up his body until their eyes locked. "I just think you should work for it."

She spun on her knees and dived off the bed. She never touched the floor, though. Mace had her by the ankle and clearly had no intention of letting her go.

"Mace Llewellyn, let me go!" She tried to pull her foot away, but Mace wasn't having it. He dragged her back as he kneeled on one end of the mattress.

"Would you look at that ass." He slowly pulled her back toward him. "That ass belongs to me, ya know."

"It does not!"

"I guess it always has. Belonged to me, that is."

"Mace, lemme go!"

"No. I'm not even remotely done with *my* ass. Not even close."

He pulled her onto his lap, ass up. Mace gazed down at her butt. Such a delightful, perfect ass. *His* ass. He leaned down and kissed the right cheek. Then he unleashed his fangs and bit her.

Dez squealed. Mace didn't even know her voice could go that high. She unleashed a stream of curses, some he never even heard of—*spunk bubble?*—reached back, and punched his thigh.

"Did you just bite me," she demanded.

Mace licked the blood away. "Uh-huh."

"Did you break skin?"

"Uh-huh."

She moaned as his tongue cleaned off her wound, her hands gripping the comforter. "Why?"

Mace kissed her ass just before he flipped her over. He shrugged. The woman asked the oddest questions. "Cause you're mine."

"You irritating, motherfucking cat!" Dez tried to scramble away again, but Mace didn't let her move an inch from him. Instead, he pulled up one leg, draping it over his shoulder, and wrapped the other around his waist. He yanked her tight against him, the length of his cock pressing against her hot pussy, while he ran his tongue over her ankle.

"By the way, Dez." She looked up at him in confusion and lust. "Love the toenails."

He didn't hear her fall out of bed until she hit the floor. Mace opened his eyes and found one of her damn dogs staring at him. Tongue hanging out with the foulest breath known to man or beast. Apparently, the dogs feared him less. As the afternoon wore on, they kept moving closer and closer to him. Testing to see how far they could go before he tried to eat one as an appetizer. Now one had his front paws on the bed and that foul wet nose almost touching his. He really didn't like how this particular relationship kept moving along. He'd hoped they would have run away by now.

He heard the cell phone ring and realized why Dez left their warm bed. He could hear her scramble for it. "MacDermot. Oh yeah. Hi. Hold on, hon."

She crawled back into bed beside him, her naked body rubbing against his as she handed him his phone. Would anything ever feel as good as that? "Your phone. Thought it was mine."

"It's not Missy again, is it?"

Dez chuckled. "Nope."

He took the phone from her. "Did you fall out of bed?"

"Shut up." She turned over and put her arm around one of her stupid dogs. That one actually lay on the bed. And his woman *spooned* it. She shouldn't be spooning the dog. She should be spooning him.

"What?" he barked into the phone.

"Hey, hoss."

"Hey, Smitty. How's it going?"

"Fine. Are we still on for tonight?"

"Hold on." Mace pushed Dez's shoulder.

"What?" She didn't turn around, but instead stroked that stupid dog's neck.

"Smitty wants to know if you wanna hang out with them tonight."

"Them?"

"Yeah. Him, Sissy Mae, and their Pack."

"Sure."

He watched her stroke that stupid dog's belly. Honestly, what next? Forget it. He didn't even want to go there.

"All right. We're in," he said into the phone.

"Great. Meet us at the hotel. We'll go from there."

"When?"

"Eight o'clock. We'll get dinner first."

"You got it."

Mace closed the phone and glanced over at Dez. Immediately his cock became hard. Damn, but the things the woman did to him. She must have catnip in her veins. He planned to turn on his side and put his arms around her, but when he tried to move his legs a one-hundred-and-fifty pound pile of raw dog meat happily sat on his feet. He didn't even realize the big bastard had gotten on the bed.

"Woman, there's a dog on my feet."

"It's his bed."

"Is this our lives from now on? I'm going to have to put up with these fucking dogs in bed with us?"

Dez turned over. She smelled of panic. "Our lives?"

"Yeah. *Our* lives. I thought I made this clear to you last night."

"Are you always like this?"

"Yes."

"Cause that's going to get on my nerves."

"Too bad."

She ran her hands through her hair. "You know, I always hated cats. Hence the dogs."

"Ah yes. You definitely want something around your house that licks its ass, chases its tail, and follows your every command until a car drives by."

She raised herself up on her elbows, her anger making her smell fucking amazing. "Dogs are loyal. They're intuitive. They drag people out of burning buildings. With cats you just hope they don't kill you in your sleep."

Mace had to be the most relentless man she'd ever known. He wanted her and apparently had no intention of giving up until he got what he wanted. What exactly should she do with a 230-pound shapeshifter anyway?

Sauer yelped as Mace unceremoniously kicked his furry butt off the bed. Then Mace was on her, kissing her, snatching the breath from her lungs. Damn, but she loved the feel of the man's body against hers. All that velvety flesh over hard muscle. One big hard muscle pressing against her inside thigh.

Now see. How exactly was she supposed to panic about their "relationship" when that demon tongue of his so gently stroked the inside of her mouth? And those big hands of his were on her breasts, tugging and rolling her nipples?

Tricky bastard. He was trying to keep her off track. Confuse her. The bastard *wanted* her to love him. *Dammit.* Why couldn't she get a nice, normal psychotic with mother issues, like every other woman in New York?

Mace flipped her over. She buried her face in her pillow and gripped the irreparably damaged headboard between her hands. He grabbed a condom, then thrust inside her, taking ownership—again.

Well he could forget anything about her loving him. She was completely okay with the desperate lust holding her captive.

That was perfectly normal. But love? No way. That wasn't happening. And the fact she squeezed the damaged wood headboard so tight she had splinters in her fingers? That meant nothing. Or the fact that she gasped like a long-distance runner on her last mile—it didn't mean a damn thing either. At least not to her.

And when she came and screamed his name into her pillow? Nope. That didn't mean shit either.

Aw hell.

Chapter Eleven

Mace pulled the thick, black cable sweater over his head and tugged it down his body. He shook the water out of his mane and put on his new watch.

Dez's arms looped around his waist from behind. She pressed her T-shirt–covered body into his and kissed him on the back.

He took hold of her hands. "How are your fingers?" It took him forty-five minutes to get the splinters out, and she whined the entire time. He offered to cut her fingers off entirely rather than using the tweezers, but she resisted that idea.

"Fine now. Was the shower okay?"

"Too small."

"Well, blame your genetics on that one."

"You still should have joined me."

"I couldn't. I had to feed the boys."

Mace glanced over. They sat staring at him. Their dog tongues hanging out. Since Dez couldn't see him, he flashed his fangs. One of the dogs started to whine.

"Whatever you are doing—stop it." She released him. "Hey, do me a favor."

He turned around and saw that she'd grabbed two leashes off the dresser. "Walk 'em for me, babe." She handed him the leashes and walked out of the room.

Mace stared at the leashes in his hand. Had the woman lost her mind? Had the world gone mad? There was no *way* he was walking these . . . these . . .

Mace looked over at the dumb beasts waiting patiently for him. "Dogs."

"You'll need these too." She came back in the room, and shoved a couple of plastic grocery bags in his hand. "Thanks, babe." She walked away.

Mace stared down at the bags in his hand.

Oh, there is no way!

No. No. No! She just asked for too much. *Demanded* too much. She wanted him to walk her dogs and to pick up their shit. Him. Mason Rothschild Llewellyn. Breeding Male of the Llewellyn Pride. Former Navy SEAL. And a lion.

Missy was right. He needed a nice Pride to take care of him. A bunch of females who made sure he ate, fucked him, and bought him stuff to keep him happy. What he didn't need was a thirty-six-year-old cop with two dogs she insisted on referring to as her "boys."

He followed Dez to the bathroom. She stood at the sink brushing her teeth with an electric toothbrush when the alternative radio station she had on suddenly busted out with No Doubt's "*Oi to the World!*," in honor of the Christmas holidays. That's when Dez began to shake her ass and bop her head from side to side. The T-shirt she wore barely covered that adorable butt of hers.

Mace closed his eyes. *Keep thinking accommodating Pride females. Keep thinking foot rubs and being the first to eat.*

He opened his eyes, and Dez bent over to spit out the toothpaste. She wore no panties. Of course, she hadn't had any on since the night before.

Mace, really having trouble breathing, turned around and went back to the bedroom. He looked at the two dogs still waiting for him.

"Well, come on. Let's get this nightmare over with."

Dez came out of the bathroom as soon as she heard the front door close. She checked both floors, every room.

Holy shit. He's actually taken my dogs for a walk. She'd only been joking. She never thought in a million years Mace would actually *walk her dogs*. She thought he'd follow her into the bathroom, throw the baggies at her, and then fuck her on the bathroom sink.

Dez stood in the middle of her hallway. Either Mace truly loved her or she just experienced one of the signs of the apocalypse the nuns always talked about.

"What have I gotten myself into?" she asked no one in particular. The sad thing was . . . she really expected an answer.

Mace turned over on the bed, letting his arms hang over the sides. A wet snout sniffed his hand. He gave a short roar and the nose scrambled farther under the bed with his canine buddy.

When had this relationship taken such an odd turn? He always controlled every relationship, and the women he'd been involved with had never minded. But, except for the bedroom, Dez never gave him a goddamn inch. She always knew what he was up to and called him on it every time.

He wasn't at all sure about the dog thing either. Irritating little bastards. Dez had made it clear, though. Love her, love her dogs. He actually picked up dog shit for her.

He pushed his mane of blond-brown hair out of his eyes. Within twenty-four hours, his hair returned to its standard length. It took him all of puberty to grow the first round, but once there it didn't like to go.

Mace sighed and looked at the clock next to Dez's bed. Where the hell was she? A shower shouldn't take this long.

He hated waiting. It was the lion in him. He didn't wait to eat. He didn't wait to go out. He didn't wait for anything if he didn't have to. True, he could leave without her. But that wasn't going to happen. Not with him having the best time he'd ever had with a woman. Cranky bitch that she was, he liked her as much as he loved her. So, for once and without any direct orders from a C.O., Mace would wait. He would wait for Dez. Christ, what was his life coming to anyway?

A tongue swiped at the fingers he had resting on the carpet. Great. Playful dogs. They'd started liking him. In typical dog fashion they found a way to make this work. Even if they forced him to like both of them.

He growled and the dogs yipped back. He almost smiled. Grudgingly.

"Are you being mean to my dogs again?"

Mace looked up, about to tell her he had just been considering what pieces of her dogs would taste good with barbeque sauce, when he pretty much stopped breathing completely.

He barely noticed the black jeans she had on or the black leather boots. No, it was that black leather bustier that had his full attention. Clearly created specifically for her, because no way could something off the rack from a fetish store have done those magnificent tits as much justice as the bustier she now wore. Tight and form fitting, it tied up the front, showing a healthy amount of cleavage that simply called to him. The bustier fit over a black leather top with long leather sleeves that molded to her strong arms and scooped nicely off her shoulders. Her tits practically defied gravity in that outfit. She didn't need a bra, and he could make out her tight nipples through the leather. The light brown skin she showed looked satiny and soft. For some reason he found her outfit almost as hot as when she stretched out in front of him completely naked, and at the moment she barely revealed anything. He wanted to rub himself up against her until he was purring and she was coming.

She'd even put on a little makeup for the occasion and brushed her hair until it fucking gleamed. No one had a right to be this pretty, least of all the woman holding onto his heart like she held onto one of her many guns. One good squeeze and she could blow his whole life apart.

"Christ, you haven't said a word. Is this outfit that bad?" He still didn't answer her. Not with him fantasizing about her, that bustier, and those damn handcuffs. He wondered how many times he could make her scream his name.

"Okay. I'm changing." She turned to walk away.

"Don't you dare." She stopped, clearly surprised by his order. And it *was* an order. "Get my ass over here."

She smirked. "What? You think you're going to give me orders when we're not—"

"Now."

What a demanding son of a bitch. Yet she did exactly what he told her to. Of course, she only seemed to operate that way when she knew some kind of sex would be involved. Otherwise, she made the man work for it.

He lounged on the bed like a lion sunning himself on a rock in the Serengeti. With crossed arms, she stood in front of him.

"What?"

He watched her with those gold eyes. "I like that top." At least she guessed that's what he said since he growled more than spoke.

Dez ran her hands down the front self-consciously. The bustier had been a guilty pleasure buy. One so expensive she saw it more as an investment. She didn't do the S & M thing. Yet she did like their wardrobes. Very few people knew that. Somehow, though, she didn't mind showing that side of herself to Mace. Although she never expected to see that expression in his eyes. It went way beyond desire to something else altogether, and Dez had no idea if she were ready to handle that.

She cleared her throat. "I've only worn it once. The cop bar down the block from the precinct just doesn't seem the right place for this thing."

His eyes narrowed. "Some guy buy it for you?"

"What do you care?"

He slowly pulled himself up until he kneeled on the bed in front of her. "Answer my question."

"No."

He watched her closely, then leered. "You bought it for yourself, didn't you?"

"Are we going or not?" She started to walk away again, embarrassed he picked up on her thing about leather so quickly, but he grabbed her arm and hauled her up against him.

"You did. Didn't you?" He brushed his lips against hers. "My kinky little puppy."

"I hate you."

He kissed the bare flesh above the swell of her breasts. "You wish."

Her hands snaked through his hair. "God, I do." She breathed desperately as he bent her back. She wanted to hate the man, but he continued to make her ache in all the best places. No man had ever gotten to her like this before.

"I thought . . . we were . . . going . . ."

He gripped her tighter. "Fuck 'em."

"No. We're going out." She pulled away from Mace.

Surprised and none too happy, he made a grab for her. She jumped back to the door.

"We're going out."

"I don't want to. Get over here."

Oh, she liked this. For once, she had the control—and without handcuffs. It sure did feel good.

She shook her head. "I'm going out now. Wearing this top. You can stay here with the dogs or you can come with me. Your call, cat." Then she slipped out into the hallway and down the stairs.

Mace crossed his arms in front of his chest and silently seethed. This had been a bad idea. He knew it as soon as they arrived at the Pack's hotel. The whole group had been waiting outside for them, and as soon as Dez stepped out of the cab, every male wolf eye turned to her—and those tits. In general, it hadn't been a bad evening really. A good dinner, some drinking since they didn't drive in, a couple of clubs, dancing with Dez, and a few near fistfights made for a festive Christmas Eve. But the male wolves were clearly into Dez, and as always she was clearly oblivious.

Now they sat in Dez's favorite coffeehouse a few blocks from where she crash-landed in his lap a few nights ago, talking and drinking espresso. Mace probably wouldn't be so annoyed if Dez sat near him, but she sat near Sissy Mae, and the male wolves suddenly found a reason to sit near the pair. He glanced at Smitty, who seemed to be seriously enjoying himself since, for once, the wolves were ignoring his sister.

His friend turned to him, and they both knew in a few more minutes Mace would start kicking some dog butt.

Dez put her hands over her ears. "We are not having this conversation."

"But you know I'm right," Sissy whispered.

"You are not right. You are very, very wrong, and I don't want to talk about this anymore."

"No, I'm not. I think you'd look lovely in white."

"You do know I'm the one person who can shoot you and make it look like justifiable homicide?"

Sissy Mae shook her head. "But you love me."

That was it. Dez stood up. "I'm going to the bathroom."

"Okay. We can talk about china patterns and the right bouquet when you get back."

Like a dog with a bone.

Dez walked to the back of the coffeehouse until she got to the bathroom. She went into the stall and took care of business quickly. She wanted to get back to Mace. She found it quite entertaining watching him get jealous.

She washed her hands, dried them, and headed back to Mace and the Pack, but she stopped when a small hand grabbed her leather jacket and tugged.

Dez turned to see a small child standing behind her. Tears poured to the floor and she pointed to the back door. "Please," the little girl whispered, her head down. "I think my brother's hurt and I can't find my parents."

Dez crouched down next to her. "It's okay, honey. Show me. And then we'll go find your parents, okay?"

The child led Dez outside as she marveled at how fucking irresponsible some parents were. It was well after two A.M. These kids should be in bed, not hanging out at a coffeehouse while their parents did whatever they did.

Dez followed the child to another small child, lying faceup in the alley. Dez snapped her phone off her hip and flipped it open as she touched the child's face. She had just punched in 911 and was about to hit Talk when the child's eyes snapped open and he smiled. Dez blinked.

Jesus Christ, are those fangs?

Then Dez watched the ground rush up to meet her.

Mace's phone vibrated against his side. He pulled it out of its holster and glanced at caller ID. He rolled his eyes as he flipped the phone open. "Yeah?"

"Mace?"

His sister sounded panicked. She never sounded panicked. She didn't allow that particular emotion. "What is it, Miss?"

"Um . . . I'm sorry to ask you this, but I was just talking to Shaw and we got cut off."

"Oh . . . kay."

"It was the way we were cut off, Mace. I'm afraid something's happened to him."

Mace caught Smitty's eye. "Do you know where he was?"

"That's what really has me worried. He told me he was at the Chapel. Mace, that's hyena territory."

"Yeah, I know. But didn't you tell him what I told you about Doogan?"

"I never got a chance. He didn't come to the house last night. He hates all the social events."

A man after Mace's heart. "I'll go over there and see if I can find him."

She sighed. "Thank you."

Mace closed his phone. "Want to go babysit Shaw?"

Smitty grinned. "Hey, our first job."

Even when human, Smitty's tail always seemed to be wagging.

Mace looked around, noticing for the first time Dez hadn't come back from the bathroom. "Sissy, where's Dez?"

Sissy frowned. "She never came back from the bathroom."

"How long has she been gone?"

Sissy thought for a moment. "A while."

Not the answer he wanted.

*   *   *

Of all Dez's experiences, flung down a flight of stairs by a small child had never been one of them.

She hit the ground, and pain shot through her left arm.

She tried to get up, but the giggling little bastards kicked her back to the ground. They wrapped a rough, heavy cord rope around her throat and proceeded to drag her across a concrete floor.

Dez fought to breathe, desperately pulling on the rope, trying to loosen it before it choked her out or snapped her neck. But she couldn't get her fingers under the rope. As she started to black out, they stopped. Dez shook her head to snap herself out of whatever abyss she'd been about to fall into. Then she pulled herself to her knees. She had her hands on the knot at her neck when another hand grabbed the rope and yanked it taut. She grabbed at the hand holding the rope and looked up into the viciously torn face of Anne Marie Brutale.

The woman sneered at her. "I'm going to have such fun with you, human."

Mace picked up Dez's phone. Her last attempted call still blinking, waiting for her to hit Send. 911. "You smell 'em?" he asked Smitty.

Sissy Mae stood next to her brother. "They smell young."

Mace closed his eyes. Not good. Anything but that. Anything but hyena children. He could see it now. They lured Dez out here by pretending to be innocent kids. As a cop, no way in hell would Dez ignore them.

Smitty cast around until he locked onto the scent. He followed it to an unlocked metal door. He walked over to it and threw the door open. The scent of hyena sucker punched Mace and made him want to retch. Nothing smelled as bad as their markings. He glanced down. The stairs seemed to go on forever. But he could smell Dez. This is where they'd taken her. He had to go after her, no matter what the cost.

"I don't have to look to know there is at least one Clan of

hyenas down here. Maybe two. I can't ask you guys to go with me. But—"

Mace turned around and found the entire Pack had already shifted. Their clothes tossed all over the alley floor. They were just waiting for him. He would have smiled if he wasn't terrified for Dez.

He didn't waste another second. He shifted, shook off his clothes, and bounded down the stairs—his Pack following him.

"I was so excited when I heard you and your cat were walking around the Village like you owned it. I sent my cousin's children to go get your dumb human ass."

Dez pushed herself into a sitting position, the wall against her back. She was in a long hallway, but she didn't know where. A healthy guess would say she was under the Chapel Club. If she hadn't been fighting for her life, she'd marvel on the hyenas' use of underground tunnels.

Dez glanced up and saw exposed plumbing, sturdy and within reach. Plus, there were doors all along the hallway, including a janitor's closet.

Anne Marie held up Dez's gun still in its holder. "Nice weapon, Detective. You ever been shot with it?" Dez didn't answer. "But where would the fun be in that, right? I wanna feel your flesh rip under my hands. Taste your blood on my tongue. We're going to have such a party, you and me."

Dez loosened up the rope on her throat with one hand while gathering the rest in the other. "Sorry about your face. Did Gina find out about what you and Doogan did to Petrov? Or was that cause of me?"

"Do you have sisters, Detective?" Dez nodded. "Then you understand. At least a little. I was trying to protect the family. First she brings in that idiot Petrov, then she lets you into our club, reeking of lion, and she thinks I'm going to let that go? Because she wants to find out who whacked her fuckin' cat boyfriend?" Anne Marie stood in front of her. Dez pushed herself to her feet and stared the crazy bitch in the eye.

"But I'll deal with her later. Because first . . ." Anne Marie whispered, "first I'm going to hurt you."

Dez knew she had only one chance, so she might as well make the best of it. She headbutted her. Anne Marie stumbled back, caught off guard by Dez's sudden attack. Dez pulled the noose over her head while she advanced on Anne Marie. Once close enough, she punched her. A right cross to the jaw. Anne Marie stumbled back several more steps, then Dez grabbed the brutalized side of the woman's face, digging her fingers into the torn flesh. She got a good grip on her cheek and spun the howling, screaming woman around, slamming her face-first into the wall.

The air changed around them—Anne Marie's scent becoming stronger, her body shifting. Dez looped the rope around Anne Marie's throat and tightened it at the moment the woman's body began to change. Dez knocked her to the ground, one foot flat against her back to hold her in place. She lifted her other foot and brought it down hard against Anne Marie's hand, breaking all her long nails. She did the same to the other hand.

Anne Marie howled in rage, completing her shift so she could tear Dez apart. But as hyena, her body would be no bigger than either of Dez's dogs. Dez had never done to one of her dogs what she needed to do now, but it was time for her to try it.

Yeah. It was time to take Anne Marie Brutale on a Nature Walk.

Mace stopped at the bottom of the stairs, the Pack surrounding him. Why the hell did he smell lion? He glanced at Smitty and realized he smelled it too. After another moment, he realized he smelled Shaw as well as Doogan and his brothers. Like he had time to deal with that little problem. This was starting to get freakin' complicated.

He glanced down the long dark hallway and realized they were in one of the infamous hyena tunnels. He knew if he followed this tunnel, it would take him back to the Chapel Club. Growling, he sprinted into the darkness, Smitty and his Pack behind him.

* * *

Thankfully her left wrist wasn't broken. It hurt like a bitch, but if it had been broken, she would never have been able to swing Brutale around like one of her dogs.

As soon as Anne Marie finished shifting, Dez gripped the rope tight and swung Brutale up and into one wall. Her hyena body bounced off, but Dez used the momentum to hammer her into the opposite wall. This time she stunned the beast. Heard the air "woosh" from Anne Marie's lungs.

Using the few precious seconds she now had, Dez tossed the end of the rope over one of the exposed pipes above her head, right by the janitor's closet. She grabbed the end and yanked down.

She pulled until Brutale hung there. A good four feet off the ground. Satisfied Anne Marie wasn't going anywhere, Dez tried the door of the janitor's closet. Locked. So she kicked it in. The door, not particularly strong, splintered and burst open. She walked in and spotted what she needed immediately. A large, heavy shelf case stood on one side of the room. Dez reached down and tied the end of the rope around one of the shelf legs. She made sure it was tight, and the bottom shelf prevented the rope from sliding up. With the rope taut, Brutale would continue to hang until someone let her loose.

Dez grabbed her gun and ran down the hall, forcing herself to remember that Brutale would never have let her live either.

Mace stopped beside the hung body of a hyena. He rose up on his hind legs and sniffed her. He smelled Dez faintly and knew she'd done this.

He followed behind Smitty and the Pack, but stopped when he saw what they were looking at.

The hallway split off into four directions. And they smelled Dez all over.

Sissy Mae sent several of her females down one tunnel. Smitty sent a few females, including his sister, and a few males down two other tunnels.

Mace took a step toward the last tunnel but stopped when he

knew someone watched him. He saw a pretty little girl, no more than eight or so, staring at him. She looked up at the hyena hanging from the pipes; back at Mace; and, with a heart-stopping smile only hyena children seemed to possess, suddenly turned and screamed, "*Giiinnnnaaa!*"

Shit! Mace and Smitty exchanged a glance, then charged down the fourth tunnel.

One hyena alone could cause enough damage. But a Clan of forty or even eighty? He had to get to Dez before she fell into the middle of them or they found her. Otherwise they'd all be dead.

She turned the corner and faced another set of long hallways. What a freakin' maze. A well-lit, confusing maze. Every corner she turned introduced her to another row of long hallways. Choosing one led her to another corner with another set of hallways and on and on.

Christ, what did she get herself into?

She stopped and took a breath. Yup. She was lost. She would have gone for her cell phone, but she'd dropped that in the alley behind the coffeehouse.

She took another breath. She would not panic. She'd get out of here. For the thousandth time she shook out her left hand. Her wrist had subsided into a dull blinding pain.

Dez moved down another hallway. She marveled at the silence. If she didn't know a club stood right above her . . . hell, she couldn't even make out the bass from the speakers. It seemed like all the walls were soundproofed.

Of course, that didn't make her feel any better. Because no one would hear her screams.

She came to another corner and stopped. Down one of the long hallways, she heard men arguing.

She moved quickly toward the sound as she pulled her Glock from her holster. She had no idea who she would find, but Dez prepared herself to be sweet as sugar or threaten to blow their heads off. Whatever got her the fuck out of here.

She followed the voices. Her body tense, her gun clasped in

both hands and away from her body. She pushed her back against the wall as the arguing turned violent. Someone was getting the shit kicked out of him.

"Do it! Do it!" a deep voice snarled.

She turned the corner and raised her weapon. Dez took in the scene quickly. One man down, a large boot against his shoulders holding him in place. The boot belonged to Patrick Doogan. She recognized him immediately now. One of his idiot brothers held a .45 aimed at the back of the vic's head. The third brother crouched beside him, the hand not in a cast buried in the vic's gold hair, pulling his head back to spit into that beautiful face.

Damn, even her shotgun wouldn't help her here. She needed her M-16. But she didn't have that either.

As a cop, she needed to scream "Freeze! Put your hands above your head and step away from the gorgeous guy!"

Fuck that. She remembered how fast Mace and Brutale moved. She didn't stand a chance with these three.

So, without warning, Dez shot the one holding the gun. The bullet hit him in the shoulder, knocking him back, the gun flying out of his hand. The other two were so startled they jumped away from their target. They were armed, but they hadn't gone for their weapons yet, mostly because they'd tucked them into the back of their tailored slacks.

"Get up!"

The vic looked at her, and immediately she recognized Brendon Shaw.

"Move!"

She wasn't about to get any closer, but she wasn't sure if she was asking the impossible as well. Severely beaten, he must have fought back. But he somehow managed to stand and stumble over to her.

"Keep going."

He did as ordered. Dez backed away, her eyes locking with Patrick Doogan's.

"I'll find you, bitch. I'll find you and fuck you and kill you."

Dez didn't bother answering him. Why? She knew he meant it.

Instead, she kept backing up, until she got around the corner. She grabbed Shaw's jacket and dragged him, but he wouldn't move.

She turned around and immediately stopped breathing. They all watched her with those cold brown eyes.

A hyena suddenly appeared from the back. The others separated, giving her a path to walk through. She came up to Dez and stood before her. A dead hyena body in her mouth, the rope still around her throat.

She knew this was Gina. Especially when she spit the corpse out at Dez's feet.

"Tell me you didn't do that," Shaw whispered, most likely because he'd lost so much blood.

"I really wish I could."

"Damn." He tried to push her back behind him. A surprisingly heroic gesture from someone she'd called "rich scumbag" in her head since he held that conversation with her tits the other evening.

She did appreciate his attempt at protecting her, but they were beyond that now. In fact, the phrase "completely fucked" kept rattling around in her head.

Dez grabbed Shaw's jacket and took a step back, but the Doogan brothers came up behind her. She realized with what quickly became overwhelming despair that the two groups had her trapped between them. Both wanting to see her dead.

Of course . . . they were archenemies. And not just because they were lion and hyena. For another reason altogether.

Dez stepped in front of Shaw. "Gina." The lead hyena watched her closely, waiting for her to make a run for it. Waiting for the hunt. "You wanted to know who killed your man." Dez stepped back and motioned to the three men behind her. "It was them."

Gina Brutale locked eyes with Patrick Doogan. He couldn't hide the truth. Not from any of them. His fangs extended as he and his brothers backed away. Gina watched him for a moment, savoring their realization that they were horribly outnumbered. She opened her mouth and let out a sound that chilled Dez's blood and made her want to start crying. It sounded almost like laughter, but it definitely wasn't.

Doogan and his brothers ran as the hyenas rushed them.

The two groups disappeared around the corner, then she grabbed Shaw's jacket and forced the man to start running in the opposite direction. Shaw had lost a lot of blood, but she didn't care. He'd lose a lot more if those lions got away or the blood-lust overtook the hyenas and they came looking for more.

Dez could already hear the battle raging behind her. Three male lions against what she estimated to be about thirty or forty hyenas. Yeah. Good luck with that.

Of course, there *was* one little problem with her escape. She still had no idea how to get the hell out of here.

Just great, Dez. She glanced back at Shaw. He did not look good.

"Can you lead us out of here?" When he stopped and dropped to his knees she pretty much figured that meant no.

"Mr. Shaw, you need to get up. Now."

He shook his head. "I can't."

"I can't carry you, Mr. Shaw."

"Forget me. Go."

There he was, trying to be a hero again. Like she had time for that. "I can't leave you here, Mr. Shaw." Christ, she really had gone back to combat mode. Well, at least she wasn't falling apart.

Dez heard scrambling against the concrete floor. Considering she typified lazy when it came to clipping her dogs' nails, she knew that sound. She crouched, her gun arm steadied against her knee. She jerked her trigger finger away in time and let out a shaky breath.

Not a hyena. A wolf.

"Sissy Mae?" The wolf yipped in response. "I'm lost and he's running out of steam."

They heard more screams, more roars, and that disturbing howl that sounded like hysterical laughter.

Sissy Mae put her head back and howled. She called to her

Pack. Dez grabbed Shaw's arm. "Get up, Mr. Shaw. We still need to keep moving."

He did his best, dragging his body up, using the wall as leverage. Once he stood on his own two shaky feet, Dez pulled Shaw past Sissy Mae. She turned the corner as six wolves charged past her. Two stopped and shifted back into males.

Naked males. She shook her head. Nope, not the time to get all lusty. Honestly, what the hell was wrong with her?

"He can't make it. Take him." They grabbed Shaw and dragged him away. "Sissy Mae, let's go!"

Sissy followed after the males. In a few moments she heard canine nails pounding concrete as they caught up with her.

Within a few turns, they found the exit Dez had come in through. The wolves dragged Shaw up the stairs. She heard more running. More beings, not human, were moving toward them.

She aimed the gun. "Sissy, go!" Sissy tore up the stairs as more wolves came from other hallways. They all moved past her and up the stairs. That's when she saw them. The hyenas were back. Not all of them, but quite a few. Covered in blood. She quickly counted. Nope. She didn't have enough bullets for all of them.

Then suddenly a lion and wolf slid in front of her. Mace bellowed out a roar, and the hyenas all made a weird yipping sound, darting back and forth, apparently searching for a way to get to her. An opening they could use.

Smitty growled, his canines flashing as he snapped at the hyenas in front of him.

Mace took a step back, pushing her toward the stairs with his body. But before Dez could hightail it out of there, more hyenas came from another hallway. The only reason they stopped was because she aimed her gun at them.

This wasn't good. At some point, the hyenas were going to bum-rush the three of them, and that would be it.

Dez desperately searched for a way out of this that would leave all of them alive, when she noticed Gina as hyena walking slowly around the corner, her sister's body again in her mouth.

Another hyena standing beside her let out a loud call, and the others challenging Mace and Smitty turned and charged back the other way. The ones facing her simply ran off.

Just like that it ended.

Gina looked at Dez, her eyes sending a clear message. She was going to let Dez go because she'd done her a favor. She'd taken out the only thing between Gina and absolute control of the Brutale family and given her the ones that had killed her lover.

Gina turned and trotted off down the hallway, her sister's body a trophy.

Okay. No more animal night in New York for Dez. She turned and charged up the stairs. As she cleared the entrance, strong hands grabbed her from behind and pushed her out into the alley.

Roasted coffee, muffins, sewage, and a light rainstorm were the welcome smells assaulting her. She wanted to take a deep breath and enjoy the cold air, but the arms that grabbed hold of her suddenly began crushing her to death. If she hadn't recognized the body attached to those arms, she might have been worried.

Instead, she couldn't breathe.

"I think you're killing her, Mace."

"Good." He pulled her closer to him and buried his face in her hair.

Dez waved desperately at Smitty. Unlike his now-human-again sister, Smitty was still naked. "Help me," she barely managed.

"Well, darlin', what did you expect? You had us worried sick."

"That's not helping," she squeaked.

The door slammed shut and Dez finally felt safe.

Sissy Mae shook her head as she quickly handed her brother's clothes to him. "I think they got some other lions. I heard it." Once dressed, Smitty gave Sissy a big, brotherly bear hug.

"That's not our problem. And good job, little sister."

The girl glowed with pride at her brother's words. Or it just looked like she glowed because Dez couldn't fucking breathe!

"Still dying!"

Mace finally released her, and she took in big gulps of air. He swung her around to face him. "That's it! No more helping strange children you don't know."

Dez pulled away from him, her breath coming in ragged gasps, the adrenaline finally leaving her body. "Are you insane? I'm a cop. If a kid comes to me, I'm gonna help 'em. So get that fuckin' thought outta ya head."

Mace took a deep breath as his gold eyes drilled holes into her. After a moment, "Fine. But next time make sure they don't have fangs."

Dez grinned. "That I can do."

Chapter Twelve

Dez opened her eyes. Then closed them again. Never again would she drink anything referred to as "Uncle Willy's 'shine." Her head throbbed. She had no idea where she was . . . or whose arms were currently wrapped around her.

The body behind her snuggled closer and purred. In that instant, her head cleared and she knew Mace held her. She smiled. What a night. In all her years as a Marine and a cop, she *never* went through anything like that before. And the fact that she survived . . . well, she felt pretty impressed with herself. But the night didn't end there.

Once away from the club, they took Shaw to a Midtown hospital. Apparently owned and operated by shifters, it was the only place that could truly care for the badly wounded man . . . or . . . whatever. The Pack and Mace were all ready to drop Shaw off at the emergency room and be done with him, but Dez couldn't do that, and for some unknown reason Sissy wouldn't allow it.

"We just can't leave him," Dez had argued. Not after his little heroic turn in the bowels of the Chapel. Of course, her sudden sentiment garnered an annoyed sniff from Mace and blank stares from the Pack. But eventually they saw her side of things. So they sat around the waiting room, chatting, eating, and . . . well . . . waiting. She even got her wrist x-rayed and bandaged. Only a sprain. No major damage.

Dez found herself liking Smitty and Sissy Mae's Pack more

and more as she got to know them. They were sweet and charming as only Southerners knew how. And they seemed to tolerate Mace well enough. Even after he roared at Smitty when he found Dez scratching his happy spot.

Eventually Mace's cousin, Elise, blew into the waiting room. It turned out she would be the only Llewellyn Pride female there that cold, rainy night. Sissy Mae and Smitty seemed dumbfounded by the lack of caring from the other females, but Mace wasn't surprised at all. Eventually the doctor told them that Shaw would survive. Elise disappeared after that, and the rest of them headed back to the Pack's uptown hotel.

That's about the time the drinking started. She really shouldn't drink. Dez knew better. Hence the Marine tattoo on her ass she had removed a few years back. Of course, now that area had a big ol' lion bite in it.

At least this time around, Mace made sure she didn't do anything too painfully stupid. He simply didn't let anyone near her.

Now it was the morning after. She still had on her bustier. Her body still ached from the beating it took the night before. Her wrist freakin' screamed "cut me off" at her. But she had Mace. She really couldn't ask for a better Christmas present than that. Hell, who could?

She sighed and snuggled closer to him. One of his hands gently caressed her stomach over the leather top while he snored. As she thought how sweet it was that he touched her even in his sleep, his hand slowly moved lower. Dez raised an eyebrow. *Tricky cat.*

She grabbed his hand with both of hers to stop its lowering course. That's when his other hand began moving. She grabbed both his hands in hers, but he kept going lower while she kept pulling him back up. That's when the uncontrollable giggling started. Christ, she was too old for giggling.

They tried to be quiet since they were on the floor with Smitty's Pack in his main suite—with that kind of drinking, one rarely made it back to her own bed. Then Mace pushed her onto her back, him on top. He pinned her arms over her head and leaned into her.

"Don't you dare, Mace Llewellyn," she whispered fiercely.

"Don't dare what, baby?"

"Get off me, Mace."

"No way. Gotcha where I want you."

"I'll scream."

"They'll just think you're having a good time."

Dez growled. "I'll scream 'walk.'"

That's when they knew the wolves were wide-awake. They all burst out laughing.

"Jesus Christ, Mace. Would you let the girl go?"

Sissy Mae pulled open the hotel curtains. Afternoon light flooded the room, and everyone groaned except Mace. He still focused on Dez, his eyes narrowed. She'd got him and they both knew it.

Sissy Mae tsk-tsk'd him. "Honestly, you cats have no sense of what's proper. Mauling a nice girl like that."

"You're kidding, right, Lassie?"

"Why you rude, son of a—"

"Now, Sissy Mae," her brother warned as he dragged his big, long body into one of the leather chairs. "Don't go gettin' all angry at Mace. You know the boy has never been in love before." Smitty looked right at his friend with challenge in his dark brown eyes. "Now have ya, hoss?"

He would kill him. Slam him down and rip him open from bowel to throat. Yeah. He loved Dez, but he didn't want to tell Dez that yet. Not when she physically flinched every time he got near the subject.

Damn, you call a man's sister Lassie and they get all defensive.

He looked at Dez. Yup. There it was. In those beautiful gray eyes. Panic. The only time the woman panicked. Anytime it involved him and his feelings for her.

Sissy Mae pushed him off Dez. He rolled away from her, his legs stretched out, his upper body raised on his elbows. Sissy helped Dez to her feet.

"Come on, darlin'. Let's order breakfast."

"Don't you mean lunch, little sister?" Smitty asked as he stretched and yawned.

Mace waited until the women went back to Sissy's room, then he glared at his friend. "Well, thank you very much!"

"Don't roar at me, boy. You called my baby sister Lassie. Only I can get away with that. Besides . . . you do love her. You fuckin' reek of it."

Mace dropped back to the floor. "I know," he moaned.

"Jes-us, Mace. My momma was right. You are more wolf than cat. Attaching yourself to one person and all."

"Cats attach themselves to one person." He raised his head to glare at Smitty. "We just don't let them know."

Smitty chuckled. "Guess I blew that, huh?"

"God, Sissy Mae. What the fuck am I going to do?"

"You New Yorkers sure do cuss a lot."

"I didn't used to, but Mace keeps bringing out the angry Bronx girl in me."

"You know what you're going to do, Dez? You're going to love him and go about your day." Sissy Mae gently unwrapped Dez's sprained wrist.

"This was supposed to be a fling—wasn't it?"

"Well, if you were a barhook on one of the bases that would be possible. But you're the great Desiree MacDermot. Mace's true ladylove. If you ask me—"

"And I didn't."

"But if you did, I'd say that boy's been waitin' on you his whole life."

"You're kind of a romantic, aren't ya?"

Sissy Mae smiled. "I'm not romantic at all, darlin'. I'm a realist. And a good one. I know what I see when it's right in front of me. And your entire body vibrates around that man."

Mace had no idea what went down between Sissy Mae and Dez but suddenly Dez wouldn't look at him. They ate brunch and Dez talked to Sissy Mae the entire time. They watched *A*

Christmas Story, and Dez leaned up against his side but still wouldn't look at him.

Eventually he couldn't take it anymore. He slid his hand down the back of her pants.

Dez made a little squeak sound and began to rub her eyes with her knuckles.

"Everything all right, darlin'?" Sissy asked with all the subtlety of . . . well, a dog. "Need anything?"

"No. I'm fine." Except that Dez's voice went up an octave. Which sounded strange with the gravelly rasp she usually came out with.

When Sissy went back to watching television, Dez slammed her elbow in Mace's gut, but he did no more than grunt.

She leaned against his ear. "Get your hand out of my pants."

Mace shook his head and gently rubbed one of her cheeks with his unsheathed claw. She jammed her elbow in his gut again. "Cut it out."

"Make me."

The couple ducked as the wolves began chucking paper goods at them.

Sissy smiled at her friends. "You two better go. Before it turns into a catfight."

Good. Exactly what Mace wanted. He pulled his hand out of Dez's pants and yanked the woman to her feet. He barely gave her enough time to grab her jacket before he snatched her out of the hotel room toward the elevators. Sissy Mae yelling something about after-Christmas shopping, the last thing he heard before the doors closed.

Dez watched Mace pull his big, undamaged body out of the taxi. Her breath caught, her breasts tightened, and visions of things the nuns definitely would never approve of ran through her head. She turned away and began walking toward the house while Mace paid the taxi driver. Maybe for once she would have a good holiday. At least she'd actually get some holiday nooky for a change. The way Mace stared at her in the cab—she was damn positive she'd get some holiday nooky. Maybe they could have some more fun on her stairs.

Dez walked up her porch and unlocked the security door. She went to open the front door when Mace came up behind her. He kissed her neck, his arm wrapping tight around her waist, pulling her close into his warm body.

When he purred in her ear, she thought she might pass out.

"We're supposed to see your family at five o'clock."

"It's already four-thirty. My parents live in Queens. We'll call 'em and tell 'em I had to work or something. We'll just lie our asses off."

He put his hand in her hair and pulled her head back. "Good plan. Because all I want to do right now is take you upstairs and fuck you blind."

Dez laughed, but stopped when he didn't.

"Uh . . . I actually need my eyesight."

"Don't worry. It'll be temporary."

He kissed her, and Dez realized that Sissy Mae was once again right. Dez's whole body vibrated at his touch. Especially when he unzipped her jacket and his big hand slid over one of her leather-clad breasts. He squeezed it, his big fingertips running along the exposed skin above the leather.

She didn't know how much more she could handle before she came right on her porch. So lost in Mace she didn't even hear her front door open.

"We wondered when you'd get here."

Dez snapped up straight at the sound of her father's voice, her head slamming into Mace's.

"Ow!"

"Daddy!"

Dez looked at her father. No. The man wasn't pleased. She tried to pull away from Mace, but he gripped her tighter. Her jacket covered up his hand, but her father was hardly stupid. He knew Mace had her by the tits and that he wasn't letting her go.

"Having fun with my daughter there, boy?"

"As a matter of fact—"

Before he could finish *that* particular statement, Dez slammed her elbow in his gut.

She probably hurt her elbow more than his gut, but it surprised him, giving her the chance she needed to pull out of the death grip he had on her tits.

Dez gave her father a warm hug.

He hugged her back. "Merry Christmas, sunshine."

"You too, Daddy." She stepped back from him. "Why are you here?" She couldn't believe for a second her father would miss Christmas dinner with his grandkids. Even for her.

"When your mother couldn't track you two down, she thought you might try to lie your way out of it." Dez flinched. Damn. She couldn't get anything past her mother. The woman always knew what her daughter was up to. *Always.* "So she decided to move the whole thing here."

Dez blinked. "Move what here?"

He stepped back and one of her nieces ran up to her. "Aunt Dez, Aunt Dez!"

Dez swallowed the panic that welled in her throat. Oh, this was bad. "Hey, Lucy. How's my girl?"

The six-year-old wore her Christmas best. The girl's dress probably cost more than the Desert Eagle Dez had bought herself a few years back. "Good. Is it true what Mommy says?"

"What's that, honey?"

"That you have issues with men?"

Dez growled. "Well you can tell your mommy to go f—"

"Okay, then!" Mace covered her face with his hand while her father pulled the little girl back into the house.

Once her father removed the little girl to a safe distance, Dez pulled out of Mace's arms.

"I am so leaving." Dez tried to push past him but he blocked the doorway with that gorgeous body she had been all ready to have her way with. *Damn family!*

"You can't leave. Your family is here for you."

"That's why I'm leaving."

Mace traced her jaw with one big, long finger. "Stay. For me."

"I'd rather chew glass."

"But once they're gone tonight, I have such plans for you and that hot little body of yours."

Dez bit the inside of her mouth. Damn him. He was using sex to entice her to stay in hell. And fuck but if it wasn't working. "Oh yeah? Like what?"

He leaned down to her ear and purred. Damn but she loved when he purred.

"I've been waiting to bury my head between your thighs all day. To take my tongue and—"

"Hi, little brother."

Mace's entire body clenched up. Dez looked over her shoulder and into the eyes of Missy Llewellyn.

Suddenly, she lost all interest in leaving anytime soon.

"What the hell are you doing here?"

"That's not very Christmas-like, little brother."

"Stop calling me that."

Mace couldn't believe it. Why was she here? For that matter, why were all four of his sisters here? When exactly did hell come to Earth?

Dez turned away from him and leered at Missy. "Well, well. Missy Llewellyn. In my humble abode. I feel blessed."

"As well you should," Missy tossed arrogantly.

"How the hell did you even know to come here," Mace snapped.

"Ah yes. Mrs. MacDermot contacted my secretary and said you'd be having Christmas dinner at her house. She felt since Christmas truly is the time for family, we should join all of you. And how could I turn that offer down?" She scrutinized her brother closely. "Glad to see you're relatively unscathed after last night's festivities."

True. He could kill her, but that might put a damper on the gift-giving portion of the evening.

Missy then turned that penetrating gold gaze at Dez. "Nice outfit, Detective. Going undercover at a fetish club?"

Dez growled. "Why don't you blow—" Mace wrapped his

hand around Dez's face again. Boy, when she went Bronx, she really went Bronx.

Rachel appeared behind Missy. "What's the problem, Missy? Afraid your tiny tits couldn't hold that top up?"

Dez glanced at Mace. He could read her easily now, and the fact that her sister suddenly jumped in to protect her from evil Missy—that might be too much of a shock for his hardened detective.

Missy spun around to glare at Rachel. "Well, I see you can take the girl out of the Bronx but you can't get the Bronx out of the girl."

Suddenly Lonnie appeared next to her older sister. "Wow. Look at the lines in your face, Missy. It's like your bitterness just dug in and stayed."

Allie, Mace's second oldest sister, stood next to Missy. "Well, I heard you'd become a prosecutor, Lonnie. It must be really hard to try and convict all your ex-boyfriends."

Rachel and Lonnie looked at each other while Mace's two other half-sisters went to stand beside Missy and Allie.

No. This really couldn't be good.

Dez pulled away from Mace. "I'm gonna go get out of these clothes before any blood gets on 'em."

She headed up the stairs. The elder MacDermot came back into the room, a toddler in his arms. An old-school Marine, tough as nails, and still sporting his high-and-tight haircut. Marine tattoos on both of his forearms. Pride for his brood, written all over the man's face. Even though, at the moment, the two sister teams were getting into a rather ugly confrontation that made Mace feel like a fourteen-year-old all over again.

"Those are some tough women."

Mace nodded. "Sorry about my sisters, sir."

"No reason to apologize. Dez can't control Lonnie and Rachel and notice she doesn't try."

"That's cause she's brilliant."

Gray eyes with dark green flecks turned to stare at Mace. "Do you really care about my daughter, Llewellyn?"

Barely realizing he did it, Mace's hands went behind his back.

His legs braced apart. Being around the man made him feel like he still needed to report to his C.O. before the night ended. "Yes, sir. More than I've cared about anything."

"Good. Because she's special. All my daughters are, of course. But Dez . . . Dez is . . ."

"I know, sir." Mace looked him in those eyes that were exactly like his daughter's. "I really do. I've always known."

MacDermot seemed to relax a bit as he nodded. "Good." He took in a deep breath, like he'd prepared himself for a fight. "Oh, and could you let Dez know I locked all her guns away in the safe in her closet upstairs."

Mace winced. They'd both forgotten about the weapons she kept stashed around the house and with kids around... "We forgot."

"Don't worry about it. I know each and every place my daughter hides her guns. Hell, I gave her most of 'em."

The older man gave a big grin, hugging the little boy in his arms tightly and walking back toward the kitchen.

The fight kept growing. This could easily turn ugly. But Mace had other things on his mind. Besides, he'd seen Dez's mother in action. If things turned bad, he had no doubt the tiny female could and would kick some ass.

Knowing that, Mace went up the stairs after his woman.

Dez tossed the sweatpants and Marine Corp sweatshirt she pulled out of her dresser on top of the closed toilet and looked at herself in the mirror. She shot a man without any warning. Faced off against hyenas and lions. But her family downstairs? That was making her break out in a rash.

Yet the weirdness hadn't ended. Not only had her entire family taken over the first floor of her house, but she had Missy Llewellyn and her cretin sisters with her.

Christ, did she really care enough about Mace to put up with those bitches?

What? Are you kidding? Of course you do, you idiot!

Dez smiled at herself in the mirror. Man, could she be more pathetic? Her eyes shifted to the right and that's when she saw

Mace standing behind her. She jumped. "Would you stop doing that!"

"I didn't do anything."

She sighed. True, he hadn't. And it would be hard to tell him to start stomping around her house because his creepy cat walk kept freaking her out.

She noticed he studied her shower closely, and for the first time in Desiree MacDermot's life she asked a lover a question she swore she'd *never* ask. "What are you thinking?"

Of course, Dez's question reeked of trepidation.

Mace shrugged as he examined her shower. "I'm wondering if this bathroom can be enlarged or if we should get another house."

She grabbed him by his sweater and pulled him around so he had to look her in the eye. "Mace Llewellyn, we are not—"

He kissed her before she could get the rest of the sentence out of her mouth and slammed the bathroom door shut with his foot. She couldn't remember what the hell she'd been planning to say. Instead, she let him roughly push her back toward the far wall, his mouth on hers, keeping Dez completely off balance.

Her jacket slid from her shoulders and to the floor. Mace released her mouth so he could kiss her neck. For a minute, she didn't even realize he was unlacing her bustier.

"Mace. What are you doing?" The minute the man touched her, she asked the stupidest questions.

"Stripping you so I can fuck you."

Of course, Mace always gave the most straightforward answers. Delicious answers. If only her entire family wasn't right downstairs. And his!

"We can't."

"Yes. We can. Just to take the edge off. We just have to be a little quiet. So no yelling."

"You're not exactly quiet either with that freakin' roar."

"You love my roar." *Dammit!* He was purring again. Right up against her ear. Suddenly, she couldn't get out of her clothes fast enough.

*   *   *

She still had no idea what she did to him. The power she held over him. But everything about her sent his feline senses into overdrive. Her smell. Her touch. The way her skin felt against his. That damn voice.

Just thinking about the little noises she made when he had his cock deep inside her made him crazy. Desperate. He forced her back against the wall, practically ripping the laces off the front of her bustier. Once he had it undone, he yanked it off her body, then dropped to his knees to tackle her jeans.

She'd already pulled his sweater off, tossing it into the empty shower. And now her hands roamed over his shoulders and through his hair. Her strong strokes across his flesh brought out the cat in him. His head grazed against her thighs as he pulled off her jeans and boots. He moved up her body slowly, rubbing himself against her the entire way. She growled and he purred back in response.

She undid his jeans, shoving them down past his hips. He pushed them down the rest of the way, snatching the condom he'd grabbed from the bedroom out of his pocket. He didn't bother taking his jeans off, though. They both knew they were short on time. Her mother would serve dinner soon, but he would have this woman or die trying.

He slid the condom on and lifted her up. Immediately she wrapped her legs around his waist, her arms around his neck. Because they had no time for slow and easy, he kissed her and impaled her against the wall at the same time—her scream lost in his mouth. Already so wet for him, he realized that hadn't been a scream of pain.

Mace stopped moving. He let himself feel her body against his. Her pussy tight around his cock. God, she felt so good.

Fuck. The families can wait.

Dez pulled out of their kiss. "What? What is it?"

He shook his head as he leaned against her. "Nothin', baby."

She cupped his chin with one hand, the other tangling in his hair. "Bullshit. Tell me what's going on."

He kissed her forehead, her cheeks, her mouth. Then he

rested his forehead against hers. "I've been waiting my whole life for you, Desiree MacDermot."

Dez was thankful Mace had her impaled against the wall like this. Otherwise, she might have bolted for the door. That would have been pure panic, though. She knew once the panic went away, she'd kick herself in the ass for running. She wanted Mace. Not just in her bed or inside her, but in her life.

Christ, she loved a cat.

Mace used his body to pin her against the wall while his hands moved over her face and throat. His hard cock still buried deep.

He waited for her. He wasn't going to ask her to say how she felt, but Dez knew he needed to hear something.

Well, she wasn't about to give him the ranch or anything. Short. Simple. And just enough to keep him happy until she'd successfully sorted through her feelings and decided how she wanted to proceed.

"You mean everything to me and I'm never letting you go."

She closed her eyes. What the hell was she doing?

You idiot!

Mace pushed his fingers through her hair. "Open your eyes, Dez."

"No."

"Wuss."

"Yup." His grip tightened and it felt so freakin' good.

"Look at me, woman."

With a sigh, Dez opened her eyes. He smiled at her. The sweetest, warmest smile she'd ever seen. "That wasn't exactly I love you . . . but I guess it will have to do."

He kissed her as his hips slowly rocked into her. Slow and steady. Sure and confident. She groaned in his ear, and that seemed to set something off in him. His thrusts became stronger. Harder. She grinned. Her voice. Her voice made him crazy. Her body would definitely go, but her voice would last for years. Thank God.

"God, Mace," she whispered in his ear, "you feel so good inside me. Don't stop fucking me. Don't ever stop fucking me."

Yeah. That did it. With a growl born of pure lust, he pounded into her. So hard she could feel her orgasm tearing up through her body. Mace pushed her head against his shoulder seconds before she started screaming. She remembered they weren't alone, so she bit into his flesh instead. But she came hard, forcing her teeth past flesh. She tasted blood in her mouth, but her body continued shaking as she came again and again.

Finally, Mace buried his head against her neck, biting his bottom lip so he only groaned as his body spasmed until completely drained.

For long quiet moments, they stayed locked together. Holding on to each other as if that was all that kept them upright.

Dez finally unclenched her teeth from his shoulder. She winced at the clear teeth marks she'd left behind. "Oh God, Mace. I'm sorry."

He lifted his head and glanced at the wound. Then he grinned. "Let's just call it your Christmas present to me."

She frowned. *What the hell is he talking about?*

Their disappearance didn't even raise an eyebrow with the two sister teams still going at it. Now, though, they'd moved on to politics.

Mace got downstairs first, fresh clothes on, his hair wet from a quick shower. And a nice clean bandage over his love bite. Dez had marked him and didn't even know it.

He briefly thought about trying to stop the sisters from fighting, but then . . . *wait* . . . *What the hell is that lovely smell? Is that turkey?* His mouth watered as he walked past the bickering women and headed toward the dining room.

He found Dez's mother putting homemade bread on the table. She smiled warmly at Mace as if she'd known him all his life.

"Don't worry. There's enough to feed you. I made an extra turkey."

Mace laughed. "A whole turkey? Just for me?"

"You're a growing boy. You need to eat. My daughter will learn." Then she shoved him into a chair.

Cool. He had her mother and he'd win over the father. Now he simply had to convince Dez. And he would. All he had to do was purr. She practically came simply from the sound of it.

"And someone named Smitty called for you. I invited him over for dessert."

Mace scratched his head to stop from laughing. "Um . . . you invited him for dessert—here?"

"Yes. Him and his family. Was that okay?"

"Mrs. MacDermot . . . that was wonderful."

"Oh good."

Dez's mother bustled back into the kitchen as Dez walked into the room and sat down next to him.

"I can't believe those bitches are still fighting."

"My sister shouldn't have messed with you in front of Rachel and Lonnie."

"What are you talking about?"

"You know how it is. It's one thing if they pick on you. It's another if some stranger does."

Dez shrugged, her wet hair and sudden shyness reminding him of the girl she used to be. "I guess."

Dez's mother moved back into the room. She smiled sweetly, then bellowed out the door. *"Dinner!"*

Mace blinked. For a tiny woman, she sure had a set of lungs.

Dez's father walked in, four children with him. He helped them get in their seats as Dez's sisters and his sisters stormed in. Still arguing.

"How can you believe for two seconds that will help the deficit?"

"I can't believe a federal prosecutor is a bleeding-heart liberal."

"I am not a liberal. I'm just not a Nazi."

Mace leaned over to Dez. "How long will this last," he whispered in her ear, enjoying the shudder that rippled through her body.

They watched the women and the rest of the family. The

fighting women ignored Lonnie and Rachel's husbands. The men were helping their kids settle in instead. Even helping with Missy and Allie's cubs. His sisters ignored everyone else in the room except Lonnie and Rachel.

"At least through second helpings. But I don't think it will last through pie." Her eyes widened. "Oh God. I forgot pie."

Her mother came out with more side dishes. "Don't worry. I bought pie. I knew you'd forget."

Dez glared at her mother. He knew that look. Any second now she'd say something that would upset her mother and ruin *his* Christmas dinner. So to prevent that, he slipped his hand between her thighs under the table.

She squeaked, causing everyone to look at her. Then, to play it off, she coughed. "Sorry. I'm getting a bit of a cold."

"I keep telling you, you don't dress warmly enough," her mother chided as Dez desperately tried to pry his hands off her crotch. But he wasn't letting go. At least, not until the turkey arrived. For good measure, he slid his middle finger against her sweatpants right where her clit would be. Her coughing became worse.

"Dear God," Missy snapped. "Would someone give that girl water before she breaks a blood vessel?"

Wow. It *was* humanly possible for six women to argue for two hours straight. Dez had no idea. She didn't argue that long with people. If she got that upset, she usually ended up hitting them or arresting them. But her sisters and Mace's were still at it. They'd moved on to other topics, but you would have thought they were arguing over things they could actually control.

Smitty and his Pack showed up just in time for pie and more arguing. Apparently invited by her mother. At that point, things got really interesting when Sissy Mae and her girls joined in. Still, not being the focus of attention for her sisters did make that pecan pie go down real easy.

When she thought the night couldn't get any more interesting, Sal, Jim, and Vinny showed up. She forgot she invited them over days earlier to get their gifts, but they were also smart enough to apologize and look slightly ashamed. Eventually Bukowski, his wife, and their kids showed up. Apparently still feeling pretty guilty about crashing her and Mace's party the previous day, he had wine for both of them. She was really proud Mace didn't comment on the vintage. Although she saw his opinion in his gold eyes.

Suddenly Dez's house had filled up with a bunch of people and Mace. A week ago, Dez had every intention of working all day and making herself a frozen turkey potpie for dinner. She smiled. She'd never admit it out loud, but this was way better.

From the kitchen, she watched the crazy bitches while she and Mace washed the dishes so her mother didn't have to. As her sisters squared off with Mace's, who was in the middle of it? Sissy Mae. No wonder Dez liked her. She was a fellow instigator.

"Wow, Missy. Are you going to let her talk to you like that?" Sissy pushed. "I mean unless you're scared of her or something . . ."

"I am not scared of anyone!"

Dez wondered how long she should wait before she stepped in when Mace's hand slid across hers in the water. He kept doing that. Whenever her mother turned her back, Mace found a way to touch her or outright kiss her. Something so cute and innocent about his actions. Especially since just yesterday the man had fucked her senseless on her dining room table.

"All right you two," her mother cheerily chastised. "Cut that out."

Mace pulled away from Dez. He was so adorable around her mother. Always treating her with the utmost respect.

"Sorry, Mrs. MacDermot."

"Silly boy. I don't mean that. I mean leave those dishes. Those arguing women can finish. You two go outside and get some air." Dez's mother winked at her. "It's getting too hot in here."

"Mom!"

Mace didn't wait for another invitation. He dried off their

hands and dragged her past their agitated siblings and out of the house onto the porch. He stepped back inside, grabbed her leather jacket and a plastic bag. He helped her put on the jacket, sat in one of the chairs, and pulled Dez onto his lap.

She watched her three friends talking with Smitty in her driveway. She had a feeling they would be joining forces with Mace and Smitty. Not that she minded. She couldn't think of anyone she trusted more. Especially if they ever needed to protect Mace.

"I got you a Christmas present."

Dez's head snapped around. "Mace, you didn't—"

"Here." He cut her off and handed her a wrapped package. "I got you one thing, but I gave it to Sissy Mae. I think you'll like this more."

"Thank you." She kissed him and then pulled the wrapping paper off. Her eyes immediately filled with tears. The man actually listened to her. He *heard* her.

"The *Cops 3-Pack*," she whispered in awe.

"If I had more time I would have checked to see if they had any other DVDs, but these were the three I found. You don't already have them, do you?"

"No," she lied. She'd burn her copies tomorrow. These meant much more. "I didn't get you anything."

Missy suddenly burst out the front door and was down the steps when the word *chicken* flew at her from inside the house.

Missy spun around and marched back up the stairs. "That's it, Old Yeller! *This is between you and me now!*"

Smitty ran into the house after her. Vinny, Sal, and Jim following, probably hoping to catch sight of a little girl-on-girl catfight. *Twisted perverts.*

Mace grinned at her. "Merry Christmas to me."

Dez laughed as Mace took off her old Guess watch. "Here. Wear this every once in a while, too. You know, like, every day. So you'll think about me when you're on duty."

Like she could ever not think about him. She watched as he put a nice stainless steel watch on her wrist. Big and heavy, definitely designed for a man. But she liked big male watches.

When she finally took a good look, she openly gawked at it,

then at Mace. "Mace. This is a Breitling." Stainless steel her ass. More like titanium. She'd seen enough counterfeits to recognize the real thing.

She did keep forgetting the man was rich.

"Don't worry about it. I've got others." *Wildly* rich, apparently.

"But why do you want me to wear it?"

"Because I want everyone at your precinct to know you belong to me."

Dez shook her head. "I'm surprised you don't want to tattoo 'Property of Mace Llewellyn' across my fuckin' forehead."

He looked away from her, clearing his throat, and settling her more firmly on his lap. "Uh . . . why would I want to do that?"

Before she could say anything beyond "thank you" or "you've already thought about doing that, haven't you," Mace pulled her close into his chest and held on to her. She relaxed against him and allowed herself to just be. Kind of a new feeling for her. She was usually doing something. Kicking somebody's ass. Taking somebody's name. But on this chilly Christmas night, she just wanted to sit with her . . . what? Boyfriend? Lover? House cat? Well, whatever . . . she just wanted to sit with her Mace and enjoy her life.

"You cold?"

She snuggled up closer to him. "Not at all. You?"

"Not with your hot little body next to me."

She'd never heard anyone use the words *hot* and *little* when discussing her body. But, hell, she would accept it for what it was. A Christmas miracle!

She heard her front door open and the nails of her dogs scrambling across the wood of her porch. She winced. She really needed to trim their nails. You shouldn't be able to hear your dogs coming a mile away because of their toenails.

She glanced back and watched as her father leashed them up. "Watcha doin', Daddy?"

"Taking these beasts for a walk." Her father liked her dogs, but he'd never really offered to take them for a walk before.

"Is it getting a little too much for you in there?"

He shrugged. "Something like that." He tied several plastic bags to one of the leashes. "I won't be long. As soon as your mother is done clearing up, I'll get them out of here." He smiled at Dez. Then glared at Mace. "You take care of her, boy. I'd really hate to have to kill you."

"*Daddy!*"

"Understood, sir."

"Good."

The old man walked down the stairs of Dez's porch, her huge dogs calmly walking beside him. Instinctively knowing not to rush the seventy-year-old man.

"I don't believe you two."

Mace stretched like the big cat he was, Dez still on his lap. "It's a male thing. So I don't want you to worry your pretty little head about it."

Dez growled. "I'm not going to argue this with you now. But tomorrow, I'm going to kick your ass."

Mace happily ran his hands over Dez's body. Even with all the clothes she had on, she still immediately responded to his touch. God, he loved that.

"So, I'm still going to be around tomorrow, huh?"

"I guess. The dogs seem to like you."

"Yeah. I was starting to notice that."

"Well, what did you expect when you insist on feeding them under the table?"

Mace ducked his head a bit. "Saw that, did you?"

"It's the cop thing. I'm paid to detect those sorts of goings-on."

"So . . . how long those dogs of yours going to want me around for?"

"I don't know. Let's not worry about it. We'll see how things are in the New Year."

He could work with that. "Sounds good. New Year it is."

Dez grabbed one of his hands and rubbed her fingers over it. After several minutes narrowed gray eyes locked onto him.

"Okay. Which New Year are we talking about exactly?"

Mace grinned and shrugged. "Well I didn't know I had to be specific. But any New Year thirty or forty years from now would be good."

"Tricky cat." Dez turned and wrapped her arms around his waist, her face buried in his neck. She became still, her breath against his throat. She was thinking. He could *feel it.*

"What's up, Desiree?"

"Just thinking about what'll happen when I go back to work."

"I wondered when you'd start worrying about that."

"I put in a lot of hours."

"I know."

"I'm always on call. I handle most of the big cases."

"I know."

She pulled away from him just enough to look at his face. "Okay. So you know. The question is . . . are you going to be able to deal?"

"Remember what you said to me the first night we were together?"

" 'Prove it'?"

Mace chuckled. "No. When I had you against the door."

"Oh." She nodded. "Yeah. I said, 'If you let me go now, I'm going to blow your brains out'."

He ran his hand across her thighs, then between them. "Well, it's the same deal, baby. I have no intention of letting you go." Her back straightened as he nestled his hand against her crotch. As always, she was hot and wet. Just for him. "So you might as well stop worrying about it. Besides, the shit Smitty and the team will get into, we'll need a cop on the inside."

Her eyes closed, she let him rub his fingers against her. "So, you're just using me . . . like a whore?"

"Yup. As often as I can."

"Okay. I was only checking." He adjusted his fingers and he must have hit a sweet spot because she almost came off his lap. He pulled her tight against him, her head nuzzling his throat, his other hand still playing between her thighs.

What a freakin' great Christmas.

"God, Mace," she whispered against his throat. "You better
. . . you better stop."

"No way. I wanna give you a taste of what's going to happen
to you tonight . . . all night." *And for the next forty years.*

As her body tightened around his hand, Mace realized their
separation for so many years had been necessary. They needed
to go off and do their own thing, become the people they now
were. They needed it so when they got here, they knew it was
where they belonged. Where they would always belong.

Dez gripped him tight, her mouth biting into his neck. "Oh
God, Mace," she whispered hotly against his throat. "God . . .
fuck. Fuck! Fuck! Fuck!" Mace had to bite his tongue to stop
laughing. Man, he really loved hearing her come. Even when she
whispered it.

Oh yeah. He belonged here. For the rest of his life. It took
him a long time to get here. And he had no intention of going
anywhere ever again. This woman was his. Forever.

Even if that meant he had to put up with those goddamn
dogs.

SHAW'S TAIL

Prologue

"**M**r. Shaw, you need to get up. Now."

Brendon Shaw, resting on his knees and probably dying, cringed at that voice. Like ten miles of bad road. Still, it gave him something to focus on. Something to keep him from blacking out completely. He couldn't allow himself to slow this woman down. He knew her . . . from somewhere. Remembered her scent from somewhere. Even knew that frightening voice.

More important, she was full-human. Even though the bastards who had done this to him were now getting torn apart by a Clan of hyenas, soon those hyenas would be coming back for them. For her. They were not a breed big on loyalty or kindness. They always took the weak ones. She was weak because she was human. He was weak because he was bleeding to death on their tunnel floors. So he had to get her out of here. Now.

Still, he wasn't a miracle worker. He had at least three broken ribs, a broken collarbone, broken kneecap, and an interesting amount of internal bleeding. If he could get someplace safe to allow his body to heal, he would probably survive. In fact, he'd heal up completely in a few days—if he lived through the night. He didn't think that would be happening, though. Either he'd bleed to death trying to get out of these tunnels or the hyenas would finish him off. Either way, he wouldn't allow this woman to go down with him. So this woman—*who the hell is she?*—had to go.

Shaw shook his head. "I can't."

"I can't carry you, Mr. Shaw."

Persistent little thing, wasn't she?

He tried again. "Forget me. Go." He could hold off the hyenas for a little bit. Not much fight left in him, but they'd be so busy mauling him and ripping his limbs off, she'd have enough time to get out—if she'd only *leave*.

She gave a soft sigh of annoyance. "I can't leave you here, Mr. Shaw."

Ahhh. Now he remembered. The cop. The cop with the great tits and Mace Llewellyn's scent all over her.

No wonder she wouldn't leave him. She was doing her civic duty—or whatever. Still, if she didn't move her pretty ass . . .

The scent of wolves hit him fast and hard. Great. Now he had to deal with wolves *and* hyenas, after getting the shit kicked out of him by low-class lions. Man, what a suck-ass Christmas Eve.

But the woman seemed to take the sight of a large She-wolf rather well, cocking her pretty head to one side and asking, "Sissy Mae?" The wolf yipped in response. "I'm lost and he's running out of steam."

Perhaps the biggest understatement of the night. He'd start coughing up blood any second, which was always such fun.

Screams, roars, and the lovely hyena laughing howl—*like nails on a chalkboard*—reminded him they were quickly running out of time. Mace's female had played it smart and pointed out to the head of the hyena Clan exactly who had killed her lion lover. That had focused hyena attention on the three bastards who were seconds from shooting him in the back of the head like some goddamn human. He'd find the whole turnabout thing pretty funny if he weren't dying.

The She-wolf put her head back and howled, calling to her Pack.

Either the dogs appeared quickly or he passed out for a while because suddenly he was standing on his own two feet, using the tunnel wall as leverage, and a good number of canines were standing around him. Two males shifted into human and grabbed hold of his arms. Normally, he'd never allow some canine to touch him, but under the circumstances beggars really couldn't be choosers.

Besides, he was going downhill fast. Things started going dark as soon as they took him to the stairs. Then he smelled trash, coffee, wet New York streets, and . . . and something else. Something wonderful and powerful and delicious enough to make his mouth water and his dick get hard. Kind of a miracle with him, ya know, bleeding to death. But, man, talk about giving him a reason to live.

He somehow managed to open his eyes, and that's when he looked into the prettiest face he'd ever seen. Beautiful hazel eyes more yellow than brown, a pug nose he had the feeling had been broken once or twice. Plus a vicious spattering of freckles across the bridge and a little less on her cheeks. Her lips were full and promised all sorts of wonderful skills, and when she grinned at him he knew he might be falling in love.

Then she said, "Don't you worry about nothin', darlin'. We'll take good care of you." While the rest of her Pack completely ignored their conversation, her grin turned wicked and so blatantly sexual, he thought he might come right there. Those pretty eyes swept him from head to foot. "I can't allow this body to go to waste, now can I? It would be unfair to femalekind." Her hand reached out and swept across his brow. Such gentle, cool fingers. Soft and caressing. Nothing had ever felt so wonderful before. "Close your eyes, darlin'. Sleep. When you wake up, I promise you'll be safe and breathing."

Unable to fight it anymore, Brendon Shaw closed his eyes and let wonderful blackness come. He didn't really know if he'd ever wake up again, like she said. But he did know one thing . . . he was *definitely* in love.

Chapter One

That scent hit him first. His nostril twitched and his lips drew back over his fangs. His body felt on fire.

The fever. Hurt bad enough, shifters would get a fever that nearly ripped them from the inside out. Once it finished moving through the system, though, the chances of surviving what would kill a normal human increased about eighty percent.

Brendon knew a really bad fever had him by the balls. His body shook and his hands kept clenching and unclenching into fists. It would be a long, strange trip back to normal, but his other options were much less pleasant.

And that goddamn scent only made things worse. It called to the lion buried inside him. Much more and he wouldn't be able to hold it back.

Much more and he might come all over his sheets.

Biting back a snarl, he forced his eyes open. He knew by the way everything around him looked, his eyes were lion's eyes. His hands damn near claws. He could feel the tips tearing into his palms when he clenched his hands.

He didn't care, though. He didn't care his entire body hurt. He didn't care the fever raced through him like some kind of California wildfire. No. All he cared about? The owner of that scent.

Scanning the hospital room he now realized he was safely in, he found her by the window. She sat in a chair, turned so he could see her profile. She had her oh-so-long legs stretched out in front of her and her extremely large boot-covered feet in another chair opposite from her. A big hardback book rested on her lap, but apparently it didn't hold her interest since she seemed quite entertained by throwing nuts up into the air and trying to catch them in her mouth. She wasn't very good at it, and he found that kind of surprising. Dogs could usually catch anything in their mouth.

And that's when it hit him. She was Pack.

"Shit."

The muttered word startled her and she turned to look at him, the nut she'd only moments before thrown in the air slamming into her cheek. She blinked and stared at him.

He stared back.

"What are you doin' up, darlin'?" she asked softly. "The doc said he gave you enough drugs to knock out an elephant for a week."

Oh man. That accent. Painfully Southern. Still, that accent with those eyes . . . all he could think about was her whispering how she was going to come with that goddamn accent.

She dropped a big, fat yellow highlighter and a blue pen in the middle of her book and closed it. He realized she held a textbook. He looked at her face, praying she wasn't some twenty-year-old. He liked his women a little older. A little more experienced.

No. This wasn't some boring, naïve kid who expected him to make all the decisions. He really knew it when she swung those long legs out of the chair and stood up. Like most wolf females, she was tall and powerfully built. At least six feet with strong shoulders and arms. No model thinness for this female. She had a body that could definitely handle a rough and tumble time in bed and leave a man desperate for more.

She was what his grandfather would have called a "tall drink of water." Those long legs encased in worn jeans and her T-shirt washed so many times it wouldn't take much but one little pull to rip it completely off her body.

She ambled over to him—and that's what it was, an amble—until she reached the bed. Her body close to his, she touched the back of her hand to his forehead.

"Good Lord." With a worried frown, she put one hand on the back of his neck and the other on his cheek. Such cool, soft hands. "Oh, you poor baby. You are on fire."

She had no idea.

"I better get the doc." She took a step away from him, but he grabbed hold of her arm.

"What's the matter, darlin'? Worried I won't come back?" She smiled and it almost ripped his guts out. He'd never seen anything prettier. "Well don't you let it bother you one bit. I'll be right outside talking to the doc." Her hand stroked his cheek and he briefly closed his eyes, nuzzling her hand and purring.

"Hhhhmm. That fever must be bad if you're making sounds I never heard before. The only sounds I usually hear from you cats are roaring and hissing. I better get the doc." Again she tried to pull away, and Brendon wasn't having it.

With one good yank, he dragged her onto his lap.

"Hey, hey, darlin'! Now wait a second."

Brendon pulled her around so she straddled his waist, her generous tits right in his face. To keep her where she was, he gripped her ass and pulled her hard against his growing-by-the-second erection.

"Look, hoss, I don't want to hurt you . . ."

He growled, kind of wanting her to hurt him. Within reason, of course.

". . . but I will if you don't get those big cat paws off my ass."

Ignoring her, Brendon buried his face between her breasts and breathed deep. Wow, she smelled so damn good.

"You need to stop that. I know you're sick and all but—"

He nuzzled one nipple then the other.

"Stop that!"

"Stay with me," he groaned against her breast, his voice sounding more animal than human.

"I am with you, and if you'd just let me go—"

"Fuck me."

"Okay. That's it."

Strong hands slapped against his shoulders and she pushed herself away from him as much as she could. He still had her around the waist, but her tits were suddenly out of his reach. He didn't like that one bit.

"You need to get control of yourself, hoss. Right now."

"Kiss me."

"No."

"Kiss me and I'll let you go." For the moment, anyway.

Even though her hands were strong against his shoulders, she didn't give the immediate "no" he would expect.

"I promise," he persisted. "Just kiss me."

She pushed away from him again, testing his strength. He held on tighter, not willing to release her. If she thought the fever would make him weak, she was very much mistaken. Instead, it had only made him dangerously strong.

"Dammit." She let out an exasperated rush of breath. "All right. Fine. But make it quick."

Reluctantly releasing her ass, Brendon slid his hands up until they braced against her back. He pulled her forward and he leaned in, those pretty eyes watching him, wary and a little bit curious.

Brendon brushed his lips against hers. A small, completely nonthreatening move. She didn't do anything back. Merely stared at him. Since she didn't try and rip his throat out, he came in for another pass, this time lingering a bit.

Still, she didn't make any moves one way or the other.

Pulling her close to his body, Brendon closed his mouth over hers. Her hands remained on his shoulders, tense like the rest of her, ready to push him away at any moment. He licked her bottom lip, the tip of his tongue tracing a line between. Her hands tightened on his shoulders but instead of pulling him off, she gripped him tight and kissed him back.

And holy hell . . . *what a kiss!*

Rhonda Lee Reed, you are a whore!

Yup. She could hear her momma's voice clear as a bell in her head. Telling her the same thing she told her when she found Ronnie in the backseat of Johnny Patterson's Pinto with Ronnie's favorite pair of red cowboy boots plastered to his roof.

And here she was again. Involving herself with the wrong kind of guy. Actually, the wrong species. Plus sick. The man had a horrible bout of fever.

He should be resting. He should be sipping fluids to keep his temperature down and moaning in agony. He should not have some stranger's tongue down his throat.

So she needed to stop this. Now.

But damn if the man wasn't an amazing kisser.

Ronnie should have known as soon as she looked into that gorgeous face the night before she was in trouble. Even bloody and broken from the beating he took, absolutely nothing could take away from his raw beauty. Sharp cheekbones and an almost muzzlelike nose did nothing but enhance the man's sinfully full lips. Lips Ronnie had no problem imagining all over her body.

It was when he opened his eyes and looked at her, though, that she felt every female hormone in her body suddenly zap to life. Those astounding dark gold eyes framed by coal-black lashes completely did her in. Add in that six-foot-six, nearly three-hundred-pound, muscle-bound body and Rhonda Lee Reed was in hog heaven.

So not surprising she'd lost utter control of this situation.

One second staring at the blindingly boring Engineering 101 textbook, wondering if her plan to go back to college continued to be one of the better ideas she'd recently had, and the next—in the lap of a damn cat with his tongue in her mouth.

At the end of the day, though, she blamed Sissy Mae Smith for this. Her best friend since she'd turned three, that evil female had gotten Ronnie into more trouble than seemed possible for two good ol' She-wolves from Tennessee. There were rock stars with cleaner pasts than her and Sissy. Not that they ever did drugs or anything run of the mill like that. Hell, who needed drugs when Sissy had no qualms about getting her drunk on tequila, wrapping a bungie cord around her waist, and shoving her off the side of a building with Sissy's famous "Would you just trust me" yelled after her? Then there was that slight run-in with the Mexican police, and that little town in East Germany that ordered them never to return . . .

Oh, and those Vegas cops—yeah, they wouldn't be going back to Nevada anytime soon either.

Honestly, Sissy Mae could start a knife fight in a convent.

Still, Sissy wasn't the one tussling with an overgrown house cat. She and the rest of the Smith Pack were off enjoying Christmas day while Ronnie stayed behind to babysit. Which, in the big scheme of things, was definitely something his Pride should be doing. Where were those damn females anyway? One had shown up, seeming extremely "put out," and once the doc told them Shaw would live, she'd skedaddled right out of there. Didn't even go in to check on him. And that's when Sissy Mae sucker punched Ronnie.

"We can't leave him alone," she'd said. "No one wants to wake up in a hospital alone," she'd said.

"And?" Sissy's big brother, Bobby Ray, had demanded. "What are we supposed to do about it?"

Ronnie knew how this would play out and had quickly ducked behind Mace Llewellyn to hide. Like Shaw, Mace was a big buck. So maybe if Sissy Mae couldn't see her . . .

"Ronnie Lee will stay. Won'tcha, Ronnie?"

If Ronnie thought she could get away with it, she would have spit the water she'd just gulped down, right in Sissy's face. Because now that Sissy had picked her specifically, no other She-wolf would stay. So either they all left and Shaw would wake up alone in a strange hospital or Ronnie would have to stay.

With an entire Pack to protect her, plus three big brothers, her pain-in-the-ass momma, and of course Daddy, Ronnie would never wake up in a hospital alone. The thought anyone would have to go through that, even a cat, made her feel like she had to do something.

Grudgingly, through gritted teeth, she'd agreed. "Fine. I'll stay."

Now here she was necking like a horny seventeen-year-old with a man she didn't even know. Okay, and true, this wasn't the first time she'd done this. She knew that. Hell, there were a number of .38 Special and Charlie Daniels Band concerts where she and Sissy Mae had left quite the indelible mark. But she'd promised herself three weeks ago, when she'd turned thirty, that those wild days were over. Instead she'd go and get her degree. Try staying in one place longer than five minutes, which meant no more backpacking across Europe, Asia, and Africa with a nutbag—aka Sissy Mae. And no more fooling around with shifters she barely knew.

What made this even worse? The poor bastard wasn't even in his right frame of mind. She should be pushing him off her and tucking his big—exquisite—body back into the hospital bed so he could get over that fever in peace. She definitely shouldn't be tightening her thighs around his waist and pulling him closer.

Only whores do that, Ronnie Lee.

There went her mother's voice again. Lately she hadn't been able to get that woman's damn voice out of her head. It was starting to make her crazy!

Slapping her hands against his big shoulders, Ronnie pushed him back. "Stop. Stop. We need to stop."

"Why?" he murmured, leaning in close to nibble her neck.

"Cause this is . . . um . . ." Ronnie had a hard time concentrating with him swirling his tongue against a spot right under her ear, but she had to try. "It's . . . um . . . something."

His teeth gripped the wet flesh of her neck and bit down. Not too hard but hard enough. Her fangs burst out of her gums as her body shook.

"We have to stop. Right now!" Never had she lost control like this before. Her fangs didn't just "slip out." Ronnie Lee always had control when it came to males. Always. That's what made it so easy to walk away the next morning. And she always walked away the next morning.

"Don't make me stop," he begged, his enormous hands trying desperately to pull her back against him. "Please."

Yup. Definitely caught in the fever, because lions didn't ask for anything. They sure as hell didn't say please or beg. It wasn't in their nature.

He gripped her waist and yanked her tight into his lap. She

could feel the powerful heat of his hard erection rubbing against the inside of her thigh. Much more of this and she'd be lost. Much more of this and it wouldn't matter if her momma never let her back in the family home.

Ronnie shoved him back while forcing herself in the opposite direction. His grip loosened and she scrambled away from him and off the bed.

"Don't," he ordered. "Don't leave me."

Trying to get her breath back, Ronnie shook her head. "I'm not leaving you, hoss. I'm just not having sex with you either."

He growled, baring *huge* fangs. "Why not?"

Ronnie walked back to her things and grabbed the painfully boring textbook she'd been hopelessly trying to read. "Because I have sense."

"Your sense sucks." Lion eyes stared at her from under a gorgeous mane of gold and brown hair that reached his shoulders. Shaw's big body leaned forward, and Ronnie gave him about ten seconds before he leaped off that bed at her. "Come here," he snarled.

She did, the book still in her hands. "What?" she asked once she stood near him.

Those gold eyes swept her from head to toe and back, leaving all sorts of interesting tingling in their wake. "Stay with me. In this bed. Now."

She nodded. "Okay, hoss. Okay." She stepped closer, brushing his cheek with her hand, and he closed his eyes on a sigh.

Her own fangs bared, Ronnie grabbed the eight-hundred-pound book in both hands and swung. It slammed into Shaw's jaw, knocking the man on his side and completely unconscious.

Tossing the book back across the room, Ronnie shook her head and sighed. "Damn cat."

"Is he supposed to be that horny?"

The doctor, a cutie-pie leopard, glanced back at the nurses who had to turn away so they wouldn't laugh in his face.

"Miss uh . . ."

"Ronnie. Just call me Ronnie. And answer my question, doc.

I mean, I could have been rolled in catnip the way that boy was acting."

Clearing his throat, the doctor took her arm and steered her away from the nurse's station. All of them shifters, Ronnie didn't worry about what they might overhear. And with such a light onsite staff due to the holiday, Ronnie didn't give a damn how loud she got.

"Ronnie, have you never taken care of anyone with fever before?"

"Of course I have. My daddy. My brothers. But they never . . . ya know."

The doctor quickly shook his head. "No. No. Of course not. They're family. But how did your father act around your mother when he was in the fever?"

Ronnie had to think about that. She'd been sixteen when her daddy had the fever after an ugly battle with a wild boar and she hadn't spent much time thinking about it once he recovered. But then she remembered how her momma kept throwing her out of the room. A lot.

"Oh."

Smiling, the doctor nodded. "Yeah. 'Oh.' He must be attracted to you, Ronnie. Otherwise, he probably wouldn't bother. Especially lions." He rolled light gold eyes that would freak even Ronnie out in the dark. "You know how they are."

He patted her shoulder in an almost friendly gesture. "If it'll make you feel better, I'll get one of the male nurses to watch him. He's a bear. Huge. Can easily handle him. That way you can go meet up with your Pack."

She almost agreed immediately but then remembered how he'd ordered her to not leave him. There was a desperation to his demand that had her frowning when she realized none of the Llewellyn Pride would be around to take care of him.

"I can't leave." Although she really should. "I promised him I wouldn't." Ignoring the doctor's raised eyebrow, Ronnie turned away and headed back to Shaw's private room.

"Use the call button if he gets really out of hand, Ronnie."

She waved in agreement and kept walking, turning a corner

and heading down another hallway. Considering shifters didn't need the hospital all that often, they sure did have a huge amount of space around this place.

After pushing the door to Shaw's room open, Ronnie froze. Shaw was gone, which would definitely concern her. But the two bodies lying on the floor concerned her more.

Ronnie moved closer, her nose wrinkling when she smelled that they were human. Both looked to be in their thirties, one with dark brown hair and a big mustache. The other blond with a brutal scar on his throat, like someone had taken a knife to it. She also smelled the gun oil from their weapons and grimaced at their incredibly tacky suits.

And what, exactly, had they done with her lion?

Ronnie crouched beside the men and found their guns, Glock .45s, expertly dismantled. The pieces tossed under the bed. Seemed her rich lion had some hidden skills. Shaw had battered these guys pretty good, but they'd definitely live.

She sniffed the air and locked on to Shaw's scent. Keeping her nose up, she followed Shaw down a long hallway and around a corner. As she reached the end of that hallway, she saw a door leading to a set of stairs that would take Shaw down and out of the building.

"Oh Lord." She ran the last few feet, slamming into the door and shoving it open. Her momentum kept her moving forward. Right into the back of Brendon Shaw who, for some unknown reason, felt the need to sit on the railing. She should have sent him flying over, but he only grunted when she collided into him.

Glancing over his shoulder, Shaw smiled at her. "Well, hi, sexy."

Ronnie pushed away from his back, taking a few seconds to tie his hospital gown back so she didn't keep staring at the man's perfect ass.

"Darlin', what are you doing out here?"

"Just watching the sun rise."

Brushing his hair out of his eyes, she said, "You're in a stairwell, darlin'. And the sun rose several hours ago."

"Really? And it looked so pretty, too."

She grinned and Shaw groaned in response. "You have the prettiest smile I've ever seen." Ronnie felt her heart warm for the big goofus. Until he added, "Just like that sunrise."

"Okay, hoss, let's get you back—" That scent hit her hard, causing her to pull back.

"What?" he asked, his gold eyes suddenly clear. "What's wrong?"

She briefly placed her hand over his mouth to keep him quiet and she sniffed the air again. The humans Shaw had dropped were on the move. She doubted they were still looking for Shaw after that beating, but no telling what they'd try if they stumbled across him. And Ronnie really didn't want to kill anyone today—if she could help it.

"We've gotta get you out of here," she whispered, knowing their voices would echo enough for humans to hear.

"Why are you whispering?" Shaw demanded, ten times louder than was necessary.

Again Ronnie slapped her hand over his mouth. "Keep it down!" She used her other hand to guide him back over the railing and onto the stairs.

"Come on, darlin'. We've gotta move."

She hustled him down five flights of back stairs to the exit that would lead her out the rear of the hospital. She knew she could take Shaw back into the hospital, but she wasn't real impressed with their Christmas day security if humans could sneak around the Shifter floor undetected. No, she'd be better off taking him someplace safe and away from the city.

"Stay here," she told Shaw, leaving him by the stairs.

Ronnie took several quick steps to the back door. She examined it and saw it had an alarm on it to alert the hospital staff of anyone coming in or out. Still not wanting to alert the men after Shaw, she quickly located the necessary wires and yanked them out, disconnecting the system. The hospital would probably know someone had tampered with it and their security guards would be there soon to check on it. Just enough time for her to get Shaw out.

Pushing open the door, she carefully leaned out so she could see if it was safe to leave. Thankfully, she didn't see or smell any humans lurking around and, even better, there was a taxi on the corner.

But before Ronnie could move, she felt big fingers brush against her lower back as they pulled the waistband of her jeans out. Eyes wide, she looked over her shoulder at the man staring intently down into the gap between her jeans and her skin.

"What do you think you're doing?"

"You have the cutest ass," he sighed out. Gold eyes looked up at her. She had no idea if the fever gave him that hungry look or her butt. "I could spend *hours* playing with this ass."

"Now isn't that a lovely compliment." She slapped his hand away. "Look, you need to get control of yourself."

Placing his hands against the door frame, with his enormous arms over her head, he leaned into her. Great, the man was hitting on her like they were at a disco.

"Let's get a hotel somewhere and work this out," he murmured.

"We need to get you someplace safe, cat."

"But I like you."

"Once you get through this fever, you won't even remember my name."

"I'll remember that ass, though."

Lovely.

A door slammed several flights up, and Ronnie could hear yelling. She couldn't wait anymore.

"Come on." She pulled the door open and took a quick look out, relieved to find the street still empty. Grabbing Shaw's hand, she pulled him out onto the street and toward the cab.

Once she got him bundled inside, she slammed the door shut and looked at the driver.

"Hey," she greeted.

The driver stared at her and didn't say anything. Lord, these Yankees were damn rude.

"I need to go to . . ." She pulled the slip of paper out of her back pocket and read the address off.

"That's Long Island," the driver stated. Like that would mean something to her.

Ronnie stared at the piece of paper. "This says Westbury."

"That's Long Island."

Shrugging, "What's your point?"

"He's saying," Shaw grumbled while trying to remove his hospital gown, "it's too far to drive—unless you have cash."

"I have cash."

"Lots of cash."

"I have lots of cash." Ronnie looked at the driver through the partition separating them. "And I'll give you a huge tip over the meter, but you have to drive now."

The driver continued to stare at her and Ronnie stared back. When she didn't turn away or back down, he paled a little bit and pulled out into traffic.

She didn't mean to scare him, but to be quite blunt she didn't have time for the little man's bullshit.

"Where are we going?" Shaw asked.

"My aunt's house." Ronnie pulled the gown back into place. "She moved out here years ago, and my momma gave me her address in case I had a problem." She looked at Shaw. "And you are definitely a problem."

"Sweet talker." He grinned even while his eyes closed.

Finally, the big horny bastard slept. Ronnie relaxed against the seat and prayed he didn't start shifting to lion randomly in this poor man's cab. There'd be no explaining that to the driver.

She hated going over to her aunt's for this reason. Ronnie had planned to call first, find out if her aunt even wanted to see her after all this time. It had been nearly fifteen years since Ronnie's momma and her aunt had that big knock-down-drag-out scuffle. Daddy and her oldest brother had to drag the women apart. Yet even though they hadn't spoken to each other in all that time, her momma always said, "Family is family, Ronnie Lee. You need her, you go on over there or call her."

Glancing over at the big man next to her, happily snoring away, Ronnie hoped her momma was right.

Chapter Two

Brendon sat up in the strange bed and looked around the room. He didn't recognize this place, but he liked it. It smelled good.

He'd like it better, though, if that She-wolf were here. Where could she have gone? He knew she hadn't left him. Not while the fever still raged through his body. Unlike the Pride, she wouldn't desert him. He knew that about her already.

Leaning back against the pillows, Brendon tried to remember how he got here. It had something to do with his brother. Maybe. To be honest, he couldn't remember at the moment, but his brother being involved wouldn't exactly shock him. Mitchell had been a fuckup since birth. Brendon's twin sister, Marissa, had written Mitch off a long time ago, but Brendon couldn't do that.

Had the kid gone missing? Again? Mitch, now twenty-eight, went missing a lot, it seemed. The brothers were born to different mothers but the same father. A father who raised Brendon and Marissa when their mother died during childbirth and her Pride seemed less than interested taking in the two of them. A father who had very little to do with Mitch over the years. Something Mitch couldn't forget or forgive.

The life of the Pride. It definitely wasn't for everyone.

Christ, why couldn't he remember? Was Mitch in New York? For some reason Brendon thought he might be. *Was that why I was looking for him?*

Brendon shook his head. He didn't know. Everything was so fuzzy. But he'd been in those tunnels for a reason, and probably when the fever finished with him, he'd remember why. Now, however, all he wanted was more time with that She-wolf. Fabulous kisser that one. Amazing. Lust inducing.

She wouldn't leave him.

Even though his body burned with fever, he couldn't see the harm in checking out the rest of the house. Maybe he could find She of the Wonderful Lips. Besides, he could explore a bit, couldn't he? That wouldn't be such a big deal, would it?

Ronnie smiled at the man sitting in the enormous SUV at the curb, waiting for her aunt.

"My hot date." Annie Jo Lucas winked at Ronnie.

"Very cute."

The older woman grinned. "Polar bear. I love bears."

Ronnie laughed. She'd completely forgotten how entertaining her aunt could be. And her momma had been right. Family was family. Her aunt didn't blink an eye when Ronnie knocked on her door holding on to a man only wearing a hospital gown. Annie Jo let them in, got Shaw settled, and even handed Ronnie a Christmas present she would have mailed to her after the holidays, like she'd done for fifteen years. True, Annie still had nothing good to say about Ronnie's mother but that went both ways.

Her aunt even talked about canceling her date, but Ronnie had no intention of getting between a wolf and a "proper layin." That would be plain wrong.

"What about you and that cat?" One dark brown eyebrow peaked up as her aunt smirked at her. "Hhhhmm?"

"I'm just doing my Alpha a favor."

"Oh. Is that all?"

"What does that mean?"

"Well I just find it surprising you haven't called in the Pack yet. Let them take care of Mr. I'm Gorgeous."

"Why should I ruin their Christmas?" The way hers had been ruined.

"Because when you're Pack, you're never alone."

"I'll call them in the morning. I promise."

Annie headed toward the SUV, Ronnie trailing behind. "You know, Ronnie, I really can stay. Help you with that boy. He is a big one."

"We'll be fine. Go! Have a great Christmas date."

"You have my cell number if you need me." Annie opened the door and blew a kiss at her date.

"I won't need you. I can handle him."

"Really?" Annie didn't sound like she believed that for one second.

"Yes. He's one man. I can handle one man."

Annie's date leaned down to look at Ronnie through the open passenger door. "Is that your lion?"

Ronnie spun around and watched Brendon Shaw—all seven feet and five hundred pounds of him now that he'd shifted to lion—trot down the nice quiet streets of Long Island, New York.

"Oh Lord!"

Laughing, her aunt waved at her. "Have fun, darlin'."

Ronnie didn't wait to see her aunt drive off with her date. Instead, she took off running after the big idiot.

Thankfully he wasn't really trying to get away. Instead he seemed to be just wandering . . . and romping.

She caught up to him nearly three blocks away, rolling around on some poor person's lawn.

"Shaw," she called out softly. He ignored her.

"Brendon!" she tried this time, whispering as loud as she dare, hearing music and the people inside the house laughing and having a wonderful holiday. "Come here!"

Shaw, on his back with big paws in the air, stared at her, his tongue hanging out. Lord, what was he doing?

"You heard me, mister. Come here!"

Scrambling to his feet, Shaw gave a low growl. If he started roaring, she was so screwed. But instead of roaring, he . . . he . . .

It was the calypso Christmas music coming from inside the house that set him off. Eyes wide, Ronnie watched the King of the Jungle shimmy his lion ass around on some poor human's lawn. They'd never understand those paw prints come morning.

Ronnie's head tilted to the side. *Is he* . . . ? Yup. He was doing the mambo. Paws crossing over paws. Head bopping to the beat. Thick, regal mane waving in the cold December air. He actually wasn't too bad. For a big cat doing the mambo.

Rubbing her eyes, Ronnie realized she had to focus.

"Get over here!" she commanded again, still whispering.

Shaw looked up at her, then he lowered his head toward his front paws, his big lion butt in the air.

Oh my Lord in heaven, he's in a play bow.

She hadn't done one of those since her first couple of years of being able to shift fully when she'd still been a pup. And she'd never heard of cats doing them ever.

Ronnie walked toward him, and he literally jumped back away from her.

Keep away. The big idiot wanted to play keep away.

She didn't have time for this. She had to get his crazy cat ass back in the house before someone saw him.

"Brendon, please come on."

Another step toward him, and another step back. *Dammit!*

He watched her, his gold eyes examining her from head to toe. Then his gaze locked on her tits . . . and stayed there.

Ronnie Lee rolled her eyes. No matter what breed they may be, all males were pigs.

However, she'd learned over the years that males could be controlled. With the right bait.

Looking around to make sure they were still undetected, Ronnie did what she'd promised she would never do again since that Motörhead concert when she was eighteen. She lifted her shirt and bra, flashing him.

Shaw charged her head-on, and Ronnie barely had time to pull her clothes back into place before she gave a surprised squeal and tore off back to her aunt's house. Lifting her legs, she cleared the eight-foot fence that cordoned off her aunt's yard from her neighbor's. Ronnie made it up the back porch stairs when she heard Shaw right on her ass. She got inside, throwing the door closed behind her, hoping to slow him down, but he rammed right into it, knocking it off its hinges. She winced, realizing she'd have to fix that before her aunt got home.

Ronnie squealed again as humongous paws slapped against her hips, forcing her to the living room floor. She scrambled onto her back, only to realize she had a naked man on top of her with his head under her T-shirt.

"God, your breasts are beautiful," he rasped. "Can I play with them for a little while?" He planted a small kiss against the side of her lace-covered nipple.

"No, you cannot. Now get off me!" She slapped at his head, trying to get him to let her go. The snoring, however, suggested he wasn't going anywhere until she moved him herself.

"Lord!" she snarled. "I am gonna kick Sissy's ass when I see her."

Panting, Ronnie scrambled out from under Shaw. She intended to think her breathing problem merely an outcome of the outrageous situation she currently found herself in and not because the cat had the softest lips known to man or God.

She stood up and cracked her neck to the side. Grabbing Shaw's hand, she dragged him across the floor and up the stairs back to the bedroom.

And the entire time she cursed Sissy Mae Smith's name.

Okay. She had to stop feeling sorry for herself. True, this wasn't how she'd wanted to spend her Christmas—fixing doors and chasing after lions—but she was here and she just had to deal with it. Like her momma would so eloquently put it, "Oh, get the fuck over it, Rhonda Lee."

Sitting at her aunt's kitchen table with her head in her hands, Ronnie stared down at the rapidly chilling cup of hot chocolate she'd made herself. She hadn't even bothered to put in the marshmallows.

How, exactly, did she get herself into these kinds of situations? First off, she knew better than to trust Sissy Mae. Second . . . oh hell. There was no second.

All of this, though, was a perfect example of how she needed to change her life. School seemed like a good start. She already had interviews set up with a few of the local universities after the New Year holiday. Hopefully they'd ignore that freshmen year grade report from twelve years ago. It had not been a thing of beauty, and her momma's reaction . . . well, She-wolf fights were never pretty. A day after the fight, Ronnie and Sissy Mae took off for Europe with their backpacks and five hundred bucks between them. Ronnie had seen a lot of the world because of Sissy's constant drive to keep moving. England, France, Germany, Italy . . . When they got done with the romance language countries, they moved on to Asia, Africa. Wherever. Wherever two She-wolves could get into trouble, they were there.

Then six months ago Ronnie Lee woke up with a German wolf whose first name she knew—and not much else. "How many times," she'd asked herself in the shower that morning, "how many times can you wake up like this?" That's when she decided she wouldn't anymore. She would no longer wake up with strangers. She'd no longer get into barroom brawls. She'd no longer randomly challenge other Packs for dominance. She'd no longer look for trouble.

Three weeks ago Ronnie Lee turned thirty and it looked like all was well on its way. For a while she'd even had a steady boyfriend. But that only lasted a month. She'd brought the poor Beta home and her daddy and brothers had kicked the living tar out of him. He hadn't actually done anything wrong either, her daddy simply didn't like him. Not surprisingly, that Beta wolf never returned her calls after that particular family dinner. So, she'd decided a few days later, she'd lay off men for a while. She had toys, and she was a woman not afraid to use her fingers. Really, what else did you need a male for except to fuck and breed with? And she was holding off on the breeding until she got her act together.

Unfortunately, kissing Shaw was like slipping back into her old patterns. Even worse, the cat had a Pride she had to worry about. Cheetahs, leopards, even tigers were mostly loners. Yet Pride females were real protective about their Breeding Males.

Of course, how protective could they be when they hadn't

even shown up at the hospital? Mace had told her Shaw must be on his way out if they didn't bother to check on him. Apparently he'd bred two healthy cubs with a couple of the Llewellyn females and that's pretty much all they wanted or needed from him.

"Nice," she muttered out loud, feeling bad for Shaw.

She spent a few moments wallowing in *his* misery—apparently her own wasn't enough—when she felt his extremely hot breath against her neck. Ronnie Lee sat up straight and slowly turned her head. He'd shifted back to lion. It amazed her how many times a body could shift while going through the fever. She'd lost count of how many Shaw had gone through. Shame there was no way to control it. Maybe then Ronnie wouldn't have one of the biggest cats in the world staring at her like a slab of prime rib.

That's what she got for sitting around her aunt's kitchen feeling sorry for herself. She never even heard the big bastard come into the suddenly very tiny room.

"Why are you out of bed? Are you *trying* to irritate me?"

He stared at her for several long seconds, then his enormous tongue came out of his mouth and slashed her from chin to forehead.

"Oh! Dammit." She wiped at her face, disgusted. "Don't do that."

Shaw took a step closer and nuzzled her under the chin, his massive gold and brown mane going right up her nose.

Trying to push him away but unable to see with all that damn cat fur in her face, "Bed! Go back to bed!"

"Come with me."

Startled, Ronnie Lee opened her eyes and found Shaw had shifted yet again. Now he kneeled naked and so damn gorgeous in front of her.

Ronnie never thought she'd go for these gold guys. They were perfectly tanned without all that messy skin cancer concern. Not an ounce of fat on that body. His face . . . perfect. Even with all the bruises and still healing lacerations, the man was so damn beautiful.

"Come to bed with me, sexy," he purred in her ear. "I promise . . ."

She waited for more. With none forthcoming, she had to ask, "You promise what?"

"Anything you want." His head dipped a bit, and his beautiful gold eyes seared through her. "Absolutely anything."

Lord, help her.

Taking his hand, Ronnie stood up. "Come on," she coaxed. "Let's get to bed."

He purred and followed.

Brendon woke up back in the room he'd found himself in five minutes ago . . . or was it five hours? To be honest, he was no longer sure. It didn't matter. He needed to get up and face the day . . . or was it night? Whatever.

Trying to sit up, Brendon quickly realized someone had bound his arms and legs to the four-poster bed.

"What the fuck?"

"Oh, look. The idiot of the jungle awakens."

Brendon blinked, trying to focus on the woman talking to him. She stood at the end of the bed, arms crossed under her breasts, glaring at him as if he'd shot her dog.

"Where am I?"

"Westbury."

Voice cracking, he yelped, "Long Island?" Why the hell would he be on Long Island?

"It was the only safe place I could think of."

Brendon nodded, quickly deciding not to care where he was as long as this female was with him. "Fair enough." He tugged at the ropes. "Think you can let me go now?"

Without a word, she walked around so she stood on his right side. Her hand slapped hard against his forehead.

"Ow."

"You're still feverish. Probably at the tail end, but I ain't takin' any more chances with you. I think I've chased enough lions around New York today. So you'll stay put until that fever ends."

Man, talk about pissed. He didn't know what he did wrong, but he didn't want her to be mad at him.

"I'm sorry."

"For what?"

"For whatever I did that pissed you off."

Finally, she gave a grudging smile. "Well, at least you don't try and bullshit your way out of things."

Brendon glanced around the room. He didn't know where he was or how he got here. All he had to anchor him during all this was this woman and her wonderful scent. "What day is it?" Something told him it was an important day.

"December twenty-fifth."

Wincing, Brendon stared up at her. *That explains the whole pissed thing.* "It's Christmas?" She gave a brief nod. "I'm sorry. I'm sorry you're stuck here with me and not with your Pack."

Her face softened a bit at that and, to his surprise, she sat on the bed next to him, her head resting against his outstretched arm. Damn, but the woman smelled so freakin' good.

"Don't let it bother you none." She patted his knee, then her eyes narrowed and she glared at him. "And would you control that thing, please."

Brendon glanced down at his lap. His cock pushed hard and demanding against the sole white sheet covering him from waist to toes.

"That is not my fault." He grinned. "That's your fault."

"It is not my fault. You have no self-control."

"You were the one who touched me intimately."

"I patted your knee."

"See? Intimate."

She laughed and shook her head. Baby-soft brown hair brushed his arm. "You're an idiot."

"Sometimes." Brendon relaxed back, letting his arms hang a bit so they didn't get tired. "Look, I really appreciate everything you've done for me tonight. I know it wasn't easy."

She shrugged like she'd taken care of hopped-up-on-fever lions every day of the week.

"I guess I owe you a Christmas present, huh?" he asked.

"A Christmas present? For little ol' me? What would you get me?"

"What do you want?"

She snuggled in a bit closer to him, and he threatened his cock with bodily harm if it even thought about rearing up again. She-wolves didn't snuggle up to just anybody, and he didn't want to scare her off.

"Let's see—rich guy asking me what I want for Christmas." She squinted at him. "You are rich, right? You're not living off those Pride females, are ya?"

Not in this lifetime. "No. I'm not living off them."

"Oh, well then, that opens up so many possibilities. I've always wanted a Maserati."

"A Maserati? Little tall for that, aren't you?"

She turned glittering hazel eyes his way. "And what does that mean?"

"That you're tall. Maybe too tall for the car."

"That better be all you mean," she muttered.

"No, I'm sure your feet can fit in there fine."

"Now see! There it is. We are not to discuss my feet." They both glanced down at the cowboy boots resting on the bed. Christ, those feet *were* big. But those boots she had on were sexy as hell. "They get me where I need to go."

"How could they not?"

"You do understand I have no problem leaving your naked ass out on the road."

"I understand."

"So you be nice to me."

"Yes, ma'am."

"Now you are gettin' me that Maserati. And jewelry. From that blue box place."

Brendon forced himself to frown so he wouldn't laugh instead. "Do you mean Tiffany?"

"Yeah. That place. I want diamonds and platinum. Necklaces and bracelets should do me fine."

"You don't really seem like the jewelry-wearing type." She didn't even have on earrings.

"I'm not. But I can sell it and put the cash in the bank." She looked at him. "It seems wrong just to take cold hard cash from you."

"I'm glad you have a moral standing."

"I do. I haven't killed you yet. Although it's crossed my mind several times this evening."

"Thank you for not killing me."

"You know, you could forget about the car and jewelry if you did me one little favor."

"Which is?"

"The next time you see a Pack, you don't think to yourself 'Hey, look at them dogs.' You think, 'Ahh. Wolves. The mightiest of the mighty. The bravest of the brave.'"

"I'd really rather buy you the car . . . and an island."

She poked her elbow into his side; a lesser man would have definitely grunted from pain. "Bigot."

"Cat hater."

She laughed and Brendon nuzzled her neck with his nose. "You smell good."

Swatting at his face as if he were a wasp, "Stop it. Stop it. Stop it. You're not helping me keep my semblance of cool control."

"Why would I?"

"Typical."

He shrugged as best he could in his bindings. "I like you. I don't feel bad cause I like you."

"You don't like me. Your fever likes me. I know once you're through this you'll go back to being an asshole cat." Leaning close to him, her lips near his, "And won't that be the fun morning-after for me."

"We can deal with the morning-after later. Let's talk about the here and now."

"Forget it, Garfield." She made to slip off the bed and his strength surged powerful and strong. He snapped the rope binding on his left arm and quickly grabbed her arm, holding her in place.

"Don't go."

"I knew I should have used the chains my aunt has in her basement. Why she has those chains I don't wanna know." She grabbed his hand and tried to pry his fingers off. "Now if you'll get your dirty cat paws off me—"

With a short growl, Brendon snapped the rest of his bindings and had her under him in seconds.

To be quite honest, nothing had ever felt so right before in his entire life.

Once again she had to ask herself, *How do you get yourself into these situations?*

True, she never should have sat so close, but he'd seemed quite lucid and she liked talking to him. There were few outside her Pack or family she had any interest in actually having a conversation with.

It definitely didn't help that she really liked this man being between her legs. She liked it way more than she should.

Big fingers dug into her scalp and then massaged. Without meaning to, she growled, her body immediately responding. In fact, if the bastard moved two inches lower, he'd find her happy spot and her leg would start shaking. How embarrassing would that be?

"You . . . you need to stop." *And I need to stop panting. And moaning.*

"I don't wanna stop." Those incredibly soft lips skimmed across her cheek. "And I don't think you want me to stop."

"Of course I want you to stop," she groaned, her hands gripping his shoulders and pulling him closer. "I want you to stop right now."

"Would it help if I said I can't control myself?" He kissed her neck and licked it, a purr rumbling up from his chest. "My animal instincts have taken over and there's nothing you or I can do about it. I've gone completely wild."

"No one is going to believe—"

Shaw kissed her, cutting off her words and making her writhe beneath him while his hips pumped against hers. With a sheet and her jeans and panties between them, this shouldn't have done much for her, but she moaned and gasped every time he pushed against her.

Ronnie spread her thighs wider, wrapping her legs around his hips, begging him for more without saying one word.

Shaw threaded his fingers with hers and pushed her hands over her head, pinning them there. The whole time they kept grinding their hips together, moving as if Shaw were inside of her. Fucking her.

He sucked on her tongue, and the sensation slammed into her clit and danced over her entire body.

She didn't try and stop him anymore. She couldn't.

Ronnie met each of his thrusts with her own until she felt an orgasm miraculously tearing up her spine and pouring out through her fingers and toes. Her grip tightened on his hands, her body arching into his.

"God!" he gasped against her mouth. "God!"

Then they were both coming. Both screaming and grinding against each other until Ronnie thought for sure she'd pass out right then. Pass out and give this man the biggest ego boost of his life.

While small spasms rippled through them and they fought to control their breathing, they clung to each other until Ronnie fell into an exhausted sleep.

Chapter Three

Brendon stretched and sighed. He'd never felt better. He'd survived the fever, his wounds completely healed except for some residual scarring. Plus he had a warm, wet woman he had every intention of spending the entire day in bed with. He just had to find out her name.

He heard movement from the corner of the room and turned over expecting to see his long-limbed She-wolf waiting for him. Preferably naked.

"Morning, sunshine."

Sitting up straight, Brendon barked, "What the hell are you doing here?"

Mace Llewellyn grinned at him from the safety of his corner. "I'm here to bring you back to the city so you don't overstay your welcome."

"Where is she?"

"Where's who?"

Brendon tossed off the sheet covering his naked body and stood up. "You know damn well who I mean! *Where is she?*"

With a bored sigh, Mace stood up. "I'm going downstairs. You've got ten minutes to shower and get your ass in the car. After that I'm heading back into the city and to Dez whether you're in the damn car or not." Mace walked out without another word, and Brendon stood in the middle of the room two seconds from roaring his intense displeasure at this current situation.

Quickly showering and putting on the sweat clothes Mace

brought for him, Brendon followed the irritating bastard's scent outside and into the black SUV at the corner. Without waiting for him to ask, Brendon gave Llewellyn directions to Marissa's place. The hotel could wait.

They drove in silence until they hit the Long Island Expressway, then he couldn't stand it anymore.

"What's her name?"

"Who?"

"Don't fuck with me, Llewellyn. Who is she?"

"She's Pack and way out of your league."

He already knew that. Didn't mean he wouldn't go for her. That he wouldn't get her. Lions were smart. A female like that came along once in a lifetime. He wasn't dumb enough to let her get away from him.

"What's her name?"

"None of your business. Oh. Sorry. I meant *Miss* None of Your Business."

Brendon rolled his eyes and stared out the window. He'd never been happier about the ending of his Pride life until this moment. Damn Llewellyns.

"So why were you in the hyena tunnels anyway?"

Tempted to say "none of your business," Brendon decided to hold his rapidly growing temper. "I've been looking for my brother."

"You have a brother?"

"Yeah. Younger. And a twin sister, too."

"Really?"

Brendon let out a deep sigh. "Yes. Really."

"I'm so . . ." After several moments, Llewellyn shrugged. ". . . not interested."

"I know. But I appreciate you asking."

"You're welcome."

Brendon watched Long Island speed by as Llewellyn broke several state and county laws rushing back to the city and, most likely, to his big-breasted woman.

When they hit the Queens Midtown Tunnel, Brendon asked, "Do you have any clients yet?"

"Clients?"

"Yeah. Your sister said you were starting a security business or something."

"Missy told you that?"

"Yeah. Right. We have deep, long conversations, me and Miss. Allie told me."

"Oh. Yeah. We're pulling it together now. Why?"

"Want a client?"

"You want me to find your brother?"

"No. I want you to find out *about* my brother. The little shit is hiding something from me, and I want to know what."

"Have you tried asking him?"

"When I actually talk to him. But he won't tell me shit."

"When was the last time you heard from him?"

"Every couple of days he leaves me a voice mail. Sometimes he'll catch me on the phone. But he won't tell me where he is. Last time I actually spoke to him was about two weeks ago. Then Petrov told me the night before he died that he saw Mitch at the Chapel. I was hoping he'd come back. That's why I was there."

"Okay. We'll see what we can find out."

"Thanks."

"And we're going to charge you out the ass."

Brendon looked back out the window, wondering where his long-legged beauty was at the moment—and if she was naked. "Yeah. I figured."

Ronnie patted her pockets, quickly realizing she didn't have her room key. But when it appeared in front of her face, she wasn't exactly surprised. The entire Pack had keys to each others' rooms.

Pack living—definitely not for everyone.

Grasping it, she turned and smiled up into the handsome face of Bobby Ray Smith. "Thanks, Bobby Ray. Where'd ya find it?"

"At the hospital with your sweater and your jacket and your big fancy textbook." He stared at her for a moment, then said,

"You should have called us, little girl. As soon as things turned bad, you should have called us."

"I handled it, didn't I?"

"That's not the point. You know how some get during the fever. Things could have gone very bad for you, darlin'."

"I handled it."

She loved Bobby Ray, but she had enough big brothers in her life. She didn't plan to add any more to the list. "I'm tired, Bobby Ray."

"Fair enough. Sorry if I pushed."

Only Bobby Ray would think of that as pushing. To the Reeds that was general conversation over family dinner before the mauling started. "Don't worry. If you'd really annoyed me, I would have gone for your throat by now."

"I always wondered where your brothers got those scars on their necks from."

"Are they coming out here?" she asked, dreading the answer.

"Probably. At least to visit before they decide. Splitting from a Pack is never easy. And my daddy will make sure it ain't easy for them." He nudged her with his shoulder, almost sending her flying through her hotel room door. "Don't you want 'em out here?"

"I love 'em, but you know my kin. They crowd me. With them around, I'll never get laid again."

"You say these things to me, knowing it's going to make me insane."

She frowned. "Why should it?"

"Because you and my baby sister have been joined at the hip since before y'all could walk. What one did, so did the other. And I prefer to think of Sissy Mae Smith as virginal and un-touched."

He let her laughter continue until she literally began to roll back and forth across the floor, then he hauled her up and stood her back in front of her door.

"I don't want to know—ever—what y'all have been up to since I went into the Navy."

"And we have no intention of telling you, darlin'." Ronnie wiped the tears from her eyes and let out a happy sigh. That had been the best laugh she'd had in days.

"I still don't know why the Pack let you go. Y'all were too young to be out on your own."

"They didn't have any choice. Besides, we snuck away in the middle of the night. By the time they realized we were gone, we were halfway across the Atlantic."

Bobby Ray stared at her for a moment. "If your brothers join my Pack, will you leave?"

Ronnie sighed. "I can't say it hadn't crossed my mind. I love them boys. You know I do. But my big brothers can be overwhelming men. When they're around, I no longer exist. I'm just 'baby sister of the Reed Boys.'"

"You know it won't be like that here. With or without your brothers, Rhonda Lee, I want you as part of this Pack. You're a mighty fighter and you are the one person who has a modicum of control over my baby sister. Most important, you're a good person, Ronnie Lee. And a mighty She-wolf. Stay and be part of this Pack because you belong. We both know you do."

She belonged. Not as daughter of Clifton Reed or baby sister of the Reed Boys, but because Bobby Ray Smith understood her worth. That meant more to her than anything ever had before.

On impulse, Ronnie went up on her toes and kissed him on his cheek.

"What was that for?" Bobby Ray smirked. "You're not falling in love with me, are ya, Ronnie Lee? I don't wanna have to break yet another young She-wolf's heart, darlin'."

Ronnie crossed her eyes. "You're gonna make a great Alpha, Bobby Ray. But you're an idiot."

"It's all right, darlin'. I understand." He patted her shoulder. "So many have loved and lost me. I couldn't expect you to be any different."

"You're right, Bobby Ray. I'm madly in love with you. My heart may never recover."

"That explains it then."

"Explains what?"

Bobby Ray scratched her head affectionately and walked off, tossing over his shoulder, "That reek of cat you've got all over you. Cheatin' on me with some cat to push me from your thoughts and heart. Cat ho."

Startled into action, Ronnie darted into her hotel room and made a beeline to the shower, ignoring the pile of Christmas presents waiting for her and tearing off her clothes as she went.

One thing for Bobby Ray to notice such a thing, but if her fellow She-wolves smelled a big, arrogant, delicious lion all over her, they'd never let her live it down.

Brendon's twin sister opened her front door, her eyes going wide at the sight of him.

"What in holy hell—"

"Don't ask." He pushed past her and walked into her apartment.

"Don't ask? How can I not ask?"

Dropping facedown on his sister's couch, Brendon said, "I don't want to talk about it."

"I guess not." He could hear her settle in her favorite king chair, her feet on the ottoman in front of it. "After getting your ass kicked like this."

Brendon's head snapped up and he glared. "I did not get my ass kicked. I got ambushed. And they had guns."

She frowned. "Hyenas or wolves?"

Brendon grabbed a pillow, resting his head on it. He did love his sister's furniture. They had the same taste when it came to their comfort. "Not in this lifetime. There's no hyena or wolf alive that can do this to me. No, it was lions."

"Lions? Lions had guns? Are you sure?"

"I was sure when they had the barrel pointed at the back of my head." His sister fell deadly silent, and Brendon looked up again to see the rage on her face. Crap. He didn't mean to get her this pissed off. Once pissed off, it was hard to rein his twin in. "Rissa, calm down."

"Calm down?" She stood up. "I wanna know who did this to you. I wanna know right now." Then Marissa Shaw let loose with a litany of curses that reminded Brendon that although his family swam in money now, it hadn't been long ago when he and his sister ran the streets of Philly causing more problems then seemed right considering their age at the time. It took a lot of work to get to this point. A lot of work to change the Shaw name from lower level lions to prime breeders.

Brendon sat up, but before he could say anything, his sister slapped her hand against his forehead.

"Ow."

"Do you still have the fever? Christ, when did this happen?"

"Christmas Eve, and I already went through the fever."

"Christmas Eve?"

"Okay, you really need to stop repeating everything I say. It's getting on my nerves."

"It's the twenty-sixth. *Where the fuck have you been for—*"

Brendon put his hand over his sister's mouth. "If you'll shut up for two seconds, I'll tell you." He hadn't wanted to talk about it, but now he had no choice. It was either that or listen to the rants of a crazy lioness.

She sat on the coffee table in front of Brendon. "Start talking."

A long hot shower turned out to be exactly what Ronnie Lee needed to calm her nerves and her worries. As she brushed her teeth and combed out her wet hair, she realized her time with Brendon Shaw had only been a fluke. A momentary loss of sanity. No matter where Sissy and she may have traveled over the years, they always made it home for the Thanksgiving and Christmas holidays. This turned out to be the first year she'd ever spent a holiday away from her kin or her Pack.

Lonely. She felt lonely. That's all. But in a few more days it would be New Year's Eve. She'd hang out with her Pack at some swank party in the hotel, get ridiculously liquored up, and this shitty holiday would be long behind her.

So, as of this moment, she would stop feeling sorry for herself and forget this particular, cat-related incident ever happened.

Giving herself a brief nod in the mirror, she headed back out to the bedroom and her open suitcase. She dug through the pile of clothes until she found a worn pair of baggy cotton shorts and a loose T-shirt. She pulled them on, shook her wet hair out, and headed toward the door.

With keycard in hand, she walked across the hallway and knocked on the opposite door. In less than a minute it opened and Sissy Mae Smith grinned at her friend. "Well, hey, darlin'. How did last night—ow!"

Ronnie twisted Sissy's nose until her friend bent to the side, then she slapped her hand off, hitting Sissy's nose in the process.

Turning on her heel she stalked back to her hotel room. And as she slammed the door she could hear Sissy's laughing response, "I *knew* you'd like him!"

"And that's the whole story," Brendon finished.

For several long moments his sister stared at him, and then she said, "You let a dog take you to Long Island?"

Brendon's head dropped forward. "That's all you have to say?"

"What else is there to say? Other than I thought you had better sense than that."

"What about Mitch?"

"What about him? He's a scumbag. I keep telling you that and you keep ignoring me."

"Our baby brother may be in trouble. How can you not care?"

"Like this." Marissa stood up and started to walk away. Brendon grabbed her arm.

"He's our kid brother, Rissa. We protect him like we protect each other."

"He's a thief and a liar and hangs around degenerates. He's not our problem. Now do you want a soda or not?"

"Not."

"Fine." She pulled her arm away and went to the kitchen, returning with a Sprite. "You want something to eat?"

"No."

"If you're saying no because you're pouting, you might as

well give it up because your hunger will win out. It always wins out."

Dammit. She was right. Brendon felt starved for food, like he hadn't eaten in months rather than a day or so.

"Fine. I'll eat. But I still think you're being cold about all this."

Marissa made an impatient noise from the kitchen. "Why? Because I'm not crying and panicking over Mitch?"

Brendon followed her in. "Yes."

"It's called tough love. You should look into it."

"No. It's called cutting yourself off from your baby brother."

"The kid's a fuckup. He's always been a fuckup. It's not going to change."

"He's still our brother."

"Tragically."

Brendon shook his head. "Give it up, sis. I think you care but you don't want me to know about it."

"I care for few things in this world. You are lucky to be one of those few, but I can only stretch myself so far."

Sitting down at her kitchen table, Brendon glanced out the big picture window that had an astounding view of the Manhattan skyline. Rissa's apartment took up the entire top floor, but she owned the building. It still amazed Brendon when he thought about where they came from, their lives in Philly. The two of them getting into situations they probably should have done some jail time for. At least some community service. They didn't talk about those days anymore. Some days it seemed Rissa liked to pretend those times never happened. That she and Brendon were somehow different from Mitch. They were different. They were lucky.

"I'm not giving up on him."

"Whoop-de-fucking-do for you." She slammed a plate full of her homemade lasagna in front of him. "Here. I made this last night. Should keep you until I finish making the ribs I have in the frig."

"Thanks." Picking up his fork, Brendon started inhaling—he wouldn't say he actually ate in the dictionary sense of the word—the delicious food. So focused on his food, it took him a moment to realize he'd felt his sister's lips kiss the top of his head.

Looking up from his meal, "What was that for?"

"For not getting your ass killed. Try and keep that theme going for me, will ya?"

"I'll see what I can do."

Brendon bent over his food again and didn't let his sister see him smile. She cared. She cared more than she ever wanted to. About him *and* Mitch.

Chapter Four

Her plan had been a simple one. Spend the evening with her fellow She-wolves. Enjoy a beer or two and relax. But that fifth shot of tequila . . . that fifth shot of tequila did her in.

She should have known better. Wolves couldn't handle their liquor. You could call it their kryptonite. If Ronnie had been lucky, she would have spent the whole night throwing up in some fancy club's bathroom. Luck, however, didn't seem to be on her side these days. Because if she had any luck she'd be unable to speak.

"I mean, that mane of hair. I could spend hours letting him rub that mane all over my body."

The three remaining She-wolves and Sissy nodded their heads. They'd lost the other five earlier in the evening when they wandered off to another club or back to the hotel.

"The man is gorgeous, there's no doubt about that." Sissy Mae poured Ronnie another shot of tequila. "What I don't understand is why you didn't make that move, darlin'. You had that big house all to yourself and a naked man desperate to get into your pants."

"A desperate man sick as a dog. I'm sorry but I don't think I could have handled that coyote ugly morning when he realized he'd fucked a wolf."

"What makes you think he'd give a shit? A male is a male, sweetie." Marty, a mated She-wolf about twenty years their senior, sipped her Russian vodka. "Trust me when I say wolf, lion, cheetah, jackal, or any of the other breeds don't give a shit when a pussy is wet and willing."

The females looked at Marty and she casually shrugged her shoulders. "What?"

Supposedly, Marty came with Bobby Ray only to help out, but Ronnie had the feeling Marty would stay. Her mate would go wherever she went, and she'd never gotten along too well with the Smith She-wolves her own age. Not surprising once Marty's past came out. She'd lived on the wild side for years, mowing through most of the Smith Pack males before settling down with her one true love and having a few pups. She never discussed her past in detail, but a few tidbits she'd dropped here and there over the last few months they'd all been hanging together convinced Ronnie and Sissy that the woman hadn't merely lived on the wild side, but instead owned prime real estate there.

Still, it gave Ronnie hope she could put her own wild times behind her and settle down with a mate who didn't irritate her too much and some pups.

"Marty's right, darlin'," Sissy insisted. "You're real pretty. Got good strong thighs. And you've got oral skills most men would kill for."

Now everyone turned and looked at Sissy Mae.

"That's lovely, Sissy," Marty sighed out.

"I was only complimenting her."

"Compliments like that create hookers."

Ronnie waved her hands, accidentally slapping herself in the face. "It doesn't matter. I'm no longer looking for the occasional sleeping arrangement. I'm looking for . . . for . . ."

"For what?" Sissy asked, and she looked like she really didn't want to know.

"Love?" Gemma, Sissy's distant Smith cousin, asked with a sad amount of hope on her pretty face.

Ronnie and Sissy snorted. "Love?" Ronnie couldn't keep the disbelief out of her voice. That word more foreign to her than Sanskrit. "No. I'd rather have rabies than be in love."

"Why?"

"Because at least you can get over rabies with some shots."

Marty laughed and shook her head. She seemed to be the only one who didn't appear remotely drunk and she'd polished off an entire bottle of vodka by herself. "Trust me, pups, one day you'll find that male who makes you love him, care for him, and want to stab him in the face all at the same time. And your lives will never be the same."

Ronnie and Sissy both shuddered in horror.

"We're so drunk," Gemma observed for no apparent reason.

"We're not drunk," Sissy corrected. "We're blasted off our asses."

Taking her shot of tequila in one gulp before slamming the glass on the table, Ronnie offered, "I don't want my life to pass me by."

Filling Ronnie's glass again, Sissy promised, "It won't."

"It's already started. It's whizzing by like a freight train."

"So? We've had some great times, darlin'," Sissy reminded her.

"We have. But I'm sorry if I don't still wanna be running wild with you when I'm fifty. Life cannot be a series of great fucks followed by barroom brawls."

Gemma scratched her head. "And why is that?"

"When you get past your twenty-fifth birthday, Perky Tits, you can ask me that again."

Looking down at her chest, Gemma grinned. "Well I'll be . . . they *are* perky!"

Sissy grabbed Ronnie's arm before she could launch herself at the adorable little She-wolf.

"Okay." Sissy kept a good grip on Ronnie while slamming back another shot of tequila. "Perhaps we should think about heading back to the hotel."

"Why?" Gemma whined.

In answer, Daria, Ronnie's second cousin twice removed, opened her mouth to say something, and then her head slammed right into the table when she passed out.

"Yup," Marty agreed. "Time to go."

They got two cabs back to the hotel and either underpaid the drivers by ten dollars or overpaid them by a thousand. Unfortunately, they weren't really sure which, but the cabbies seemed happy and Marty kept snickering.

Arms around each other, they stumbled back into the Kingston Arms. A fancy, shifter-owned-and-operated establishment. Unlike some resort towns their kind owned, here the Pack couldn't exactly go running around in their animal form since full-humans stayed at the hotel, too. They had no way to keep them out. But shifters received the best of everything at a very low rate.

"Oooh. Bar." Sissy Mae stumbled into the fancy hotel bar, but Ronnie and Marty caught up to her.

"Oh no you don't. Upstairs with you," Marty chastised. "She is so going to regret this when she wakes up tomorrow."

"I'm relatively certain we all will." Together they stumbled to the elevators, and as they waited, Ronnie glanced back and realized Marty studied a large glass case by one of the bars. Ronnie had barely noticed it the many times she'd passed by it. It looked like a typical trophy case with important hotel awards or whatever. "Whatcha lookin' at?"

"I'm reading this article on the owners of this hotel."

"Fascinating." Ronnie looked at Sissy and they both rolled their eyes.

"Oh it is," Marty enthused. "Here. Let me read you a bit . . ."

"Please don't," Sissy muttered in Ronnie's ear.

Clearing her throat, Marty began reading, " 'The Kingston Hotel in downtown New York was only a few days from the wrecking ball when entrepreneurs Alden, Brendon, and Marissa Shaw purchased the old hotel and turned it around. Since then the still family-owned Kingston Arms Hotels have become exclusive havens for the very wealthy, with establishments located around the world. The elder Shaw makes his home at all of the locations from time to time.' " Taking a deep breath and not even bothering to hide her smile or laughter, Marty finished with, " 'Only son *Brendon* still lives in Kingston Arms New York.' "

Ronnie stared at the older woman. "No. Way."

"Sorry, darlin'. Looks like you'll be seeing him again whether you want to or not."

"You know, you could enjoy this a little less."

"I could." Marty stepped into the elevator, holding the door open for the rest of the She-wolves. "But I plan to enjoy this to the full extent of my capabilities."

"I hate you," Ronnie mumbled as she shoved her cousin inside.

"Oh, I know you'd like to, darlin'. I know you'd like to."

Brendon glared down at the top of his sister's head. "Are you crying?"

"No," she muttered while discreetly trying to wipe her eyes.

"You are," he accused, pushing her off his arm where she'd been resting. "You're crying at *Born Free*!"

"Well, it's just so sad."

"You cry at a movie but not about your brother?"

"Why would I cry about him?"

Brendon returned his gaze to the television. He knew he should have gone back to the hotel but, to be honest, he wasn't really in the mood to be on his own. So here he sat, watching *Born Free* and listening to his sister cry. Not exactly what he'd call a wild evening.

He could have gone out. Probably could have found some companionship, too. But he didn't want that. Brendon didn't want to wake up next to a no-name piece of ass he didn't want to talk to in the morning. At twenty-three that was all he could think about. At thirty-three it was starting to get a little creepy.

"You're thinking about her again, aren't you?"

Busted. "What are you talking about?"

"Don't bullshit me, Bren. You're thinking about Benji."

"Don't call her that."

Now that the movie ended, Marissa grabbed the remote and changed to *Resident Evil*. Not exactly *Citizen Kane*, but better than *Born Free*. At least she wouldn't cry.

"What do you care what I call her? When did you get so protective of dogs?"

"Since they saved my ass."

"Yeah, but that was more Llewellyn."

"He may have got them down there, but they didn't have to help me. You and I both know some Packs would have happily left my ass there for the hyenas."

"Yeah."

"And she didn't have to stay with me in the hospital. She didn't have to protect me from those two guys who snuck into my room. She sure as hell didn't have to take me to her aunt's house. So do you think we can elevate this Pack beyond dog status?"

"Christ! Okay. Okay. Geez. When did you get a soul, anyway?"

"Just do me a favor and lay off."

"Fine. Whatever."

"Fine. Whatever," he imitated back to her. The snarl he received would have scared a lesser man.

Chapter Five

Brendon and Marissa reached for the last grapefruit at the same time. Eyes locked on each other, they tried to stare the other down. Then Brendon roared and Marissa jerked back with a vicious hiss. Feeling smug, he took the grapefruit and cut it in half. He tossed the other half to Marissa, laughing when it hit her in the face.

"Bastard."

"As are we all," he joked around a mouthful of grapefruit.

"So what are you doing today?" Marissa buttered her toast and turned the page on her copy of the *Wall Street Journal*.

"I gotta stop by the Pride and see the kids. You wanna go?"

She nodded, then stopped. "Is that bitch going to be there?"

"Do you mean Missy?"

"I hate her."

"Yes. I know. In fact, I think the entire universe knows."

"The only thing that gives me ease is that you never bred with her."

"You kidding? I'm almost positive she has fangs in her crotch. Snap a man's penis right off."

Marissa burst out laughing.

"If you come with me, you can give the kids their gifts."

She nodded but didn't answer.

"You did get them gifts this year."

"Of course I did." She bit into her toast. "Cash is a gift."

"Marissa."

"Don't give me that tone. Look, I don't know what to give children. And there's absolutely nothing wrong with a Baby Gap gift card."

Brendon sighed. "You're pathetic."

"Yeah. But you love me anyway."

"I have no choice." Brendon looked around for toast already made, didn't find any, so he reached over and took it out of Marissa's hand. "Look, have you ever thought of having your own Pride? We have cousins you sort of . . . tolerate."

"We've had this discussion and I don't want to have it anymore."

"All right. Then in twenty years you can be the kids' old bitter aunt."

"Well, I'm already their young bitter aunt, so it's really not that big a stretch. What else are you doing today—and get your damn hands off my sausage."

Brendon dropped the sausage he'd taken from his sister onto his plate. "Nothing. Kids then hotel. As it is, the kids will take a few hours and I've got to make sure everything's okay at the hotel. Then I've got me a She-wolf to track down."

Marissa slammed her fork down. "You must be joking," she barked.

"Nope. I know she's around somewhere. I just have to find the Smith Pack."

Reaching over, Marissa slapped her brother in the head.

"What was that for?"

"Hello? Cat." And she motioned between the two of them. "Dog." She made a throwing-away motion; Brendon just didn't know why. "Mortal enemies."

"Actually that's more hyena."

She clenched her fists. "What I mean, you big-haired idiot, is that she is *not* the female for you."

"Why?"

"What do you mean—wait a minute. Why do you have that look?"

"What look?"

"The same one you had when you went for the grapefruit.

The 'this is mine and I'm never giving it up' look. You've never had it about a female before. At least pick a cheetah maybe. Or a leopard," she cried desperately. "She'll spend most of her time in the trees anyway. But a *dog*? A dog with a group of dogs behind her? Are you insane? They howl. They bay. They whine."

"They saved my life."

Marissa let out a big sigh. "You're gonna keep throwing that in my face, aren't you?"

Brendon grinned. "Yup."

"Stop! Oh God! Please stop!"

Ronnie grabbed the ringing hotel phone beside her bed, ripped it out of the wall, and threw it across the room. Moaning in absolute agony, she carefully laid back on the mattress.

No sound. No light. No nothing. She would allow nothing into her "safe space."

She remembered last night clearly. No lovely blackouts for her. No. Ronnie Lee must remember every humiliating second. Like telling her Pack she wanted Brendon Shaw to run his mane all over her body.

Even worse . . . she couldn't stay here knowing Shaw may show up at any time.

Of course, her rational mind kept telling her it didn't matter. It didn't matter if she found Brendon Shaw standing outside her room doing the mambo again. The reality remained he wouldn't remember much after such a bad fever. He probably woke up in bed thinking it had all been a weird dream. Nothing more. Nothing less. So worrying about an impromptu meeting in the hotel lobby . . . kind of dumb. Even for her.

Very, *very* slowly, Ronnie Lee turned onto her side and forced her vicious bout of nausea down. She was a Reed, dammit. She wouldn't let some cat get under her skin and have her running scared like a big girl.

Then, as she slipped into a deep sleep, she promised herself for the thousandth time—*No more tequila.*

* * *

Brendon ignored his daughter climbing up his back and getting comfortable on top of his head while his son gripped his leg and tried to bite his knees with his less-than-deadly human baby teeth. The little guy wouldn't come into his fangs until puberty hit, and his mother would probably drop him off at Brendon's house and not come back for him until he turned twenty-one.

"There you are." Allie Llewellyn closed the door to the solarium behind her, blocking out all that yelling. "I figured you'd have to escape as soon as the fighting started."

"I should have never brought Marissa when Missy's here." He realized his mistake in the first ten minutes of their arrival. As soon as Missy, head of the Llewellyn Pride, walked into the enormous Llewellyn compound living room, Marissa was in her face demanding to know why none of the Llewellyn Pride had stayed with Brendon at the hospital and why none of them had bothered to call her. When Missy snarled that she was *not* an answering service it went straight downhill from there.

Three hours later and the two females were still going at it.

Allie stretched out in a lounger and stared at him. "You seem unusually cheerful, considering all the yelling and drama."

"It must be the holidays."

Laughing, she said, "Okay. What's her name?"

"That's on a need-to-know basis, and you don't need to know."

Brendon actually liked Allie. Not when she was around Missy but one on one. Allie and Erik's mom, Serita, were relatively nice and they'd made breeding with them quite entertaining.

"You do understand that Missy's not going to like you getting involved with someone from another Pride. At least not without a trade contract."

"Our contract involves the kids and the kids only."

"I'm not arguing. Just letting you know. And there's some slight whining in there because I'll have to hear about it. Constantly."

Blocking his daughter's tiny fist from making contact with his eye, he asked, "It sounds like she's still raging over Mace and his Bronx m'lady."

Allie laughed at his use of "m'lady" in a sentence. "Oh yeah. She's still raging all right. Besides, we're down to two males now. Petrov's gone. You're gone. And Mace won't let her trade him out for more. Her life is in shambles." Allie rolled her eyes. "Personally I could care less. Little Miss Evil Kitty over there"— she pointed at her daughter—"is more than enough trouble at the moment. I certainly don't need to add to it with another cub until she's a tad older."

"Makes sense." Brendon picked up his son and placed him on his knee, ignoring the teeth he sank into his forearm. "But Missy needs to understand, I won't let her use my kids as leverage against me."

Allie shook her head. "I won't let that happen, Brendon. I'm not saying she won't try, but I won't let her get away with it." She smiled at him. "I like you. You irritate me much less than most males. Besides, our darling little brat will rip my long silky locks out if I ever try to get between her and her daddy."

"And Serita?"

"Missy will be lucky if Serita doesn't start her own Pride. They've been fighting like two cats in a bag lately. Besides, we both know she can't use the kids. We all read that contract we signed. It's quite airtight."

"Damn right it is." Three high-priced lawyers who specialized in shifter law and his sister made sure of that.

"I don't blame you at all," she said with a sigh, leaning back into the lounger and staring up at the ceiling. "Nothing is sadder than an old Pride lion who hasn't seen his cubs for decades." Like his dad hadn't seen Mitch.

Allie yawned, her eyes fluttering closed. "You coming out to dinner with us, Brendon? We have reservations at that new sushi place uptown. The chef is supposed to be a god."

He'd rather remove body parts before sitting through some overpriced nouveau riche meal with Missy. But before Brendon could state that out loud, his cell phone went off. He checked caller ID and answered. "Yes?"

"Hello, sir. It's Timothy."

"I know. I checked caller ID." After eight years as his personal assistant, one would think Timothy would already know that about his boss. "What's going on?"

"I received a message from Louise." Louise had been Brendon's secretary longer than Timothy had been his assistant. "You wanted me to check the local hotels and find a Smith Pack?"

"Yeah. Did you get something?"

"Sir, they're here."

"Here? You mean in New York?"

"No. I mean at the Kingston Arms. They've been checked in for more than a week under the name ... uh ... Sissy Mae Smith."

Brendon stared at the wall, completely oblivious to his daughter gripping his hair and hanging from his head like a monkey.

"You're sure?"

"Yes, sir. I even went and checked the other hotels in the Tri-state area that cater to your"—Timothy cleared his throat—"kind, because Smith is such a common name, but the only Smith Pack I could locate is at this hotel."

Letting out a deep breath, Brendon grinned. "Good work."

"Do you need me to do anything else, sir?"

"No. I should be back at the hotel in a few."

"Yes, sir."

Brendon ended the connection. "I've gotta go."

Without opening her eyes, Allie smiled. "Figured."

After unattaching his daughter from his hair, Brendon swung her around in his arms and kissed her neck, then kissed the top of his son's head. "Both of you be good."

"Don't forget," Allie reminded him, "we're heading out tomorrow to Grandmother's property in Sag Harbor for the New Year."

"Okay. I'll come over in the afternoon to send you off."

He put his children beside Allie and opened the solarium door. The arguing hit him in the face. It would take time to get his sister to back off. Time he wasn't in the mood to give.

"When she's done, tell my sister I went back to the hotel."

Allie opened one eye and stared at Brendon. "You're leaving her here?"

"I don't feel like dragging her out. I'll even leave the car. I'll catch a cab."

Laughing, Allie closed her eyes again. "Okay. But neither your sister nor Missy will be happy. So I hope whoever she is, she's worth it."

Oh, she was.

A good long sleep and a little worshipping of the porcelain god, and Ronnie felt much better. Although she still didn't feel like hanging out tonight and she didn't know how the rest of the She-wolves were managing it.

Big dinner plans and some club hopping for the whole Pack, courtesy of Bobby Ray. He even tried to drag poor Mace and Dez into it, but from the end of the conversation Ronnie heard, Mace had no intention of getting out of his bed anytime soon as long as Dez was in it.

Ronnie smiled when she thought about the two of them. They were a cute, if unlikely, couple. And she loved the panic in Dez's eyes every time she caught Mace staring at her like he could simply eat her alive. The man was in love. No two ways about it and nothing Dez did or didn't do would change that so she might as well suck it up. So to speak.

The Pack stood in front of the hotel's front desk. At some point they would find permanent dens, and that search would be down to the females. Until then, they would continue to enjoy the luxury of the Kingston Arms.

Bobby Ray retrieved another stack of business papers from the desk staff. He and Mace had already hired a lawyer and apparently Sissy Mae had started working with realtors for a big-enough space to house their office. Clearly Mace and Bobby Ray weren't men to waste time on "what if"s and analyzing. They just went for it. Ronnie liked that.

"Are you sure you don't want to go?"

Glancing down at the pile of legal papers Bobby Ray had

shoved into her arms and the ripped, seen-better-days cutoff shorts, scuffed and decades-old cowboy boots, and the worn Lynyrd Skynyrd T-shirt that once belonged to her daddy, Ronnie shrugged. "I know this is the perfect outfit for the thirty-degree weather we have outside, but I think I'll stay in."

"You don't have to be a smart-ass. I was just askin', Ronnie Lee."

Feeling bad for sniping at him, she pushed her shoulder against Bobby Ray's. "Sorry. But I blame your sister for my cranky attitude."

"Told you not to go drinking with her anymore."

"I know. I know. But she's so persuasive." Ronnie Lee juggled the papers in her hands and reached out and yanked Sissy Mae's hair.

"Ow! What was that for?"

"For leading me down the path of sin and drunkenness."

"Looked to me like you were gettin' there fine all on your own."

Bobby Ray slammed another four thick envelopes filled with papers from his lawyer on top of the pile she already carried. "Just drop these off in my room when you go back up."

"Sure."

"If you need us, we all have our cells." Bobby Ray frowned. "And why did management call me about your ripping the phone out of the wall?"

"It wouldn't stop ringing."

Shaking his head, Bobby Ray turned to one of the other males, and Ronnie focused on Sissy Mae. "How do you do it?"

"Do what?"

"Remain so perky and fun loving after a drinking bout like the one we had last night?"

"Easy. I take a couple of aspirin before I go to sleep."

"That's it?"

"That's it."

"So my momma's right. You are Satan."

"Can't prove it."

Ronnie started to laugh until the scent hit her. That big delicious cat scent that three days ago she would have sworn she'd never like, much less lust over.

Swallowing her slight case of panic, Ronnie Lee reminded herself she was a Reed and she wouldn't go running because of some cat. Besides, he'd forgotten all about her. Right? No use making a fool over herself for a male who wouldn't even remember her.

Determined to stand her ground, Ronnie watched Shaw stride into the hotel lobby, looking amazing in a thick cable-knit forest-green sweater, faded blue jeans, and scuffed work boots. As soon as he appeared staffers came from everywhere, demanding his attention and asking him to sign things. He dismissed all but one with a wave of his hand. She had a feeling the *much* smaller man, a full-human, walking with him to the front desk was Shaw's personal assistant. *Lord in heaven, the man has a personal assistant.*

She held her ground until he stood no more than forty feet from the Pack, then she panicked. Ducking her head, Ronnie took a step back. Sissy Mae glanced over and abruptly moved in front of Ronnie, blocking her from Shaw's sight. That was the one thing Ronnie did love about Sissy. She'd give her shit later about being a wimp, but she'd protect Ronnie now, no questions asked.

Lord, but did she need that.

To her growing horror, Shaw stopped beside the Pack and glanced up from the paperwork his assistant had shoved into his hands. He looked at Bobby Ray and she started to step away, run really, but Sissy grabbed her shirt and held her in place. Smart woman. As predator, Shaw would immediately notice a female sprinting out of the room.

Knowing something was going down, both Marty and Gemma stood beside Sissy Mae, further blocking Ronnie from Shaw's sight.

"Your Mace's friend, right?" Shaw asked. "From the tunnels the other night."

"Yup," Bobby Ray answered back . . . eventually. Bobby Ray didn't believe in rushing much of anything. Especially words.

"Thanks for that."

"Welcome."

She silently sighed. *Males.*

Shaw turned to say something to his assistant, and Sissy gave Ronnie a shove to move her from the room. Perfect timing.

Ronnie sprinted to the elevator and repeatedly mashed the call button. "Come on," she begged. "Come on."

Finally, after what seemed like forever, the elevator doors slid open and Ronnie rushed inside. She juggled the big manila folders and papers in her hands so she could push the button for her floor. Once it lit up, she leaned back against the wall and let out a sigh of relief when the doors began to close.

But when that big hand reached in and slapped itself against one of the big metal doors to stop it from closing, she barely stopped herself from letting out a yelp of surprise. Ronnie pushed herself up against the wall and held her breath as Brendon Shaw walked onto the elevator with his assistant.

"Comp them for their rooms."

"Sir?"

"Did I stutter?"

"Not usually, sir."

"And make sure they have everything they need while they're here."

"Yes, sir. And your sister called."

"What did she want?"

Ronnie glanced up at the numbers and willed the floors to go by faster.

"Um . . ." The assistant glanced at her. "It can wait, sir."

"Timothy, spit it out."

He shrugged. "She just said, 'Tell him bite me.'"

Instead of being angry, Shaw let out a deep laugh. He had a nice laugh. Low and real. She liked it.

"She's pissed at me. I left her alone with Missy Llewellyn."

"I'd be mad at you, too, sir," Timothy joked, laughing right along with his boss until the elevator stopped on the twenty-fourth floor. "I'll be here late, sir, if you need me for anything."

"No. Don't be here late. Go home and see your . . . uh . . ."

Smirking, Timothy asked, "My boyfriend, sir?"

"Yeah. Whatever. Can't we just call him Frank?"

Now grinning, Timothy stepped off the elevator. "If you say so, Mr. Shaw."

"I do. Go home. I'll see you tomorrow."

"Night, sir."

The elevator doors closed and Shaw let out a breath. Out of the corner of her eye, she could see him glance at her. He stared at her bare legs for a bit, then looked away.

She knew then he didn't remember her. Like she guessed, once the fever wore off, he'd gone back to being a big arrogant cat with no use for "dogs."

What annoyed her was how irritated she felt by it. She'd nursed the man through his fever and then had one helluva orgasm with him. You'd think he'd remember *something*.

She should have known better and felt damn grateful she hadn't fucked him. The humiliation if she had . . .

The elevator stopped on the thirty-eighth floor—a shifter-only floor—and she stepped out without looking at him. She went down the long hallway until she stood in front of Bobby Ray's room, digging into her back pocket for his keycard while trying not to drop her pile of papers.

She'd just swiped the card, unlocking the door, when the bellowed "*You were going to pretend you didn't know me, weren't you?*" had Bobby Ray's precious papers and envelopes flying everywhere.

Brendon couldn't believe how angry she'd made him. Did she really think he wouldn't notice her? That he hadn't smelled her as soon as he walked into the lobby? He'd kept his mouth shut to see if she'd say or do anything to acknowledge who she was, but when he saw her duck down to hide from him, his heart sank.

He could have let her walk away. He almost did as he watched her scurry from the lobby like a frightened mouse. But he'd been simply too angry to let her get away with it. It didn't help, either, how damn good she looked in those shorts and boots.

"*Weren't you?*" he yelled again.

She turned and faced him, her hand over her heart. She slumped against the wall. "Lord in heaven, you scared the *shit out of me!*"

"Good!"

"Well you don't need to keep yellin'. I hear you just fine." She glanced down at the papers and folders all over the floor. "Dammit. Now I gotta get these back in order."

Papers? She was worried about papers? Who gave a flying shit?

He watched her crouch down and pull everything together. "Is that all you have to say to me?"

"Your fever gone?"

"Yeah."

With all the papers in one hand, she stood and slapped her free hand across his forehead.

"You still feel kind of warm to me. You should probably be laying down and getting some rest before you start working again. Anyway, that's my opinion. You can do what you like."

She turned and again swiped the keycard, unlocking the door. Before she could escape inside and shut him out, he grabbed the papers out of her hands, ignoring her plaintive "Hey!", and tossed them into the room. He could smell this wasn't her room. It belonged to a male and he didn't want her in there. Brendon slammed the door shut.

"What the hell do you think you're do—"

Brendon shut off her tirade by kissing her. He couldn't help himself. He'd never seen a female look finer in a pair of cutoff shorts, cowboy boots, and a T-shirt that had been in the washer so many times and seen so many years, he could easily see the aqua blue lace bra she wore under it. One good tear would have it off her in seconds.

To stop himself from doing exactly that in the middle of the hallway, he dug his hands into her hair and plunged his tongue between her lips. Her hands slammed hard against his shoulders, and he thought for sure she'd push him away. Maybe even claw his chest open. She-wolves could be mean when provoked.

But her fingers gripped his flesh hard and she yanked him closer, rising on her toes to meet his mouth, her tongue sparring with his.

Brendon didn't want to give her a chance to have any doubts, to worry what her Pack would say, so he slipped his hands under her perfect ass and lifted her. He maneuvered her legs around his waist and headed toward the back elevator down the hall. The elevator that would take him directly to his apartment on the top floor.

He made it about ten feet when one of her hands released his shoulder and slapped against the wall.

She pulled out of their kiss. "Wait. Just wait."

He growled.

"And don't growl at me." At least she was panting. Panting was good. "Where the hell are we going?"

"My apartment."

She shook her head, confusion and lust all over her beautiful face. "We can't . . . we shouldn't do—"

Again he kissed her to shut her up and because she tasted so goddamn wonderful.

He set off again, her claws scraping a line down the wall as he hustled her toward the secluded elevator.

She pulled her lips away again. "Wait!"

He stopped and stared at her.

"I'm relatively positive we're not supposed to be doing this."

"Who says?"

"The laws of nature and God."

"Laws are made to be broken and God just wants us to be happy." Fucking this woman would make him so damn happy. "Come on. Let's go break some laws."

"No, no, no! Let's think about this a minute. Just give me a second."

He didn't release her. And since her breasts were right there . . .

She gasped, her hands grabbing his head and pulling him in tighter as he suckled her nipple through her T-shirt and bra.

"You are so not giving me a minute to think."

"I know," he said around her nipple. "I don't want you to think. Thinking is what had you running out on me."

"I didn't . . . I couldn't . . ." She panted harder. "Stop sucking it like that."

"Okay. How about this?" He drew her in deeper and she cried out.

Her hand slammed hard against the wall, claws once again out. "Your room," she demanded. "Your room now."

Brendon didn't argue, he just moved.

The ding of the private elevator nearly snapped Ronnie out of her idiocy—but not quite. Not with a man who could kiss like this. If the way he used his tongue remotely mimicked his skills with his cock, she was in for a time.

Thought you were an adult now and you weren't going to do this sort of thing anymore? Remember? New year . . . new life.

There it went again. That damn voice in her head. The one that sounded suspiciously like her momma. The one she never listened to even when she should. She probably should listen to it now, but the man's kisses were drugging. Ronnie couldn't think past his lips touching hers. His tongue gliding along the inside of her mouth, caressing and tasting. She couldn't think past what he'd do once he got inside her, the very thought making her shudder and her pussy clench tight.

The elevator didn't directly open to his room, but to a hallway and a door right across. Shaw pushed her up against the wall while he fished keys out of his back pocket and unlocked the door. He carried her inside and shoved her up against another wall as he slammed the door shut and threw the four bolt locks.

Not until he had her right where he wanted her did he release her legs, his hips rocking into her body. She moaned, slipping her hands under his sweater and into the back of his jeans. She squeezed his ass and laughed when he groaned against her mouth.

Shaw's lips trailed down her jaw to her neck, his teeth scraping along the throbbing pulse point in her throat. He continued on, bringing his mouth back to her breast and pushing her shirt up while pulling the lace bra cup down. His warm mouth enveloped her nipple, hungrily tugging on it.

She dug her hands into his hair to hold him in place, wondering if he could bring her over the edge by sucking on her breast. She'd heard some men had the skill, but she had yet to meet one.

Ronnie's body tightened in anticipation, every muscle tensing, preparing for the release it knew was coming.

She opened her eyes to watch the man playing her body so effortlessly, and that's when she saw him walk out of Shaw's kitchen.

He froze at the sight of her, juice from the green apple he'd just bitten into dripping down his chin. He wasn't like the ones at the hospital. He wasn't human. Not fully anyway.

Growling, fangs bared, Ronnie slammed her fist into the side of Shaw's head.

"Ow!" He pulled away, his hand rubbing the cheek she'd wounded. "What the fuck was that for?"

Pulling her bra up and her shirt down, she snarled, "If you think I'm that kind of wolf, you've got another thing coming!"

"What?" Shaw looked genuinely confused and a little hurt.

She pointed toward his kitchen.

Frowning, Shaw stood straight and turned. The two males stared at each other for several long seconds. Then Shaw was on him, grabbing the male around the throat and slamming him up against the wall.

"*Where the hell have you been?*"

Roaring, the male shoved Shaw back and turned so he could slam Shaw against the wall.

"*None of your goddamn business!*"

Ronnie rolled her eyes. Brothers.

They had to be. Only family could ever get a body this pissed off.

Shaw pushed his forearm against the other's throat, turned, and slammed his brother against that poor abused wall.

"I almost got killed looking for you!"

"Who told you to look for me? *I told you to mind your own goddamn business!*"

They both roared at each other, literally, and Ronnie decided it was a good time to leave. She quietly unlocked and opened the door, but before she could sneak out into the hallway, Shaw's gold eyes lasered over to her, nailing her to the spot with one look.

"Don't even think about leaving."

Ronnie would have argued with him. Told him it was best he and his brother talk alone. Or that he was being an ass and he could go find another fuck somewhere else. But before she could say a word, Shaw's brother shoved the bigger man to the floor and the two went at it like . . . well . . . like two big cats.

It wasn't pretty.

Although the canine part of her sure did enjoy the show.

Chapter Six

They hadn't shifted yet, but it had crossed Brendon's mind. Especially when the little shit sank his fangs into the side of Brendon's neck. Without his protective mane that shit really hurt!

This wasn't how he'd planned to talk to Mitch when he finally caught up to him. Brendon had it all worked out. In nice, easy tones, he was going to ask his brother what was going on and whether he was okay.

Unfortunately, he'd been so wound up from making out with the She-wolf and sexually frustrated because of all the things he wanted to do to her but hadn't been able to yet, he'd unleashed his full fury right on his baby brother's head. As usual, Mitch dived right into that fight.

Honestly, the boy had no sense at all sometimes. Although he did have a mean right cross, and sometimes it felt like his fangs were extra sharp.

Brendon grabbed his brother around the throat, letting his claws dig into the skin enough to make Mitch nervous. But before he had time to gloat about his brother's sudden stillness, water, cold and imported directly from Denmark, ploughed into his face.

Both brothers snarled and separated, looking up into the smug face of one gorgeous She-wolf.

"Didn't have time to bother with the tap." She held the empty water bottle in her hand. Water that cost him five bucks a pop. "Although why a body would go all the way to Denmark to get *water*, I'll never know. Ain't American water good enough for ya?"

She put the empty plastic bottle on top of a side table. "Anyway, sorry about that, but I figured there had to be a better way for you two to work out whatever it is you've gotta work out. And, to be quite honest, you won't let me go and I haven't got all night to sit around here waiting for you two to get bored. So"—she held her hands out to both of them—"why don't you two try talking this out rather than ripping each other's throats out. I'd hate to have to explain all that blood to those poor maids."

Not knowing what else to do, Brendon grabbed her hand and Mitch grabbed the other. She pulled and both of them stood up, towering over her.

"I have three older brothers," she explained with a smile. "If I didn't stop some of their fights, those boys would have fought all damn day and one of them would have died from blood loss. That would have upset my momma no end, and she would have found a way to blame me."

Using the tips of her fingers, she turned Brendon's head a bit so she could look at his neck. She grimaced, sucking the air in between her teeth. "Lord, boy. You really need to learn how to pull back when it's your own kin."

Mitch's eyes narrowed dangerously. "And who are you exactly?"

"Be nice," Brendon growled, his hands clenching into fists.

"Don't start that shit again." She stepped back. "Look, I'm right downstairs. Why don't I—"

"No. You stay here." Brendon grabbed his brother's worn leather biker jacket and yanked him toward the door. "Don't leave. I'll be back."

"Where the hell are we going?" Mitch demanded.

"I'm getting you a room and you're staying the night. And don't even think about giving me any shit about this."

Pulling open the door, he shoved Mitch through it and toward the elevator. He glanced back at the She-wolf. "I'll be back in a little while. Make yourself at home, but promise me you won't leave."

She opened her mouth to argue, he could see it on her face, so he added, "Promise me or I'll start kicking his ass again, right here."

His brother turned away from the elevator and snarled, "You wish—"

"Shut up." Brendon snapped at his brother while staring at her. "Promise me."

Exasperated, she rolled her eyes. "All right. All right. For the sake of family harmony, I'll stay. But not like for twelve hours or something. My Pack might notice if I'm gone that long."

"Don't worry. I'll be back." He started to close the door, but he stepped back and looked at her. "One other thing."

"Yeah?"

"What *is* your name?"

She looked torn between being amused, embarrassed, and appalled.

"Rhonda Lee Reed. Everybody calls me Ronnie Lee or Ronnie."

"Anybody ever call you Ron?"

"Not and live to tell about it."

Brendon grinned. Yup. He liked her.

"All right, Ronnie Lee. Make yourself at home and I'll be back in a bit."

"Yeah. Yeah. But you better have TV," she mumbled as he closed his front door.

He walked over to his brother and the elevator doors slid open. Grabbing the younger man by the back of the neck, he threw him inside. "And that's for trying to rip my throat out, you little shit."

How she could initially miss the fifty-inch, flat-screen plasma TV attached to Shaw's wall, she had no idea. Then again, his tongue down her throat and his hands on her tits might have had something to do with it.

Settling down onto the man's butter-soft leather couch and

picking up his gargantuan remote to start flipping channels, Ronnie shook her head. He hadn't even known her name. She almost fucked a man who didn't even know her name. Lord, she hadn't done something *that* trashy in a very long time.

So then why wasn't she running for the exit instead of sitting on a lion's couch, reprogramming his inadequately programmed remote?

Because . . . because she liked him. Stupid idiot that she was, she liked a cat. She liked a male who would never want more from her than a quick, anonymous fuck so he could tell his friends he did a She-wolf.

Even as she thought it, though, she realized that didn't seem Shaw's way. He could have anyone he wanted. Human or shifter. Any breed. But he wanted her. He made that clear in front of Bobby Ray's room. She just couldn't figure out if this was a mistake or not.

Then again, as long as she kept it simple, maybe it wouldn't be. Maybe they could have a fun, meaningless fling. Lord knew it wouldn't be her first.

Of course, if it was all so damn easy, why had her stomach tied itself into knots?

She should go. She should write a little note telling the cat thanks but no thanks. She should. Really.

Ronnie kept thinking that, too, even as she stretched her legs out on his couch and smiled when she realized she'd had the good fortune to catch some *CSI* reruns.

Brendon scrubbed his face and leaned back, staring at his brother. After three hours and two enormous sandwiches from the kitchen—he knew the kid hadn't had a decent meal recently—he still didn't know a damn thing.

"At least tell me why you showed up in my apartment after all this time."

Mitch paused for a moment, truly contemplating his answer. Brendon knew that expression. Knew Mitch would only tell him enough truth to get Brendon off his back. He'd done it enough times before. Eventually, Mitch shrugged and took another bite.

"Marissa left a message on my voice mail," he grumbled around a mouthful of food.

"She did?"

"Yeah. And she was way pissed. She blames me for this, doesn't she?"

"Don't worry about her. So you came here to check on me?"

Mitch rolled his eyes. "If that helps you sleep better, bruh."

"It's nice to know you care."

The middle finger salute given, Mitch went back to his steak sandwich. "So who did it?"

"Doogan brothers." For a split second Brendon saw surprise register on his baby brother's face before he quickly masked it. The kid had a talent for that.

"They killed Petrov before Christmas," Brendon continued. "Shot him in the back of the head."

"They used guns?" Mitch made a sound of disgust. "Tacky."

"Doogans," Brendon reminded him, leaning back in the chair. "They wanted the Llewellyn Pride. They killed Petrov. And they almost killed me."

"Is that what happened to your face?"

Brendon chuckled. "Yeah. That's what happened to my face, but it's healing."

"Where are they now? The Doogans?"

Brendon knew that look on his brother's face. He'd seen it on Marissa's enough. Knew what the kid would do if he had the chance. Too bad for him he wouldn't have the chance.

"Hyenas ate 'em."

Mitch stared at him for a long time. Nearly a minute. Until he said, "Excuse me?"

"Hyenas ate them." Brendon lifted his hands and let them drop. "Like forty of them. Ripped the three of them apart. Considering the bastards were about to shoot me in the back of the head—they kind of deserved it."

"Good point. Although I don't see a bunch of hyenas helping you."

"They didn't. A really well-endowed cop and a Pack of wolves helped me."

"Is that where you met She of the Sexy Shorts?"

"She stayed with me through my fever. She protected me from a couple of guys. Got me out of the hospital and stashed me at her aunt's."

Again that look passed across Mitch's face clearly stating he knew more than he was spilling. Only, for once, he looked a bit panicked. "What guys?"

"I don't know. White. Humans. That's all anybody knows." Completely useless information in a court of law.

"You didn't ... uh ... I mean ..." He cleared his throat. "How badly did you ... uh ..."

"They're still breathing, if that's what you're asking me."

Mitch nodded, guzzled his beer.

"Anyway, she stayed with me, man. She didn't desert me. And she looks amazing in those cowboy boots."

Mitch put down his beer. "You like her."

Brendon grinned. He couldn't help himself. "Yeah. I like her."

"And what's your precious Pride have to say about that?" He never could keep the disgust out of his voice when he mentioned them. Just like Marissa. They'd hate it if they knew how alike they were.

"I've only been hanging around lately because of the Doogans. I wasn't going to let them get near my kids. But we've been done with each other for a while now. They got what they wanted out of me and I got what I wanted out of them. So everyone's happy."

Mitch smiled. "How are my niece and nephew?"

"Beautiful. Kitten-cranky."

"I love that age."

"They'd love to see you."

"Maybe."

"What's going on, Mitch?" Brendon asked yet again.

His face perfectly blank, Mitch stated, "Nothing."

A stranger might have believed him, but Brendon knew better. Unfortunately, Mitch had the Shaw stubbornness. He wouldn't tell anyone anything until he damn well wanted to.

"So basically you came to check up on me. You were worried about your big bruh."

"I wasn't worried. But I knew if you were dead, I'd want your stuff."

"Oh, that's very nice."

"Come on. Can you blame me?" Mitch gestured around the opulent room. "This gorgeous hotel. Staff waiting to do my bidding. Beautiful woman right upstairs . . . even if she is a dog."

Brendon ignored the flash of uncharacteristic jealousy over a female he suddenly experienced. "She-wolf."

"Whatever."

"You'd still have to fight Marissa for it all."

"I could take her. Once I took a bat to her head."

"Such family love we have."

"We're like the lion equivalent of *The Waltons*."

Brendon laughed and shook his head. "You're the biggest idiot."

It made him feel really good when Mitch smiled.

Chapter Seven

B rendon opened his front door not expecting but hoping to find Ronnie still there. And he did. Asleep on his couch, the television playing an *X-Files* repeat low in the background. Her body curled into a tight ball, her feet and hands twitching in sleep as she dreamed. She sort of looked like she was . . . well . . . running. In her sleep.

Forcing himself not to laugh, he crouched in front of her. Carefully, Brendon brushed her brown hair off her face. She made little whimpering sounds in her sleep and then her lip pulled back in a snarl.

Perhaps the cutest damn thing Brendon had ever seen in his entire life. He kissed her cheek and Ronnie snapped awake . . . and up. Their heads slammed together. You could almost hear the "thunk."

"Ow!" Brendon rubbed his nose where her cheek made contact. Christ, his body had taken more abuse in the last few days.

"Sorry," she said while gripping her own head.

"I didn't mean to startle you."

"No. No. It wasn't your fault. I dreamed I was fighting a puma. A full one," she added, which explained why she might be so jumpy. A Pride of shifters might decide not to attack a lone wolf because they know her Pack would come after them, but the full-bloods had no such worries about repercussions.

Which explained why Brendon left hunting in wild animal

parks to the hearty and insane, of which his father turned out to be both.

"Did I hurt you?" she asked with a giggle.

"No. I'm fine."

She felt his forehead. "I still say that fever is there. Not a lot, but a bit."

"My fever's gone. Stop worrying."

"My daddy thought he was over the fever once after he got in a tussle with a wild boar. Then he passed out in the Piggly Wiggly. Went down head first. *Bam!* Took out their entire candy display."

That quick, the woman had his heart right in the palm of her hand. To quote her, "Bam!" She probably didn't even realize it, and Brendon sure as hell had no intention of telling her.

"I'm okay," he reassured her before he could say something stupid. Like "marry me."

She shrugged. "Fine. Males wanna take chances with their health, no female around can convince 'em different."

Ronnie sat up, scratching her head and yawning. "You work everything out with your brother?"

Brendon gave a sharp snort. "Not really. My brother's not big on telling me or my sister anything."

"Y'all from the same Pride?"

Sitting down beside her on the couch, enjoying simply having her there, "Nope. His mother belonged to the West Philadelphia Pride and our mom to the South Philly. Our mom died when we were born and her Pride didn't want us."

"Why not?"

He shrugged. "Got me. Sometimes cats just get that way."

"So your dad took you in?"

"Yeah. He raised us. Was determined to do things differently."

"Differently than what?"

"His father. He died in prison. Art thief."

Ronnie pulled her legs up onto the couch, her arms around them and her chin resting on her knees. "I used to have an Uncle Louie who robbed banks until he was shot in the head."

Brendon leaned back and put his feet up on his coffee table. "Ya gotta love family, huh?"

"Not really. But you can't pick your family. It's just the way it is. Your brother can't be that bad, though."

"What makes you say that?"

"I don't think you'd be worried about him if you thought he was hopeless."

"Know that much about me already, huh?"

"Nah. Just a feeling I have. And I'm usually pretty right about people. Got it from my great-grandmother. She was Black-foot tribe . . . or . . . something."

"And you have three brothers."

"Yup." She shook her head. "They wouldn't like your pretty face one bit."

"Don't give a rat's ass about your brothers. Do *you* like my pretty face?"

"Yeah. I do." She gently stroked his cheek. "But if my brothers come to New York and find you sniffing around me, what the Doogan brothers did to you in those tunnels will seem like a cakewalk compared to the Reed boys."

Brendon leaned into her, his eyes locked on her lips. "I'll take my chances," he whispered and moved in.

Should have kept his eyes open, though. It would have prevented him from going face-first into his couch.

By the time he sat up, she had his front door open.

"Where are you going?"

"My momma says to hell in a handbasket, but I'm fightin' that."

She got as far as the elevator before he caught hold of the back of her denim shorts and proceeded to drag her back into his apartment.

"You're not walking out on me again."

"I can't stay. I can't do this."

"Do what?"

"Have sex with guys who don't even know my name." She grabbed the doorjamb and held on for dear life. "I promised myself no more of this wild child bullshit. I'm thirty now, I gotta be responsible."

"And being with me isn't responsible?"

"And I repeat—you didn't even know my name and you'd already started sucking on my nipples. So, yeah, I'd say this is us about to be irresponsible."

He had to pry her fingers off the doorjamb and haul her into his apartment. "Your name was the first thing I planned to ask you when I came out of the fever, but you were already gone."

She scrambled out of his arms and backed up into his apartment. Thankfully, she didn't smell frightened, but she did seem wary. He just didn't think it was about him.

"I swear it's nothing personal," she insisted, "but it is for the best."

"Don't leave, Ronnie."

She shook her head. "I can't stay. I *won't* stay."

Brendon realized there was only one thing he could do. A risk. But he had to try. "I understand." He walked away from the door so he no longer blocked her exit. "I'm sorry."

"No, no. You didn't do anything wrong, darlin'. It's all me." With one last look at him, those beautiful eyes filled with regret, she headed toward the door.

Letting out a low, mournful sigh, he sat on the armrest of one of his club chairs, his head hanging down.

"What . . . what's wrong?"

"Nothing. I'm fine. You better go."

He didn't look at her and when he heard the door open, it took all his strength not to run over and slam it before she could leave.

He waited. The door didn't close.

"Are you sure you're okay?"

"Yeah, yeah. Go on. I'm just tired."

Another moment of silence, a growl, and then the front door slammed shut. Cool hands grabbed his jaw and lifted his head. "Look at me."

He did . . . and Christ, those eyes.

"I bet it's that fever. I told you it hadn't finished with you yet."

"I'll be okay. Really. I'm sure I'm only tired."

"Come on." She took his arm and put it around her shoulders. "We're taking you to bed before you pass out or start running down Fifth Avenue on all fours."

Brendon let her help him up, and he led her straight to his bedroom. As she helped him onto his bed and proceeded to take off his boots, he realized that yes, he would be going to hell for lying his ass off.

Somehow he knew, though, that Ronnie Lee Reed would be worth every second he'd burn.

He could be faking it. Hell, he probably *was* faking it.

And if she were to be real honest with herself, she didn't really care. He'd given her a guilt-free excuse to come right back inside and take this man to bed . . . uh . . . to help him through the fever. She wouldn't *get* into bed with him.

Unless he needed her to.

Clearing her throat, she dropped his frighteningly large work boots at the side of the bed. "We should . . . uh . . . get your jeans off, too."

"Okay." He pushed himself up on his elbows and let out that sigh again.

"Now don't go exerting yourself. I don't mind helping." Yeah. Helping. She didn't mind helping one bit.

Forcing herself to be completely impartial, she reached for his jeans. "We'll get you out of these and into bed. By morning you should be right as rain."

She pulled his jeans down past his hips, realizing too late the man wore no underwear. Swallowing past the lump of lust in her throat, she locked her knees tight and yanked his jeans down his legs.

"I really appreciate you taking care of me like this."

"Oh, it's no bother." No bother at all when a man had thighs like these. Big. Hard. Perfect. She could "hee haw" her way to orgasm on those thighs.

Crouching at the end of the bed to finish pulling off his jeans, she tried not to think about the mouthwatering cock a few inches from her mouth. She didn't do very well, but she did really try.

"Ronnie?"

Ronnie closed her eyes. *If you look at him, you're a goner. Whatever you do, don't look at him.*

"Ronnie. Look at me."

Damn, damn, damn!

Still crouching by the bed, Ronnie slowly lifted her head.

"Open your eyes."

"I don't think I should."

"Okay. Keep 'em closed."

Strong hands gently gripped her face, big fingers sliding into her hair, angling her head a little up and to the side.

"Keep 'em closed," he whispered, his warm breath against her mouth. "Keep 'em closed and just kiss me, Ronnie Lee."

Shaw's lips brushed hers. Tongue stroking, teeth nipping. Ronnie grabbed hold of his wrists and whimpered. She opened her mouth, and Shaw dived in. His tongue tangling with hers, both of them groaning.

Then, with his fingers still buried in her hair, he pulled her to her feet. Before she could even blink, he had her on her back across his lion-sized bed.

Yup. Goner.

Chapter Eight

Absolutely. This woman was absolutely worth any stint in hell he may have to do. Her smell. Her taste. That canine "yip" sound she'd make every time he nipped her neck. All of those things were driving the lion buried inside him out of control.

"Christ, you smell good."

Ronnie didn't answer him, but slid her hands under his sweater and yanked it up. He stopped kissing her long enough for her to pull the sweater over his head and throw it across the room.

"If you value your clothes," he said while kissing her throat, "you'll get them off in the next thirty seconds. I won't be responsible for what happens after that."

She pulled out of their kiss and dragged her body out from under his.

"My daddy's," she explained about the T-shirt before it went sailing across the room. Her lace bra went flying next.

"No," he growled low. "The boots stay on."

Brendon had never met a female who looked at him with such raw sexual hunger. Exactly like the way Ronnie looked at him now, her hands sliding up the cowboy boot she'd been seconds from taking off, up her leg, until she reached the fly of her shorts. Clasp opened, zipper down, and then she wriggled that gorgeous body out of the scraps of denim.

"Come here," he ordered, and watched with narrow eyes as she backed away from him, still on her knees.

Her lips curved into a smile and her eyes shifted from human to wolf. She reached the top of his bed, shoving his pillows to the floor before leaning back against his headboard, her arms hooked over the top.

She spread her knees wide so he could see the wetness of her pussy and her trembling thighs. Softly, she said, "If you want this, hoss, you better come over here and get it."

No one had ever accused Ronnie of being shy. If she knew what she wanted, she went after it without a second's thought. Being wolf, this wasn't exactly surprising.

This bit of her character put off most human men or attracted the really scummy ones. Wolf males saw a challenge. A chance to dominate. They always thought they had to. And once they made her come they thought they owned her. They were always so shocked when they woke up in the morning and found her long gone.

She could say in all honesty that although she'd had some wonderful lovers, she'd never met her match.

Until Brendon Shaw dropped to all fours and crawled across his bed to her. Fangs slowly slid from his gums, and his claws kept catching on his sheets. He didn't rush over to her, slam her down. He moved like the king of the jungle he believed himself to be. Like he knew he'd get what he wanted eventually. She liked that he hadn't dived face-first into her muff in the hope of forcing that orgasm out of her so he could get in and get off.

Nope. Shaw meandered his way across that bed like the world belonged to him. Once he reached her, he nuzzled her thigh and licked the back of her knee. His hands smoothed across her skin, exploring every inch, taking his time. He even rubbed his mane of hair across her breasts and stomach, the feel of it exciting her more than any tongue or finger ever had.

Eventually he moved lower, his tongue swiping up between her legs, licking the wetness already coating the inside of her thighs. Then he purred, and Ronnie's eyes crossed. She gripped the headboard and gritted her teeth. "Let him work for it" had always been her motto, but his skills were such, he didn't have to work very hard.

Big hands slipped around the back of her legs and lifted her hips up, resting her thighs on his shoulders. Her cowboy boots pressed against his back, and his hands took firm hold of her ass. His tongue swept inside her and Ronnie cried out, her hips rocking against his mouth. Brutally fast, that orgasm crawled up her spine. Her body tightening, her claws gripping the back of his headboard, tearing at the wood.

Yet the man didn't seem to be rushing anything. Licking her slow and easy, still purring up against her flesh. Ronnie looked down to see that oh-so-happy smile he sported while giving her head—and she came like a freight train all over that pretty face.

Shaw rode it out with her, keeping a tight hold on her until her ecstatic cries turned to exhausted whimpering.

Grinning like he owned the universe, he lowered her legs until they rested against his thighs. Ronnie still had her arms holding the headboard, so Shaw ran his hands over her body. When his big thumbs grazed her nipples, she squeaked.

"Man," he sighed, "you are easy."

She'd been called that before, but for once she didn't get pissed because she knew he didn't mean it as an insult. "Don't get cocky, cat. We ain't done yet. We've got miles to go before you sleep."

He laughed and kissed her, pulling her body flush against his. "You are so beautiful," he said against her lips while his hands roamed over every inch of her. "I can't wait to get inside you."

"And why exactly are we waiting?"

He shrugged, kissed her shoulders. "Trying to be a gentleman or . . . whatever."

She snorted. "You know what I do with gentlemen? I chew them up and spit them out and leave the remains for the hyenas." Ronnie wrapped her arms around his neck. "Gentlemen don't make me hot. They don't make me squirm. And they sure as shit never make me come." She dug her hands into his hair, loving the way he never had true control over it. A big healthy mane. "If you were a gentleman, I wouldn't be here with you. I'd be anywhere but here with you."

Shaw leaned back, his hands brushing her hair off her face. "But you are here with me."

"Yeah. I am. Now it's time for you to get to work. Show me how you're king of the jungle and all that."

He laughed and joked, "You sure that's a good idea? Once you've had the king, you'll never go back to the lowly Alpha Male."

He knew how to have fun in bed. *Thank God!* Nothing Ronnie hated more than a man who had to be serious all the time. In bed or out. But especially in bed. Here you are, naked and groping each other. Seemed like the perfect time to joke, tease, have fun. But some men acted like they were "taking the beach" at Normandy during World War II.

Ronnie slipped her right hand down, gripping Shaw's cock and totally enjoying the way he groaned as she slowly pumped it.

"Talking. Talking. Talking. But I'm still waitin' for the proof, hoss."

Teasingly he rolled his eyes. "If you insist on me having actual intercourse with you to prove my point—and thereby ruining you for other males—I guess I have no choice but to oblige."

He reached over into the side drawer, her going with him since she now rested on his lap and still had his cock in her hand.

Pulling out a long strip of condoms, he held them up and asked, "Think we'll need all of these tonight?"

"If you want me bragging about you in the mornin', then you damn well better."

"Here." Brendon handed her a condom. "Make yourself useful."

She grinned while tearing open the packet, and he tried not to panic at the riot of emotions assaulting him at the moment. Instead he stroked her, caressed her, reveled in the softness and hardness of a female predator's body. He traced scars riddling her shoulders, back, and torso. She didn't hide them, nor did she stop him from touching, exploring. He really liked that about Ronnie Lee. She didn't shy away, it seemed, from anything.

The condom slipped over his aching cock, and she rolled it down to the base. She wrapped her hand around it and squeezed.

Letting out a groan, "Evil."

Ronnie chuckled, probably not realizing the hold she had on him went deeper than the hold she had on his cock.

Gripping her ass, Brendon pulled Ronnie firmly into his lap until his cock slipped just inside her. Her arms again wrapped around his neck, her face buried against his throat. Brendon impaled her with one firm thrust, loving the gasp of surprise she let out and the way her fingers tightened in his hair.

He held her like that for a long while, enjoying the way she wrapped around him and how she felt in his arms.

Perfect. That was how she felt. Absolutely perfect.

He held her in his arms like he would a fragile, weak-boned full-human. Like the slightest move could break her. Hurt her. She nipped his neck, reminding him of what they were. Not enough to break skin or accidentally mark him as her own, but enough to startle him back into action.

The next thing she knew Shaw had her flat on her back again. The gentle kitty cat had left the building, replaced by the killer cat. Not that she minded either way. She enjoyed both.

Lacing his fingers with hers, he pinned her hands down on the bed beside her head while he stared at her with the eyes of a lion. She could even feel the tips of his claws against the back of her hand. And . . . yup! Those were fangs.

She grinned at him, flashing her own canines. Daring him to fuck her right.

He snarled and then he moved. Fucking her hard, so hard. Using his weight and the strength of his arms to keep her in place while he pounded into her.

Lord, that felt good! So damn good.

They snarled and snapped at each other, and he made sure to hit her clit on every brutal thrust.

"Yeah," she said when she felt another orgasm starting to move through her system. "Yeah, yeah, yeah," she chanted over and over again until she came so hard she could only scream.

Still pinning her down, Shaw kissed her, their fangs scraping against each other, their tongues licking and stroking. His big cock slammed into her, pushing her toward another orgasm. Demanding it. She couldn't resist it. Couldn't stop the way he made her feel. She shook beneath him, the strength of her orgasm wiping her mind clean. She couldn't even scream anymore, could only gasp and whimper.

When Shaw came, he roared so loud Ronnie wondered if all fifty-three floors heard him.

He dropped on top of her, panting hard, their hands still locked even though both sets of claws and fangs had retreated.

They were quiet for a while, until Ronnie said, "Well that's definitely the most fun a body can have while naked."

She smiled when he snorted a laugh into her neck.

Chapter Nine

Brendon felt amazing. Better than amazing. He'd left his blinds open and he could see the dark skyline of his city.

Still dark out and he had no idea why he would be up this early—but he did know that he felt amazing.

Hair brushed the inside of his thigh, and he glanced down his body.

No wonder he felt so damn amazing. No wonder he was up so early.

Ronnie deep throated him again, her hand massaging his balls while she did.

"Christ, Ronnie," he rasped when she swirled her tongue around the tip of his cock, then took him deep again.

She sucked hard and released him. "Oh, don't mind me none."

Brendon laughed. "You're kidding, right?"

"Nah. Go back to sleep." She tore open another condom and put it on him. "I just need to borrow part of you for a time, is all."

He would have laughed if she didn't feel so goddamn good sinking onto his hard cock.

Her head fell back, and Ronnie let out a long, luxurious moan. "Yeah. That's exactly what I need." She started moving. Slow and easy, a smile of pure joy on that gorgeous face.

She looked into his eyes while she rode him. "You don't

mind, do you? If I take dirty, disgusting advantage of your sleeping body?"

"Anytime, sexy. Any goddamn time you want to."

"You may regret that. I can be real demanding." She leaned over him, her hands gripping his shoulders. Her rhythm never changed and her pussy clutched him on every rocking thrust.

"So you're a glutton. Always demanding more?"

"As much as I can get, hoss. I might be too much for you. More than you can handle."

He gripped her hips hard enough to bruise. "No, sexy. You're just right." Brendon used his hands to speed up her rhythm. Make her rock into him harder, faster.

Their groans grew louder, more desperate. Their bodies slick with sweat.

"Christ, Ronnie. You're amazing."

She laughed. "I bet you say that to all the girls who wake you up with a blow job."

Brendon slapped her ass, eliciting a yelp as her pussy clenched him hard. "I'm saying that to *you*."

"All right, hoss. All right. No need to get cranky."

He rubbed her where he'd slapped her ass. "You liked that, didn't you?"

She leaned down, licked his nipples, and Brendon barely stopped himself from coming.

"Liked what?" She very gently gripped one nipple between her teeth, then tickled it with her tongue.

Brendon closed his eyes and briefly thought about the Phillies baseball team season. He'd have to remember to get tickets this year. Maybe he could convince Ronnie to go along with him for a couple of games.

"Like what?" she asked again, her hands running along his shoulders, her hips and pussy rocking him into oblivion.

"When I slapped your ass. You liked it."

"Do you really think I'd answer that question?"

He arched into her. "You just did, sexy. You just did."

Ronnie gave a frustrated whimper.

Brendon opened his eyes to see Ronnie shake her head, a frustrated frown on her face.

"You need help going over, baby?"

She nodded, whimpered again. "I'm so close."

He pulled one hand away from her hips and placed his thumb against her mouth. "Suck on this like you sucked on my cock."

Without hesitation, she took his thumb into her mouth and sucked hard, her tongue swirling around a bit before going back to sucking.

I can't believe I slept through most of that blow job.

Dragging his finger from her mouth, Brendon brought it down the middle of her body until he hovered over her clit. He stared up into her face, wanting to watch Ronnie while he did this. While he gave her this.

He touched her clit with the pad of his thumb and made small circles.

"Oh God, yeah," she panted. "Oh yeah."

Brendon increased the pressure a bit and Ronnie exploded, her orgasm ripping through her, leaving her shaking and gasping. And smiling. She always smiled when she came. He kept up the pressure and the movement until she caught his hand with her own.

"Stop. Stop." Ronnie laughed and leaned back, shaking out her shoulder-length hair. "Whew! *That* was exactly what I needed, darlin'."

Taking Brendon's hands and placing them on her breasts, she said, "Now I need to know what you need."

He grinned, loving that she cared enough to ask. "For you to finish that blow job."

"Oh baby. That I can so do."

Ronnie woke up when the morning sun hit her full in the face. She took a moment to enjoy the feel of Shaw's back pushed up against her own. Took a moment to enjoy the scent of a male surrounding her. Shaw's scent. But she only gave herself that one moment. Now it was time to go. Like she did nearly every morning she woke up in a man's bed. And Shaw would be no different. No different from the other men in her life that she wrung pleasure from and then left before they ever woke up. Before they ever had a chance to ask her to stay.

Moving with the stealth she'd been born with, Ronnie slipped out of Shaw's bed and started toward the door. Quickly, though, she realized she had to pee like a race horse. Taking a detour, she went to Shaw's adjoining bathroom, pausing for a moment in the doorway. Good Lord, the man had a huge bathroom.

Huge bathroom, huge apartment, huge cock.

She used the toilet, washed her hands and face, brushed her teeth using her finger.

"You're procrastinating, girl," she said to herself in the mirror. "Just get your clothes and go."

Ronnie slipped back into the bedroom, picked up her clothes and boots, and headed to the door. She stopped right in front of it, staring at it.

All she had to do was put her hand on the knob and open the door. She glanced back at Shaw. Still asleep, he wouldn't know she'd left for hours. She looked back at the door.

Open the door, Ronnie Lee. Open the door and leave.

But the thought of going back to her boring hotel bed held absolutely no appeal. Usually, she couldn't get out of the room—and away from the male she'd just had sex with—fast enough.

For the first time ever, she didn't feel that overwhelming desire to escape. The realization unsettled her, but she blew it off. Merely the holidays, she told herself. People got lonely around the holidays.

Dropping her clothes into a chair, Ronnie walked back over to the bed. A deep breath, and she slipped back under the covers, resting on her side. It felt nice and right, but she blew that off, too. She was just tired, is all.

Shaw turned over and wrapped his arm around her waist, his face nestled into her hair, his cock snug against her ass. She rested her hand on his arm, smiled, and went back to sleep.

* * *

Brendon waited until he knew she was asleep before he let out the breath he'd been holding. True, he would have stopped her before she made it through his front door, but he wanted her to come back on her own. Wanted to see if the pull she felt was as strong as his own.

He didn't feel smug in the knowledge she came back. More like relieved. He'd fallen hard and fast for this female. This woman. He had no intention of letting her go now, but he wasn't stupid enough to believe it would be easy to keep her. Ronnie didn't like anyone having a hold on her. Not a man or her family. Not even her Pack. If she knew Shaw wanted her to stay in his life forever, she would have sprinted out the door like in one of those Bugs Bunny cartoons, leaving a big Ronnie-shaped hole in the wood.

No, he'd have to be crafty. He wouldn't trick Ronnie. He didn't want her to stay because she thought he was dying or something. He wanted her to stay because she loved him. Because the wolf in her realized it had found its mate. So he'd have to be crafty to keep her around until she realized it. Until she admitted it not only to him but to herself.

Thankfully, cats were known for being crafty and extremely patient.

Already planning his next move, Brendon pulled her closer and smiled in pure pleasure when she gripped his arm tight—afraid to let him go.

Ronnie stood in front of Shaw's refrigerator and continued to debate the pros and cons of its contents.

She absolutely detested eggs, so that was out. The man had enough bacon to feed the French Foreign Legion, but then she'd have to cook. She worked really hard to avoid using that stove thing.

She could eat some fresh fruit, but . . . nah.

"Uh . . . excuse me?"

Ronnie didn't bother glancing over her shoulder at Shaw's brother. She'd heard him at the front door as soon as he slipped the key in the lock and she smelled him as soon as he got off the elevator. And she didn't feel self-conscious because Shaw's Philadelphia Flyers hockey shirt reached below her knees, covering her naked ass.

"He's in the shower," she answered his unasked question.

"Do you want me to leave?"

"No. Just didn't want you walking around the apartment calling out his name like some stray cub, thinking he's ignoring you when he's only in the shower." She winked at him. "Figured it was best to tell ya up front."

At her smile, he seemed to relax. She had no idea why he might have been uptight. She'd been nothing but polite to the man while he rolled on the floor trying to kill his own brother.

"Breakfast or lunch?"

"I know the clock says lunch, but I'm just getting up after my own shower. My stomach wants to be fed but I don't see anything I have the energy or inclination to tussle with."

"Um . . . can I make a suggestion?"

For a man whose own brother referred to him as "scumbag" he sure seemed awfully polite.

Stepping back from the fridge but keeping the door open with her butt, Ronnie gestured toward the cold storage. "Be my guest."

Mitch crouched in front of the open refrigerator and dug around the back. Really, the damn thing was huge. Take out the shelves, you could comfortably fit a family of four in there.

"My brother usually has . . . ah . . . there it is." He glanced at what he held in his hand. "Expiration date's good, too. Here." He handed her a medium tub of low-fat vanilla yogurt.

If she hadn't been having wild sex with his brother all night, she might have kissed him. "Yes!" She grabbed a spoon, then leaped up onto the counter without using her hands. An old She-wolf trick. She crossed her legs at the ankles and opened the fresh yogurt. "How did you know?"

Mitch shrugged and closed the refrigerator door. "I used to date a She-wolf when I was sixteen." He opened the fridge door again, grabbed a water, and reclosed it. "Went to her house for Thanksgiving dinner. At dessert, they had five kinds of pie, six cakes, and this enormous bowl of plain, low-fat vanilla yogurt." He leaned at the far end of the counter, forcing her to turn a little to see him but keeping a healthy distance. "By the end of the evening, a few slices here and there of cake and pie were gone, but the yogurt bowl . . . completely cleaned out. When I asked her, she said wolves love yogurt."

"Did you mock?"

"No. Then I wouldn't have gotten laid."

"This is very true."

Ronnie ate her yogurt, her feet banging against the counter doors.

"Ya know," she finally offered as she steadily worked her way through that tub of yogurt, "you seem awful polite for a lowlife." She shrugged when he stared at her. "You wear that rebel without a clue motorcycle jacket, appear to shave only once or twice a week, got a couple of interesting scars on your neck, but . . ."

"But what?"

She shrugged. "You bathed this morning. You use conditioner. What nails you do have are clean. And I don't know many lowlifes who would have dug around in a fridge to get his hated brother's lay-of-the-moment a yogurt without trying to get some pussy himself, and yet you are halfway across the room. Out of respect."

He picked at the wrapper on his ridiculously overpriced water bottle and stared at her. Finally, he said, "I don't hate my brother."

"I know. Not sure Shaw does, though."

"And that bothers you—why?"

"It doesn't. Just passing on the information."

Mitch smirked and looked so much like his brother when he did. "I think you like him."

"Not at all. I often have sex with men I can't stand."

"I don't mean that kind of like. I mean, you *like* him."

Reaching the bottom of the yogurt tub, she joked, "You're right, Mitchy. And would you pass him a note in study hall for me?"

He snorted. Then he froze, his gold eyes glued to the swinging kitchen door. Ronnie's eyes narrowed, a female scent hitting her hard.

The door flew open and a tall, beautiful, and clearly feline female strutted in.

She stared right at Mitch. "Here to mooch off Brendon again?"

"I don't need to mooch. I can just steal from his wallet."

"And I'm sure you do." Her nose crinkled. "Why do I keep smelling wet dog?" Gold eyes turned to Ronnie. "Oh. That must be you."

Mitch straightened but Ronnie held her hand up to stop him. "It's okay, Mitch." She slid off the counter, turning to face the lioness who had to be Shaw's sister. She looked exactly like him, only female. Sleek and elegant in designer jeans and sweater and designer boots, she still couldn't hide the cold eyes of a predator. Or the rough edges of the less-than-wealthy upbringing Shaw had mentioned over late-night bowls of cereal.

"You'll have to accept us eventually," Ronnie said simply, her eyes downcast.

"I will?"

Ronnie smoothed her hand over her stomach. "Of course. Once I have our baby."

The female went from fifteen feet away to two with one leap, coming at Ronnie just like she goaded her into doing. As soon as she landed, Ronnie slammed her hands against the female's chest, forcing her back and right into Shaw's arms as he walked into his kitchen.

He'd been having the best day, too. Got to sleep in, nice sore cock from great sex, and a sexy little She-wolf all to himself. But leave it to his own relatives to try and ruin everything.

He glared down at his twin. "Why are you here?"

Growling, she struggled out of his arms. "To check on you and to make sure that idiot," she pointed at Mitch, "didn't steal all your good china. But I had no idea you were entertaining canines. *Or getting them pregnant!*"

"Pregnant?" Brendon knew he was potent, but to go through latex . . . wow.

What should really worry him? That the idea of Ronnie carrying his baby didn't scare him at all. He'd bet she'd look beautiful pregnant.

Then it hit Brendon like a brick to the head where his mind had happily wandered.

Look at that. Your heart can *just stop in your chest but you keep on breathing.*

To keep himself from asking if Ronnie wanted to go maternity clothes shopping, he looked at her and softly asked, "Pregnant?"

Ronnie shrugged. "Nah. I was just fuckin' with her. As soon as she tried to kill me she would have smelled I wasn't pregnant."

Okay. He really liked this female. He'd always loved a woman with a healthy sense of humor. But one who refused to be intimidated by his sister made him all horny and anxious to get her back into bed.

Trying not to laugh in the face of his sister's blinding anger, he said, "Ronnie, this is my twin sister, Marissa. Rissa, this is Ronnie. She and her Pack saved me the other night." He yanked Marissa back. "So be nice," he snarled in her ear.

She didn't apologize and Brendon didn't expect her to, but she stopped talking and looked away.

"Ronnie, could you give us a minute?"

"Yeah. Sure." Thankfully, she didn't seem angry he'd asked her to leave.

She pushed through the door and Rissa turned on him. "Couldn't you at least fuck one of the small ones? She's built like a linebacker."

Not surprisingly that swinging door slammed back open,

denting Brendon's wall as Ronnie walked in yelling, "*You tree-climbing heifer!*"

"*You car-chasing slut!*"

Mitch came around the counter and grabbed hold of Marissa while Brendon put his arms around Ronnie and pulled her back. Unfortunately, the two females were in full rage, and even Brendon's roar didn't get them to shut up.

But Mitch's quiet "You know, lions really don't climb trees" brought the yelling to an abrupt end, and the three of them looked at him.

He shrugged. "I mean . . . we *can* climb trees. Especially ones with low branches. But then we can't get down again. Leopards, however, are quite spry. So they take their prey up into trees. So other predators like us or hyenas can't steal their meal."

After a long moment of silence, Ronnie shook her head and pulled out of Brendon's arms. Without a word, she walked out of the kitchen. He waited until he heard his bedroom door close, then he looked at Marissa.

"I think you better get used to something."

"What?"

"Her." He stepped up to his sister. "Cause if I get my way, she'll be around. A lot."

"Are you giving to the ASPCA, too? I didn't know you'd become so altruistic."

Knowing he was way close to popping his own sister in the mouth, Brendon picked her up and dumped her in front of Mitch.

"What the hell am I supposed to do with her?"

"Take her to your room. The two of you can have lunch and discuss other fascinating cat trivia."

Marissa stepped away from Mitch. "Brendon—"

"*Out!*" He took a deep breath. "Out of my sight. Until I'm ready to see you again. Of course that may not be until after New Year's."

"Fine! Do whatever you want. And when you get fleas, don't come complaining to me."

Mitch shoved Marissa out the door. He stopped and looked at Brendon. For a second, Brendon thought he had something really deep to say. But the kid only shook his head and said, "I'll see ya later, bruh."

His family left and he walked into his bedroom to find Ronnie back in her own clothes.

"Ronnie—"

"Forget it." She turned and glared at him. "I'm leaving you. And I never want to see you again."

He swallowed the lump of panic in his throat. "If you'll give me a—"

She cut him off. "Shaw . . ."

"Yeah?"

"I'm just kiddin'." She burst out laughing. "You should see your face!"

His eyes narrowed. "You think that's funny?"

"I think it's hilarious."

"You're mean."

"Not as mean as that sister of yours. I've met snakes nicer. But compared to my momma she's a lightweight. And I don't scare easy."

"That's good. Now get over here."

"You want me all the way over there? That's like a really long walk."

"Don't make me come get you, Ronnie Lee."

"Oooh. And what if I do make you come get me? Whatcha gonna do, Yankee?" He watched her nipples harden under her worn T-shirt. "Whatcha gonna do to poor little ol' me?"

Slowly, Brendon moved around the bed. "I gave you an order you didn't follow." He made a tsk-tsk sound. "That requires punishment, Ronnie Lee."

"Punishment?" He watched her fight a smile as she took steps away from him. "You'd punish me?"

"Yeah. I would. And I know I'd enjoy every minute of it."

"That's not a good idea, hoss."

"Oh?"

"I'm a fighter. I won't go down easy. No pun intended."

"Good. I don't need any weak females in my bed. Now get over here and take your punishment like a good little pup."

"Sorry, pussy. Can't do it."

Now a few feet from her, Brendon shrugged. "That's too bad, sexy."

He made a wild grab for her and she expertly dodged him, avoiding his arms and audaciously slapping his ass as she passed.

"You little brat!"

She laughed and leaped up on his bed, charging across it. He didn't bother running for her, instead leaping right from the spot where he stood. She'd reached the door when he tackled her from behind, knocking her to the ground.

Brendon used his arms to protect her while he made sure he fell on his side.

She struggled even as she laughed hysterically.

"Shaw, you crazy bastard! Let me go!"

Jumping to his feet, Brendon grabbed hold of her ankle and dragged her back to the bed. "Oh, I'm not letting you go, sexy. Not for a while anyway." Not ever.

He grabbed her waist and lifted her, tossing her on the bed. She tried to sprint away, but he slapped one hand against her back, and the power of it kept her right where she was. He had to be careful, though. Too hard a slam from his hand or paw could snap her back like a twig.

Ronnie kicked and cursed and laughed, trying her best to get away from Brendon. He sat on the edge of the bed and dragged her over his lap.

"I have to say, Ronnie Lee, I love this ass." He reached between them and expertly got her shorts loose.

"Don't even think about it, Shaw," she squealed when he pulled the denim off her ass.

"Too late." He brought his hand down on one cheek.

"Ow! You bastard!"

"That was just mean, Ronnie Lee." He slapped her other cheek.

"Stop. Stop!" She reached back and tried to cover her butt.

"Now, now, Ronnie. You know how important it is to get your punishment."

"Don't," she begged, even while she giggled. "I'll do anything."

"You say that, but I don't think you mean it." He raised his hand and she wiggled desperately.

"I promise. Anything!"

Brendon pretended to think about it for a second. "Anything?"

"Yes."

"Okay. Stay with me today. We'll go out, have some fun, then come back here tonight."

Ronnie blinked in surprise. "Spend the day together? I don't know . . ."

He raised his hand again.

"Okay! Okay! I'll spend the day with you."

"And tonight."

"You said the day."

He brought his hand down on her ass and she howled. Literally. "All right! Tonight, too."

"Promise?"

"Yes. I promise."

"Good."

Brendon didn't say anything for a minute, and finally she looked over her shoulder at him. "What?"

"You wet, sexy?"

Smirking, she looked away. "Maybe."

He shoved her back on the bed and pulled her shorts completely off.

"What are you doing?"

"I can't leave you like this. All wet and horny because of little ol' me."

She rolled her eyes. "Oh puhleeze!"

Brendon pushed his basketball shorts down and put her legs on his shoulders. He grabbed the last condom from the box on the nightstand, making a mental note to pick up more while they were out. "No need to beg, sexy. I'll take care of it."

"Are they all like you?"

"All what? Cats?"

"Yeah."

"They want to be, but they're not kings of the jungle. Only I am." She looked up at him with one raised eyebrow. He shrugged and added, "Duh," before he buried himself balls-deep inside her and "took care of it."

Ronnie pulled out a pair of black jeans, a black sweater that would show some cleavage, and her favorite pair of black cowboy boots. Shaw really seemed to like her in cowboy boots. Now if she could get *him* in a pair of cowboy boots, all would be right with her world.

Smiling, Ronnie made a small pile of her clothes and then stood by the bed trying to figure out what else she might be forgetting. She knew she probably forgot something. Especially with her mind wandering back to last night with Shaw. She could say in all honesty she'd never had such a good time before in bed, and she'd had many good times in bed. Yet something about being with Shaw felt so right.

Whatever. Until the last year or so, Ronnie had never been a big-time worrier, concerned with how events would play out a few months or years down the line. And she wouldn't start now with Shaw. She'd keep this relationship as simple as she kept all the others. They'd have a good time now and end it when it got boring. She gave what they currently had about a three-day shelf life. She figured by New Year's Eve they'd both be looking for something more in line with who they are. Shaw would want back into some Pride, and Ronnie would be on the lookout for the wolf of her dreams.

Until then, until they were both so bored they couldn't stand the sight of each other, she and Shaw would merely enjoy the moments—and have astounding sex.

Satisfied with her plan, Ronnie didn't even bother to turn around when her bedroom door opened. She knew Sissy and Marty walked up behind her.

"Hey, y'all."

When they didn't answer, she looked at Sissy, shocked by the anger she saw there. "What? What's wrong?"

"Do you think we don't know?"

"That the whole Pack doesn't know?" Marty added with more venom than Ronnie ever heard from the woman.

"If y'all are talking about Shaw—"

"You doin' more than one lion?"

"You know what, Smith? That ain't none of your business." She didn't know why Sissy should be so pissed. In the bar the other night she'd practically thrown Ronnie face-first into Shaw's lap.

"Everything that happens in this Pack is now my responsibility."

"You don't even know anything happened," Ronnie reminded her friend. "You haven't even been here."

"We have proof."

Huh? "Proof of what?"

"The disgusting things you two were doing," Sissy snapped.

Ronnie rubbed her eyes. "What the hell are you two talking—"

She stopped when Sissy Mae tossed down the first eight-by-ten picture on the bed. Staring blindly, it took Ronnie several seconds to understand what she was actually seeing.

"You're a whore, Ronnie Lee Reed," Sissy said while tossing down more photos. Lord . . . so many sexual positions. So many disgusting, inappropriate things for two beings to be doing to each other. "And now everybody in the Pack knows it."

"You," Ronnie said through gritted teeth, "showed this to everyone in the Pack?"

"Had to," Marty sighed. "Had to prove what a whore you are."

Ronnie picked up the picture of a male and female having oral sex. "You two spent time on this?"

"Sure." Marty shrugged. "Quick stop over at FAO Schwarz to pick up Ronnie"—Marty lifted up the stuffed wolf she had hidden behind her back—"and Shaw." Her other hand held the stuffed lion.

"Then we used Bobby Ray's digital camera so we could capture the true essence of what you two have been up to since yesterday."

Ronnie kept staring at the pictures. She couldn't help herself. "Where did you find the little latex thong? *And the whip?*"

"Wolf ingenuity, darlin'."

Idiots. Her Pack was filled with absolute idiots.

Marty picked up another picture. "I had heard you have some oral skills, my dear. I must say I'm impressed."

Sissy held up a different photo, Ronnie's stuffed representative in a position with the Stuffed-Shaw that no amount of money in the world would get the breathing Ronnie to try. "And she's not afraid to experiment. Are ya, my kinky little friend?"

Ronnie grabbed several other photos: Stuffed-Ronnie getting it from behind. Stuffed-Ronnie sitting on Stuffed-Shaw's face. Stuffed-Ronnie wearing a leather bustier and a little leather mask. They'd tied her paws to the makeshift cardboard four-poster bed and stuffed-lion Shaw was—*oh good Lord in heaven.*

"You showed these to the Pack?"

"Oh yeah. Over breakfast in that fancy restaurant they have downstairs. Couple of tigers were there too, came over and looked cause they heard us laughing. Then they laughed."

"And the jackals. Don't forget the jackals."

"Oh. Those jackals were so entertained."

The title Alpha Female of the Smith Pack completely forgotten, Ronnie slowly rounded on her childhood best friend. "Sissy Mae?"

"Yeah, darlin'?"

"Run."

Chapter Ten

She smelled good. She'd used his shampoo and soap, and he liked how those scents clung to her.

She'd also slipped into a worn pair of black jeans, a black V-neck sweater, and black cowboy boots that sounded sexy as hell "clopping" against his hardwood floors. Even her leather motorcycle jacket made her look like one of those biker wolves that roamed the West Coast and Texas.

"What's wrong?" she asked as soon as she saw his face.

"Nothing. You ready to go?"

He started to stand, but she pushed him back to the couch and crawled into his lap, her knees on either side of his thighs.

"Now come on, darlin'. Something's not right. What is it?"

Ronnie put her arms around his neck and looked at him, waiting for him to answer. It occurred to him she actually cared.

Brendon had kept most things to himself or between him and his sister. There were few he trusted with his personal information, but those hazel eyes patiently gazing at him made him feel remarkably safe.

"My brother took off again."

She winced and he knew he'd been right. She did care. "I'm sorry, darlin'." Her fingers tangled in his hair. "I know you're worried about him. And I think you're right. He's definitely hiding something. But you can't protect him if he doesn't want you to. Whatever it is, I think it's something he has to work out for himself."

"I know. But I feel like I should help him. I didn't know about him until he was fifteen and I wasn't there to protect him like I should have been."

"That's not your fault."

"I know. Doesn't make me feel better, though." He sighed. "It doesn't make me feel less responsible for him being such a . . ."

"Fuckup?"

He nodded. "Yeah."

She brushed his cheek with the palm of her hand. "I hate to tell you, but he doesn't exactly look helpless. Plus it doesn't seem like he wants anybody's help. And, as my daddy would say, 'fuckup' is relative."

Shaw gave a short laugh. "Your father sure has a lot of interesting sayings."

"You have no idea. He'd also say there's absolutely nothing you can do about any of this. Your brother's grown. He needs to make his own decisions. All you can do is hope he starts doing the right thing and that he doesn't set himself on fire in the process."

Brendon frowned in confusion. "Huh?"

"Forget it. Long story. Now"—she smiled and he felt his mood lighten instantly—"you promised me we'd get out of here."

"That I did."

"Then don't keep me waiting, hoss."

"In one second." He leaned his head down and rubbed his cheeks against her face, neck, chest, and finally her hands when she giggled and tried to push him off.

"What the hell?"

"Okay, now we can go." Standing, Brendon placed her on her feet.

He moved toward the door while she sniffed her hands.

"Hey . . . Hey! *Did you mark me?*"

Grabbing the back of her jacket, he pulled her toward the door. "Stop squawking, sexy. It's totally temporary."

* * *

"*Daaaaaaaaaddddddddddddyyyyyyyyyyyyyyyyyyy!*"

Ronnie's eyes crossed. The kid hit notes that made her feel like barking in response.

The little girl pulled away from her mother and charged head-on into Shaw's arms. He picked her up, lifting her in the air. She squealed in glee again, her little legs kicking out.

Ronnie stepped back, not wanting to intrude and refusing to ask why Brendon Shaw brought her over to meet his goddamn kids. *Means nothing, Ronnie Lee. Figured he'd just take care of it while he was out.*

Yeah. That reasoning *did* sound stupid, didn't it?

Not wanting to obsess about it, Ronnie did the only thing she could think of. She watched the quiet city street for any danger. She'd do the same thing if this were a Pack pup.

"What's my baby girl up to?"

"Going to Grandma's. New Year's hunting!" she cheered.

Apparently Shaw's child had one decibel level, and Ronnie's head had already begun to throb.

A young couple walked down the opposite sidewalk, and Ronnie watched them with an intensity bordering on the psychotic. She couldn't help it. She didn't know them, wasn't sure she liked them, and Shaw's kids were right behind her. The pair must not have liked what they saw on her face because they sped up and disappeared around a corner. That's when Ronnie realized Shaw had called to her.

"What?" She turned and found Shaw holding his daughter against his chest with one arm while he held the other out toward her. He wiggled his fingers and she took his hand.

"Baby, this is daddy's friend, Ronnie. Ronnie, this is my daughter, Serena."

"Hi, Serena."

The little girl snuggled her father's face while piercing gold eyes sized her up. *Baby predators. Ya gotta love 'em.*

"You smell different," she finally said.

Ronnie nodded. "I do."

"And you smell like Daddy, too."

Glaring at Shaw, Ronnie said, "That I do."

"So you're Pride?"

"Uh . . ."

"Don't be rude, Serena," a lioness chided while watching the butler or chauffer or whoever load up one of the waiting limos. "We'll be back about a week after the New Year, Brendon."

"That's fine, Allie." He and his daughter rubbed noses. "When you get back you'll be staying with me for a while, baby."

The girl cheered and kissed her father's face.

Another lioness walked out, a small toddler in her arms. "Hey, Brendon."

"Hey, Serita."

"Glad you could stop by before we left." She watched the limo driver try and put a bag into the trunk. "No, no! Not like that. Oh, I'll do it!"

She turned to Shaw, saw his hands full, and then turned to her sister who raised one eyebrow. "Hands full."

Must be that one tiny Louis Vuitton purse she has on her arm.

"Here." She looked at Ronnie. "You don't mind, do you?"

"Uh . . ." Before Ronnie could answer either way, the little boy reached out for her, and the lioness practically threw him into Ronnie's arms.

Shaw grinned. "You okay?"

"Yeah. Sure." She'd held children before. Lots of them. She had more than thirty-five cousins last count. Still, this wasn't some wolf pup. This was a lion. Future Breeding Male. It felt a little overwhelming. What if she dropped him or something?

"I'm assuming Missy's not here, Allie." Shaw rubbed his cheek against his daughter's while he reached out and affectionately brushed his son's head.

"Nope. She left early this morning with the other kids. Thankfully. If I had to hear her complain one more time about Mace and that woman, I would have ripped her arms off."

"Low-class Po-rican whore."

Shocked, they all looked at the little girl in Shaw's arms.

Allie winced when Shaw glared at her. "I'm sorry, Brendon."
She tugged her daughter's hair. "I told you those were bad
words, Serena. And you're not to say them." Allie looked back
at Shaw. "I'll talk to Missy when I see her."

"You better. I'd hate to have to enforce the terms of our contract because your sister can't watch her mouth."

"I said I'll take care of it. Hey!" Allie snarled when her sister
tossed one of the bags out of the trunk. "That's one of my
bags."

Ronnie hugged the boy in her arms. Only two or so, if she
was guessing right, with an incredibly out-of-control baby mane
of hair. Not a full mane yet, but one day it might rival his father's. "Contract?"

"Do you actually think I'd go into this without an iron-clad
contract?" he murmured, kissing the top of his daughter's head
and smoothing his hand down her back.

Lord, a breeding contract. Only lions would think of that.
Wolves were much more... "in the moment." A bottle of
tequila and a quiet spot in someone's backyard during a party,
and whole Packs were created with matings lasting fifty or sixty
years.

Curious, she asked, "What did they pay you ... exactly?"

"Pay me?"

"You know ... to ... uh ..." She lowered her voice to a
barely there whisper, "Breed?"

Shaw blinked, then he exploded. "*What?*"

Ronnie took a quick step back while his daughter giggled.
"You made him mad."

"I just thought—"

"Well, you're wrong." He looked hurt she'd even think it.
"The contract is only regarding the cubs. Everything is spelled
out. Custody. Visitation. And basic ground rules. That's it.
Everything else is by ... well ..." He glanced down at his
daughter's head.

Ronnie grinned. "Mutual agreement?"

"Exactly." He shrugged. "I wasn't raised in a Pride. I wanted
to see what it was like."

"And?"

He nodded his head. "I love my children."

Chuckling, Ronnie hugged and rocked the little boy in her arms.

Shaw's expression warmed as he watched his son bury his face in Ronnie's neck. "He likes you."

"Like father, like son apparently. He's been nipping my neck for the last five minutes."

"Be grateful he doesn't have his fangs yet."

"Okay. Time to go." Allie tried to pull her daughter away from Shaw, but the little girl held on like her life depended on it, refusing to let her father go. Shaw took her to the limo himself and buckled her into her car seat with surprising efficiency.

Her little guy, Erik, Ronnie finally discovered, didn't put up a fight when his father pulled him from her arms, but he did look deep into her eyes for several seconds, then kissed her cheek before letting anyone put him into his own child seat.

As the limos pulled away, Ronnie turned to Shaw. "Good Lord, is that boy like you."

"So tell me about your mom."

He didn't expect that question to send her tripping over her own two feet and flying into the bookstore's erotica section he'd followed her to. Luckily he had fast hands and caught her before her head could make contact with the *Kama Sutra*.

"Whoa! Are you okay?" The few times she'd mentioned the woman it hadn't been very positive. Brendon simply hoped to find out why.

Ronnie gripped his arms and let him put her back on her feet. "I'm fine. I'm fine."

"You don't have to answer me if you don't want."

Shaking her head, "No. No. I don't mind."

"You two argue a lot, I guess."

"Not often. Only anytime the sun rises or sets somewhere on the Earth."

Brendon laughed and didn't immediately release her. He liked having her in his arms. "Okay, so you two have your, uh, issues."

Ronnie tried to pull out of his arms, but when he didn't release her, she shrugged and leaned back. "Yeah. We don't get along much. Never have. My daddy said we started arguing when I was still in the womb." She leaned forward and grabbed one of the books off the shelf. "Said he'd walk in the room once and found her yelling at her stomach, telling me to stop kicking her so damn much."

Keeping one hand around her waist, Brendon took the book out of her hands. "Let's see what we have here." He quickly read the blurb on the back. "Nope. Forget it. There's no spanking. You'll get bored."

She elbowed his stomach. "I will not get bored." She snatched the book back. "I don't need to read about spanking, ya know?"

"True. Why read about it when I can slap your ass myself?"

She slammed her foot into his instep. And, if he were a lesser man, it would have hurt like hell. He tried to get the book back but she held onto it, the two of them laughing as they struggled over it. It took them a few seconds to realize they were being watched. Slowly, they looked over their shoulders at the human male ogling them. They stared at him for several moments, then Ronnie snarled and snapped. The man couldn't run fast enough.

Grinning, Ronnie looked up at Brendon. "I love doing that."

She mentioned the schools she had interviews set up with, and Shaw drove her to the closest one. They got out and walked around the deserted campus for a good thirty minutes before Ronnie had to sit down on a bench by a Japanese garden so she could put her head between her legs.

"I can't do this. I can't go back to this."

"Why not?" He sat down next to her, his hand smoothing down her back. "Ronnie, it'll be fine."

"I'll be trapped. Like an animal. In these tiny classrooms. And they'll expect me to be back at a certain time on certain days—for *four years*." At the moment, four years sounded pretty much the same as forty.

"You're not real good with everyday routine."

"Why should I be? What's so great about routine? The same thing everyday. Is anything more depressing?"

"Routine doesn't always mean boring."

"Ha!"

Shaw scratched her head, leaning over to kiss her temple. "What are you planning to study anyway?"

Shrugging, she replied, "Probably engineering. It's what I studied in college the first time around."

When he didn't say anything, Ronnie looked at him. He stared off across the campus, a deep frown on his face.

Insulted, she slammed her fist in his shoulder, making him wince. "I know this accent confuses you superior Yankees, but being Southern does not make you stupid."

"I never said—"

"Shut up."

Shaw quickly complied, but she knew he was trying not to laugh. So was she.

Clearing his throat, he said, "Was that the textbook you had at the hospital? The one you hit me with?"

"You deserved it. And yeah. One of my old engineering textbooks." She rubbed her hands over her face and rested back against the bench. "I started reading it, and it all rushed back to me. How boring this all is. No wonder Sissy Mae didn't have to twist my arm to get me to bail. And bail I did."

He chuckled. "But I thought you were ready to change your life. Settle down—"

Ronnie sat up abruptly and slapped her hand over his mouth. "Let's not use those words right now."

Intense gold eyes watched her, and he pulled her hand off his mouth. "What if you meet the right guy, Ronnie? Would you settle down then?"

"You mean the right *wolf*?" She wanted to get the distinctions clear because she didn't much like the expression on that gorgeous face.

"Why limit yourself?"

"Mostly because I don't want funny-looking children."

Shaw rolled his eyes. "Don't tell me you believe that breedist bullshit. Just because two different breeds mate doesn't mean—"

She had her wallet out and her pictures unfurled before he could even finish. "One summer we stayed with Sissy Mae's cousins in North Carolina. Momma's Smith Pack, daddy's a black leopard. This is their daughter when shifted."

Ronnie handed Shaw the picture of her, Sissy Mae, and her cousin lounging around many years ago after the Fourth of July family hunt.

Shaw jerked back. "Christ."

"Yeah. Exactly. Do *you* think that snaggle tooth is attractive?"

He shuddered but tried to hide it. "Okay. That's one instance."

"Really? Have you seen a wolf with a full mane? Or a cat with a long muzzle?"

He shuddered again. "Okay. Okay." He motioned to the picture. "But what does she look like human?"

She flipped a couple of pictures over and showed him a picture of the three friends on the North Carolina beach in bikinis a year or two back.

"Whoa." Shaw took the wallet out of her hand. "She's hot." He glanced at Ronnie and back at the picture. "North Carolina, right?" He shoved Ronnie off the bench. "That's where I can find the snaggle-toothed babe?"

For a second there, he ran so fast she wasn't sure she'd catch up with him.

Brendon glanced around the dance studio and frowned. "Explain to me why we're here."

For some unknown reason she'd dragged him into one of those ballroom dancing studios and had signed up for one of the advance classes. She wouldn't tell him why, but she kept giggling, which had begun to make him very nervous.

"Would you relax already? You are so uptight."

"I'm not uptight. I just don't like to be confused. It's a cat thing."

Ronnie scrunched up her nose and glared at him. "Are you trying to imply that wolves like to be confused?"

"I'm not trying to imply anything. You're the ones who chase your tails for apparently no reason."

She went to slam her foot on his instep again, but he dodged her this time. Then the pulsating beat of Latin music started, and the teacher got in the middle of the room.

"All right, everybody. Let's all partner up and get started."

Ronnie Lee grabbed his hand and dragged him to the middle of the dance floor.

"Have you lost your mind? I don't know how to do this."

"Oh yes you do."

"No, I don't."

Ronnie started moving to the beat, shaking that delightful ass as only she could. "Come on, darlin'," she coaxed. "You did a great job the other night."

"The other—" *Oh God!* He glanced around at the dancing couples. "I . . . I thought I dreamed that."

She grabbed his hands and started taking him through the mambo. "Nope. You didn't dream a thing. I had no idea you could move so well." She took a step back and swung her head from side to side like, he now realized, he did *that* night, only with full mane swinging in the cold December wind.

"Oh Christ, shoot me now."

"Now, now. No need to be shy around ol' Ronnie Lee." She turned and rubbed her ass against his cock in time to the music. "One day I'll have to teach you the two-step, but this'll do for now."

Taking her hand, he spun her around and caught her in his arms. "You are never to tell anyone about this, Rhonda Lee."

"Lips are sealed, darlin'—except during sex."

"Good girl." He started to move and then abruptly stopped, looking at her in a panic. "That night . . . I didn't do anything else, uh, embarrassing?"

She snorted while she watched and emulated the foot moves of the other dancers. "I got two words for ya, hoss. Play. Bow."
Oh please, someone shoot me now.

Ronnie took a step back, wrinkled up her face, and shrugged.

"What does that mean?" Shaw looked down at what he wore. "It doesn't look right?"

"It looks fine." Actually, the man looked astounding. "Tuxes are just . . ." She shrugged again. "Boring."

He threw up his hands. "And what would you suggest?"

"What are you asking me for? I don't care what you wear."

"I'm asking you because you'll be with me when I wear this on New Year's Eve."

Ronnie took another step back. "What? When did I agree to that?"

"You didn't. But you're my date for New Year's."

"And you decided that when exactly?"

"When I met you."

"And you assumed I'd say yes?"

"Yeah. Unless you have another date."

"If I had another date, I wouldn't be here with you now." Annoyed, she walked up to him. "I date one male at one time. I may not date 'em for long, but I don't overlap."

Shaw slipped his hand behind her neck, the skin tingling where he touched her, and pulled her close.

"Good," he murmured. "I'd hate to have to kill a man for being in my way."

"Don't get too attached, hoss. This is temporary." Fun, but temporary. Right?

"You going somewhere I don't know about?"

She tried to answer him, to tell him that soon she'd be gone just like she'd done so many times before. But he massaged the back of her neck and she had to grab his hand when her leg started to shake.

Staring at her, Shaw looked down at her legs and she stumbled away from him before he could start again.

"Man, am I hungry!" She cleared her throat so she wouldn't

yell the next sentence like she'd yelled the first. "How about some dinner?"

"I know a perfect place. Great Italian and amazing desserts."

"Perfect."

"What about the tux?"

Shrugging, "If it's the best you can do."

"It's Armani."

She pointed at her jeans. "And these are Old Navy. Don't care when I'm hungry. Let's move, hoss."

Brendon took another bite of the mass of dark chocolate fudge cake with Belgian dark chocolate candy, "enrobed" in dark chocolate sauce monstrosity they'd ordered for dessert. The plate it came in took up half the table. Luckily they only ordered one and decided to share.

Ronnie scooped up another spoonful. "Okay, have you ever been in love?"

They'd spent the whole day together and Brendon had never enjoyed himself quite so much with a female. Ronnie kept things light and funny, seemed to enjoy life in general, and adored his kids. Now they ate at one of his favorite restaurants for dinner, grabbing seats outside so they could watch the world speed by while they downed two prime rib dinners. Rare.

Brendon crunched on the walnuts his half of their chocolate dessert contained. "Once," he said after a moment of thought. "When I was thirteen. Her name was Denise Leweskie. I learned how to polka for her."

He expected Ronnie to laugh at him, his sister sure as hell had in seventh grade until he shoved her into his gym locker with his unwashed jock.

But Ronnie didn't laugh. Instead, she said, "That's nothing. To impress a polar bear I met in Switzerland, I once got on two tiny sticks and flew down a snow-covered mountain."

Brendon blinked. "Do you mean ski?"

"Yeah. Never again. Which is exactly what I said when I went flying off that mountain. I also said it in the hospital, too. And while I was in traction."

Focusing on the dessert in front of him to prevent himself from laughing in her face, he asked, "Didn't you take lessons first?"

"Lessons? Oh no. I didn't need lessons." He glanced up and found her shaking her head in disgust at her own idiocy. "You see, Sissy said I wouldn't need lessons. 'You're a shifter,' she said. 'We can do anything,' she said. And the fact that I'd had six hot chocolates laced with tequila had me believing she was right. So, there we are on this mountain some-the-fuck-where in Switzerland, at midnight—"

"Midnight?"

"Yeah. And I was standing at the little kid's run, thinking to myself, 'Girl, have you lost your goddamn mind?' and Sissy says, 'If you're going to impress a polar, Ronnie Lee, you better get over to that other run . . . way up there.' So, like a damn fool, up there I went."

"And how old were you exactly?"

"Nineteen, I believe. Nineteen and dumb as a load of bricks. Dumb and horny."

"And the polar bear?"

Ronnie gave a slow grin that made his cock hard. Brendon had to admit, he was beginning to love that smile. "Let's just say he made the nights go very fast in a lonely Swiss hospital where the staff, mostly jackals, mocked me."

Brendon couldn't believe the next words about to come out of his mouth, but he discovered he couldn't help it. "Ever seen that polar bear since?"

She looked surprised at the question. "Are you kidding? That was a long time ago. I'm not even sure I'd remember his face or he'd remember mine. Besides, he was only visiting Switzerland; he was originally from Norway. And, last I heard, me and Sissy are still banned from there."

Jealousy over some big, dumb bear flew out the window as he stared at Ronnie. "You . . . you were banned from Norway? The *country*?"

"Yeah. Talk about an uptight people. Apparently they have no sense of humor."

Brendon stared at his filled spoon for several seconds. "Um . . . are there any other countries you're not allowed in?"

"*Whole* countries?" She shrugged. "Well, there's Korea."

"North or South?"

"Both."

Brendon put his spoon down. "Both?"

"Yeah. And then we were banned from Japan, but they lifted that. Peru and Morocco also temporary. Now Belgium did say never to return, but that still doesn't seem fair. For once it was not our fault. And Germany . . . well, let's just say that whole thing about the Autobahn having no speed limit—not entirely accurate."

The "recommended speed" on portions of the Autobahn was eighty miles an hour. Other than that, most of it was pretty free-wheeling. Brendon and his sister, after making several million, had vacationed over there, rented Ferraris, and hit the Autobahn. They raced each other for hours, but locals still passed them.

"And those cops are mean," she added.

"You got pulled over on *the Autobahn*?"

Ronnie shrugged again. "Eventually. When they caught us."

Brendon leaned back in his chair, his arms crossed in front of him. "You're never driving my car."

Confused, Ronnie asked, "Why not?" Then her eyes brightened. "What kinda car ya got?"

"It doesn't matter. You're not driving it. Ever."

Brendon had more than one car. His Mercedes got him around the city. But he had a sweet Jag he would never put into the hands of this female. She could take care of his kids but never his car.

She pouted for about two seconds, then she looked panicked and tried to duck down.

"What?" Christ, he hoped it wasn't some ex-boyfriend. Something told him he'd be meeting a few of those over time. They probably had some "Ronnie Anonymous" association to help them get over the addictive nature of this woman.

"Well hey, y'all."

Brendon looked up into the face of a She-wolf. She looked familiar. He probably saw her with the Smith Pack.

"You don't mind if we join you?"

Ronnie sat up straight. "As a matter of fact—"

Too late. She'd pulled out a chair and plunked herself down at their table. Another female stepped up. A human. A human Brendon recognized.

He smiled. "Detective MacDermot."

"Shaw." She glanced at Ronnie and shrugged. "I tried to make her keep going, but she insisted."

"Now, now. Ronnie loves me." The She-wolf motioned to a chair. "Sit, Dez. Sit." She placed her elbows on the table, interlaced her fingers, and rested her chin on top of her hands. Big, innocent, brown eyes turned to him, and she smiled. "Now tell us, Brendon Shaw. Are you having a good time with my friend here?"

If Brendon were a lesser man, he would have run for his life.

Ronnie sighed and looked at Dez.

"Sorry," Dez muttered. "I really did try and stop her."

"I'm having a great time," Shaw answered, a warm smile on his face. "The best time I've had in a long while."

Sissy sat up straight and grinned at Ronnie. "Good. Very good."

Shaw pointed at Sissy's face. "What happened to your eye?"

Ronnie scratched her nose to stop the smile. "Yeah. Tell him how you got that black eye, Sissy."

Glaring, "Walked into a door."

Ronnie glanced over at Dez only to find her staring at what was left of their dessert.

"Want some?"

"It looks really decadent."

"Cause it is, darlin'. Here." Ronnie reached over to an empty table beside them and grabbed a spoon. She handed it to Dez and pushed the enormous bowl toward her.

Dez, with an unholy gleam in her eye only other chocolate

lovers could truly understand, dug her spoon into the dessert. Halfway to her mouth, she stopped when she realized Shaw stared at her.

"What?"

Dez wasn't exactly a subtle gal, but that could explain why they all liked her so much. Before they met her, they figured she'd be more like a cat with Mace being a lion and all. But she was way more doglike.

"I wanted to thank you."

Her eyes narrowed. "For?"

Shaw gave a small frown. "For saving my life."

"Oh. That. Yeah. You're welcome." She motioned to the bowl in front of her. "Think I can eat now without you staring at me?"

Yup. Subtle.

"Y'all should come out with us tonight," Sissy offered, ignoring Ronnie's pointed glare. "We're meeting the Pack and Mace at a club on the East Side."

"Forget it," Ronnie snarled before Shaw could say a word.

"Why? You ashamed of your new boyfriend?"

"He's not my boyfriend."

"I'm not?"

Shocked, Ronnie turned to a pouting Shaw. "What?"

"Oh my God! This is the most amazing thing I've ever tasted."

Ignoring Dez's orgasmic reaction to their dessert, Ronnie leaned forward. "What are you talking about?"

"I'm hurt. I got the marriage license for nothing."

"The marriage—*Have you lost your mind?*"

"I already added you to my will. And, of course, our future snaggle-toothed children. All ten of them."

Sissy laughed so hard she cried, and Dez banged her free hand on the table. "Freakin' amazing. This chocolate has to be imported."

Shaw motioned to the waiter for the check. "Why don't we go back to the hotel and talk about this and start the breeding process immediately. No more pills for you, and the condoms can go too."

"Not on your damn life, cat!" One gold eyebrow perked up at the slightly hysterical sound to her voice, and Ronnie cleared her throat. "We're going to the club with the Pack. Remember?"

"Oh?" The pout returned. "I guess. If you really want to."

Damn tricky cats!

"And ya know, this cake," Dez continued, completely oblivious, "it's completely flourless. Amazingly dense. And rich."

"I guess if you're insisting." Shaw grinned, acting like he won something. "We'll go hang with your Pack."

"I'll get you for this."

"Yeah," he agreed. "Tonight."

Dez pointed her spoon at the bowl. "The candy . . . I think it's imported dark chocolate. I'm betting 72 percent cocoa. You do know this is evidence of God?"

Shaw let out a sigh of satisfaction. "You know, Detective, I have to say I'm going to enjoy you being part of the Llewellyn family."

Chapter Eleven

"He likes you so much," Sissy enthused, ignoring yet another one of Ronnie's sighs. "Aren't I right, Daria? He can't keep his damn hands off her."

"Yup," Daria agreed. "He's always touchin' her. Flirtin' with her. I didn't know cats could be so friendly."

"Me either. I think he's sweet as hell. Don't be stupid, Rhonda Lee. You gotta keep this one."

"But he's a cat," Marty added. "The Reed boys ain't gonna like that none."

"It don't matter if he's cat or wolf. Reed boys won't like any male getting too close to their baby sister. And that's a fact."

"Can we talk about this some other time?" Ronnie growled.

"Lord, girl. What are you doin' in there?"

Yelling through the bathroom stall door while she hovered over a toilet no amount of money or protective sheets of paper would ever allow her to sit on, "*I am tryin' to pee!*"

"Well hurry up. We need to analyze this."

"I don't want to analyze anything. And move away from the goddamn door."

They did, allowing Ronnie to finally pee in peace. Once done, she stormed out of the stall and over to the sinks. She washed her hands and Sissy sat on the counter.

"You like him."

Ronnie took the paper towels Marty handed her. "Yes. I like him. So?"

"Then don't do anything stupid, Ronnie. He really likes you. I can tell."

"Leave it alone, Sissy Mae."

"Tell her, Marty."

Marty folded her arms over her chest. "I have faith Ronnie will make the right decision without our help."

Suddenly feeling smug, Ronnie tossed the wet paper towel into the trash can and headed toward the door. "And stop trying to get me to drink tequila tonight."

"Might get you to loosen up a bit."

"Do you remember the last time you said that to me?"

"No, but—"

"We were in Prague. 'Loosen up,' you said. 'What can it hurt?' you said."

They entered the hallway, pushing past some of the most beautiful humans in the world like they were no more than bums on the street.

"Are you still not over that?" Sissy sighed.

"Do you think a Prague jail is fun? It's not."

"That was not my fault. Perhaps you forgot the hyenas that were involved."

"I forget nothing, Sissy Mae Smith. So unless you want me to shove a glass of tequila up your ass, you'll stop bugging me."

Brendon nursed his drink and tried to ignore the make-out session going on next to him at the bar. Eventually, he had to look past the couple at Smitty, who stood on the other side. He raised an eyebrow, and Smitty gave a slow easy grin that must have had females passing out at his feet.

The wolf turned and rested his elbow against the bar, focusing on the couple. Brendon mirrored him and they both watched until Dez's eyes snapped open and she looked at the two men staring at her.

With an incredibly strong shove for a human, she pushed Mace off her. "Why don't I go see if I can find a booth or something." She practically sprinted off, and Mace Llewellyn glared at them. "Bastards."

He stormed off after his female and Smitty moved to the stool next to Brendon, which kind of surprised the cat. Actually, the whole night had been a surprise. The Packs Brendon had met since owning the hotel had been barely tolerable, and some had been downright violent. But Smitty and his Pack really didn't seem to give a shit about him and Ronnie. He appreciated that, because the more time he spent around that woman, the more his feelings for her grew. But he only had to take one look at her face to know the thought of anything remotely permanent freaked her the hell out.

It entertained Brendon to watch her constant struggle between wanting to find a nice "wolf" and settle down and wanting to remain that traveling wild child on her own timetable.

It would not be easy to convince Rhonda Lee Reed that he could give her everything she ever wanted. But he'd always been determined, and he had no intention of giving up now.

"So . . ." Smitty began.

"So . . . ?"

"You and our little Ronnie, huh?"

"Yup."

"My sister says you like her."

"Yeah. I like her." Brendon shrugged. "I like her a lot."

Smitty gave a surprised chuckle. "Man, you and Mace sure do confuse things."

"How do we do that?"

"We're the loyal ones. The ones who love forever. Y'all are the alley cats. Not to be trusted. Y'all are ruining what I've been using in my favor for many pleasurable years, and I don't appreciate it one damn bit."

Brendon laughed. He could see why Mace liked Smitty. Smart and funny hidden under a veneer of slow-moving Southern male.

"Sorry, but I never saw her coming."

"Most don't." He sipped his beer. "A lot of people think Ronnie just follows Sissy Mae around like a lemming. I think she even thinks it sometimes. But she's smarter than that.

There's no one else I would have trusted my baby sister with when she went traipsing over to Europe."

Smitty looked over at him. "Her brothers are probably going to be coming this way soon, Shaw. If you're not serious about her, I'd suggest you end it right quick."

"I'm very serious. But she scares easy."

"So does Sissy. They're afraid of becoming like some of the Smith females. Trapped in a small town, mated to men they love but can barely stand with five or six more Smith males to raise. The two of them wanted more, and they went out and got it. I admire that myself."

"Me, too."

"Then I best warn ya . . . the Reed boys, they love their sister something fierce. But she uses them and her daddy to keep any male serious about her away. You want that little gal, you'll have to face them boys head-on. They're gonna mess that pretty face up some, but I doubt they'll kill ya . . . unless they *really* don't like you. Which, with the Reed boys, is a definite risk cause they don't like many."

Brendon shook his head and faced Smitty. "Why are you telling me this? Warning me, I mean?"

"I don't know really. You don't irritate me much. And you're kinda funny. Plus, I guess, because Ronnie and Sissy are two peas in a pod. The two of them can convince the other of anything and often do. But maybe if Ronnie finds somebody . . ."

"Then maybe Sissy will stop fighting it?"

"Don't get me wrong. I'd rather take a bowie knife to my eye than think of my baby sister with any male on this planet. But I don't wanna see her alone and bitter because she's trying to not be like our momma. Because the harder she tries not to be like our momma, the more like our daddy she becomes. And, hoss, I simply can't have that."

Brendon motioned for two more beers from the bartender. "Then I guess I'm on deck to make this thing happen, huh?"

"Better get your cat ass in gear, too, son. Because that Ronnie . . . she don't stand still long for any male."

*   *   *

The four females stepped into the main part of the club. Music pulsated, lights flickered and flashed, and bodies writhed on the dance floor. It surprised Ronnie the little interest this held for her anymore. At one time, she and Sissy would have been right in the middle of all those people dancing their asses off.

Sissy stood beside her. "You wanna dance, darlin'?"

Ronnie looked at her friend. "Do you?"

She scrunched up her face a bit. "Not really."

"Me neither."

"Lord, we're gettin' old, aren't we, Ronnie?"

"Nah. Not old. Maturing. Maturing's a good thing."

"Who taught you that lie?"

Ronnie started to laugh, but stopped abruptly and stared out over the dancing crowd. A few of them shifters, but most of the writhing bodies were humans. Still, she'd always been good at recognizing scents.

Sissy Mae watched her. "What is it?"

Ronnie sniffed the air and growled. She took several steps forward and her eyes caught sight of one of them. She remembered the scar on his neck, bruises still on his face from his run-in with Shaw, and the persistent smell of gun oil.

She started toward him, watching as he headed to a back door and slipped out. Like most humans, completely oblivious to being tracked.

Not clear why, Ronnie went after him. But she knew she didn't track him alone. Without having to say a word, the She-wolves were right behind her, slipping out of the crowd and following. The best part of being in a Pack—you were never alone. They always had your back. They always protected their own. No matter what internal fighting may go on as each member tried to stay out of the Omega spot, they were always a unit. With a helpful howl, they'd have the males by their side as well. But they didn't need the males. They rarely did when it came to hunting a full-human.

Ronnie reached the emergency exit the man had slipped

through and pushed open the door. Ten feet below, the exit door slammed shut. Ronnie grabbed the railing and leaped over it, landing in a crouch.

Cracking her neck, she shoved open the door and walked out into a large back alley. At the mouth of the alley, the scarred male leaned against a late-model Ford, talking to the other man Ronnie remembered from Shaw's room. Each leaned over the roof, speaking in low tones.

Ronnie sauntered over, loving the cold December air against her skin. She always got a little hot and bothered when she stalked. Nothing she loved better.

Neither male realized she was there until she placed her hands on either side of the scarred male. Her fingers gripped the metal roof, and she barely held her claws in. She'd pull those out only when necessary.

"Well, hello, darlin'," she purred in his ear.

Stunned, both men froze. The male facing her quickly saw the other females behind her as they slowly made their way around the car. Surrounding them as Ronnie surrounded the scarred human.

He slowly turned, gripped her hands, and pushed her away. "Can I help you?" Ronnie grimaced. The male's New York accent was thick and powerful, grating on her sensitive wolf ears.

"I was just wondering," she softly stated while stepping close again, her hands resting on his chest as she leaned into his lanky body, "what your fascination with Brendon Shaw might be?"

The male snorted, dismissing her. "Mind your own business, sweet cheeks."

Using very little effort, Ronnie slammed the scarred human back against the car, then pinned him there with her body.

"I'm sorry. Maybe I wasn't clear, darlin'."

The She-wolves moved closer. Gemma climbed up on the hood of their car and Sissy Mae got close to the other male, sniffing his neck while she rubbed up against him. Any other time, Ronnie would bet the male would love that move. Right now, he looked terrified.

"What do you want with Brendon Shaw?" she asked again.

The male stared at her. They were of equal height, but Ronnie easily outweighed him. She felt the gun attached to his slacks, but she had no fear he'd ever get close to it if he tried.

"Nothin'. I don't want nothin' from Brendon Shaw."

"I saw you at his hospital room. I know you were there."

He smirked, so Ronnie leaned forward and snapped at him. She didn't bare her fangs, but she added a little growl for effect.

"Answer me, boy. I'd hate to have to ruin that face any more than necessary."

His smirk turned feral and he said, "Lady, get the hell away from me before I arrest you for assaulting an officer."

Ronnie raised an eyebrow. "You're a cop? You expect me to believe that?"

The other male pulled out the long chain hidden under his orange sweater. The badge hanging at the end of it blinked at her in the streetlights.

Fuck, fuck, fuck!

Holding her hands up, Ronnie stepped back. Damn, but she really didn't want to go to jail tonight. Although New York jails couldn't possibly be any worse than the ones in Mexico and Russia.

"You're cops," she said flatly.

"Yeah, brain trust. We're cops."

With a motion from Sissy Mae, the other She-wolves slowly backed off.

The humans opened the car doors, but Ronnie couldn't leave it at that.

"What do you want with Brendon Shaw? Why were you at the hospital?"

The male on the driver's side ignored her and got into the car, immediately starting it up. Poor guy couldn't wait to get out of there. The other looked at her and smiled. "Let's just say," he offered as he climbed into the vehicle, "we're not here because of *Brendon* Shaw."

*   *   *

"You know, the first time you ever spoke to me, you held a conversation with my tits."

A lesser man would have spit his beer across the table. Brendon, however, choked it back and looked straight at a scowling Mace and smirking Dez across the booth they'd absconded.

With a shrug, he said, "What can I say? They're so . . . *there*. It's hard not to talk to them like they're individual people."

Dez's eyes narrowed, but Mace grunted and turned away. It took her all of five seconds to realize he was laughing. "What's so damn funny?" she demanded.

"Nothing." Mace cleared his throat and looked back at her, trying, Brendon noted, not to let his eyes stray anywhere near her very prominent breasts. "Just thinking about how much I lo—"

Dez's hand landed across Mace's mouth so fast and hard, Brendon almost jumped.

"I thought," she growled, "we had this discussion."

Mace pulled her hand away and kissed her fingers. "You discussed. I didn't agree to a damn thing."

"Tricky cat."

"You say that like it's a bad thing. Besides"—he nuzzled her palm—"you know you lov—"

Dez's free hand slapped across his mouth. "Stop it!"

Sure, most people would walk away, give the pair some alone time. But Brendon was cat and, to be quite honest, he found the whole thing absolutely fascinating. Humans could be so weird. Especially human females. Didn't they live to hear someone say they loved them? When did that change?

Really, give him a predator female any day. They were much easier to deal with and a lot less drama.

"Well"—Ronnie dropped into the booth next to him—"I almost got arrested again."

Then, of course . . . there was Ronnie.

Taking a deep breath, Brendon asked, "Why did you almost get arrested . . . again?"

"For, according to him, assaulting an officer." Now Ronnie, completely oblivious, had Dez's full attention. "Although I didn't assault him. He was just pissed off I had him pinned against his car with my knee real close to his nuts."

After several long seconds, Brendon shrugged again. "You know . . . I have absolutely no response to that statement."

Dez did, though. "Explain to me why you had a cop pinned up against a car."

"I didn't know he was a cop. I thought he was some scumbag. Looked like a scumbag. And, he was the one ol' Tigger here beat up in his hospital room."

Brendon winced. "I beat up cops?"

"Sure did. They had badges and everything."

Dez snorted. "Unfortunately, that doesn't mean shit. What were their names?"

Now Ronnie shrugged. "Got me. Yet their scent did have a strong hint of jackal. But they're completely human."

Taking a deep, cleansing breath, Dez asked, "Okay, I'm not going to let that statement freak me out, so let's try this. What did they look like?"

After thinking for several moments, "One had dark blond hair and a scar across his neck."

"A scar? Like someone cut him from ear to ear?"

"Yeah. Exactly."

"Was the other one a little runty, dark-haired guy? With a mustache?"

"Yeah! That's them."

Dez nodded. "Yup. You beat up cops."

Brendon frowned. "Then shouldn't I be in jail?"

Ronnie rested her head against his shoulder and yawned. "They said they don't want you. I think they want your brother."

Completely drained, Brendon rested his elbows on the table and rubbed his eyes with his knuckles. "What exactly has that dumb fuck done?"

"You can't assume he did anything." When Brendon glared at her in disbelief, Ronnie shrugged. "Innocent until proven guilty. And if he is guilty, I'm sure he has an explanation."

"Why do you constantly protect that idiot?" Brendon hated how much he sounded like Marissa, but suddenly he saw how idiotic he must sound to her. Always making excuses for Mitch. Mitch who was wanted by the police. *Nice one, asshole.*

"I protect him cause he's your kin." She brushed her knuckles against his cheek. "I protect him like I'd protect you or your cubs. Although"—she gave that adorable smirk—"your sister is on her own. Because Mitch may or may not be a criminal, but at least he's nice to me. He gave me yogurt."

"Yogurt?" he asked to give himself a few seconds to get control of his suddenly exploding emotions. Not over Mitch. Hell, he'd gotten used to these times with his baby brother. But the fact that Ronnie protected him and his family like she would her Pack. Brendon didn't even know if she realized it yet. Realized how much that simple admission said to him.

"I love yogurt, and he dug it out of the back of that inhumanly large refrigerator you have. He did it for me. Hardened criminals don't do that unless they're expecting to get some pussy out of it."

Brendon took her hand, kissed her knuckles. "That was eloquent, Ronnie."

She snorted in response and then climbed into his lap. He wrapped his arms around her and pulled her in close to his chest.

Ronnie nuzzled his neck and licked his jaw. "Any chance you're ready to go home, hoss?"

Nibbling her ear, Brendon whispered, "More than ready. What would you like to do when we get there?"

She wrapped her arms around his shoulders. "Let's not worry about family or cops or anything else tonight." She kissed him and pulled back with a grin. "Tonight I'm a coquettish schoolgirl and you're the dirty next-door neighbor boy trying to talk me out of my virginity."

Dez choked on her beer, and Mace had to pound her back to help ease the cough.

Brendon ignored it all, instead staring into Ronnie's dark

hazel eyes. Because of the darkness of the club, they glinted when she moved. "The coquettish schoolgirl?"

"Trust me, darlin'." She slipped off his lap and stood, grabbing his hand to drag him out of the booth. "I've got the perfect skirt."

Chapter Twelve

She'd practically shoved him into his elevator and told him she'd meet him upstairs in a little while. That had been forty minutes ago and he was starting to get antsy. Something about that female, something that made Brendon insane and wild. Something that made him want to do whatever necessary to make her a part of his life forever. Not just because she was a great time in bed—and Christ, was she ever—but because she had a heart as big as Asia. He loved how Ronnie cared about those in her life and did what she could to take care of them. Protect them.

He loved how she loved life. The woman had done more in her thirty years than most people in their sixties, but still she acted like everything was wonderful and new. She always found something interesting to learn.

Christ . . . he loved her. He loved her and she was home. They were home. She just hadn't realized it yet.

The knock on the door surprised him since he'd given her his key. He dropped his beer on the table and headed to the front door. He didn't need to check the peephole because he could smell her on the other side. He smelled her excitement and anticipation. The scent made him hard and desperate, but when he opened the door he froze.

He thought she'd been kidding. But nope. Not his Ronnie. There she stood in a way-too-short plaid skirt, white blouse, and white Keds. She'd put her hair into a ponytail at the top of her head, and she even had on small wire-rim glasses. She held a notepad and textbook against her chest, and she stared down at the floor.

"I'm . . . I'm here for your tutoring session," she stammered out, and all Brendon could do was lean against the door, staring down at her. She glanced up at him. "Ain't ya gonna let me in? My momma will be real mad if I ain't back in an hour." Her accent was thicker, her voice a little higher and insecure sounding.

She wanted to play to get his mind off his brother, and he was more than happy to oblige.

"Guess you better get in here then." He stepped back from the door and she walked in, doing her best not to brush up against him.

"Wanna beer," he offered, making sure to slam the door behind her.

She jumped and turned around. "Uh . . . no. No. That's okay."

"You sure? Might loosen you up."

"I don't need loosening up, Brendon Shaw. I need to get this trig down your throat, so I can go home for dinner." She stormed over to the living room and slammed the books down on his coffee table, then sat primly on the edge of his couch. "I'm just doing this cause Coach Wilson asked me to."

"Makes sense. You being president of the math club and all."

Brendon sat down on the couch next to her. "So tell me, Ronnie Lee, why don't you like me?"

"Don't like you? Who said I didn't like you?"

"You do, pretty much. You never say hi to me or sit next to me in history class." He brushed the hair falling from her ponytail off her neck. "You look right through me."

Her eyes closed when his fingers touched her throat, and a small shudder rippled through her body. "That's . . . that's not true. I just . . . we don't . . ." She shook her head. "I can't think when you're doing that."

"Doing what?" he softly demanded as he kissed her neck again. "Don't know what you're talking about."

"We need to study."

"Study later. I need you to reassure me now."

"Reassure you?"

"Tell me you like me, Ronnie Lee." He nipped her neck. "Even better . . . show me."

Ronnie's eyes crossed and she clenched her knees together. She thought she'd have to drag Brendon Shaw into this little role-playing thing. Not a lot of males, human or shifter, were real comfortable with it. Or they did it wrong. Diving right for the good stuff and not even bothering with the little scene she'd created.

Not Brendon. She could easily imagine him as head of some Texas high school football team, luring young girls to the death of their virginity. As much as she was ready to straddle him and fuck him into oblivion, she had no problems extending the game a wee bit more. How often would she get someone worthy of the effort?

"You stop that right now, Brendon Shaw! I'm not like those slutty cheerleaders." She slapped her hand against his face to push him back and squealed when his tongue licked her palm. "I . . . I'm a good girl."

"You don't have to be, Ronnie Lee." One of his big hands cupped her breast, the thumb teasing her nipple. "Let me show you how much fun it is to be bad every once in a while."

"I . . . I can't. It's wrong. What if my momma finds out? Or the preacher? They'll see it on my face. I know they will and I'll burn in hell."

With him kissing her neck and massaging her breasts, it took Ronnie a good thirty seconds to realize Shaw had slowly pushed her onto her back.

"No one will know, Ronnie Lee. I promise."

"You'll tell everybody."

"I won't. I know what your daddy will do to me if he finds out." He unbuttoned her blouse in record time, slipping it off her shoulders. "It'll be our little secret, Ronnie Lee. Yours and mine."

Brendon's big hands slid under her skirt and took hold of the plain white cotton panties she had to dig through her entire suit-case to find. She always made sure to keep a pair with her, and she'd never been so grateful before.

"But . . . I've never done *it* before."

He slid the panties down her legs. "Not ever?"

"No. Not ever."

"I'll be your first?"

She gave a shy nod. Amazing, since she'd never been shy a day in her life. Even when she *had* lost her virginity.

"Don't worry, baby. I'll take care of you."

She thought Brendon would just get on top of her and go for it, not that she minded, but he didn't. He played the game of the only-slightly bad boy next door. He rested on his side, staring down at her, his head propped up by one arm.

"Since this is your first time, we've gotta take this slow. I can't rush you or I'll hurt you."

Oh man.

"And I don't wanna hurt you, Ronnie Lee."

"Okay."

The fingers of his free hand slid down her chest, stopping briefly to unhook the front clasp of her bra and gently cup and squeeze her breasts. Then his hand continued its journey down her body until it reached her legs, slid back up her thighs, and under her skirt. The only thing, besides her white Keds, she still had on.

He slid one finger inside her, and Ronnie's eyes closed.

"No, baby. I want you to look at me. I need to know if I'm hurting you."

Oh Lord. The man is good!

Slowly, shyly, Ronnie opened her eyes.

"Good girl. Now tell me if this hurts." His index finger slowly pumped inside her, going in only so much like there was a hymen actually left to break. Normally this wouldn't do much for her, but the way Shaw watched her and made her watch him, while still keeping their little game going, had her arching into his hand. "You like that?"

She gave a shy nod and fought her desire to tackle the man onto his back and take him by force.

"How about this?" His middle finger joined his index, still moving slowly and carefully inside her. "Does that feel good?"

"Yeah."

"Good." He settled himself comfortably on the couch, his head still resting in the palm of his hand.

The entire room filled with the sound of their heavy breathing and his fingers stroking inside her, all that wetness making squishy sounds that might have embarrassed a lesser female.

"Now I'm going to try something else, Ronnie Lee. You might get a little scared at first, but what you're feeling is completely normal. Okay?"

She nodded and grabbed hold of his shoulders when his thumb brushed against her clit. Her legs moved restlessly over his couch and her breathing turned into hard pants.

"That's right, baby. Just go with it." Shaw watched her with wild eyes, like he couldn't wait to see her come. Merely the out-of-control high school quarterback triumphant over making the uptight math wiz come all over his hand? Nah. Ronnie knew better. Shaw simply liked to get women off. A rare and mighty attractive trait in a male.

His thumb pushed hard against her clit and moved in circles. Ronnie couldn't hold back anymore. Her body bowed, her head thrown back, glasses flying across the room. She vaguely heard them slide across his hardwood floor, then she came. The power of it exploding through her, her fingers digging into Shaw's shoulders as she rode his hand.

By the time she floated back to the here and now, Shaw had his clothes off and a condom on, probably from the box he'd picked up earlier at a little drugstore.

She knew he really liked her skirt when he still didn't take it off—merely lifted it out of the way—while settling between her thighs.

"You ready for me, Ronnie Lee?" he demanded between deep kisses.

Ronnie could only nod. She didn't want to say anything stupid. Like "marry me." She didn't want to fall for this guy, but how could she not? Sure, he was great in bed, but hell, so were a lot of guys. No, Brendon Shaw was a full-fledged, honest-to-God sweetheart with a wicked sense of humor.

And he liked her. He didn't just lust for her, he liked her. She could tell. She'd known enough men to know when they only wanted a woman for sex and when they liked her.

And she liked him. A lot.

His hands gripped her hips, raising them a bit. "It'll hurt a little at first," he whispered in her ear. "But then I promise it'll get better."

She grinned, loving the fact he was still rolling with the game.

"Will it be like what just happened?" she panted, loving the feel of his cock sliding inside her.

"Better, baby," he groaned desperately in her ear. "Christ, so much better."

"Brendon Shaw, you do *not* know how to share."

Brendon looked up from the glass of cold milk he'd just dunked his Oreo cookie into. "Hello? Male lion. Duh."

After more than an hour on his couch, they'd somehow ended up stomach-down on his living room floor with a hell of a lot of junk food. But apparently they both favored the chocolate cookies with the creamy center. Too bad for Ronnie there was only one bag.

Determined, Ronnie reached for another cookie and Brendon pulled the bag back, closer to his body. Ronnie snarled and Brendon roared back.

Her eyes narrowed. "You *roared* at me?"

"And I'll do it again if you can't keep your paws off my Oreos."

She moved fast, he'd definitely give her that, landing on his back before he could even blink. Couldn't say he really minded, though. With both of them being naked, it felt really nice to have her wiggling around back there.

"Give me that cookie!"

"Get your own, scavenger."

Ronnie gasped in outrage and gripped his earlobe with her teeth while her hand reached out and made a wild grab for his cookie.

"Get those fangs off me, woman."

"Start sharing," she demanded between teeth firmly clenched on his ear.

"I don't share." She bit down harder at his statement. "Ow! Okay. Okay! You can have a little nibble."

"I want the whole cookie, cat." She released his ear and reached over, snatching it out of his hand.

He flipped onto his back, grabbing hold of her hips before she could wiggle away from him. Realizing he had her, she shoved the entire cookie into her mouth and grinned around it.

"I can't believe you stole my cookie."

She chewed a bit and stuck her tongue out, showing crumbled, spit-covered cookie and cream.

"Oh, very nice."

"Come on, Shaw. Kiss me."

"No way." He turned his face away and she landed a crumb-covered kiss on his cheek.

She swallowed and sighed in pleasure. "That was the best cookie I ever had."

"I bet."

"Don't be jealous."

"I'm not. I just think it's sad we're fighting over one cookie and I've got a whole package of them right there."

"Oh. You do."

Ronnie made a move for the cookies, but he held her back.

"I want another cookie. Now!"

"Okay. On one condition."

She leaned back and stared down at him. "This doesn't involve me wearing a full nurse's uniform with spiked heels, does it?"

"Not tonight, no."

"Latex? Furry handcuffs? Entertainment involving me, a vibrator, and—"

"Please stop." Brendon ordered his cock to behave and it pretty much laughed at him. "Those things will be for later." Maybe even tonight if he could track down the nurse's uniform. "Right now, I want you to promise me something."

"What?"

He had to proceed cautiously here. "If you have to leave for any length of . . . uh . . . time, you'll let me know."

She reared back, and if he hadn't had a firm hold of her, she probably would have bolted. "That sounds like a commitment."

"No, no," he said quickly, already smelling her panic. "Not a commitment. A courtesy. That's all. The polite thing to do." Southerners, from what he could tell, were big on courtesy and politeness. "You wouldn't want me to worry if you and Sissy Mae are only off shopping, would you? Especially with all this stuff going on with my brother."

"You're not asking me to stay forever, are you?"

"Nope. Just let me know when you're heading off somewhere." That way if she's leaving him, he can convince her to stay forever.

He could be very persuasive when the situation called for it.

"This is so you won't worry, right?"

"Right."

"Not because you're expecting me to settle down with you or anything."

"Never," he lied. Unfortunately, there were times when a man needed to lie to his woman. The wild look of panic in her eyes . . . lying was very important at the moment. He needed to lure her over before he pounced and made Ronnie his forever.

"Okay. That I'll agree to. And just that," she tacked on with a large amount of unnecessary vehemence.

"Perfect."

"Are we now done with this frightening conversation?"

"Yes."

"Good. I want more cookies."

"Get your own damn cookies."

"Give me those cookies or I'll kick your Yankee ass."

Laughing, his hands sliding along her naked body, "You know there are much nicer ways of getting me to give you those cookies."

"Oh." She blinked. "You're right."

Before Brendon could move, Ronnie pulled out of his arms and turned to face away from him.

"Ronnie, what are you—"

Suddenly he had a face full of her pussy and Ronnie's mouth around his cock. She sucked, causing his eyes to roll back into his head, then wiggled her ass a bit.

"Get to work, hoss," she said after releasing him with a wonderful pop sound. "We get done here, we can tussle over the cookies some more."

Brendon gripped her hips and pulled her lower. "You know, sexy," he sighed before taking her to heaven, "I *love* tussling with you."

Ronnie groaned deep and long when he pushed his tongue inside her. "Me too, hoss," she panted out. "Lord in heaven, me too."

Chapter Thirteen

Ronnie was kind of surprised she could walk at all as she made her way out into Shaw's living room. Room service had already delivered a huge breakfast, and tightening the belt around her Kingston Arms robe, she sat at the table across from Shaw. He had the *Wall Street Journal* in front of his face, and there was something amazingly domestic about it all. It shocked her she still hadn't made a run for it. She would have before.

Pouring herself a cup of coffee, she checked under the silver covers keeping the food either hot or cold.

When Ronnie found a big bowl of plain yogurt under one of those covers, she nearly squealed. Tossing some fresh fruit over the yogurt, she picked up the bowl and spoon and sat down in the chair. She'd finished off half the bowl by the time Shaw lowered his paper and looked at her.

Raising one eyebrow, "You didn't think to offer me any?"

Ronnie shook her head. "Nope."

"How many times do I have to tell you, kings of the jungle eat first."

"And She-wolves love to chase cats into trees, then laugh and laugh. So don't push me."

Grinning, he picked up a slice of thick-cut bacon. "So what do you want to do today?"

"Don't you have to work or something?"

"I am working. I'm staying out of my staff's way. They love when I do that."

"You're one of those nitpicky bosses, aren't you?"

"Damn right I am. I know what I want. I won't take any less."

She refused to comment on that one. Not when he had that intense look again with those gold eyes locking on her.

"Do you like museums?" he asked. "We can check out a few. Then I can fuck you in the Guggenheim bathroom."

"Such respect for the artists."

"I try." He stared at her. "You look good in my robe, sexy."

"Thank you kindly."

"Open it."

She hid her smile by shoveling a spoonful of yogurt into her mouth. "I'm eating," she said around her food.

He rested his elbow on the table, his chin in the palm of his hand. "Open the robe, Ronnie Lee."

With an annoyed sniff that even she didn't buy, she put her nearly empty bowl on the table and loosened up the belt at her waist. Keeping her eyes on him, Ronnie pulled the robe down over her shoulders and licked her lips. "Like this?"

Brendon growled and she thought he'd come over the table for her when his cell phone went off. His growl turned into a snarl, and he snatched his cell phone off the table. "What?"

He glanced at her and Ronnie opened the robe completely, arching her back. His eyes locked on her breasts and he gave a small whimper. He frowned. "Mace who?"

She covered her mouth to stifle her laugh.

Brendon flinched. "Oh. Llewellyn. Yeah. What's up?"

Ronnie watched the humor go out of his eyes. "You can't tell me over the phone? Yeah. Okay. Okay. One o'clock. I'll be there." He sighed and disconnected.

"What's wrong?"

"Mace needs to see me. Has information on my brother."

Ronnie stood up, pulling the robe back on. "Come on." She stepped over to him and held her hand out. "Let's get showered and dressed. Once you're done, we can still do that museum thing if you want." Although she doubted that would be happening, she wanted to act as positive as possible. But if Mace didn't have bad news, he would have told Shaw over the phone.

"You don't have to go."

"Do you want me to go?"

He didn't answer at first, staring at the table. Finally, he slipped his hand into hers. "Yes. I want you to go." He let out another sigh and allowed her to pull him out of the chair. "I'll need you to keep me from beating the shit out of Mitch. Who knows what the little idiot has gotten himself into now."

Brendon stared blindly while they chatted around him. He stared blindly at the corkboard with its pictures and diagrams. He stared and stared and stared, not sure what he was actually seeing. Realizing he knew nothing about his own blood. His own brother.

Around him they talked about the offices Mace and Smitty had so quickly secured with Sissy Mae's help, including a gorgeous cheetah receptionist who looked organized, highly competent, and like she could probably outrun a gold medalist sprinter. They chatted about the weather and the annual New Year's Eve party at the hotel. They chatted about a new club on East Fourteenth. Llewellyn and Smitty dropped their bomb and then let him deal with it on his own while they drank bottled water and chatted about their lives.

Finally, after he'd stared at the corkboard—and that one picture that said so much—for longer than many might consider normal, he exploded, his roar shaking windows and the glass on tables.

Silence, not surprisingly, followed until he heard Ronnie ask, "Could y'all leave us alone for a minute?"

They left without making a sound, and hands that were becoming as familiar as his own cupped his face. Ronnie turned him so he gazed down at her. One look into those hazel eyes and Brendon pulled her into his arms, burying his face in her neck.

"How could he not tell me?"

Ronnie's arms held him tight and she said, "Because he's being a passive-aggressive prick. But he's not hopeless."

"I'm going to kick his ass when I see him."

"Call him. Tell him to come to the hotel. You'll feel better once you know he's safe. 'Round his own kind."

"I should let him deal with this on his own."

She kissed his cheek. "You'll never forgive yourself if anything happens to him. We both know that."

He nodded, knowing she was right.

"So call the little fucker up and tell him to get his skinny lion ass over to your hotel."

"And my sister."

"If you must."

He released her so she could hand him the phone she took off his jeans.

Dez walked into the room from a separate door, carrying two bottles of water. She glanced around as she stepped closer to them. "Where is everybody?"

"They ran to safety," Ronnie joked.

Those strange green-gray eyes narrowed and Dez asked, "Did Mace roar at you guys? I told him not to keep doing that."

"No." Ronnie patted his shoulder. "That was ol' Shaw here."

"Oh." Dez seemed to immediately lose interest, turning and staring at the corkboard Mace and Smitty had set up. She frowned and pointed at a picture of Mitch. "Who's that?"

Sighing as he speed-dialed his brother. "Him? That's my brother."

"I didn't know your brother was a cop."

Brendon glanced up at the picture of his brother in full Philadelphia PD uniform. His graduation picture. The graduation and career Brendon had never known about.

"Yeah. I didn't know either."

Chapter Fourteen

Brendon looked up as his brother sauntered into the suite that had been reserved for him.

Hands in pockets and a cocky stance, he stared down at Brendon. "What?"

"You said you'd be thirty minutes. That was three hours ago."

"I was busy. What do you want?"

Standing, Brendon walked to the small fridge in the corner. He grabbed himself a beer and offered his brother one. Mitch waved it away.

"Busy doing what?" Brendon asked, popping the top on his Heineken. "Dealing? Breaking someone's kneecaps? Pimping?"

Mitch shrugged. "Something I don't think you should know about. It's for your own protection, big bruh."

"I see." Tempted to use the beer bottle, Brendon used his elbow instead, slamming Mitch to the ground. With his foot firmly planted against the back of the little shit's neck, he said calmly, "Let's try this again, *Detective* Shaw. What were you busy doing?"

"Fuck," Mitch growled while trying to dislodge his brother's foot.

"No, I'm sure you haven't been fucking. You'd be much more relaxed."

"Get off me, you asshole!"

"*I'm* an asshole? Do you know how long you had me believing you were some scumbag I had to reform?"

"Yeah. Now you can brag about me to your yacht club friends."

"First, you idiot, I don't belong to any yacht clubs. Second, what did I ever do to you to make you so goddamn pissed at me? I tried, Mitch. I really tried. But no matter how hard I try, you continue to be an asshole."

Abruptly, the fight went out of Mitch. He sort of laid there. "I didn't want anything from you," he said softly. "I didn't want your help. I didn't want your handouts. I wanted to prove I didn't need you."

"Proven." Brendon lifted his foot off Mitch's neck and stepped back, turning away. "You don't need me. You don't need Marissa. You're an army of one. Good for you."

"At first."

Brendon turned and looked back at his baby brother, who'd pushed himself off the floor. Some days it was like looking into a mirror, but Mitch didn't have as much brown hair in his mane yet. He would soon when he got a little older. "At first?"

"At first I was going to show you all. Show up for Thanksgiving dinner with my gold shield and enough attitude to choke a walrus."

"And?"

"I went undercover. I became part of this crew. Irish mobsters. Old school. Christ, Bren, I did things . . . *saw* things." Mitch shook his head and turned away. "In the end it was safer they didn't know you or Marissa existed. I didn't want them to have any leverage over me. I didn't worry about Mom. Her Pride is twenty strong with four Breeding Males. But Marissa doesn't have a Pride . . . I couldn't risk her. Either of you. So I let you believe I was a scumbag. It was easier because you both stayed away from me."

Brendon swallowed past the lump in his throat. "Two cops were looking for you the other night."

"Nah. They weren't looking for me. They were watching out

for you." Mitch laughed. "Poor guys. First you beat them up at the hospital, then your girlfriend and her Pack of She-wolves scare the shit out of them. They were doing me a favor, but I'm pretty sure their wives won't invite me back to dinner anytime soon. They're jackals and not real friendly as it is."

"So they weren't trying to arrest you?"

"No. I'd heard about you being in the hospital before Marissa ever called me." Mitch took a deep breath. "The truth is, Bren, I'm supposed to be in protective custody right now. I'll be giving testimony on the crew in a few months, and the city put me in this shitty little hotel with three other cops. Humans. I couldn't stand it. I couldn't leave, the room was tiny, the scent of those humans on some days . . ." He shook his head at the memory. "Too much. A few more days and they would have known exactly what I was. I took off. Been hanging in New York since. I asked Monahan and Abbott to watch out for you and Rissa as soon as I went into protective custody."

"Why?"

"The people I brought down . . . I was afraid they'd find out about you. Afraid they'd use you to get to me."

"What about the trial?"

"The prosecutor is one of us. A leopard. She knows where I am and how to get in touch with me. She said she knew I wouldn't last five minutes in that hotel. But cases like this take months if not years to come to trial. They can't expect me to stay trapped for that long. I'm better off taking care of myself."

Mitch ran his hands through his hair. "I'm really sorry, Bren. I never meant to—"

"Forget it." And Brendon meant it. "It's over. Now we know and we can figure out what we're going to do from here."

"I don't want you involved, Brendon."

"Shut up, Mitch." Brendon sat down on the couch. "Just . . . shut up. It's too late for you to protect me. It's too late for you to protect Rissa. You'll stay here. We'll amp up security. Mace Llewellyn and Smitty can get us people. Our own kind. Until this is all over, until you're done with the trial, we have no choice." Brendon stared at him. "I won't lose you, little brother."

The suite door opened and Marissa walked in, carrying a duffel bag with a change of clothes.

"Well, I'm here as ordered." She frowned, her eyes darting between the two of them. "What? What's wrong?"

Brendon sighed. "I'm in love with a She-wolf and Mitch is an undercover cop mobsters are actively trying to find and kill. They'll probably try to kill us too since we're family."

Marissa dropped her bags, her face white with shock. Slowly she walked closer to the two males. She glanced at Mitch, shoved him out of the way, turning both barrels on Brendon. *"How the hell could you fall in love with a She-wolf?"*

The two brothers looked at each other . . . and grinned.

"You all right, darlin'?"

Ronnie Lee smiled at Sissy Mae as her friend walked over to her. She knew Sissy would eventually come looking for her. They'd been traveling buddies for so long, they knew each other's moods as well as their own. Now the two friends stood outside a fancy New York hotel in the biting cold, their lives about to go around a new bend in the road—for better or worse.

"Called my momma tonight," Ronnie admitted.

"Lord, girl. Why would you do that?"

"Glutton for punishment, I suppose."

"I guess so." Sissy leaned against the wall next to her. "She tell you your brothers are on their way here tonight?"

Ronnie sighed, big and long. "No. She failed to mention that."

"Probably wanted it to be a surprise." Probably. Ronnie could tell from their tense phone call her mother knew something was going on. Most likely hoped her brothers would ferret out the information and get back to her. Then she could really shove it down Ronnie's throat.

Once her brothers got here, the party with Shaw would be

over. She didn't have to see them tonight, but they'd track her ass down by morning. In her estimation, she had one more good night with her lion, then she'd have to walk away. It gave her the perfect excuse. At least that's what she kept telling herself.

"Did she tell you you're hopeless and no good?"

"No. This time I didn't care enough to call on Christmas and how could I be so mean to my daddy. Oh. And there was lots of sighing."

"There's always lots of sighing where your momma is concerned. Didn't you know? The weight of the universe rests on those shoulders." Sissy Mae nudged Ronnie's shoulder with her own. "She does love you, Rhonda Lee. In her own special, mean-as-a-snake, everyone-is-against-her way."

"Yeah. I guess she does."

"What are you going to tell her about Shaw?"

"Nothing. Why?"

"What do you mean why? You gotta tell your momma something. The boy's so in love with you, he can't see straight."

Ronnie had always been the rational one. The one who, unless seriously drunk, always said, "Are we sure we want to do this?" But clearly all that wonderful rationality went flying out the window when she swung her fist at Sissy's face.

Sissy Mae caught that fist, too. In an instant, her eyes shifted from friendly human to Alpha Wolf as she shoved Ronnie back against the wall. Becoming Alpha Female wasn't any easier than becoming Alpha Male. You needed your wits and the ability to make split-second decisions. You also needed to be able to scare the bejesus out of people. When Sissy leaned in close to Ronnie and bared those pearly white fangs, brutally snarling, Ronnie knew she'd stepped over the line.

Turning her head away, she pressed back against the wall, cowering as Sissy came a hair's breath from her face, snarling and snapping. Making it clear who was Alpha Female and who was just a Beta.

Ronnie kept her eyes down and her body submissive. If she had her tail, it would be tucked up between her legs. When Sissy

Mae felt she'd cowered enough, she released Ronnie's hand and stepped back.

"Someday you'll have to tell your momma about Shaw. One, because your brothers will notice a big cat rubbing against you and purring. Second, the boy is not walking away from you anytime soon, Ronnie Lee. And you might as well get used to it."

Ronnie didn't know if she momentarily hated her friend more for making her cower . . . or for being right.

After five full hours of their arguing, Brendon lost his patience and stormed out of the suite. Mitch and Marissa didn't even notice.

Sleep. A few hours of sleep and he knew he'd feel so much better and a damn sight less mean. Because after refereeing between those two, he felt really mean.

He stepped into his apartment and headed toward the kitchen. Pushing open the swinging door, Brendon froze.

She sat at his counter, a magazine open in front of her, a pile of M&M's next to that. What he found most disturbing was how she'd separated the colors out. Black and reds in one small pile, in little pairs. Greens in another. Yellows and oranges in another. No blues, which made him think she'd put those back in the bag or ate them. Nothing like the slightly obsessive-compulsive wolf to make life interesting.

"You're here." *Christ. Is that the best you can do, you idiot?*

She didn't even look up from her magazine. "Yup. Looks that way, now don't it?" She turned a page. "If you want me to go, all you have to say is go. We both know it don't take much to get me to leave."

"Stay if you want to. Go if you want to."

What the hell was wrong with him? Why the hell was he goading her? He didn't want Ronnie to leave. Ever. Isn't that what he just spent five hours shoving down his twin's throat? So why push her out the door now?

Ronnie looked up from her magazine. "You gonna be an asshole the rest of the night?" she asked calmly.

"You know," he responded sarcastically, "I think I might. So feel free not to be here for it."

There. He'd given her an out. Now she could go and he could be even more miserable. *Good plan, Bren.*

Ronnie closed the magazine and slid off the stool. She'd put on another pair of ratty cutoffs and a Coors Beer T-shirt. The woman really knew how to wear clothes most women wouldn't be caught dead in.

A few steps and she stood in front of him. He looked into her beautiful eyes and didn't see tears or even pain. She didn't look hurt. More amused. But before he could figure that out, her fist slammed into his jaw, knocking his head to one side.

"*Motherfuck—*"

Leaning in close to his ear as he massaged his sore face and cursed up a blue streak, "Talk to me like that again and lose one of those lion balls you're so proud of, hoss." Her forehead brushed against his wounded jaw. "And now you're going to have to convince me to stay. Think you got the balls to make me stay, Brendon Shaw?"

Without another word, she pushed past him and headed out of his kitchen. Maybe out of his life.

And there was no way in hell he was ever letting her go.

Typical shifter male. They handled stress in the worst ways. Especially when it involved their kin. Her daddy only got real crabby when he and Momma had a fight. Something about her pushed all his cranky buttons. Still, after a good fight, her brothers often had to drag Ronnie out of the house to a movie—or two—until they all felt it was safe enough to head back home.

Ronnie made it to the door before Shaw caught up with her. His big body stepped in front of her, blocking her way out of the apartment.

She barely stopped her smile in time.

"You gonna move?" she asked.

"Nope."

Ronnie stepped away from him, claws unleashing. "This

won't be pretty, Shaw. I got in a little tussle with Sissy Mae tonight and I'm not my usual fun-loving self."

"Kick your ass, did she?" he murmured, ignoring her annoyed growl and tossing his leather jacket aside. "Sorry I missed that. Especially if you guys were naked and there was oil or mud involved. Now come here."

"Like I'd ever make it that easy." She took several long steps back. "You want me, hoss, you better come and get me."

Forgetting—again—lions had quite the leap in them, she almost didn't move in time.

She took off across his living room, clearing furniture easily, and headed down the hallway. He made no sounds as he moved up on her, but the one thing Ronnie knew about lions—the females did most of the hunting. The males came in for the kill bite and to feed. Otherwise you could find their lazy asses sleeping in the shade while the females did all the work.

Shaw reached for her, and she ducked under him, heading back the other way.

"You little . . ."

She laughed, loving the chase. Needing their ridiculous frolicking to take her mind off everything else.

He caught up with her, and she felt the air move as his arms swung for her. She dropped to her knees and Shaw tumbled right over her, landing with a painful thud. She stopped long enough to look him in the eye. He gazed at her, clearly stunned.

Licking her lips, she whispered, "Gotta be faster than that, pretty kitty." Then she popped to her feet and jumped over him, heading down the opposite end of his ridiculously enormous apartment. His roar shook the walls, and Ronnie moved faster, knowing he was right behind her. Knowing he'd get her.

Ronnie charged into one of the unused bedrooms, slamming the door behind her. She'd made it into the bathroom when the bedroom door slammed open. She had a distinct feeling the man had kicked it off its hinges.

She went through the bathroom into the adjoining bedroom and out the door. Only Shaw hadn't followed her, he'd backtracked to this door and she ran right into his arms.

He slammed her against the opposite wall, his mouth crushing hers while his hands kept her claws from tearing him apart. She fought him. No fake fighting either. She kicked and bit and knew she hurt him by his grunts of pain.

She tasted blood and she knew her fangs had scraped him hard.

Panting, he pulled away from her, gripped her tight around the waist, and stormed off down the hall. She thought he'd take her to his bedroom so he could have his dirty, disgusting way with her—at least that's what she hoped for—but apparently the kitchen was closer.

He pushed through the swinging door, and the next thing Ronnie knew, he had her facedown over his kitchen counter.

A bloody lip, sore jaw, and a couple of bruised ribs. Seemed a small price to pay to have Ronnie Lee Reed bent over the island in the middle of his kitchen.

She still had her claws out and insisted on putting up a hell of a fight. Grinning, Brendon pushed his knee between her legs, forcing them apart and raising her a bit so she couldn't get a clear shot at his nuts—again. He laid one hand flat against her back, keeping her pinned to the spot.

His free hand rubbed his throbbing jaw. "You've gotta hell of a right cross, sexy."

"Thank ya kindly."

"You were kind of rough on me, weren't ya?"

She laughed even as her claws dug into the marble countertop, trying to pull herself out from under his hand. "Are you kidding? You had every one of those hits coming."

"You're right. I was a total asshole to you." Brendon moved his hand so he could stretch out over her, resting against her back. She tensed beneath him.

"I'm sorry, Ronnie," he whispered in her ear. "I'm sorry I was an asshole."

She held herself rigid for several long moments and he waited for her to start swinging.

Instead she let out a breath and turned her head to look at him. "Don't do it again."

"I won't."

"Cause next time I won't be so nice."

He flinched, wondering what her "mean" must be like. Then Brendon decided he didn't want to know and he hoped he never stupidly found out.

"I'll keep that in mind."

"Do."

He nuzzled her chin. "So you forgive me?"

"If I must."

"You must." He kissed her forehead, her cheek. "I like having you around, Ronnie. I don't want you mad at me."

"Then don't piss me off," she said with a smile.

"I promise to try really hard to keep the pissing off to a minimum."

She snorted. "At least you're realistic."

"I like doable goals."

She pushed back against him, her ass rubbing against his hard cock. "You still have that condom we were going to use if we made it to the Guggenheim?"

"As a matter of fact . . ." Brendon dug into his back pocket and slapped the condom down on the counter.

Ronnie reached one hand back and gripped his cock through his jeans. "I say we find out how sturdy this fancy counter is."

Brendon pulled her hand away before she made him come in his pants. The female had wicked fingers. Grabbing both her hands, he slapped them on the counter and held them down with his own.

"All the way over, Ronnie."

She looked back at him and nipped his chin. "I will, but you better make it worth my while."

Ronnie bent forward, resting her cheek against the cool marble counter. Shaw released her hands and ran his fingers up her arms, over her shoulders, and across her back.

"Keep your hands on the counter," he ordered while reaching around her waist and undoing her cutoff shorts. The ragged denim dropped to the floor, and he groaned while his hands palmed her bare ass.

"No underwear? You're a horny little thing, aren't you, Ronnie Lee?"

"Never been a big fan of wasting time. Besides. You're a ripper. Girl could lose her best underwear with a guy like you ripping them off all the time."

Shaw ran his hands over her ass, and her back arched. The man had the best hands. Rough and insistent most of the time, but he knew how to back off when she wanted him to.

"Good point," he muttered, and she heard him unzip his jeans. His cock came out so fast, she knew he hadn't bothered to drop his pants. The condom wrapper crinkled and then his knee pushed her legs farther apart.

Ronnie braced herself for it, knowing the first time with Shaw always had enough edge of pain to make it interesting. Two big fingers slid between her legs, and she gasped as they pushed inside her pussy.

"Christ, Ronnie. You're already so wet." She didn't respond, only grunted while his fingers pulled out and shoved back in. "And hot," he whispered against her hair. "So goddamn hot."

She pushed back against his hand, loving the way his body tensed when she made it clear what she wanted.

His hand suddenly withdrew and Ronnie whimpered, feeling the loss until his cock replaced those fingers and Shaw's hips slammed her forward, thrusting into her in one long, hard stroke.

Flush against her back, his cock seated firmly inside her, Shaw rested against her, the two of them panting into his marble counter. Hands resting on top of hers, his fingers scratching the skin.

He waited and she didn't know why. She didn't want him to wait. She wanted him moving.

Ronnie leaned her head back, rubbing against his cheek, her

nose nuzzling his chin. Then she nipped his jaw, hard, and Shaw bared his fangs, snapping at her.

His left hand slid into her hair, pulling her head back and leaving her neck exposed while his body rocked into hers. Closing her eyes, Ronnie let the feel of his cock forcing its way into her over and over again take her where she wanted to be. Lost among the sensations only Shaw seemed able to give her. His face buried against her neck, harsh breaths panting across her flesh as he rode her hard. His fingers only releasing her hair long enough to get another good grip and hold her tighter.

Letting her instincts take over, Ronnie risked losing some hair to lean back a bit and snap at Shaw again. She didn't even realize she had her fangs out until they grazed her lip.

With a short, powerful roar Shaw pushed her farther forward and pulled her head to the side, gripping her shoulder with his teeth. A typical predator move to keep a dangerous lover from causing permanent, life-ending damage.

But Ronnie winced when she felt Shaw's fangs dig past her T-shirt and into her skin. Her eyes snapped open when she realized, too late, what he was doing.

"Wait—"

He either didn't hear her or didn't care because those fangs tore through flesh and muscle, sinking deep into her shoulder and holding her steady as he fucked her brutally hard and with absolutely no mercy.

Her heart soared while her stomach dropped, and Ronnie barked, trying to get loose. Shaw dug in deeper, a short warning growl making it clear he wouldn't let her go. The She-wolf inside her stopped fighting, smart enough to know its mate even if Ronnie wasn't.

Shaw's free hand slid between her legs and held steady, letting his thrusts push her clit into his fingers. Even as she fought it, even as she tried not to let it happen because she knew it would be the final nail in her coffin, the orgasm ripped through her system with a vengeance.

Screaming, Ronnie exploded. Her claws tore into the marble

counter leaving deep gouges, and her body shook from the strength of her climax.

Shaw finally unclamped from her shoulder and roared out his orgasm. His entire body shuddered behind her and his grip tightened around her body.

Slumped over the counter, the two of them panted and didn't speak.

Ronnie didn't know what to say. What did you say to a man who just made you his for eternity?

Especially when she had the distinct feeling the big-haired idiot hadn't even realized it.

Chapter Fifteen

Only the sounds of their harsh breaths filled the large kitchen. Brendon still rested against her and he could feel her body shake beneath his with every rough pant.

She's mine.

That one thought kept ringing through his head. Over and over.

She's mine.

She'd always be his. Just as he would always be hers.

Brendon's lips curved into a smile and he hugged her close. *She's mine.*

"Get off me, Brendon."

Whoa. That didn't sound good. Especially when she used his first name. She never called him by his first name. And she'd never sounded that cold before. Not ever.

"Now. Get off me now."

Slowly, Brendon stood straight, gently pulling out of her. He stepped back, quickly disposing of the condom and tucking himself back into his jeans.

Ronnie pushed away from the counter and reached down to grab her shorts. He watched her silently pull the denim on, tug her shirt back into place, turn, and head out of his kitchen. The entire time she never said a word and she never looked at him.

He followed her as she walked to his front door, opened it, and walked to his elevator. She pressed the call button and the doors immediately opened. She stepped inside, pushed a button, and finally looked up at him.

Confused and a little panicked, he demanded, "Where are you going? You promised you'd tell me if you were going to be gone for a while."

"You're right. I did." She gave a casual shrug. "Europe."

Refusing to believe he heard her correctly, "What?"

"Europe. I'm going to Europe. See ya."

Then the doors slammed shut in his face.

Ronnie walked out into the main lobby, her eyes focused on the floor. She needed to go. She needed to run. She needed to do something but stay here and face this. She couldn't face this.

She pushed open the front door of the hotel and stepped outside. After walking past the doormen who helped new arrivals, she stood on the corner. It could have been minutes she stood there or hours, she didn't know.

"You may wanna put on some shoes."

Ronnie looked down at her big feet and realized that not only did she not have on shoes, she still only had on a pair of shorts and a T-shirt. No wonder she felt cold.

She looked up into the handsome face of Mitch Shaw.

Concerned, he asked, "Sweetie, are you okay?"

"I'm leaving. Before I get trapped any more than I am, I'm leaving," she spewed out.

"Leaving? Now? You sure that's a good idea?"

"I always leave." She headed down the street.

"But why? You and Bren—"

"No. No." She stopped and spun on him, slamming her hands against his chest like she'd done to his sister. Unlike his sister, however, Mitch didn't move. Not even a flinch. "Me and 'Bren' nothing. I'm going before I start driving a minivan and worrying about the school system."

"You can't just leave him."

"Well, Lord knows I can't stay!" She knew she sounded hysterical. People on Manhattan streets were actually staring at her. Took a lot to get their attention.

Shaking her head, embarrassed, Ronnie walked off, Mitch right behind her.

"Why are you following me?"

"I'm walking with you. I was leaving anyway."

Ronnie stopped again and turned, Mitch walking right into her. If he hadn't grabbed her, she would have hit the ground after bouncing off all those muscles.

She immediately noted the duffel bag on his shoulder. "You're leaving, too."

He looked slightly ashamed. "Yeah. Me and Marissa had this fight. She kind of stormed off and . . . I thought maybe if I—"

"Ran away?"

Gold eyes narrowed. "I don't see you sticking around."

Without answering, Ronnie again turned and walked away. She didn't want this conversation. She didn't want to talk about this. She wanted to leave. She wanted to go far away. As far away as possible.

"Ronnie, wait." Mitch grabbed hold of her arm. "Please wait. I'm sorry."

"He loves you, Mitch. You can't leave without telling him."

Mitch gave a low chuckle. "He loves you, too."

She shook her head. "I can't hear this. I can't—" She tried to pull out of his grasp, but Mitch wouldn't let her go.

"Let's do this." His free hand cupped her chin, his fingers smoothing along her cheek. She knew that move. He was trying to soothe her. Calm the yipping dog before she started barking at the neighbors again.

"Let's go back inside," he offered, "and talk. I'll buy you a hot chocolate. We won't go anywhere until we talk. Okay?"

She knew she should leave, but she didn't want Mitch to go, too. That wouldn't be fair to Shaw. "You'll stay?"

"If you stay."

She couldn't let Mitch run off again. Shaw would lose his mind if his kid brother took off again. "Okay. For hot chocolate only."

Mitch grinned, looking so much like Shaw it made her heart ache. "Yeah. Although we may want to get you some shoes before you take off. Walking around New York in December with no shoes . . . probably not a good idea."

He steered her back to the hotel, leading her inside and to a small restaurant tucked away behind the more glitzy popular places. They sat down and a waiter glided over to take their drink orders. Once he glided away, Mitch frowned at her. "You look like you're freezing."

"Freezing? Not really." But her teeth chattered when she spoke.

Giving a snort of annoyance, Mitch took his jacket off and reached over, placing it around Ronnie's shoulders.

"Tell me what happened, Ronnie."

She shrugged under his big heavy jacket, pulling it tighter around her. "Nothin'."

"Ronnie, he marked you. I can smell his scent all over you."

Placing her elbows on the table, Ronnie rested her face in her hands.

"This isn't what you wanted?"

"It would have been nice if he asked."

"True. But would a wolf have asked? Or would he have just taken his life in his hands and hoped for the best?"

Ronnie dropped her hands to the table, moving them when the waiter placed her enormous cup of hot chocolate in front of her. Giant imported marshmallow right on top.

"Don't you see, Mitch? I'm trapped now. I've gotta tell him where I'm going. When I'll be back. If I'm arrested."

Mitch blinked and leaned back in his chair. "Um . . . are you arrested a lot, sweetie?"

"In this country? Not really."

"That's good to know. But wouldn't you want someone to bail you out when you're arrested?"

"That's what my Pack is for. And I don't need to give them constant updates on my whereabouts."

"True, but now you've got Bren. Think of it like an extra pair of thermal underwear. Sometimes you're in a situation when you really need two."

Ronnie started to sip her hot chocolate but stopped and put

her cup back down. "Darlin', that is one of the dumbest analogies I've heard in a long time."

He shrugged. "Cut me some slack. I'm winging it here." Mitch's face turned solemn. "Bottom line is, babe, you'll break his heart if you leave him."

"Cats don't mate for life."

"Who told you that?"

"*National Geographic* and the Discovery Channel. The males come and go, jumping from Pride to Pride. And wolves don't share anything but our food, but even that we tussle over."

"All of that's absolutely true—for cats who live to be about twelve and reside in the Serengeti. Last I looked, this was New York and me and Bren have another fifty or sixty years to fill. I know Bren wants to spend it with you. And neither of us have any intention of spending the rest of our lives being traded around by a bunch of females who can barely stand us."

"He just wants me cause I stayed that night. They left and I stayed."

"That's not why. He's grateful to you for staying that night. He wants you cause you look fierce in those shorts." Mitch grinned when she smiled. "And he loves you because you make him happy. I've never seen the big butthead smile so damn much."

"He makes me feel . . ." Ronnie stopped and looked back at the table.

"What, Ronnie? He makes you feel what?"

"It's what he doesn't make me feel that's the problem."

"Which is?"

She took a deep breath. "Restless. I never feel like I have to leave when I'm with him. I never wake up in the morning with one foot already out of the bed."

"And that's a problem because . . ."

"Because I always leave. Now I only want to stay, and it's freakin' me the hell out."

"You're freaking out because you know your life is changing for good. If you weren't freaking out, I'd be worried." He took a long sip of his hot chocolate. "How about I make you a deal?" Mitch suggested softly.

"What deal?"

"You stay . . . and I'll stay. At least for a little while."

"I shouldn't care whether you go or stay. I *shouldn't* care how it affects him at all."

"But you do care, Ronnie. And that's okay."

"Fine." Ronnie pushed her cup aside. "I'll stay."

"Good. Now let's go find him before he tears the friggin' hotel apart looking for you."

He'd checked her room. The front lobby. Even a couple of the restaurants. She'd disappeared.

Hell. What she'd done was left him.

Now he had to stand here dealing with Sissy Mae Smith. A lesser man would have killed her by now.

"Let's think . . . where could she have gone? Did she take her passport?"

"I have no idea," he replied.

"No idea."

That's what annoyed him. She kept repeating everything he said back to him.

"Did she give you a hint of where she might go?"

"She said Europe."

She tapped her fingers against the solid oak of the front desk. "Europe."

Brendon dropped his elbows on the desk and buried his face in his hands.

"Now, now, darlin'. No use crying. We'll find her eventually."

"I'm not crying. I'm trying to stop myself from ripping out your vocal cords."

Surprisingly, she laughed. "My Lord, Brendon Shaw. You are just the cutest little thing when you're upset."

When she pinched his cheek, all he could do was laugh.

Sissy Mae glanced over his shoulder. "And look. There she is."

Brendon turned around. The relief hit him first, quickly followed by blinding jealousy when he saw his brother walking with her. She even had on the treacherous bastard's leather jacket. Mitch had never let anyone else ever wear that jacket—until now.

"Hhhmm," Sissy Mae mused. "I wonder where those two have been together for such a long time."

A small, rational part of him knew Sissy was merely fucking with his head; based on stories from Ronnie, he knew that's what she did for amusement, like some people knit or play video games. That didn't stop the jealousy from coming up and choking him.

Brendon stalked over to the pair, ignoring the smile Ronnie Lee gave him that quickly turned into a dark frown.

"What the hell is going on?" He didn't even look at Ronnie, he only focused on Mitch.

"Nothing, big bruh. Just . . . ya know . . ." Mitch placed his hands on Ronnie's shoulders and smoothed them down her arms. "Trying to make Ronnie feel better."

In that instant, everything melted into this one moment. The attack, the truth about Mitch, Ronnie running out on him—all of it slammed right into Brendon at that moment, leaving him filled with a rage he hadn't experienced since his wild days running the South Philly streets with his twin.

Carefully, Brendon lifted Ronnie up and out of the way, not even hearing her warning growls or the words she said to calm him down. Then he slammed his hands into Mitch's chest, sending the little shit back five feet.

"Maybe you're an idiot," Brendon snarled. "Maybe slightly brain damaged." He shoved his brother again. "Whatever the fuck is going on with you, you need to remember she's mine."

Mitch lowered his head and glowered at Brendon, lips pulling back over bright, white fangs. "Then, maybe, big bruh, you should learn how to keep your female without needing me to do it for you."

Brendon's rage centered and narrowed to a fine, honed point and, like the lion he was, he went for his brother's throat, not really caring about all the snarling and growling in the middle of his five-star hotel.

"What did you say to him?"

Sissy gave her that innocent look. "Me? I didn't say anything, darlin'."

"You're lying to me, Sissy Mae."

"Lying is such a strong word."

The scent hit her first and Ronnie spun around, coming nose to chest with Rory Lee Reed.

"Baby sister," her brother's deep voice greeted her. "Typical. We just get into town and we find you and Sissy Mae dead center of a shit storm."

"What's going on anyway?" Ricky Lee Reed asked, curious as always.

"Nothin'," Ronnie choked out, grabbing hold of Rory's arm and trying to drag him away, hoping Ricky Lee and Reece would automatically follow like they always did. But apparently Sissy Mae had other ideas.

"Those two lions are fightin' over Ronnie Lee."

Slowly her brother looked at Sissy Mae. "Excuse me?" Rory asked.

"See the bigger one?" She helpfully pointed out Shaw. "That's Brendon Shaw. He marked your sister tonight. If you take a good sniff you can catch his scent *all* over her. And the slightly smaller one . . . that's his baby brother, Mitch." She grinned. "I think he's mighty cute. Now see, Brendon is all jealous because he saw Ronnie Lee and Mitch walking together. Poor baby, I don't think he's used to being possessive over a female."

Ronnie Lee turned on her friend. "*Have you lost your goddamn mind?*"

Rory nudged his sister. "Watch your mouth, Ronnie Lee."

"How long has this been going on?" Ricky asked, his big hands shoved into the front pockets of his jeans.

"Just a few days. But your sister moves fast as y'all know."

She'd kill her. She'd absolutely kill her best friend.

Reece glanced around at the growing number of observers. "Think we better deal with this. Can't let some cats embarrass the Reed name."

"Wait." Ronnie jumped in front of her three brothers before they could move. "Don't hurt him."

"At the very least don't hurt his face," Sissy piped in helpfully, but she slapped her hand over her mouth when Ronnie gave her a withering glare.

"Why shouldn't we?" Rory demanded in that calm, low voice of his. "That bastard's been messing with our baby sister to hear Sissy Mae tell it." Rory's hazel eyes stared down into hers. "You gonna give me a reason why I shouldn't tear him apart, Rhonda Lee?"

Ronnie cleared her throat and looked around. A few of the Pack males had wandered over, always lured by the sound of a good fight. Now they stood behind her brothers, staring at her and waiting. Unfortunately, Smitty was out with Mace. The one rational wolf among a bunch of junkyard dogs. Dammit!

"Answer me, Rhonda Lee," Rory pushed. "Answer me or move out of my way."

She couldn't answer. She couldn't. Until Rory shrugged and tried to go around her.

"I love him!"

Rory stopped, his eyes again focusing on her. Reece and Ricky Lee stepped closer, watching her but saying nothing.

"What did you say, baby sister?"

"I . . . I said I love him." Ronnie's cheeks burned with embarrassment. She suddenly felt like that high school virgin she'd played with Shaw the other day. Sure, she'd told her friends and family she loved them. But she'd never said it about a male before. A male she had regular sex with. And Lord help her, but it was true.

"You sure about that, baby sister?"

"Yes. I'm sure."

The three brothers passed glances and then pushed her back, advancing on the fighting Shaws. Apparently they didn't care that she loved him.

"Just remember . . . not his face!" she called after them in a last-ditch effort to save *something*.

Rory reached down and grabbed the back of Shaw's neck, yanking him up, but Shaw had his claws dug into his brother's shoulders, so Reece grabbed Mitch, pulling him the opposite direction, and Ricky Lee went about pulling claws out of important body parts.

"Y'all need to simmer down now," Rory warned softly. "A lot of full-humans around and they're watching."

Shaw closed his eyes and took deep breaths. Mitch shook his head, trying to get the hair out of his eyes. Unfortunately, he sent some blood flying in the process.

Rory grabbed Shaw by the hair and pulled his head around. He squinted into his face. "You'll heal."

"We should clean up this one, though."

"Yup. Come on."

The Reed brothers pushed the Shaw brothers ahead of them toward the elevator.

"Where the hell are you going?"

"Don't you never mind, Ronnie Lee. We'll send him back in one piece."

Rory winked at her and ambled off, the rest of the Pack males following behind.

Once the elevator doors closed, Ronnie turned to Sissy Mae. "What the hell was that?"

"That, my friend, was male business."

"Male business?"

"Yeah. Shit too stupid for a female to ever think about getting in the middle of."

"Ahh."

"Come on, darlin'. Let's get you into some clothes before you freeze to death. And a nice big vat of tequila."

"Good plan."

But before either could take a step, Marissa Shaw exited one of the other elevators. Her gold eyes searched the lobby, and when she locked onto Ronnie, she marched right over to her.

Ronnie grimaced. "Aww, shit." She'd really hoped her night of excitement was over. Apparently not.

"Don't fret none, darlin'. I got your back."

"You said that in Budapest. I still have the scars, too."

"You are such a whiner."

Marissa Shaw stepped in front of them, her eyes locked on Ronnie.

"Uh . . . hi, Marissa."

"After a delightful fight with that idiot baby brother of mine," she launched with absolutely no preamble, "Brendon's phone rang. It was Missy Llewellyn."

Ronnie frowned. "Missy?"

"Yes. Missy. Apparently her sisters had just told her about you and Brendon." *Uh-oh.*

Marissa's arms crossed in front of her chest and she braced her feet apart. The woman was definitely sturdy and powerful. A typical predator.

"Look, Marissa—"

The lioness held her hand up, silencing Ronnie. "When she asked me what was going on, I was forced to tell her about you and Brendon. About how Brendon told me he loved you and how I was almost positive he was going to mark you as his own."

Sissy Mae opened her mouth, probably to confirm that, but Ronnie slammed her foot into the woman's instep. Sissy's mouth opened in a silent scream, but she kept her pain to herself.

"Maybe you should talk to Bren—"

"I had to tell her that a She-wolf would be helping to raise the Llewellyn Pride's cubs. And that they would have little half-wolf sisters and brothers one day. Plus there was nothing she could do about it because of the contract. I also had to tell her that every Pride on the East Coast would know she lost one of her favored Breeding Males, not to some rich Pack from Boston or Connecticut but to a Smith Pack She-wolf from the back-woods of Tennessee."

Ronnie would have probably been good and angry if tears

hadn't started to slide down Marissa's face. *Oh good Lord in heaven, she's sobbing.*

"I had to tell her all those things and I have to say that nothing, absolutely *nothing*, has ever made me happier."

Ronnie blinked. "What?"

"You, my She-wolf friend, have given me hope when I only saw darkness. You've given me joy, when I've only known misery. *You*, Ronnie Lee Reed, have made me happier than I've ever been before."

Then Marissa wrapped her arms around Ronnie and held her in a tight bear hug. Eyes wide, Ronnie looked over at Sissy who, also wide-eyed, stared right back at her.

Wow. And she thought her family was weird.

"That's . . . uh . . . really great, Marissa." Ronnie awkwardly patted Marissa on the back. "I'm glad I could be of help."

"Oh, you were. I haven't had that kind of fun since I stopped stealing cars."

That's when Sissy Mae covered her mouth and turned away, her shoulders shaking.

Ronnie carefully pushed Marissa off her. "I am so happy I could bring you this kind of joy."

Marissa stood straight and wiped her eyes with the back of her hands. "Why don't we get some dinner and champagne to celebrate this auspicious event of making Missy Llewellyn the most miserable bitch on the planet?"

Ronnie glanced down at Mitch's jacket that she still wore and her bare legs peeking out from under it. "I'm not exactly dressed for most of the restaurants in the hotel."

Slinging her arms around both Ronnie and Sissy's shoulders, Marissa reminded them, "Hello? Own the joint. We can go into any damn restaurant we please, wearing any damn outfit we want to." She started walking, both She-wolves trapped in her iron grip, unable to escape. "I'm in the mood for steak. How about you ladies?"

What could Ronnie say? She'd never be able to outrun a lioness. "Sure. Sounds great."

Boy, would she make Shaw pay for this little nightmare.

* * *

How could Ronnie desert him like this? For two hours he'd been trapped with her brothers, five other wolves who he didn't bother to learn the names of, and his idiot baby brother. Who, at this moment, stood on the balcony with Ricky Lee and howled at a nonexistent moon.

Rubbing his eyes in the hopes of stopping the unbearable pounding in his head, Brendon asked again, "Are you sure?"

"I was standing right there. I ain't deaf." Rory Reed forced the Mason jar back into Brendon's hand. When he started to pass it off to another wolf, Rory gave him that glare again.

With a sigh, he took a long swig of the clear liquid and grimaced as it burned a hole in his esophagus. After a few moments, he cleared his throat and handed the jar back to Rory. "She actually said those words?"

"Yup." Rory took a deep drink, looking completely unfazed by the amount of liquor he'd imbibed in the last two hours. "She said, 'I love him.'"

"Did she mean it?"

"Well, she's never said it before."

"She's never stopped us from putting a hurt on a male before either," Reece Reed added. "Most of the time, she actually steers us over there. So she must like you some."

She must like you some? Talk about vague.

The howling became louder and Brendon couldn't stand it anymore. "Mitch! Would you stop making that annoying, goddamn sound!" The howling cut off abruptly, but now Brendon had the attention of every wolf in the room. Clearing his throat, he added, "It's so annoying when a cat does it, don't ya think?"

The wolves nodded and Rory held the jar out to him again.

"No, thanks. I really don't—"

They all stared, and Brendon realized he didn't have much of a choice. So he took the jar and gulped down more stuff he felt pretty confident could eat through titanium.

Man, he would so make Ronnie pay for this nightmare.

Chapter Sixteen

R onnie went to knock on her brother's door, but it already
stood ajar. Kept that way by one long arm.

"Oh Lord."

Ronnie pushed the door open and it slammed right into
Ricky's big head. She kept pushing until she could easily enter.
Disgusted, she stepped over her brother and stormed into the
middle of the room, staring down at all of them.

With an angry growl, she kicked Reece in the head. "Wake
up!"

Still holding onto his bottle of 'shine, Reece grumbled and
turned over. Then he started snoring again.

"*Rory Lee Reed!*"

Rory sat straight up. "What? What?"

"Where is he?"

"Um . . . ?"

Ronnie waited for her brother to answer until she realized
he'd passed out again while sitting up.

"Goddamnit."

A toilet flushed and the bathroom door opened.

"Hey, sweetie." Mitch walked by and gave Ronnie a friendly
scratch on the head.

Well at least one of them had survived. "Are you okay?"

"I'm gonna hurt in the morning from all that liquor. But right
now I feel very little pain." Reaching down, Mitch grabbed

Reece, lifted him, carried him to one of the two queen-sized beds, and carefully placed him on the mattress.

"Did you really drink Uncle Willy's 'shine?"

"That stuff in the glass jar? Yup. Sure did. Hence the not feeling any pain."

But he wasn't slurring his words or walking funny or passing out midsentence. He looked sober as a judge.

"Where's Shaw?"

"Bed, I think. He bailed when Rory dropped. And that was after those three guys over there dropped."

"But he's okay?"

"He's fine. An asshole, but fine." He flashed her a killer grin every Shaw male seemed to have, then he picked Ricky up and laid him out next to Reece.

Fascinated, Ronnie watched as Mitch did the same thing for Rory, carefully laying him on the bed. It was the nicest thing she'd ever seen a man do for another man.

Until Mitch started picking up the other wolves and placed them on top of each of the Reed boys in a lovely sixty-nine position. Thankfully they were all dressed, but she knew when her brothers woke up . . .

"That is *wrong*," she finally gasped out, tears rolling down her face from laughing so hard.

"Yeah. I know." Mitch grinned "But admit it. It's so fuckin' funny."

Where she got an air horn from at two o'clock in the morning, he had no idea, but the damn thing blasted him right out of bed and halfway across the room.

"*What in holy hell are you doing?*" he roared while covering his ear. He knew it must be bleeding. He'd probably be deaf for life. Still, the crazy She-wolf he felt the need to mate with didn't seem too concerned with the damage she may have caused.

"Mornin', darlin'."

Brendon glanced out his big windows facing the city. "It's still dark out. So it's not morning in my universe."

"I know. You city people sure are used to being lazy and getting up when the day has just passed you by. But we have a few things to straighten out before you get to sleep."

Uh-oh. "What kind of things?"

"First, never leave me alone with your sister again. She scares me, which isn't easy."

"What happened between you and—"

She hit the button on the air horn and he slammed back against the wall, his entire body shaking with rage. He'd bet hard money she got that damn thing from Timothy.

"Was I finished speaking?" she asked cheerfully. "Nope, sure wasn't. Now where was I before I was so rudely interrupted? Oh, yes. Your sister is insane, and you're not allowed to desert me if she's around."

"Fine," he spit out. He might actually wear his teeth down into nubs at this rate. "Anything else?"

"Yeah. I want three pups, which you'll clearly have to teach how to fight because a wolf with a mane . . . not a pretty idea. And our children's misery will be all your fault."

"Ronnie—" He quickly held his hands up when she pointed that stupid air horn at him again.

"Did I look done talkin'?"

He stared up at the ceiling, praying God would give him strength. "No."

"Also, every once in a while, I may take off for places unknown. I will leave a note and call you regularly. I will return, but I have to feel I can leave whenever I want or I will go insane like your sister. And if I go insane I'll make sure to take you with me." She raised an eyebrow and again he held up his hands, letting her know the floor was still hers. "You *will* let me drive your car . . . all of them."

"Now wait one goddamn minute—" He slammed into the wall again, his hands over his ears. "*Stop doing that!*"

"Stop," she replied calmly, "interrupting me." She cleared her throat and continued. "You will no longer be a Breeding Male unless you're breeding with me. You marked me, now you're stuck with me. I don't share cock, underwear, or toys. It's that simple. Any female lions come sniffing around you, no one will find their remains for a very long time. You, of course, will not go sniffing around anyone else because you already know how mean I can be. Now, last, and this is most important. There will always be Oreos in the cupboard, and you will share, Brendon Shaw. With me and definitely with our children. You'll eat first only if the rest of us aren't in the room. Okay. Are we all clear?"

Brendon nodded and she smiled. "Good."

He held his hand out. "Can I have that?"

"This?" She held up the air horn. "Sure." With no effort, she snapped the cheap plastic part off the can and tossed the can to him. "You didn't think I'd give you the thing whole, did you?"

"Doesn't matter. I was only going to snap it in half anyway." He tossed the can aside and stepped toward her. "Now you're gonna say it."

"Say what?"

"You know what." He kept moving forward, and she started to stumble back. "You said it in front of your brothers, you can damn well say it to me."

"Oh. That." She rushed out of the bedroom, down the hallway, and into his living room. "I was just saying that so my brothers wouldn't hurt you." She stood on one side of a large couch. "I'd feel real bad if they did that."

His eyes narrowed. "Ronnie Lee . . ."

"Brendon Shaw . . ."

He faked right and she darted left; he had her in his arms before she even got around the couch.

"Put me down!"

"Say it."

"No."

He flipped her over and held her by her feet. "Say it, Ronnie Lee."

Laughing, she squealed and slapped at his legs. "No! I won't say it. Now put me down."

"Fine. Don't say it." He took hold of her ankle in one hand and slapped her ass with his free hand.

"You bastard!"

"Stop whining. You know you love it." He slapped her again. Again she squealed.

"Stop!"

"Say it, Ronnie Lee. Say the words."

"Pull me up first."

"No. Say it."

"Fine, you bastard. I love you. Happy now?"

Ronnie squealed again as Shaw flipped her back over. But before she could tell him what an asshole he was, he kissed her with so much passion, so much love, she felt her insides melt. He shoved her into one of the club chairs, yanked off her shorts, and buried his face between her spread thighs.

She cried out from the pleasure of it. Not only the pleasure he gave, but from the joy her words brought him. She didn't realize how much it would mean to him. Or how much it would mean to her to make him so happy.

Digging her fingers into his hair, she whispered, "I love you, Shaw. I love you."

Big gold eyes stared up at her from her lap. "Say it again," he demanded. "Say it again."

Typical lion . . . just a glutton.

"I love you."

Suddenly his arms were around her and his mouth crushed hers. She let his passion flow from him right into her. Let him show her how much this all meant any way he wanted to.

"I love you," he panted against her lips. "I love you, Ronnie." He pulled her off the chair and spread her out on the floor. "I'll always love you."

She knew that. And for once the thought didn't scare her at all.

Chapter Seventeen

Ronnie never knew a cat's obsessive cleanliness could turn into such a pleasure.

Arms tight around his shoulders, legs tight around his waist, Ronnie let Shaw hammer into her. Again and again. She lost count of how many times she'd come just during this morning session, but she had a feeling this would be a regular thing. Not that she minded. A girl had to stay clean, didn't she?

Fangs gripped the skin on her throat and another orgasm started to flash through her. "I can't," she begged over the running shower. "Not again."

"You can. You will. Christ, Ronnie, you feel so good." She exploded at his words, at the sound of desperation in his voice. And this time she made sure to clench her pussy so hard, she dragged his cat ass right along with her.

He roared against her throat and the pair of them slid to the shower floor, water pouring down on them.

Ronnie finally opened her eyes and smiled at Shaw. He had that look again. The one that used to freak her out. The one were he stared at her with such love she didn't know quite what to do.

"I love you," he said again. He said it a lot. She didn't mind.

She leaned forward and kissed him. "I love you, too."

"Can you walk?"

She chuckled. "With a little help, sure."

"I have a surprise for you."

"What surprise?"

With great effort, Shaw stood and lifted her with him. He held onto her as he shut off the shower and stepped out into his way-too-big bathroom.

"Tell me."

"Sure you don't want to wait?"

"I'm sure. Tell me."

"No." He placed her on the bathroom counter and kissed her nose. "But I'll tell you some of it."

"Okay."

She watched him walk away to grab a towel, and she started wiggling, running out of patience. "Tell me," she whined.

"Okay. Okay." He began drying her off with the towel. "Tonight we do the New Year's Eve party thing. I have to go, being the host and all."

"Yeah. Yeah." No biggie. She already had a dress for it. She had shoes too, but Shaw made it clear he wanted her in her boots. He really loved those boots.

"Then tomorrow, on New Year's Day—"

"Hey, bruh."

Gritting his teeth and shielding Ronnie's body with his own, Shaw glared at his baby brother over his shoulder. "What?"

"I need to borrow a tux if I'm going tonight."

"Can't you buy one?"

"Do I look made of money to you? Hello? Cop's salary."

"Hello? Heir to a fortune. Go downstairs and tell Timothy to hook you up. And stop just walking into our apartment."

"Why? It's not like Ronnie has anything I haven't seen before." Mitch wiggled his eyebrows at her, making her giggle.

"It's like you want me to kill you," Brendon seethed. She almost hated herself for enjoying his jealousy.

Mitch leaned over a bit to see her better. "Hey, sweetie, where's my jacket?"

"Sissy Mae has it."

Mitch frowned. "Why?"

"Because she said, 'Ooh. Nice jacket. I'm taking it.'"

Now he looked pissed. "And you just gave it to her?"

"Alpha Female, remember? Besides, she'd snarled and snapped at me earlier. I wasn't about to go through that again. You want your jacket back, you're on your own, O King of the Jungle."

"Fine. Whatever." Mitch disappeared from the doorway and Ronnie started to tell Shaw to finish about the surprise when Mitch came charging back—all three Reed brothers on his ass.

"Come back here, you twenty-hour-sleeping bastard!"

Brendon shook his head. "I need to change that lock."

"Won't matter. Every wolf knows how to pick a lock, hoss."

"Great."

"Don't give me that look. You wanted me. You got me. That includes my Pack. Now tell me about my surprise." She wiggled again, and Shaw laughed.

"I can almost see your tail wagging."

"Ha ha."

"Okay. You and I are going on a trip tomorrow afternoon. Taking Dad's private jet, too."

"Cool. Wait." She frowned. "Did you check it against the list?"

Shaw sighed. "Don't worry. You can legally go where I'm taking you."

"Don't get that tone. I gave you that list so you wouldn't get disappointed when you try to go to Singapore or Madrid or—"

"Yes. I appreciate the helpful and *long* spreadsheet with all the *many* places you can't go."

"Well that statement was riff with sarcasm." She wiggled again. "Tell me where we're going!"

"Nope. It's a surprise. But you're totally going to thank me when we get there."

"You lying, conniving son of a bitch! Let me go, Brendon Shaw!" Ronnie tried to dodge past him again and he grabbed her around the waist, forcing her up the porch steps while he continued to argue with his sister long distance.

"Look, Rissa, I'll be home in about a week," he barked into the phone. "You should be able to manage the hotel until I get back. This isn't brain surgery."

"I know that but it's been a while, Bren. And all I'm saying is a little warning before you went traipsing off with your Huckleberry Hound would have helped considerably."

"Get over it. I've gotta go." He disconnected and took firm hold of Ronnie so he could haul her over to the door.

He'd hoped she'd be too tired to put up much of a fight. The hotel party lasted until five in the morning. A great night of drinking, food, and Ronnie. He couldn't think of a better way to bring in the New Year. After the party, Brendon took her back to their apartment and fucked her senseless for several hours, gave her only three hours to sleep, then carted her off to the airport. He got her on the plane and wouldn't let her get any sleep by bringing up her college plans, which she still hadn't made up her mind about, but the discussion caused a nice bit of panic that kept her wide awake.

But as soon as they got off his father's private plane and she realized where they were, he'd been having a hell of a time keeping track of her. She tried to ditch him at the rental car place and then at a gas stop on the way. And he'd already had to chase her into the surrounding woods once. He had no desire to do it again . . . unless, of course, they were naked.

Before she could squirm away, he knocked on the door and the fight in his female became decidedly worse.

But as soon as the knob turned, she stopped fighting and turned to face the horror on the other side.

If he didn't have Ronnie already in his arms, he'd have assumed she'd just opened the door . . . and aged a few years. *Wow,* he thought in surprise, *she's gonna be hot when we hit fifty.*

"Rhonda Lee." Powerful arms crossed over a Randy Travis T-shirt. "What brings you here—after all this time?"

"After all this time? I was here four weeks ago."

"But Christmas passes and no word from you. Think that's fair to your daddy?" With a resigned sigh, Tala Lee Evans motioned to them with a wave of her hand. "Well, y'all might as well come on in since you're here. Your brothers got here a couple of hours ago."

"Why are they here?" Ronnie demanded without going inside.

"You'll have to ask them. I'm assuming they wanted to spend New Year's Day with their parents. Unlike some other ungrateful children I could mention."

"That's it." Ronnie threw her hands up. "I'm leavin'."

Brendon caught up with her on the porch steps and had to pry her fingers off the banister.

He carried her into the house, and her mother motioned to the living room, apparently unfazed by her grown daughter having to be physically forced back into her childhood home.

"Go on in," Tala sighed. He'd never heard a female sound so put upon before. Almost every sentence started after a deep, heartfelt sigh. Yet he didn't get any real anger or annoyance from her. Just drama.

Tala watched Brendon carry Ronnie into the living room and place her down. Still, he had to take firm hold of her jacket before she could take off.

"So . . . a cat," Tala said.

With a nod, "Yes, ma'am." One hand still held Ronnie's jacket while he stepped forward and extended his hand. "Brendon Shaw."

Tala stared at his hand and, with that dramatic sigh, "Want some coffee and sweet rolls, Brendon Shaw?"

"That would be great, ma'am." He briefly wondered if she'd always call him by his full name.

"Well then, you may as well sit down for a spell." She glanced at Ronnie. "Your brothers are in the barn. They'll be back soon." She raised an eyebrow at her daughter and walked out without another word.

"What was that about?"

Ronnie slapped Brendon's hand off her jacket. "My momma thinks I'm going to have sex with you in her pristine living room."

He wouldn't exactly call Tala Evans's living room pristine. More like tidy and comfortable. But just this morning he'd begun to notice that Ronnie's clothes seemed to find permanent spots on the bedroom floor. He had a feeling his female was a messy gal, so she probably did think her mother's house was pristine.

"Aren't we going to have sex in her pristine living room?"

"Yes," she snapped in exasperation. "But she shouldn't *assume* we will. My own momma thinks I'm a whore."

"Only with me."

When she glared at him, he wandered away to look at the pictures of Ronnie and her brothers from birth until now. They filled the small room, proving just what Brendon had been thinking. They may argue from sunup until sundown, but clearly Tala loved her children. Even Ronnie. He guessed *especially* Ronnie.

"I can't believe you tricked me into coming here," she grouched, her arms crossed over her chest.

"I didn't trick you," he drawled, and smiled down at a picture of Ronnie as a howling pup. "Tricking you is putting you in the car, driving you five miles from home, and releasing you in a field. Which would be very wrong." He barely ducked her fist and laughed as he pulled her into his arms.

"I wanted to meet your family, Ronnie, and waiting until one of them died—which was your suggestion—is unacceptable."

She growled and pouted but rested her head against his chest and her arms around his waist. "You owe me for this, Shaw."

"I owe you for a lot, sexy." He kissed the top of her head and then her cheek. She went up on her toes and touched her lips to his. That was all it took. Her fingers tangled in his hair, moans easing up the back of her throat while Brendon pulled her tight against his body, holding onto her the way he planned to hold onto her for the rest of his life.

She reached down with one hand and gripped his cock through his jeans, making him instantly hard and ready. Her nipples were hard under her sweater, and he was mere seconds from pushing her onto the couch and fucking the living—

"Rhonda Lee Reed!" The snarled words slammed across the room, startling the two away from each other. "I know I don't have to tell you that you will *not* be having sex with that boy in my living room."

Suddenly Brendon felt like a horny fifteen-year-old caught on his girlfriend's couch. He even had to turn away for a bit to get his cock back under control.

"And let me tell you something else"—Tala slammed down a tray with two cups of coffee and freshly made sweet rolls—"y'all are sleeping in separate rooms."

Ronnie gasped in outrage. "What? I'm not sixteen, Momma. You can't—"

"Oh yes I can, little girl. This is my house. Will be until they bury my bony ass in the backyard. Until then, I will not have your poor father hearing the two of you having . . . relations. Understand me, Ronnie Lee?"

Giving a dramatic sigh of her own, Ronnie turned away and stared out the window. Nothing like a Reed female standoff.

So Brendon answered for them both. "We understand, ma'am."

Those dark hazel eyes, so much like Ronnie's, looked Brendon over. "At least the cat's got some damn sense," she muttered. "Now when your daddy gets back from his still, Ronnie Lee, y'all better have more control than what I just witnessed."

Tala walked back into the hallway but stopped and turned toward Brendon. *Uh-oh.* "Ham do you for dinner tonight, Brendon Shaw?"

Startled she asked, and realizing he was being invited to dinner among wolves, Brendon quickly answered, "Yes, ma'am."

"Good. Gotta have pork on New Year's Day. It's good luck. I'm even making my famous redeye gravy and biscuits. You'll like it." The "or else" definitely implied.

"Sounds wonderful, ma'am."

She grunted and headed back to her kitchen.

Ronnie turned away from the window and punched his arm. "You suck up!"

He pushed her back. "Shit starter."

They glared at each other for a moment, then the two of them grabbed hold of available body parts, viciously tickling while tripping their way over to the couch. They barely controlled their laughter, made worse for the fact that they didn't want Ronnie's mother, who had wolf hearing no less, to catch on to their wrestling. Or, as Ronnie liked to call it, "tusslin'."

Suddenly the weeklong vacation in Tennessee seemed way too long with the idea of separate rooms, and at the same time Brendon couldn't think of anyone he'd rather sneak around with, trying to cop a feel.

The one thing he could say about his Ronnie Lee, she made nearly anything fun.

The front door opened, and he and Ronnie scrambled to separate corners of the couch.

A large, unfriendly hulk of a wolf stopped in front of the living room and stared at them.

"Hey, Daddy!" Ronnie jumped up and ran to her father, throwing her arms around his neck. She kissed his cheek and the old man hugged her back. But those wolf eyes stayed locked on Brendon.

"I missed you, Daddy."

"I missed you, too, little pup," Clifton Reed said gruffly. "Who's this?"

Ronnie walked back to Brendon's side as he stood up to face the man who had hurt a lot of males he felt weren't worthy of his daughter.

"Daddy, this is Brendon Shaw. My mate. Brendon, this is my daddy. Clifton Reed."

"Mr. Reed." Brendon stepped forward and shook the old wolf's hand. "Nice to meet you, sir."

The old man grunted. "Boy." He looked back at Ronnie. "Your brothers are bringing in wood for a fire. Look like it might snow. Where's your momma?"

Ronnie sighed good-naturedly. "Where she is every day at this time for the last thirty-five years y'all have been mated. She's in the kitchen."

"That's all that needed to be said, little pup." With another grunt in Brendon's direction, the wolf walked off.

Ronnie beamed up at him. "He likes you," she whispered.

Brendon frowned. "Likes me? The man grunted at me. Twice."

"You're still breathing, aren't you?" Brendon didn't even know how to respond to that, which Ronnie took as agreement. "Exactly."

The front door opened again, and heavy footsteps could be heard as Ronnie's brothers marched in the room, their arms filled with either wood or Mason jars filled with that paint thinner they tried to pass off as liquor.

Rory stopped first, staring at the pair. "What y'all doing here?"

"He tricked me," Ronnie said simply.

"You decided to get involved with a cat." Rory dropped a pile of wood by the fireplace. "What exactly did you expect?"

Ricky Lee took off his heavy winter jacket and carelessly tossed it onto a chair.

"Don't you leave that coat lying around, Ricky Lee," his mother yelled from the kitchen.

"How does she do that?" he demanded while snatching the coat back up and taking it to the hall closet.

Ronnie opened her mouth to reply and Rory cut her off without even looking at her, "And don't say Satan, Rhonda Lee. It wasn't funny twenty years ago, it's less so now."

"Are you guys staying with Smitty's Pack?" Brendon asked as he walked around the room, taking everything in. Enjoying this side of family life he'd never experienced before, but might now that he had both Marissa and Mitch admitting blood connections.

"Yup. Already talked to Daddy. He knows it's for the best."

"Besides," Reece added, his big fingers affectionately scratching Ronnie's head as he passed her to help himself to the entire plate of sweet rolls, "he likes the idea of us keeping an eye out for this little monster."

"I don't need y'all watching out for me."

"Is that right?" The big grin on Rory's face had Brendon's eyes narrowing. Crouching by the fireplace, Ronnie's brother looked back at Brendon. "Rhonda Lee ever tell you how she and Sissy Mae made money while traveling the world?"

"No. How did she—"

"Hookin'," Ronnie Lee tossed in desperately. "I was a prostitute. A damn good one too."

"Stop lyin', Rhonda Lee," her mother called from the kitchen. "I doubt you were good at all."

Brendon grabbed hold of Ronnie before she could go after her mother.

"She was not a prostitute," Ricky Lee said, scooting by Ronnie but not before flicking her forehead with his middle finger.

"Try illegal racing," Rory said, and his grin grew.

Brendon blinked. "What?"

"You heard me, hoss."

"Her and Sissy Mae," Ricky Lee added.

"Sissy Mae would set 'em up and Ronnie Lee would knock 'em down." Reece laughed. "They still sell her T-shirts in Japan and Korea."

Her face red with embarrassment, Ronnie Lee walked away from them all and threw herself into one of the plush recliners.

"What was their motto again, Ricky Lee?" Rory asked, his hands held in front of a now-roaring fire in the fireplace.

"A rich boy and his money will soon be parted."

"That's right. Sissy Mae would find some rich boy with no sense and a hot car. Challenge him to a race, and the brain surgeon over there would race him. By the time they were done with him, they'd have the winnings, the poor sap's car, and sometimes real estate."

"Which they'd sell and invest. Sissy Mae can turn a dime into ten thousand dollars in an hour."

"That She-wolf does have a gift."

"I don't want to discuss this anymore," Ronnie snarled.

Nodding, Rory stood up. "She's right. Might as well save the really good info for tonight's dinner."

The three brothers headed for the hallway, but Rory stopped and asked, "How did you two get here so fast anyway?"

"Took his daddy's jet."

"Hey!" Ricky cheered. "Did you hear that, boys? We're taking a jet back to New York City."

"Who the hell invited you?" Ronnie practically yelled.

"Ronnie Lee, you can't expect us to go coach now that you've snagged yourself a rich boyfriend."

Ronnie flashed her fangs at Ricky and Rory stepped between them. Staring down at his sister, he said, "Be nice, Rhonda Lee, or I'll have to tell Momma how the barn burned down that time."

Her eyes narrowed. "You swore you'd never tell."

Her brother snorted and winked at Brendon. "Rory Lee Reed in a jet. Has a nice ring to it, don't it?"

Laughing, the three brothers walked out, and by the time Brendon turned back to Ronnie, she already had one of the windows open and was halfway out of it.

He rolled his eyes and grabbed her, dragging her back into the house.

She struggled in his arms. "I won't stay!"

Brendon spun her around and kissed her. Within seconds, they were practically tearing each other's clothes off.

"*Rhonda Lee!*" her mother bellowed from the kitchen. "Get that ass in here right now, little miss!"

Startled, the couple jumped apart.

Ronnie pulled her shirt back down while Brendon adjusted the front of his jeans.

"What is it, Momma?" Ronnie Lee called out, somehow keeping her panting under control.

"Y'all come into this kitchen and keep me company while your daddy and the boys hunt down that boar for dinner."

Like a teenager, Ronnie rolled her eyes. "But—"

"Now, Ronnie Lee."

"Fine!"

Stamping her foot, Ronnie started to storm off, but Brendon grabbed her arm, pulling her back a bit.

"Don't start a fight, Ronnie."

"Me? *She* started it—"

"Ronnie."

"Fine. You wanna side with her, go ahead. Hope you enjoy sleeping alone tonight, hoss."

She turned and started to storm off again when Brendon said to her retreating form, "I packed the skirt."

Ronnie froze in the doorway, her body tense, fingers gripping the door frame. After several moments, Ronnie turned and whispered, "Keep it down, Brendon Shaw. If my momma finds out what we did on your parents' couch she'll skin me alive."

Flowing right into their little game, Brendon moved in front of her and placed his hands on the archway, his arms and body leaning over Ronnie Lee. If he remembered correctly, he did the same thing to her at the hospital. It was a signature Shaw move he often used in high school. "I promised I wouldn't tell and I won't. But I need to see you tonight."

"I . . . I can't. I have a calculus test next week."

"Meet me, Ronnie." He leaned in closer, his lips brushing against her forehead. "Promise you'll meet me."

"Where?"

"My car. Tonight."

She swallowed. "Your car?"

"Yeah. I wanna see if those boots look as good against the inside roof of my car as they do against this floor."

Ronnie looked honestly surprised for several moments before a beautiful grin spread across her face. She shook her head and instantly went back to their game. "Are we gonna do what we did . . . before?"

"Did you like what we did before?"

Looking appropriately embarrassed and turned on at the same time, she nodded. "I . . . I did."

"Then, yes. We'll do what we did before. As many times as you want."

"Rhonda Lee Reed. Get your ass in here now!"

Her grin returned. "Coming, Momma," she called back. She

looked at Brendon, sizing him up. "At least I better be. Tonight. In that car."

Brendon laughed. "That I definitely promise." He brushed a finger across her cheek. "Love you, Ronnie Lee."

She went up on her toes and kissed his lips. "I love you, too. Now," she grabbed his hand with her own, intertwining their fingers, "let's go have some fun molesting each other when my family ain't lookin'."

Grinning, Brendon let Ronnie lead him to the warm Evan–Reed family kitchen. "Rhonda Lee Reed, I absolutely *love* how you think."